GLIMPSE
OF
DEATH

LESLIE WOLFE

 **ITALICS**

ITALICS PUBLISHING

$I\!I$ ITALICS

Italics Publishing Inc.
Cover and interior design by Sam Roman
Editor: Joni Wilson
ISBN: 1-945302-12-7
ISBN-13: 978-1-945302-12-1

Acknowledgement

A special thank you to Bob Erwin, who has made the research for this novel a joyride and has shared his tremendous knowledge of all things biological under the sun, from practical applications of DNA sequencing to genetic prediction modeling of complex traits.

Taken

He watched her from across the street as she left the coffee shop. She was beautiful, this one. Her long, wavy, brown hair coiled and bounced in thick, silky strands around her shoulders, dancing with every step she took. Her smile was dazzling, even from a distance, and her eyes were half-closed, the way they get when laughter touches them and lends a glow of happiness.

He licked his lips and swallowed hard. Soon enough, those eyes would be looking at him. He felt a twitch below his waist, and a crooked smile curled the corner of his mouth.

She stopped right outside the coffee shop and turned around to look at the man who'd held the door for her. Then she reached out and took his hand, weaving her fingers through his, and her smile widened. The man leaned forward and kissed her on the lips, lingering a little, then turned away and quickly disappeared around the corner. She unzipped her purse, her eyes still following him as he vanished, and took out her car keys.

That was his cue. Time to move.

He ran his sweaty palms against his thinning, blond hair and arranged it into place, although not much could be done with the few remaining strands, pushed backward by an aggressively receding hairline. He straightened his posture and arranged the knot of his tie, then buttoned his jacket. He scrutinized the reflection in the tinted car window and saw a moderately attractive, professionally dressed man, looking the part he was about to play.

He quickly crossed the street and caught up with her just as she was about to get behind the wheel. He delayed his arrival long enough to give her time to be seated but caught the doorframe before she could close it.

"Dr. Katherine Nelson?" he asked, flashing a wallet with his fake police ID.

The young woman didn't bother to check his credentials. They never did. But even if she checked, the fake he carried was quite good; it could probably pass for the real thing with most uneducated civilians. He'd paid good money for it, worth it to the last dime. It made things so much easier. He didn't have to lurk in the shadows anymore, worrying about muffling their screams and getting kicked, bit, and scratched. He could go out in broad daylight and get the job done.

"Yes, that's me," the young woman replied, her voice trembling a little.

"I'm afraid I have some bad news for you. Your husband, he—"

"What happened? What's wrong?" she almost yelled, panic instilling a crystalline, high pitch in her voice.

He didn't even have to be creative. They never let him finish his damn sentence anyway.

"It's better if you come with me, Dr. Nelson. It's faster that way."

She grabbed her purse and slammed her car door, then trotted quickly behind him, as he crossed the street and headed toward his car. The rhythmic sound of her high heels hitting the asphalt made it unnecessary for him to look over his shoulder to make sure she was still coming.

He led her to a black, unmarked Crown Victoria he'd bought at a police auction a couple of years before, and held the door open for her. Then he took his seat behind the wheel and shoved the key in the ignition.

"Please," Katherine said, turning toward him, "tell me what happened to Craig. Is he okay?"

He reached into his pocket and pulled out a syringe, then quickly removed the cap. She watched him with bewildered eyes, turning pale, faltering. She pushed herself backward as far as she could, flailing desperately for the door handle, but unable to take her eyes from the approaching needle. Her mouth opened, but no sound came out.

"Your husband is in a world of trouble, Dr. Nelson." He grabbed her shoulder with a steeled grip and shoved the needle into the side of her neck, swiftly pushing the plunger, before she could react. "You see, his cheating wife was kidnapped today."

Waiting Room 2

The three men knew one another well, but barely exchanged glances. The occasional word was muttered under their breaths, almost whispered, although no one else could hear them talk. Other than that, they waited.

Hospital waiting rooms are all the same, no matter where they happen to be. Fluorescent lights, with undecided hues of bluish purple, and the nonstop humming of the ceiling-mounted lamps. A vending machine, also humming every now and then, holding the typical offering of junk food, rich in chemicals and empty calories. A few wide chairs in green, faded fabric, and a wall-mounted TV, with the sound set on mute.

At least they had their privacy.

Hospitals tend to be courteous to law enforcement, probably due to the repeat business the profession tends to deliver. Passing, or even enduring, relationships are formed among officers, agents, and their family members on one side, and nurses and doctors on the other. They cross paths, unfortunately, much too often. In their case, the small, private, waiting room was the least the hospital could do.

The three men had been waiting for a while—a few hours now. Not a word.

FBI Special Agent in Charge Alan Pearson had loosened his tie an inch or two, then crossed his arms at his chest. That had happened more than an hour earlier. He hadn't budged since, although somewhat irritated with the restlessness of Detective Todd Fradella, from Palm Beach County Sheriff's Office. The young detective couldn't sit still; he paced the floor like a caged animal, annoyingly running his hands through his shoulder-length hair, randomly stopping in front of the window, as if something of any interest could actually be seen through it, in the late-afternoon sunlight.

As for Detective Gary Michowsky, he didn't move much either; but his lips did. He sat in the same chair, his hands clasped together tightly in his lap, and stared into emptiness. His jaws clenched spasmodically, and he constantly bit his lips, munching on them from the inside, angrily. He tried to stay calm and quiet, but his anguish showed.

Fradella stopped his pacing in front of Pearson and shoved his hands deep inside his jeans pockets.

"It's taking a while," he said, breaking the tense silence.

The two men stared at him disapprovingly.

"I hope she's okay," he continued, almost apologetically. "I mean, when it takes so long—"

"Shut it, Fradella," Michowsky snapped.

Pearson unfolded his arms and sighed. "Come on, guys, take it easy," he said, staring at Michowsky.

Michowsky fidgeted in his seat, then gazed at the shiny, floor, following the random design of the cement mosaic tiles.

"It's on me," he eventually muttered. "All this. On me."

Pearson frowned, and Fradella turned to look at his partner.

"How d'you figure that?" Pearson asked.

Michowsky remained silent, biting his lips some more.

"Did *you* stab her?" Pearson pressed on. "Was that you, detective? Or was it a psychopath you two eventually put in the morgue?"

Michowsky shot Pearson an angry glare, then lowered his eyes again. There was nothing to say, and he didn't want any consolation coming from any of them.

"When this is over," Pearson continued unfazed, making a gesture with his hand, "I'll need a statement from you. I know it was a good shoot, but she's under internal rev—"

Michowsky glared at Pearson again, just as briefly, interrupting him.

"Yeah, I heard about that nonsense. I'll give you my statement anytime you want. It *was* a good shoot."

The door opened and a tall man dressed in a surgical gown walked in. The three men gathered around him, all talking at the same time, asking the same question, but with different words.

The doctor raised his hands in a pacifying gesture. "Hello, I'm Dr. DePaolo. We met earlier, I think," he said, locking eyes with Pearson and then Michowsky. "She's strong and she's a fighter; she has a good chance to make a full recovery," he said, and smiled encouragingly, while wiping his brow with his sleeve. Tiny beads of sweat had accumulated there, and the edge of his surgical cap was moist.

"It was a close call for a while," he continued, "but I believe she'll pull through. The next few hours are still critical. She waited too long." He cleared his throat, then continued in a stern tone. "XStat is designed to stop the bleeding while help is on the way, officers. You can't get stabbed, XStat the wound, patch it up with a bandage, and go back to work like nothing happened."

The three men looked at one another, then, one by one, lowered their eyes.

"She lost a lot of blood," Dr. DePaolo continued. "She's in ICU now, still sedated. I'll show you where that is, if you follow me."

He walked briskly and quietly on the endless corridors, then led them to a room on a restricted part of the floor. The room had a glass wall and a French door, also made of glass. Inside the room, surrounded by stacks of beeping equipment and digital screens, a tiny figure lay immobile on the bed.

Tess looked thin and pale against the white bed sheets; Gary almost didn't recognize her. By her side, a nurse took readings from the machines and jotted notes onto a chart.

Pearson frowned and tapped gently on the glass. The nurse quietly opened the door.

"Why is she restrained, Nurse… Henderson?" he asked in a curt tone, reading the name off the ID tag she was wearing.

Gary hadn't noticed the restraints, but now that Pearson mentioned them, he frowned as well. Her wrists were tied to the bed rails, and she constantly shook her head, slowly, without opening her eyes, moaning.

"She's very restless, although she's heavily sedated. We can't risk her moving too much and tearing her sutures."

"I'll place a uniform at the door," Fradella said. "Just in case."

That wasn't a case Gary could think of, but he didn't find it necessary to disagree. After all, it was Tess Winnett in there, fighting for her life.

"Are you family?" the nurse asked.

"Work family," Michowsky replied, earning himself a curious look from Pearson. "Why? Need anything?"

"She's worried about her cat. She keeps mumbling something, I can't understand what, but it's something to do with a cat. Can someone check her home and make sure her cat's okay? Maybe then she'll be able to sleep better."

He stared at Tess, puzzled for a few seconds. He wished he could ask her what she needed. Cops had turned her apartment upside down, and he'd been there too; it was still an active crime scene. No one had mentioned a cat, and he didn't remember seeing food bowls or cat toys anywhere.

Then he remembered something else.

He pulled out his phone and said, "I think I know what that's about."

He dialed 411, then requested the information, "I need the number for a Media Luna Bar and Grill, or something like that. Yes, in Palm Beach. Yeah, connect me; I'll hold."

A few seconds later, Michowsky broke the silence again.

"Yeah, um, hey, Cat, you might want to know that Tess is in the hospital." He stopped talking for a split second, then continued. "University of Miami Hospital, third floor, room 3104."

The call ended without any additional words. Michowsky had expected a few questions, but none came. All for the better. He felt exhausted, the exhaustion brought by feeling some relief, after a long period of tension.

The nurse smiled and nodded a silent thank you in his direction. He sat on a vinyl chair across the hallway, and let out a long breath of air.

"She won't be up for a while," the nurse said. "Why don't you go home? I can call you when she wakes up."

"I'm not going anywhere," Michowsky replied, resuming his earlier posture, with his hands firmly clasped in his lap and his shoulders hunched forward. Pearson nodded and did the same, leaving an empty chair between them and taking the one next to that. Fradella resumed his pacing, including the occasional stops in front of a nearby window, now completely engulfed in darkness.

A few minutes later, a uniformed officer arrived, quietly greeted Fradella and Michowsky, and pulled a chair for himself right next to Tess's door. The nurse frowned when she saw him sit there, but then got absorbed in her work and her frown vanished.

Michowsky's phone chime raised disapproving eyebrows everywhere on the hallway, even from passersby. He took the call immediately, shooting apologetic glances in all directions. A minute later, he stood up, ready to leave.

"Fradella, I've got to go. They found Lisa Trask, the missing person from last week. She's been dead for at least a day. You stay here; I'll do this solo. Call me as soon as Tess wakes up."

"You got it. Where did they found the body?"

"You're not going to believe this… in her own backyard."

He nodded an acknowledgment toward Pearson and hurried out, not noticing the worried look that appeared on Pearson's face the moment he'd mentioned where the body had been found.

Crime Scene

3

It took Michowsky almost an hour to get to the crime scene; traffic was still heavy, despite the early darkness of the southern Florida winter day.

Florida winter… what a perfect contradiction in terms. There's nothing wintry about it, other than shorter days and longer nights, pleasant temperatures, and lots more tourists, enough to make the highways unusable for a few months a year.

By the time he arrived at the Trask residence, the street was filled with emergency vehicles with their flashers on, and the area surrounding the house was cordoned off with yellow tape. Neighbors huddled together in small groups, talking incessantly, concern and curiosity written all over their faces. Nothing churns a peaceful, suburban neighborhood more than a dead body found in someone's backyard.

Michowsky recognized the medical examiner's van and muttered, "Good," happy he wouldn't have to wait for Doc Rizza's arrival.

He flashed his badge at the young uniformed officer who kept the gawkers at bay and entered the backyard, following the trail of crime scene unit technicians who ran back and forth from their van to the location of the body.

The backyard was flooded in light, coming from several portable halogen projectors. He hurried toward the far end of the yard, where the techs had removed a portion of the shrubs marking the edge of the property, to allow easier access.

She lay naked on the ground, as if she were waiting for someone. Her beautiful face, serene and immobile, rested on her folded arm. Her long, luscious hair covered her in part, undulating gently in the evening breeze. Her left arm rested in a relaxed position, and her legs were straight, crossed at the ankles. Her eyes were half closed, and a hint of a smile lingered on her pale lips, as if to welcome an unseen lover. Despite the deathly bluish pallor of her skin, she looked almost alive. It was all in the posturing.

"Seems alive, doesn't she?" Doc Rizza asked, touching Michowsky's shoulder.

"Yeah," Michowsky replied. "It almost seems like she's—"

"In bed, waiting for her lover?" Doc Rizza asked. A hint of sadness colored his voice.

"Yeah," Michowsky repeated, running his hand across the back of his neck. "Any preliminary findings?"

"Got a few," Doc Rizza replied, signaling his assistants to start preparing the body bag and stretcher. "She's been dead about thirty hours. Preliminary cause of death is strangulation. You see the petechiae, here, and here, around the eyes?"

"Uh-huh," Michowsky replied. "What did he use?"

"I'm guessing a rope of some kind. I found a few fibers in the abrasions on her throat. I'll run trace and DNA."

Michowsky jotted a few notes in a small notepad. "I'll have some uniforms search for that piece of rope. Maybe we get lucky... Dumpsters, bushes." He cleared his throat quietly. "Was she raped?"

"You'll have to wait for the autopsy results, but if I were to venture a guess, I'd say yes."

Michowsky's eyebrows shot up. Doc Rizza rarely ventured guesses of any kind. He took pride in his rigorous adherence to scientific facts. "Observation, not speculation," he liked to say.

"You see these ligature marks on her ankles?" He crouched next to the victim and pointed at her feet. "The abrasions are more pronounced on the inside of her ankles, here, and on the Achilles tendons, consistent with her legs being tied apart. This type of ligature mark is common in sexual assault victims. I'll know more in a few hours."

"Got it. Thanks, Doc."

"I'm not done yet," Doc replied, then stood up with a groan. "This isn't your primary crime scene."

"I didn't think so," Michowsky confirmed.

"She was moved, a few hours after she was killed. There's livor mortis on her breasts, inner arms, abdomen, and feet."

"Huh... that doesn't make sense," Michowsky said, speaking more to himself.

"Yes, it does, if you picture her bent over a table or a high bed, with her ankles tied to the posts, and her wrists tied forward. After she died, she was left in that position for at least three or four hours, judging by the levels of set lividity. The blood pooled in the areas touching support surfaces: her feet, arms, chest, and abdomen. Then she was moved in this position we see here, prior to full onset of rigor mortis."

"You're saying, dumped here, while almost in rigor? Are you sure?"

"Very," Doc Rizza sighed and shot Michowsky an almost offended look. "There's absolutely no sign of insect activity, and no sand or dust settled on her skin. She hasn't been here long."

"That's ballsy," Michowsky replied, pointing his flashlight into the thick forest stretching behind the Trask property line. "What's that way?"

AJ, Doc Rizza's assistant, approached with his smartphone in hand, and showed the two men the screen. They saw a satellite view of the area, with a little blue dot marking their position, at the edge of the home's backyard.

"There's nothing but this stretch of woods, up to the highway behind it. It's not even that far to the road; maybe 100 feet or so in a straight line," AJ explained. "I guess he came through there, not through the street."

"Don't guess, AJ," Doc Rizza scolded him in a parental tone. "That's not what we do."

AJ's shoulders dropped. "Sorry, Doc."

"You might be right, though," Michowsky said. "It's the logical way to get here unseen, especially when carrying a body. You can't just pull your car to the curb and enter the backyard via the sensor-floodlights pathway, and in the eyes of the entire neighborhood, right? It's not even that late. People are still coming and going." He stretched his back a little. "I'll get a search team started; we need to go over every inch of that patch of woods."

"Still not done, Gary," Doc intervened. "See this ring? It's a little loose on her finger, and it's thinner than the tan line. Ask the husband if this was hers; I, for one, don't think so. I'll get prints and trace started on it anyway."

Doc carefully removed the ring and put it in an evidence bag, then sealed it and signed the seal. Michowsky took a picture of the ring with his phone, then Doc put the evidence bag together with all the other evidence, in the collection bin.

Michowsky scratched his furrowed brow, then ran his hand over his buzz-cut hair.

"Why bring her here, Doc? Why risk it? She's been missing for a week; this is the last place anyone would have looked."

Doc Rizza sighed, and sadness touched his eyes. "I can't answer that for you, Gary, but I know someone who can. If not today, then soon. Fradella told me she came out of surgery a couple of hours ago. How is Tess? Have you seen her?"

"Yeah, through a window. She's…" His voice trailed off.

"She's going to be fine," Doc said. "That's what I'm hearing. Fradella's been texting me every hour with updates."

Michowsky watched for a few seconds as AJ prepared the body bag, and Doc Rizza packed up his utensils. "Where's Buchanan, do you know?" he finally asked.

"Who?"

"Gloria Buchanan, the missing persons detective who handled Lisa Trask's disappearance."

"Ahh…" Doc Rizza replied. "My apologies. You see, I mostly cross paths with homicide detectives in my line of work. I think she's over there, talking with Mr. Trask."

Michowsky turned and located Buchanan. She stood near the home's back door, facing a young man holding a toddler in his arms. The young boy, oblivious to everything that went on, reached playfully for his father's hair, grabbing fistfuls of it and tugging away.

He approached them and introduced himself. "Mr. Trask, I'm Detective Gary Michowsky, homicide. I'm very sorry for your loss."

The man shook Michowsky's hand. His eyes were red and swollen. "Ramos," he said. "Enrique Ramos. My wife kept her last name and rarely used mine," he added, avoiding Michowsky's glance. "Her parents were, how can I put this, not happy with her ethnic choice of husband."

"Oh, sorry about that; I didn't know," Michowsky said quickly.

Enrique shrugged and continued to look away, while his eyes welled up again. "She wasn't there earlier," he eventually said. "There's no way she was there when I took the dog out. I came home from work, I took Buster out, but she… wasn't there."

"We know that," Michowsky replied, in a gentle tone of voice. "There's evidence that points to that fact. She was brought here very recently."

"When did she die? Maybe if I had—"

"Mr. Ramos, there's nothing you could have done," Michowsky said. "Nothing. She died yesterday."

"Oh, God…" His breath shuddered, escaping his chest with a sob. Then he forced some air back into his lungs and raised his eyes to meet Michowsky's. "That's exactly where she saw him, you know."

"Saw whom?" Michowsky asked.

Detective Buchanan handed him an open case file. "The man with the rope. There was an open investigation on this address even before she went missing."

Michowsky lifted his eyes from the file and looked at Enrique.

"A couple of days before disappearing, my wife saw a man back there. But it wasn't the only time she'd seen him. First, she saw him in the office parking lot, when she was leaving work. She thought it was just some random creep. But after she saw him in our backyard, we called the police. No one did anything. Now she's dead."

Michowsky started to read the report in Buchanan's case file, but then decided against it. "Can you tell me exactly what she saw?"

Enrique cleared his throat and sniffled quietly. "He was standing there, behind those shrubs. He was holding a piece of rope as if getting ready to strangle someone. I remember her saying the rope was coiled around his fists multiple times. He was looking straight at her. She was terrified. She screamed, but by the time I came outside, he was gone."

Michowsky turned to Buchanan. "Any sketch? What did he look like?"

"None. Mrs. Trask didn't see his face," she replied, sounding a bit defensive. "We had nothing to go on. We logged the report though."

"She said she could only see his hands and the rope. He kept his face hidden in the dark." Enrique took a deep, shattered breath before continuing. "He strangled her, didn't he?"

Michowsky averted his eyes for a split second. "We'll know more once the autopsy is completed. Please, Mr. Ramos, take care of yourself and your son, and we'll do everything in our power to catch the man who killed your wife."

Enrique didn't seem convinced, but lowered his head and turned toward the house.

"One more thing," Michowsky said, pulling out his phone. "Was this her ring?"

The young man looked at the photo for less than a second.

"No, absolutely not. She wore her wedding ring every day. It had a thick, gold band and three diamonds. I've never seen this ring before."

A Life

4

Melissa Henderson climbed behind the wheel of her red Acura and pulled the door shut. Then she let out a long sigh, and closed her eyes for a minute or two. Finally, some peace, after a long day's hustle in the emergency room. She did catch a break that morning; she'd been assigned to care for a wounded federal agent, and that brought a nice change in scenery, the occasional break from the demanding ER shift.

She couldn't linger too long though; she had to rush home to her son. She started the engine and shifted into gear, getting ready to leave. Then she removed her nametag and let it drop into its usual place, in the center console cup holder. Not too long ago, she used to change out of her nurse's outfit before leaving the hospital, to hang on to her individuality, her femininity. Now it didn't make sense anymore; she was too tired, and no one looked at her anyway.

Her eyes stayed glued to the nametag; she picked it up again and ran her fingers across its shiny surface. *M. Henderson*, it read. How very appropriate. It was all him… all her life was about him these days, the man she'd married eight years ago, Derek Henderson. Only a single letter was about her, the M standing for her given name, Melissa. How accurately that nametag reflected the realities of her existence.

When had things turned so bad? She couldn't remember, no matter how hard she tried. He'd been her very own Prince Charming, her own dark, tall, and handsome Mr. Right, sweeping her off her feet when she was a young nurse's aide fresh out of school, and he was an accountant, finishing up his CMA certification. In a matter of days, they were seriously in love, and she still recalled his burning gaze as he undressed her, wanting her, craving her like a drug. She missed that heated gaze, the things it did to her body. She missed the man she'd fallen in love with.

Where does love like that disappear?

She felt a rebel tear form at the corner of her eye, and wiped it away angrily with the back of her hand. Too late for that. What was gone, was gone, but it hadn't vanished overnight.

Between chores, work, long hours away from home, and raising their son, Charlie, none of that passion had survived. That's how love dies, buried among recycle bin duty, folding lingerie, dishwasher cycles, and grocery shopping. PTA meetings, play dates, double shifts in the ER, taking a screaming kid to the dentist, and then finally home, after a shower, curled up in a ball on the couch, wishing she could sleep forever.

It wasn't entirely her fault. Derek was ambitious, and she'd loved that about him, many years ago, before she understood that ambition would make him want more and more out of life, while giving less and less to their family. It started gradually, soon after Charlie was born, when she fought chronic sleep deprivation, more painful to bear than a physical ailment. He started staying in the office later and later each day, working more, dreaming of that big promotion he was going to get. It came, eventually, more than once. He was a forensic accounting investigator now, an expert auditor, making almost three times more money. He wasn't happy though; it still wasn't enough. It was never enough.

He was never there, not for her, not for Charlie. Even when their son was an infant, Derek nudged her to do all the chores, invoking her professional nursing skill as a mandatory qualification to change a diaper, or wipe a runny nose. He sat in front of his computer, working, and beckoned her whenever Charlie needed anything. "Melissa, he's crying," he'd say, without even looking in Charlie's direction. "Melissa, he needs a new diaper. It stinks of shit in here. But you're used to that, aren't you?"

Yes, she got used to that, and soon stopped expecting anything from him. She was happy just to see him come home, smile briefly in her direction, pretend to care about Charlie for a minute, then disappear into his home office. For a while, she'd missed sharing life with him. Now she didn't anymore; him out of the way meant she could move faster, go through chores quicker, and maybe, just maybe, catch half a movie with a TV dinner.

Soon there was no trace of passion left in their middle-class, boringly dysfunctional couple. Family life had stolen it away, eroding it day after endlessly overworked day. Outside of reading the occasional trashy novel during her hospital lunch breaks, there was no romance in her world anymore; all gone.

Still it was all acceptable to her, in some twisted way. Too tired to even assume she deserved better? Maybe... She sometimes wondered about that, what her life could have been, or could still be. What if she started over? What if...? But no, she couldn't, not ever, do that to Charlie. That's what she'd promised herself.

However, something had changed the day before, something causing her to wake up from her self-abandoning lethargy and see things differently. The night before, when Derek had come home from work, late as usual, he slapped Charlie across the face. Hard. So hard, he sent his little body tumbling across the room. It didn't happen out of the blue; Charlie had spilled some OJ on his father's white shirt, but that didn't matter; there was no excuse. She would have washed and dried that shirt in no time, but Derek didn't even ask. He didn't make a sound, or say a word; he just turned toward his son, then his hand came down and delivered the blow without warning or precedent. His face was scrunched in anger and his eyes shot daggers of hatred and irritation. All she could do was get Charlie out of there, and eventually put him to bed, after two hours of inconsolable sobs.

That was the line she wasn't going to let anyone cross. Not Derek, not any other man.

She hadn't even noticed when she'd arrived home. She looked around out of habit, and didn't see Derek's car anywhere. It was too early for him anyway; these days he almost never got home before nine or ten at night.

She parked in the driveway and waved at the next-door neighbor, who smiled back and nodded her way. He seemed like a nice man; she wondered if he could hear their arguments through the closed windows, and cringed at the thought.

She rushed inside and hugged Charlie, putting a happiness in her voice she didn't feel.

"Hey, there, young man, you know what you're doing today? You don't, do you?"

"No, Mommy, what?"

"You're going on a big trip, baby. You're going to visit Grandma, all the way to Arizona. You'll go on a plane, all by yourself. Only grownups do that, you know?"

Charlie frowned and shifted his weight from one foot to the other, unsure what to think.

Melissa paid the sitter and sent her off with a thank you and a promise she'd call when she needed help again. Then she started putting a small suitcase together, with the bare necessities for her son's travel.

Charlie stood in the bedroom door, watching her. "Are you coming with me, Mommy?"

"No, sweetie, not this time. Mommy can't leave work just now. But Grandma will be there, waiting for you at the airport."

She stopped counting underwear to give him another long hug, and swallowed a sob.

Charlie remained confused. "Are you sending me away because I made Daddy mad?"

She froze for a second, feeling her heart break. "No, Charlie, that's not why. Grandma misses you, and she wanted to spend the spring and summer with you, before you go to school. She already bought you a lot of presents."

A timid smile appeared on his lips.

"Yep, she's got you a Batman action figure, and a Transformers robot too."

"SpongeBob?"

"Absolutely!"

His smile stretched out, showing his missing teeth and making his eyes sparkle.

"I have a Transformer, Mommy. I want a Hatchimal now. I've seen one I like. It's blue, with big, yellow eyes."

"Well, tell Grandma when you see her, okay? She'll take you shopping."

"Cool," he replied in an excited voice, proceeding to stomp his feet rhythmically in a dance of simple joy.

She zipped the small suitcase and took his hand. "Ready, baby? Let's go. We don't want to miss your flight."

Melissa called her mother from the car. Hearing the sound of her voice made her want to cry, but that wasn't the time nor the place for a meltdown. She took in a sharp breath of air.

"Mom? We're on our way to the airport. Make sure you're not late."

"I'll be there when the plane lands, don't fret about it."

"Call me when you have him, all right?"

"I will, Mel, I promise. He and I will get along just fine." Silence took over the conversation for a second or two. "Are you all right, honey? I'm worried about you."

She couldn't answer. She was too busy fighting back her tears. Eventually, she was able to articulate in a low, strangled voice, "Not now, Mom, okay?"

Half an hour later, a flight attendant took Charlie's hand and walked him through the boarding gate onto the jetway. Melissa waved at him, although he couldn't see her anymore, long after the gate had closed.

Cat

5

The man approached in a determined stride, walking so quickly it made his shoulder-length, salt-and-pepper hair wave with each step. His half-undone, Hawaiian shirt partially revealed a tribal tat, a stylized drawing of a tiger's face, with hypnotizing eyes and long whiskers, imprinted on his chest. Somewhat faded by the passing of time, that ink job still drew everyone's attention, turning heads, especially women's. He wasn't young, but he had an ageless, timeless quality that made him stand out. That, his military gait, and the look of fierce determination on his stubbly face made everyone he encountered on that endless hospital hallway move out of his way, then turn their heads to stare a little longer.

He stopped abruptly in front of Tess's room, making both the uniformed officer guarding it and Fradella hop to their feet. The man grabbed the door handle and whispered in a low, menacing voice, "I'm going in."

"I'm sorry, I can't let you do that," the officer replied. "Let's see some identification."

Fradella approached but stayed silent, observing, ready to intervene.

The man turned to Fradella and asked, "Didn't you call me?"

Fradella hesitated for a second, then correlated the earlier call his partner had made in reference to Tess's mysterious cat, with the tiger eyes staring at him from the man's hairy chest. He took a step back, getting out of his way.

"No, that was my partner, Gary Michowsky. I'm Detective Todd Fradella, homicide."

"Yeah, whatever."

He slid the door open and rushed to the bed. "Ah, goddammit," he growled, then immediately untied Tess's hands. He pulled a chair next to the bed and took her hand in his, gently.

"I'm here, kiddo, right here," he whispered.

Tess groaned and fluttered her eyelids, trying to open her eyes.

"Cat..." she said softly, then licked her lips. "Don't let him... don't let him touch me," she mumbled.

"He's gone, kiddo, he can't touch you again. You put him in the ground, where he belongs."

"Don't leave me, Cat... I can't sleep. Not while they touch me."

"I'll be right here, I promise. No one will touch you. Now sleep. I'll watch over you."

"Just like… old times," she managed to say, before falling asleep.

Cat pulled his chair closer without letting go of her hand, then lifted his gaze and saw Fradella, frozen in the doorway, with a thousand questions written in his eyes. He glared in his direction and Fradella took the hint, pulling the glass door shut and walking away.

Room with a View

6

The room was completely dark, but he had no trouble getting around. He moved silently while he pulled a recliner in front of the window, far enough to keep the light coming through the tinted glass from touching him. That's when he got the best view; when they didn't know he was watching.

They couldn't see him; not with the lights off in his room. He'd applied a one-way privacy film to the glass, on his side, making sure he could see in the adjacent room unobstructed and undetected. The only time they could see his side of the world was when he turned the lights on. That rarely happened, but when it did, it happened for a reason, and one of them was always invited.

He'd installed microphones in the adjacent room, to catch every nuance of their dialogue, every sigh, every sob. He'd furnished their room more generously than his. It had a nice, comfortable bed with clean sheets, a nightstand, one armchair, a massage chair, even a shower cabinet with hot water. The only thing obstructed from his view was the toilet, protected with a matte, plastic curtain to convey an illusion of privacy, and to keep their image untainted in his mind.

He called that room "the guest room"; it made it easier to think and talk about these things if they had names. His room, he called "the room with a view." How appropriate. He sunk back into his comfortable recliner and waited for the show to begin. Katherine Nelson was about to wake up.

She stirred in her sleep, then stretched her arms while squeezing her eyes shut. Sarah hustled when she saw Katherine move and sat on the side of the bed next to her. Finally, Katherine opened her eyes.

"Who the hell are you? And why the hell are you naked?" she asked, while taking in her unfamiliar surroundings and beginning to panic. "Where am I?"

"Shh," Sarah whispered, touching her arm. "Calm down, it's important. Trust me."

"Why would I do that, huh?" Katherine asked, raising her voice and getting out of bed quickly.

"Because I've been here longer than you have, and I know," Sarah replied quietly, lowering her eyes.

As if her knees no longer supported her, Katherine sat on the side of the bed. "Where is *here*? What is this place?"

"I—I don't know. I've been here almost a week, I think. I lost track. He… takes me sometimes."

"This can't be happening," Katherine snapped, then sprung to her feet and rushed to the door. She banged loudly against the solid-wood panel, yelling from the bottom of her lungs. "Hey! Let me out of here! Hey!"

After a while, Katherine lost her breath, and turned away from the door. She trotted to the dark window and stuck her face against it, trying to see.

Behind the dark window, he steepled his hands under his chin and leaned forward. She was beautiful, this one. She was better than all the rest. He thought she looked just like her, just like he recalled his mother's elegant physique—her long, dark hair, her thin, delicate fingers, her slender figure. A distant memory of her was all he had left, a memory dating all the way back to when he was a third grader, and school let out early because of a storm. That storm had destroyed their lives. Or… was it him?

That day, the school bus had dropped him in front of his house mid-morning. He remembered how happy he was to be home early. The wind was blowing hard, throwing leaves and small debris everywhere, but he didn't care. He trotted to the front door, excited to make use of the house key he was so proud of carrying. Most days, his mother dropped him off at school, and picked him up mid-afternoon, when classes were done for the day.

He unlocked the door and took off his shoes, just like she'd taught him to do, to keep the carpets clean. He dropped his backpack near the entrance, and started toward the kitchen, when he spotted his mother's high-heeled shoes and blouse scattered on the living room carpet.

"Mom?" he called quietly, afraid something was wrong, afraid he was all alone.

No one replied. He quietly climbed the stairs, barefoot against the thick carpet, and headed toward his parents' bedroom. The door was ajar, and he pushed it open a little more, enough to see if she was in there.

She was… and what he saw scared him to death. He scurried to his bedroom and sought refuge in the familiar darkness of his closet, hidden between scattered clothing items and stuffed toys he'd grown too old for.

He didn't recall how long he'd stayed hidden in there. He only remembered that soon thereafter the storm came.

Captive

7

Katherine stared at the young, naked woman sobbing quietly on the bed. Her eyes shot daggers of anger, but the woman didn't see them; she had averted her eyes and stopped talking.

"Are you part of this circus? Huh?" Katherine asked, still fuming.

The woman's sobs intensified, but she didn't reply.

"How do I know for sure? How *could* I know?"

Her anger slowly subsided, watching the frail woman heave with sobs, hiding her face. Her dissipating rage left room for some clinical judgment, and she started noticing things. The woman wasn't hiding her face from Katherine, but from the dark window. She had bruises on her thighs, buttocks, and arms, some old and almost healed, some new. There were abrasions on her wrists and ankles that had just started to heal. More bruising, old and new, was visible on her throat, and the skin was friction burned, most likely by a rope.

"Damn it, woman, what's your name?" Katherine asked in a more resigned tone, and crouched in front of her, to seek her eyes.

"Sarah," she eventually replied, sniffling. "Sarah Thomas."

"All right, Sarah, I'm Katherine."

Sarah smiled shyly between tears. She still hugged herself, and rocked forward and backward gently, trying to soothe herself, just as a child would.

Katherine sat on the bed next to her. "Let's take this one step at a time, all right?"

"Uh-huh."

"How long have you been here?"

"I—I don't really know. A week, I guess? You lose track, you'll see…"

Katherine rolled her eyes and some of the anger returned. "Oh, God, I hope not!"

"What day were you taken?" Sarah ventured to ask. "What date was it?"

"February 18," Katherine replied, frowning. "It was early afternoon."

"Oh," Sarah said, and a few more tears rolled down her cheeks. "It's been eight days already."

Katherine's jaw dropped. Was it possible? Every now and then she saw it on the news, or read about it online, some poor woman found chained in a dungeon, as if people were living through the Dark Ages all over again. Or kidnapped women held as sex slaves in a freak's basement. Some serial killer caught, after murdering multiple women, all looking alike.

She'd never paid much attention to the news pieces she heard or read; she'd always dismissed them, thinking it only happened to people living high-risk lives, to prostitutes, to those isolated people who live at the edge of civilization, in the middle of rural America's darkest nowhere. But that never happened to people like her, to third-year medical residents with a husband, a child, and a good, clean life. Or did it?

Now she wished she'd paid more attention; maybe somewhere in those stories she could have found a clue, an idea, something she could use to break herself free.

She saw her reflection in the mirror and, next to hers, she saw Sarah's, and repressed a shudder. They could have been sisters. Same body shape, skin color, hair... what they call a type. A physiognomy type. Not good.

She took a deep breath of air and focused on feeling the air as it filled her lungs. It was time to get a hold of things.

"Sarah, how did I get here?"

"*He* brought you, a few hours ago. You slept like a log, just like I did when I got here."

"Who's *he*?"

"The—ugh, the man who took me. Who sometimes comes and—"

"Describe him for me, please."

Sarah clasped her hands together nervously. "He's tall and thin," she whispered, turning her face away from the dark window. "Blond, balding."

"How did he kidnap you?"

"He said he was a cop, and something had happened to my husband. I... fell for it."

The description sounded familiar. They'd been kidnapped by the same man, using the same ruse. Katherine almost touched Sarah's shoulder, but refrained from putting her ice-cold hand on the woman's bare skin. "Then what happened?"

"I woke up here, on this bed... Lisa was still here; she talked to me until I stopped crying."

"Who's Lisa?"

Sarah bit her lip and stared at the floor. Her shoulders hunched forward, and a tear rolled on her cheek. "The one they took before me."

Katherine frowned. "And where is she now?"

Silence engulfed the room thick, palpable.

"They killed her."

Katherine felt a wave of panic rush through her veins, bringing her boiling blood to her head. She jumped to her feet and ran to the door. She banged on it with both fists, kicked and screamed until she fell into an exhausted heap on the ground, hugging her knees and sobbing hard.

After a while, she felt a timid touch on her arm, and lifted her swollen eyes to see Sarah, crouched next to her.

"Come on, you have to stop crying," she whispered. "It's not going to do any good. Come on, let's sit you on that chair," she continued, helping her up.

Katherine let Sarah lead her to the chair and sat, unable to say anything or fight anymore. Her sobs eventually subsided, while Sarah spoke gentle words of encouragement. She didn't hear much of what Sarah said; instead, she tried to recall how her son looked when he laughed, or what her husband had told her the last time they held hands. She invited her mind to wander away, into a place of safety and happiness. Then slowly, for the second time since she'd been taken, clear judgment regained control of her brain.

"You'll pull through this," Sarah was whispering, "just like I did. You just have to submit... do what he wants. Be strong."

"The hell I do," she snapped. "I won't give in, not until they make me."

"There's no other way," Sarah insisted, suddenly worried. "He'll hurt you."

"By the looks of it, sweetie, he'll hurt me anyway," Katherine replied dryly. "He didn't exactly bring me here for a day at the spa."

"Let me show you something," Sarah whispered in her ear, then grabbed her wrist with trembling, frozen fingers and led her to the bed. She stood facing the wall, next to the bedpost, turned away from the window, and pulled Katherine right next to her. Then she pointed at some scribbles on the wall, hidden behind the bedpost.

"See here? All these names? These women have been here before us. This is Lisa," she added, running a finger over the name in a silent gesture of remembrance. "I'll have to add mine now."

Katherine froze, staring at the list of scribbles with dilated pupils. "How many are there?" she whispered in Sarah's ear.

"Fourteen. I'll be fifteen. I have to do that soon."

"Why?"

"It won't be long, now that you're here. A day... maybe two. You can't really tell."

Katherine let herself drop onto the bed, feeling a sudden weakness in all her joints. She sat there, hunched forward, unable to speak or think. She breathed shallowly and felt her heart pounding against her chest. There was nowhere to go, nowhere to run. She was going to die there, in that godforsaken room.

Sarah took a strand of Katherine's hair and ran a hairbrush through it.

"Don't touch me," Katherine yelped, jumping to her feet, startled. "Take your hands off me and never touch me again."

Sarah stared at her in disbelief. "You don't understand," she replied apologetically. "I have to… I have to get you ready."

"The hell you do," Katherine replied and stepped forward, inches away from Sarah. She gave the young woman another scrutinizing look, then asked again, "Why on earth are you naked?"

"That's what he wants," she whispered, lowering her eyes and blushing a little.

"But you have clothes?" Katherine insisted, pointing at a heap of clothing piled on the floor.

"It's not all mine," she said, shooting the pile a furtive, scared look.

"Somehow, I don't think the original owners will mind that much. So, why do it? Why stay naked?"

"We have to obey," she whimpered, crying again. "He can see and hear everything."

Katherine bit her lip. She wasn't going anywhere with Sarah. Maybe she was too scared to make sense anymore. Maybe she'd seen firsthand what not subduing could bring, but Katherine didn't care either way. She wasn't going down without a fight, and for sure she wasn't going to strut her stuff naked in front of that damned, dark window.

"What's in there, anyway?" she asked, pointing at the window.

Sarah took a step back, as if she'd seen a monster. Her eyes rounded in fear and immediately looked away from the window.

"If you're lucky," she whispered, "you'll never find out."

Questions 8

Melissa prepared another IV drip and tiptoed around the man dozing in the chair next to the bed. She'd learned he was the Cat her patient had been calling for. How fitting. Moving quietly, she hung the new IV bag and removed the old one. She connected the lines and turned to leave, but as she did, she locked eyes with the man, now awake.

She managed a smile. "Good morning," she whispered.

"Uh-huh," he replied in a coarse, low voice.

She hastened by him and released a long breath of air when she made it back to the cabinet, after putting several feet between the two of them.

For some reason, the man intimidated her, although he'd done nothing to earn that. She had the feeling he'd wring anyone's neck if they harmed Tess Winnett, the recovering federal agent in her care, including hers.

She shrugged away her concerns, and her mind wandered to the questions keeping her awake at night and troubled at day. Moving on autopilot, she marked the time on the patient's chart, and proceeded to record her vital signs. She found it difficult to concentrate on what she was doing, and found herself needing to correct her erroneous entries more than once. She just needed to focus, survive the work day somehow, then go home and cry her eyes out.

She kept playing the events of the previous night over and over again in her head, hoping that at some point they'd start making sense. They still didn't. She'd arrived home from the airport and Derek wasn't there. She waited for him, dreading the argument that was bound to ensue. After all, she'd shipped their son across the country to Arizona without even telling him. He was going to be mad as hell.

Finally, at some time after ten in the evening, she heard him come in. She rose to meet him, and he looked briefly in her direction, took his jacket off, and sunk into the couch, looking exhausted. She offered him a beer; he accepted with a small smile that didn't reach his eyes. Then she told him Charlie was going to stay with her mother for a while, and all he said was, "Okay." He loosened his tie and kicked off his shoes, leaned back, and closed his eyes.

He lay like that for minutes in a row, beer in hand, eyes closed, seemingly asleep. She gave him some time, and then came near him, to remove the beer bottle before he spilled it, and cover him with a blanket. That's where the details went blurry on her, and she kept replaying them in her mind to no avail.

Did she feel the smell of jasmine perfume first? Or did she reach for the beer bottle before sensing that foreign scent? She couldn't recall... not that it made much of a difference. When she tried taking the bottle, she must have startled him from his sleep, because he tensed, snatched the bottle away from her timid grasp, and growled under his breath, "What the hell is wrong with you?"

She froze, unable to find an answer, but he wasn't expecting one. He just closed his eyes again and leaned back, just like he'd done earlier. She stood there, watching him, more and more aware of the troubling smell he'd brought home with him. That scent churned her gut with an unspeakable fear that wouldn't go away.

Melissa was familiar with the scent of jasmine perfume, just as well as she was familiar with betrayal, with being cheated on. She hated that perfume with a vengeance, and the memories it brought. Memories of dating Beau, her high school crush, and thinking the gods of love were all smiling on her. Memories of the two of them making love in her parents' home, whispering in each other's ears, then walking in the park at dusk, holding hands, and swearing they'd be together forever.

Then came reality, the reality of jasmine perfume on Beau's collar, and his lame attempts at denying he'd been fooling around. She claimed she was okay with it, just to get him relaxed enough to admit what drove her crazy not to know, and so he spilled it. He'd fallen in love with Jasmine, her best friend. He felt bad about it, but there was nothing he could do.

She stood there, frozen in place, long after he'd left her house. She kept thinking what to do next; should she go tell Jasmine, her so-called best friend, what she thought of her friendship? Good thing Jasmine was so vain she had to wear the perfume that bore her name every day, and gallons of it. That lying bitch in heat had left a scent trail so thick on Beau it was impossible not to catch it. Melissa was happy she did, better sooner than later, but who knows how long the cheating had been going on. The scent might have been on him before, but Jasmine was her friend; her scent was everywhere. She wished she could somehow destroy Jasmine with her bitter words.

She did nothing of the kind; her heart was broken. That day she'd lost her first love, her best friend, and her ability to ever trust a man again. Soon thereafter she graduated from high school and moved to Florida for nursing school. That chapter of her life had closed forever. The smell of jasmine perfume though, she would never forget.

There it was again, almost eleven years later, clinging like the smoke signal of betrayal to her husband's collar. Was he having an affair? Was that why he'd been so distant, so cold lately?

She remembered how she stood there the night before, unable to move, frozen in place next to the couch where her husband lay. Panic riveted her feet to the floor in that particular spot, and all she could do was breathe and feel her heart thumping against her chest, beat after shattering beat. Now, a million thoughts flooded her brain, unsettling, horrifying thoughts. If he was having an affair, what could she do? How could she find out? Should she confront him? If she did, would he turn violent? He wasn't a violent man, or so she'd believed, up until he hit his own son.

What if she were wrong? What if it were all in her mind? No, the smell of jasmine was there, undisputable, but maybe there was some other explanation for it. Maybe he was working all those long hours because tax season had started, which was his season to work the longest hours. Maybe a new coworker wore gallons of jasmine perfume, and it somehow clung to his clothes, without him ever touching her. Maybe he and that colleague hung their jackets on the same coat rack in the office. That must be it.

Her weary mind grabbed hold of that idea, hugged it, built visuals around it. She could see it now; the coworker was an overweight, menopausal, unattractive woman who'd lost her sense of smell and didn't realize how much perfume she poured on herself. In their office, there was this wooden coat rack, where all of them hung their jackets so they could roll up their sleeves and work hard the entire day. After all, tax season was just starting.

Or was he, in fact, cheating on her?

The sound of broken glass gave her a start. She looked at her feet and realized she'd dropped a handful of test vials. She mouthed, "Sorry," and promptly cleaned everything, then thoroughly washed her hands.

"Are you all right?" Cat asked.

She hid her tears. "I'm fine. Sorry about that."

Melissa pulled on a fresh pair of nitrile gloves and took another set of test vials, then approached Tess. Cat watched every move she made with intense eyes.

"She'll be okay," she said, speaking softly.

He frowned a little. He didn't seem to believe her, or want her anywhere near her patient.

She wondered who he was. He was old enough to be her father, possibly even grandfather. Whatever their relationship, they shared a special bond. He cared for her deeply, and she trusted him more than anyone else. When people talk under anesthesia, they speak only the ultimate truth, and Tess Winnett had called his name.

"Her vitals are improving," she added, gesturing at the monitors. "She'll wake up in a little while."

House Call

9

Gary pulled over at the curb and gave the Pembroke Pines house a thorough look. He'd somehow expected more show of status from a family who'd been so offended with their daughter marrying a Hispanic man. Apparently, it was a simple case of racism, rather than the typical entitled attitude encountered with wealthy families when it comes to their daughters.

"Ready?" Fradella prompted him.

"Yep," he muttered, a little embarrassed to be nudged like that by his junior partner. He was more thoughtful about things, he liked to believe; he wasn't slower, just more careful. He liked to prepare himself, organize his thoughts, especially before interviewing grieving parents. He could rush through everything, just like Fradella did, but that wouldn't make him a better cop. He wouldn't solve more cases, or make fewer mistakes. Lately, all he could think of were his mistakes, the ones he'd made throughout the years, and the unexpected consequences they carried.

He pressed the doorbell and heard the chime through the colorful, oval, glass insert. A man in his seventies opened the door widely, inviting them in before they'd showed any ID. The detective knew better and remained outside, then presented his badge.

"Mr. Trask?" Michowsky asked. "Detectives Michowsky and Fradella, Palm Beach County."

The man nodded and invited them in with a hand gesture. They followed his lead and took a seat in the living room. A woman, also in her golden years, sat in an armchair, knitting.

"Ah, we have guests," she said, smiling. "Get a pot of coffee going, dear."

Michowsky's puzzled eyes shifted from the man's distraught face, to the woman's blissful demeanor.

"She's... not like she used to be," Mr. Trask said. "It's Alzheimer's. This is the first time I'm actually glad about it. She won't feel the pain of losing Lisa. She won't know."

His shoulders hung and his eyes remained riveted to the floor. He covered his mouth with a wrinkled hand, covered in bluish veins and liver spots.

"Mr. Trask, we're very sorry for your loss," Michowsky said. "We have a few questions."

The man continued to stare at the floor, but invited him to speak with another hand gesture.

"Are you aware of any issues in your daughter's marriage?"

"Other than marrying a good-for-nothing border bunny?" the man asked with a dry scoff. His sadness had vanished, replaced by anger.

Fradella and Michowsky exchanged a quick glance.

"Mr. Ramos is a civil engineer," Fradella asked, "is he not?"

"Yeah, yeah, whatever," Mr. Trask replied. "That didn't give him the right, you know."

Fradella looked Trask in the eye. "Right to what?"

"To marry my only daughter."

Michowsky shot Fradella a quick glance. There was no point in aggravating a mourning father, regardless of how ridiculous his views were.

"Did they ever argue?"

Mr. Trask shrugged. "Don't know if they did. They weren't speaking with us that often. He took our daughter away from us, and then he took her son too."

Michowsky frowned. "What do you mean?"

"Dylan's not Enrique's kid. She was seeing someone else before, a nice, young man with a good, steady job. Dylan is his son."

"How did Enrique take Dylan? You lost me there," Fradella asked.

"He adopted Dylan. Now I can't get custody, with Lisa gone. He's probably not even going to let me see him."

"How about Dylan's biological father?" Fradella pressed on. "Was he unhappy with the adoption?"

"Nah... he renounced his parental rights, unfortunately. He got himself another girl, had a career ahead of him to focus on. I don't blame him. It was Lisa's fault, not his. She left him, for that awful man."

"What kind of career? What does he do?"

"Dylan's real father? He's a store manager at the local Whole Foods. That's a real job, you know, with lots of responsibilities."

Michowsky and Fradella exchanged another quick glance, then stood and thanked Mr. Trask. There was nothing more to be gained from the interview.

Back in the car, Fradella whistled. "A grocery store manager is a more desirable and noteworthy suitor than a civil engineer? Since when?"

Michowsky laughed bitterly, as he started his engine and pulled away. "Since some people are struck with color blindness. If your skin's a certain color, these people become blinded by hate."

"Hmm... so we got nothing," Fradella summarized. "Where to next?"

"Lisa Trask's last credit card charge was at a hair salon on Coral, the day she disappeared. She dumped almost three hundred bucks in there; she must've had plenty of time to chat."

"Didn't Buchanan interview the hairdresser?"

"Do I need to explain the difference between a missing person's interview and a murder case interview? This hairdresser, um, Justina," he added, reading off his notepad with a furtive glance, "might have been the last person to see Lisa Trask alive."

"Okay," Fradella conceded. "I think the husband looks good for this, though."

"Why?" Michowsky said, keeping his eyes on the dense traffic.

"Lisa could have been in that house the entire time, drugged, or tied up. Then the husband reports her missing, goes through all the circus while the missus is conveniently locked in a room somewhere, then when the heat's gone, bang! He *finds* her, in his own backyard!"

Michowsky laughed. "That's why you can't rush through an investigation, Todd. You have no motive, no forensics in the home, nothing. She saw the man with the rope while her husband was inside the home, so it wasn't him. You got nothing."

"Statistically, you know I'm right though. Most of the time it's the husband."

Michowsky let out a long sigh and shook his head. "Let's see what Doc Rizza finds on the body. Until then, humor me. Treat this case as if we're sure the husband didn't do it. I'm willing to bet you this nice, crisp twenty," he added, grinning widely while extracting a bill from his wallet with one hand, "that Doc will find us some trace evidence on Lisa's body. Maybe even DNA, if we're lucky."

Fradella studied Michowsky for a second. "All right, it's a bet. But why are you saying that? What makes you so sure?"

"Call it my gut," he replied cryptically. "Twenty-five years of doing this job, and something Tess Winnett once said."

"Spill it."

"She said strangulation is personal; the most personal way of killing there is. The more heated and personal the act of killing gets, the more likely the killer made a mistake."

The Stylist

10

They pulled into the small parking lot allocated to Waves and Shine, the hair salon Lisa Trask had visited right before she vanished. The salon shared the parking lot with a bank and a posh restaurant, marking the one-stop-shop for well-off women running errands in the exclusive neighborhood.

Michowsky entered first and was immediately greeted by a young, beautiful woman with a dazzling smile, who gave his buzz-cut hair a slightly confused look.

"You'll look fabulous today," she recited the habitual greeting with enthusiasm. "Just give us some time. Who's your miracle worker?"

"Oh, so I need a miracle to look fabulous today?" Michowsky couldn't help it, but sweetened the quip with a smile.

The greeter's jaw dropped.

"We're looking for Justina," he continued, and showed his badge.

"Over there," the young woman replied. "I'll take you." She stopped next to a tall, thin blonde dressed in black, and whispered in her ear.

"All right, get someone to fill in here," Justina told the greeter, then turned to them. "Detectives?"

"Michowsky and Fradella," Gary replied. "We have a few questions for you. Can we talk somewhere more private?"

She turned and led the way to the back of the salon, then exited through an emergency door. They followed her into the alley behind the building, where Justina immediately lit up a Marlboro.

"Might as well enjoy it, right?" she explained, holding the cigarette with thin, long fingers. Her fingernails were manicured, her eyebrows waxed to perfection, her lipstick intact. She was a poster girl for a salon like that.

Michowsky noticed the tattoo of a pair of scissors on her inner left forearm and smiled. "Your personal brand?" he asked.

"You might say that," Justina smiled. "I love doing hair."

Michowsky took out his phone and showed her Lisa's picture. "She was in here last week, on the tenth. Her name is Lisa Trask. You might recall talking about her with a Detective Buchanan?"

Justina blew out a lungful of smoke. "Yes, I remember Miss Buchanan, and, as I told her, I have no idea where Lisa went after leaving the salon. We don't ask."

"But you had her in your chair for quite some time, right?"

"It must have been more than two hours, yes. She always gets her hair straightened, then we put in those large curlers, to get the wavy appearance rather than the curly. She also does a few highlights and lowlights for depth and volume, and a cut and style at the end. She's a regular."

Fradella whistled, the second time that morning. "She did so much stuff to her hair, when she looked good the way she was?"

She chuckled lightly. "The way she was, Detective, was the result of hours of work and hundreds of dollars spent. There's no natural beauty; not one that matters, anyway."

"Is it true that you chat with your clients about all kinds of personal stuff?" Michowsky asked. "My wife tells me she doesn't need a shrink, because she's got a great hairdresser."

Justina's eyes flared briefly. "If she has a good relationship with her stylist, yes, I can understand how that could be true," she replied a little dryly, emphasizing the word "stylist."

Michowsky took a mental note to be mindful of what she liked to be called. "And did you? With Lisa Trask?"

"Talk about personal stuff? Yeah, we did."

"Where was her mind at? What do you recall?"

Justina frowned and searched Michowsky's eyes. "It's the second time you used past tense. What's the deal, Detective? What happened to Lisa?" She nervously flicked away her cigarette butt.

"I'm afraid I have bad news. Lisa was killed."

Justina gasped and immediately covered her mouth with her hand. Then she lit another cigarette and inhaled deeply.

"All right, what do you want to know?" she asked in a lower, more forthcoming voice. There was no need to keep secrets anymore.

"Anything you can tell us," Fradella encouraged her.

"She was sad and concerned about family issues; from what she shared, her father and her husband didn't see eye to eye, and she suffered to see her son deprived of a healthy relationship with his grandparents. She didn't want her son's mind to be poisoned by what she called, 'my father's ludicrous hate.' So, she just managed to keep them apart, but was sad she couldn't have a real family life like that."

"Any arguments or fights with the husband? Or the father?"

"None that she shared; this was more of her internal angst."

"What kind of person was she?"

Justina smiled. "She was… young at heart. Her eyes still wandered, you know, even if she was married and had a young child. She was in my chair, getting her foils in, when a courier came to deliver a package. Her eyes escorted the guy's tight butt all the way in, then all the way out. I remember she chuckled and said, 'There's no harm in looking, is there?' I laughed out loud."

"How about an affair? Any other men in her life?" Michowsky asked.

"None that she mentioned. She seemed happily married, but not buried alive, how some people believe women should be, once they've tied the knot. We're still alive, Detectives, you know? We can still crave attention and appreciate male beauty."

"Anything else you recall?"

Justine hesitated, thinking. Her second cigarette was almost finished, and she gave it a frustrated look. "She mentioned in passing some weirdo had creeped her out at her house. You guys must know about it; she said she'd filed a police report."

"Uh-huh," Michowsky replied, then handed her his business card. "Call me if you remember anything else."

"I will," she replied, and leaned against the wall. They walked around the building toward the parking lot, and before turning the corner, Michowsky saw Justina light up a third cigarette. He couldn't help but wonder if Justina had shared all there was to share about her client's confidences.

"I'll drive," Fradella offered, and reached out for the keys.

Michowsky gave him a good stare, but handed him the keys anyway. "Dare I ask why?"

"No reason," he replied, "just for fun. And sharing the job responsibilities, of course."

Michowsky didn't reply, deep in thought. An enduring crease still wrinkled his brow. "I wonder, if she was a regular here, isn't this place a little above her pay grade? Seems rather high end to me."

"Huh… Lisa was an analyst at a national bank, twenty-four, married to a civil engineer. Maybe it was too expensive for her," Fradella acknowledged. "Worth keeping in mind. But if she didn't have any other vices, it might have been okay for her to spend three hundred bucks on herself every now and then."

"Yep, you're right, we got nothing," Michowsky admitted with a long sigh.

In the Dark

He sat in the dark, watching the two women. They weren't talking anymore. One was curled up in the armchair, with her legs tucked underneath her. The other one feigned sleep under the bed covers, but her shivering breaths gave her away. She was proud, the new one. She reminded him of his mother like none other before her. The way she threw her hair over her shoulder when she was angry. The sparks of rage in her eyes, when she banged against the window with both fists, yelling and screaming profanities in endless fits that left her breathless, wounded, but unbroken. Just like his mother.

He closed his eyes and tightened his fists, allowing unsettled memories to invade his mind. Transported, he could see himself as the little boy hidden in the dark closet, too afraid to crawl outside and face a world that was too scary to take on by himself. He had no idea how much time had passed since he sought refuge among scattered clothes and old toys. He might have dozed off, or just lost track of time, until his father had opened the closet door and made him squint and blink repeatedly under the piercing rays of light coming from his bedroom's ceiling fixture.

"There you are, little buddy," his father said, kneeling in the closet, right next to him. "Time to get out of there, all right?"

His father extended his arms and reached around him, but he pulled back, squirming and whimpering.

"What's going on, huh?" His father's voice was warm and encouraging, but he kept staring at the carpet. Then the next thing he knew, he was in his father's arms, feeling safe. He stayed like that for a while, quiet, while his dad held him and rocked him gently, back and forth, and listened to the sounds of the approaching storm. The wind howled and blasted furiously, smashing against the low-pitched, Hawaiian wind chimes that hung on the porch. Heavy rain hit the windows and rapped against the roof, and every now and then a loud thunder strike made him jump out of his skin.

When the downpour eased up for a minute or two, he caught the courage to speak. "Is Mom in trouble?" he whispered, almost too faintly for his father to hear.

"No, little buddy, she's fine. Why would you think that?"

His eyes welled up as he recalled what he'd seen earlier, in his parents' bedroom. "He seemed very angry. He pulled at her hair with both hands, even if she was begging for forgiveness."

His father's arms turned rigid. "Who?" he asked in an ominous voice. "Who was angry with Mommy?"

"A man… I don't know."

"And where did you see this man, little buddy?"

"In her bedroom, I told you that." He squirmed a little, but then remained cuddled up in his father's arms and buried his face in his chest when a lightning bolt lit up the room.

"Was Mommy crying?"

"Uh-uh. She was on her knees in front of him, like people do in church. But he didn't care, and pulled her hair. It was warm in the house too."

His father frowned and lifted him to his eye level, searching his face. "Why do you say that?"

"Because they had no clothes on."

"Oh, God," his father said, and he felt his chest shuddering among short, raspy breaths.

"She didn't scream, Daddy; she was brave. Will she be okay?"

He didn't answer. He stormed out of the closet, carrying him in his arms, and started looking for her. Still holding him, he kicked the doors open with his foot, one by one, looking for her. Every few seconds, he shouted her name, and hearing his dad shout was terrifying. He eventually let him go, and he crawled on the living room couch, curled up in a corner, and waited for the storm to pass.

His father had paced the floor for a long time that night, waiting for his mother to come home. When she did, he didn't say or ask anything. The moment she walked through the door, he pounced and hit her hard. "You goddamned whore!"

One more blow and she was on the floor, yelling senseless words, kicking and clawing at his face, but he soon overcame her. He cornered and straddled her, and she couldn't move anymore, couldn't fight back. He held her wrists above her head with one hand, and tried to strangle her with the other, while she kicked and writhed on the floor, trying to free herself from underneath his weight.

"With your son in the house, you fucking slut?"

She choked and gasped for air, fighting hard. He let go of her neck only to slap her again, then reached for her scarf. He grabbed the silky fabric and rolled his fist around it a couple of times, so it wouldn't slip. Then he wrapped it around her neck, and let go of her wrists to grab the other end of the scarf and pull.

"Daddy!"

The piercing sound of his son's voice stopped him in his tracks, and he turned to look at the boy. In that moment, he lost focus and loosened the grip on the scarf for a split second, enough for her to wriggle free and kick him in the groin, as hard as she could. He gasped and buckled on his side, crouching and holding his abdomen with both hands. She didn't need more than that. In an instant, she got up to her feet and dashed out the door. A second later, he heard her car's engine roar, then it disappeared, covered by the sound of rolling thunder.

That was the last memory he had of his mother. Torn clothing, bloodied lip, and an eye swollen shut, running for her life, choking and yelling and swearing. He'd never seen her since, nor heard from her again. The storm had come and gone, leaving shards of their family behind.

It wasn't until years later that he truly understood what had happened that day, and it didn't help him forgive her. It just deepened the anger he felt, for having been abandoned and deprived of his childhood... and for what?

Regardless, his eyes always searched the crowds for her. He wanted to see if she was really as beautiful as he remembered. He yearned to ask her why she'd betrayed the both of them for a stranger. He craved to punish her for her betrayal, for the endless pain he and his father had suffered, all those years. He ached to finish what his father had started.

Memories started to fade away, withdrawing into the darkness they'd emerged from, and rendering him back to his adult reality. When he opened his eyes, he let go of the chair's arms, and felt the tension in his fingers ease. He'd been holding on too tight, so tight his fingers hurt and cracked, white-knuckled and numb. He rubbed his hands for a minute or so, watching the two women in the guest room.

They stood and talked quietly now, one naked, one still fully clothed. Yes, that one... that one had the defiance he remembered seeing in his mother's eyes.

When he entered the guest room, both women gasped and turned to face him, frozen with fear. He approached the new one and looked her in the eye. He saw the terror in her steady look, but also a shred of pride, of character. He lifted his hand and caressed her face gently, but the woman pulled away and grunted, visibly disgusted, turning her face away from him. He grinned and turned to the other woman.

"Get her ready," he said, then turned and left the guest room before she could answer.

Preparations

12

Katherine didn't dare to breathe until the door closed after the man, leaving the two of them alone, locked in the room from hell. Instinctively, the two young women huddled together, holding on to each other's arms, and still stared at the closed door, fearing he'd change his mind and come back.

"Who the hell was that?" Katherine asked in a whisper. "That wasn't the man who took me. This one's taller, stronger—"

"Yeah, I know," Sarah replied. "He's... there are two of them."

"Oh, great..." Katherine said, then swallowed hard. "I thought you said *he* comes and takes you sometimes, *he*, as in one man."

"Yeah, this one never touches me; only the other one does." Sarah averted her eyes and blushed a little.

Katherine started slowly pacing the room, deep in thought. Two deep lines of worry marked her brow, flanking the root of her nose. What if they were never getting away? What if this was it? Sometime in the future, if ever, the cops would catch these animals and dig up the bodies they'd buried who knows where, and she'd end up on some list, in a local newspaper, maybe on TV, and that's it. That's how these things typically ended. No future, no hope, nothing. Just darkness, and a fate that made her afraid to breathe, afraid to exist. Her hands trembled constantly now, and her heart rate was well beyond the clinical limit for tachycardia.

She watched Sarah pull open drawers and get some items together, but didn't pay attention. She had a single thing on her mind.

"How can we get out of here?"

Sarah turned her head toward her and looked at her with weary eyes. "We can't. There's no way."

"Have you tried? Have the others tried?" Katherine pointed at the list of names scratched on the wall, behind the bedpost. "I can't believe so many women just gave up, resigned to their kidnappers' whims. They must've tried something."

Sarah scoffed bitterly. "That's what you think? That we just gave up and accepted our fate without even trying?"

Katherine frowned, waiting for her to continue.

"Whatever we do, they see," Sarah explained. "Whatever we say, they hear. The walls are solid; Lisa knocked on every corner of these walls, searching for a way out. The door is massive, solid wood, and bolted shut; we can't break through that. So, tell me, what exactly did we miss?"

Katherine pursed her lips, thinking of other options, then whispered, "I'm sorry." She approached Sarah and gave her a hug, just to place her lips near the young woman's ear.

"How about we jump the guy when he comes in here next time?" she whispered. "It could work; just poke his eyes out with your fingers. I know where to apply pressure to weaken him in a matter of seconds."

A little stiff at first, Sarah hugged her back, tentatively. "It's been tried before, or so Lisa told me. Their vengeance was horrible. I—I just can't, I'm sorry." She pushed Katherine away gently, and returned to the dresser.

Katherine stood, watching the other woman clutter the dresser with all sorts of cosmetics. She organized them by categories. She had facial treatments and makeup in one pile, then nail polish, manicure accessories, and hand creams in another. A wax heater was warming, filling the room with the familiar salon scent. She couldn't take her eyes from the long, metallic, nail file; it could work so much better than a finger for stabbing the bastard in the eye. They had options, but she couldn't do it alone.

"All right, let's get started," Sarah said softly, with a sigh she tried to hide.

"Get started with what?"

"Getting you ready," she replied, keeping her eyes lowered. "You heard him."

"That's what he meant? Primping me for them, to find me more attractive while they rape me? Absolutely not," she replied coldly. "You got to be kidding me, right?"

"No, I'm not," Sarah replied in a sad whisper. "We have to do it. All hair must go, all of it. He doesn't like it. Fingernails done, fresh makeup every day. That's the rule."

Katherine looked at Sarah's naked body, scrutinizing every inch of her skin, and ignoring the blushing young woman's visible humiliation. There wasn't a single hair anywhere on Sarah's body, except for the hair on her head, that she could see. All of a sudden, she felt a wave of immense sadness swell her heart. She felt sorry for the young woman in front of her, for what the sick bastards had put her through, and for what her own uncertain future held. Her eyes welled up, but she blinked back her tears and welcomed the rising anger that brought bitter bile to her throat.

"I'm sorry, Sarah, I'm not going to do it," she replied calmly, then shoved her clenched fists in the pockets of her black Anne Klein pants.

"Please… we have to," Sarah insisted, shooting a quick, scared glance at the dark window.

Katherine turned toward the window and propped her hands on her hips. "Read my lips, willya?" she said loudly. "Hell, no!"

Waking Up

13

Tess became aware of her eyelids at first, stubbornly stuck and refusing to peel off her eyes. She forced them to open, and the first ray of light blinded her, making her turn her head away from the window. The sudden movement made her dizzy, so she closed her eyes again and breathed deeply, trying to stop the room from spinning. She felt her throat, parchment dry, and tried to swallow, but didn't feel any relief.

"Here you go, kiddo," she heard Cat's voice, and opened her eyes again to find the tip of a straw next to her thirsty lips. She tried to smile, then sipped a few gulps of tea. It was delicious, or so it seemed, quenching her thirst and easing the metallic taste in her mouth.

"Look who's up," the nurse said in a chipper voice, arriving promptly by her side and noting her vitals. "How are you feeling today, Special Agent Winnett?"

"Like I've been stabbed and sewn back together," she replied in a coarse voice, and let a faint smile appear on her parched lips. "It's Tess. You've seen my insides; I think you can call me by name."

Cat smiled widely. "Happy to have you back," he said, and squeezed her hand in his.

"Thanks…" she whispered, "for being here."

He didn't let go of her hand, and she relished the feeling of safety and comfort his presence gave her.

The nurse wrapped a blood pressure cuff around her arm and began pumping.

"We got 96 over 57," she said, seemingly satisfied. "All right, Tess, I'll let the doctor know you're awake. He'll be happy to hear that."

The nurse slid the door open, and Tess saw a uniformed cop pull out a phone and speed-dial a number.

"She's awake. Yes, sir," he said, then hung up and dialed a new number.

"Don't go calling any more people now," the nurse said. "Not today. She's not up for too many visitors. The doctor won't allow a whole gang in there."

Tess must have dozed off for a little while, because the nurse was back at her bed, changing her IV. She tried to read the name on her nametag, but her blurry vision wasn't helping much. It was as if two different images ran circles around each other, failing to overlap and become a single, crisp view.

"What's your name?" she asked.

"Melissa Henderson," the nurse replied, not taking her eyes off the job she was doing. "I'm your day shift, post-op nurse."

"Can I call you Melissa?"

"Sure you can, sweetie."

Tess smiled and looked at Cat for a second. From Special Agent Winnett to sweetie within the hour. That was the Southern way, and Tess loved it. She closed her eyes, just for a little while.

When she woke up again, a tall man who looked vaguely familiar was holding her wrist with a dry, warm hand. He wore white hospital scrubs, and the traditional stethoscope hung around his neck. Instead of a chart, he carried an iPad, and wore a pleasant smile, even if a little smug.

"Agent Winnett? I'm Dr. DePaolo. I operated on you yesterday, and you did me the favor to recover quite well. Thank you for that; I like good stats," he said. He spoke cheerfully, a little louder than she would have cared for.

"Thanks," Tess replied.

He took a flashlight out of his pocket and checked her pupillary reflex, muttering, "Uh-huh," after checking each eye. "Do you know what day it is?" he asked, frowning a little.

"Um, the day after the surgery, right?" She racked her brain to extract more information. "The nineteenth... Tuesday."

"Perfect," he replied with a satisfied smile. "You've had a grade III splenic trauma, but we managed to save the organ. Through some kind of miracle, the blade missed the colon. That means you have no dietary restrictions; just take it easy for a while, enjoy our chicken broth and Jell-O. You don't want to be bloated and put pressure on your sutures before they heal. Eat low-residue foods, with plenty of protein."

She smiled nervously, a little worried, seeing how the doctor's frown didn't go away.

"That's where the good news stops, Agent Winnett. You've lost a tremendous amount of blood, and came within an inch of losing your life. You went into stage three hypovolemic shock, and we've given you four units of blood. You might need more."

He waited to see if she had questions; she didn't. She just kept her eyes focused on him, listening.

"You might experience some mental confusion, dizziness, and pain. However, considering what I've seen so far, you should start feeling better soon. You'll make a full recovery, Agent Winnett; you just need to rest. Only don't do this again, all right?"

She smiled. "It's a deal."

"We'll see you again tomorrow morning," he said, then promptly left the room.

Tess tried to lift herself higher on the pillows, but sharp pain in her side got her to give up on that idea.

"There's a remote for that," the nurse said, and put the small, tethered device in her hand.

She lifted the head portion of the bed without any effort, and felt better just to be able to sit up for a while.

"And this is for your pain medication," Melissa added, handing her another device. "In case I'm not here and you need some more."

"I'll go easy on that," she replied. "I hate being zombied out."

"Why am I not surprised?" the nurse said with a chuckle, then resumed her activities, preparing another batch of test tubes. "None of you tough guys like the pain meds much."

"I'm hungry, you know," she told Cat, as if she shared a big secret. "That soup would be nice."

The door opened again. Michowsky and Fradella hesitated in the doorway for a split second, then came rushing in.

"Hey, you guys," she said, ignoring the nurse's furrowed brow and Cat's frustrated groan. "Good to see you two."

"Good to see you're back in the land of the living, Winnett," Michowsky replied, feigning humorous indifference. His eyes told a different story though, and Tess looked at him long enough to notice his unspoken anguish.

"Thank you for saving me," she said, and took his hand.

He didn't reply for a while, just held her hand quietly. "Any time," he finally said, then swallowed hard.

"Sorry we had to leave," Fradella said. "We have a new case, another weird one."

"No worries, guys, the job comes first. Why is it weird?"

She felt energized to be talking shop again. She felt the blood rush through her veins, and her brain clear itself of the painkiller fog.

"Ah, you know Fradella," Michowsky replied. "He sees serial killers everywhere. Yesterday he thought it was the husband who did it. Today, he has a different opinion. But I don't think it's a serial killer. Not this time, anyway. It's a single murder, nothing more, albeit a little strange."

"Tell me about it," she asked, then took the cup of soup Cat offered and sipped from it. It wasn't all that bad, but it wasn't good either. With food like that, her recovery was going to take a while.

"Um, maybe some other time," Michowsky replied, shooting Cat a concerned gaze.

Cat looked at Tess for an instant, then stood up and stretched his back. "I could use a shower and some real food," he said. "Back in an hour?"

Tess nodded with a smile, and he disappeared.

"Come on, spill it," Tess insisted.

"All right," Michowsky replied, lowering his voice in an attempt to keep the nurse from hearing their conversation. "This girl, first she sees a guy in her office parking lot with a rope in his hand. She thinks he's a creep, ignores the whole thing. Two days later, the creep with the rope appears in her own back-yard and scares the crap out of her. They report it to the cops. Then she goes missing for a week, then turns up dead in the same backyard, the same spot where rope guy had stood. Strangled with a rope, no less."

Tess nodded a few times. "Yep, serial killer."

"Told you so," Fradella said, sounding almost excited.

"Only one victim," Michowsky argued. "Not enough to call it a serial."

"Several serial killer attributes come across in this MO, even if he hasn't killed more than one person, or we haven't found more than one of his victims yet. That's possible too."

Michowsky stared at the cement pattern on the floor. "All right, let's say I buy that."

"He even has a signature, Gary. I'm guessing she was raped?" Tess asked, causing the nurse to lock eyes with her for an instant, then look away. Tess smiled apologetically.

"Yeah, she was."

"Postured too?"

"Yep."

"Huh... What does Doc say?"

"It's too early. We just found her last night. He's working on it," Michowsky replied.

"There's something else," Fradella said. "The killer changed her wedding ring with another ring, smaller, cheaper."

Her brow furrowed deeper. "How are you working this?"

"We spoke to the vic's husband, parents, and the last person to see her alive, her hairdresser. Got some insight."

"Stylist," Fradella corrected him, and they both chuckled.

"Yeah, my bad. We're running digital footprint, social media, phone records, while waiting for Doc Rizza to give us the autopsy results, trace, and DNA. He seems positive he can get us trace and DNA for this case, something solid to work with. He's found stuff on the body."

"Run a state-wide search for any rope-related sightings of creeps any-where." She met Michowsky's inquisitive gaze with a sheepish grin. "Put an active alert in the system. You know, just in case it's a serial killer."

"Yeah, I kinda thought of that, but didn't get to it," Fradella said.

She sighed, feeling a little tired. "Then you might not need me after all."

"We hope we might not need you," Michowsky confirmed, "but something tells me we will."

Lunch

14

Melissa checked the monitors in Tess's room one more time before heading to the cafeteria for lunch. She shot her patient a quick smile and waved. "I'll be back in a jiffy."

The fed seemed okay; she was quite popular, considering the constant flow of visitors, and deliveries of balloons and flower arrangements that had started pouring in. More than anything, she seemed like a nice person. She was tough, but not completely callous, like most law enforcement, bitter for having been wounded on a job that paid too little for its demands and brought nothing but grief in their personal lives.

She closed the door behind her and headed toward the elevators, letting her mind wander. After a few steps, her shoulders dropped and her head hung, but she didn't even notice the change in her own demeanor. Her personal anguish washed over her brain every time she wasn't completely immersed in her work. It drained her, flooding her reason with unreasonable fears and unspeakable pain.

Was Derek cheating on her? Or was she losing her mind? One moment she was cringing, visualizing Derek making passionate love to a beautiful, young stranger. The next, she cringed again, imagining herself throwing a hissy fit at him, and being proven wrong.

Moving on autopilot, she entered the cafeteria, still crowded after the lunch rush hour, and grabbed a tray. She stood in line, looking at the day's meal offerings, but not noticing them. A minute later, she set her tray on a table, filled with a slice of meatloaf, mashed potatoes, and some gravy, then she went back for the cutlery and napkins she forgot.

"Hello, Miss Henderson," a man said, cutting into her path. She had to stop, so she wouldn't run into him. He wore the gray scrubs reserved for imaging technicians, and the color looked good on him. He was new; she hadn't seen him around much.

"Oh, hey, Mike," she replied, forcing herself to sound if not friendly, then at least decent, polite. "It's Mrs. Henderson, by the way."

The young man smiled with his entire face. "There are facts of life I choose to ignore." He pulled out of her way with an exaggerated, gallant gesture, then asked, "May I join you for lunch?"

She made an apologetic gesture with her hands. "Maybe not today, Mike. Some other time?"

"Sure, just say when. I'll be waiting," he replied, and ended his phrase with a wink.

She smiled apologetically. He seemed like a nice guy, this Mike, whatever his last name was. Moderately attractive, but smart, albeit a little shy, boyish even. He was a little awkward around women, and she'd never seen him socialize with anyone. Maybe in another life, in another time, she could have accepted to share a hospital lunch with him and become friends, but nothing more. There were facts of life she couldn't choose to ignore, like the fact she loved another man, who happened to be her husband. Her cheating husband?

Melissa's smile died, quickly replaced by the earlier look of anguish she had done such a poor job of hiding. She started to eat her food, and it was tasteless. She normally loved mashed potatoes and gravy, but not today. They tasted like soap, the cheap, flavorless kind. She pushed the tray aside.

"Not so fast, Mel." A tall woman dressed in dark-blue scrubs dropped her tray on the table and took a seat next to her. It was her best friend, Sophie, a top-notch ICU nurse and a kind soul, who'd taken an interest in her and mentored her through her first year on the job.

She lifted her eyes and met Sophie's concerned gaze. "I'm not that hungry today, Soph."

Sophie touched her arm. "You're also not yourself today, Mel. You look like shit. What's up?" she asked in a lower voice.

She let a long sigh escape her lips. Who better to help her stay sane? "I... think Derek might be having an affair," she said, feeling tearful all of a sudden. Saying the words out loud made it real, much more real than she was prepared to handle. She struggled to contain a sob, and reached for the water bottle. She took a couple of swigs and felt better, more in control of her emotions.

Sophie pushed the food tray back in front of her. "Have some potatoes and talk to me."

"I can't be sure, that's what's killing me. He's so distant these days... we don't talk anymore, we don't do anything together anymore. He's always at work, always busy, and I'm—"

"Wait, don't tell me. You're a full-time nurse in a large hospital, full-time mom, and wonder what you've done wrong?"

Melissa smiled tentatively and took a bite of meatloaf. She was grateful for having Sophie there. "I don't want to accuse him, but not knowing drives me crazy. Last night I smelled perfume on him, and I... can't deal with it very well. Oh, God..." She discreetly wiped a tear, and shot a couple of glances around, to see if anyone noticed anything.

Sophie leaned forward a little, and patted Melissa on the forearm. She gently shook her head, and let a frustrated breath of air escape. "Then find out, Mel. Don't ask him. Most men lie. Even if you do ask him, you're still not going to know."

"How am I supposed to find out?"

"Men are like children. They think they can lie to us, but they can't, mostly because they don't pay attention to anything around them, and because they're careless slobs. If he's cheating, there will be traces for you to find. Look carefully at his clothes. Check his car. If *she* exists, she's been in that car, leaving her hair behind. Pull his credit card statements, see what he spent, where, how much. If she exists, he takes her out."

"You're so smart, Soph. No man could pull a number on you."

"Maybe, but that wasn't always the case, you know." She shrugged, probably pushing away a bad memory. "I guess you could call me experienced, rather than smart."

"Sorry... I didn't know," Melissa said, dropping her plastic fork on the tray. "I always say the wrong things, don't I?"

Sophie chuckled. "No, don't worry. Doesn't matter anymore. It hasn't mattered since I caught the bastard and moved on with my life. Never looked back since." She smiled with pride. "No man deserves our pain. Eat your food; I'm not going to tell you again."

They laughed a little. Sophie was like that, she could make the toughest challenges simple, and make her laugh, no matter what the crisis was.

"One more thing," Sophie said. "Follow him. Is he really working late? Verify that. Once you start on the path of suspicion, at least be fair and square. Suspect everything. But don't get caught."

Melissa nodded. "Yep, got it."

"What are you going to do if you find out it's true?"

She leaned back in her chair, letting her head hang low. "I don't know. The thought terrifies me."

"Would you be able to forgive him?"

She shook her head and bit her lip. "I don't think so. This is where I draw the line."

"Smart girl," Sophie said, and gulped down the rest of her tomato juice, the usual beverage for her hospital meals.

"Then what should I do? File for divorce? What about Charlie?"

"That's why, my dear, you have to be smart about it. You can't just yell at him and file for divorce, no matter how much you wished you could do that. Get some proof of his indiscretions. It will help you in court, and it will help you with the custody battle." She scoffed, deep in thought. "That is, if he's even going to care enough for a custody battle. He might not want Charlie, you know."

Sophie had a valid point. Considering the type of parent Derek had been throughout the years, it wasn't like he bonded with Charlie very much. More recently, he behaved as if the poor boy annoyed him to death.

As if reading her mind, Sophie continued. "If he's mean to Charlie in any way, make a note of it somewhere, to keep track of dates and what happened. It will help."

Melissa nodded, suddenly feeling cold, frozen inside. "Oh, God," she whispered, "it's becoming real, isn't it?"

"Listen," Sophie said, "first, you don't know anything yet. Don't freak out over maybes. Save your energy so you can deal with the absolutes. And until proven guilty, give him the benefit of the doubt. Who knows? Maybe he deserves it. You're young and sexy, he should be on fire around you. Reach out, see if you can kindle that fire again somehow."

She felt a shudder, remembering how he hit Charlie. That single event had killed her libido indefinitely. She couldn't bring herself to tell Sophie about it, though. She kept clinging to the hope that it was an isolated incident, never to happen again.

Sophie gave her forearm one last squeeze, then hopped to her feet. "I got to run, I'm already late. Hang in there, Mel, and let me know if I can help."

She nodded one more time. "Thank you, Soph, you're a lifesaver."

She watched Sophie walk away with a determined stride, then let her head fall in her hands the moment she vanished from view.

Spy on him? She felt cheap, dirtied by her mistrust. Yet there was no other way to know for sure.

Pathology

15

Cat quietly snuck back into Tess's hospital room, and closed the door behind him without making a sound. Then he closed the blinds more than halfway, to give them some privacy. He wore a satisfied smile on his face, and Tess couldn't help but smile back.

"What's going on?" she asked. "What's with all the secrecy?"

"Where's everyone?" he asked, ignoring her question.

"Gone. Gary and Todd went back to work some time ago, and Melissa, the nurse, is on her lunch break. Why?" She frowned a little, but not enough to erase the smile from her lips. Then a scent caught her attention, and she flared her nostrils inhaling it, welcoming the savor, anticipating the taste. "You didn't…"

He nodded vigorously, and retrieved a small Styrofoam box from his jacket. "Hell, yeah. The doctor said protein, didn't he?"

They chuckled as Tess opened the box and took in the aroma of the double cheeseburger, set on fresh lettuce. He handed her a plastic fork, and she immediately took a bite. "Oh, this is so good!"

He sat in the chair next to her bed, watching her eat. "Take it easy, kiddo, don't rush."

"Are you kidding me? What if they come in here and take it away before I'm done?" she replied with her mouth full.

They heard voices in the hallway, and Tess quickly slapped the lid back onto the Styrofoam box and hid it under the covers. Then she wiped her mouth discreetly, and swallowed the last mouthful just as Melissa walked back inside.

The nurse stopped in her tracks and took in the scene. Blinds closed, a rattled, fidgety patient, a guilty-looking visitor. She'd probably seen it before.

She started laughing. "Come on, you two, 'fess up."

"What are you talking about?" Tess asked, as innocently as she could.

Melissa propped her hands on her hips. "I'd have to be dead not to smell that burger. Eat it while it's warm, if you still have it, but skip the bread and the onions. No pickle, either."

Cat lowered his head and shook it gently, but his shoulders heaved as he laughed quietly.

Tess mustered whatever dignity she had left and pulled the box from underneath the covers. She opened it and took another bite, trying not to laugh. Laughing tugged at her stitches, and it was still quite painful.

Melissa waited patiently by the bed for her to finish. When she did, she took the box and disposed of it in the bio-hazard trash can, where no one would look.

"We need to get rid of that smell," she said. She took an air freshener spray from a closet and discharged it generously into the air, then opened the blinds and pulled the door wide open, to let some fresh air in.

"Thank you, Melissa," Tess said.

"Don't mention it," the nurse replied. "No, I mean seriously, don't mention a word. It's against hospital policy to eat outside food while you're in post-op recovery."

A quick rap on the door frame, and Michowsky popped his head in. "We're back!"

Tess waved them in, and lifted her backrest another notch.

After Fradella, Doc Rizza walked inside, carrying a flower arrangement.

"Thank you so much, Doc, they're beautiful!"

The chubby, balding medical examiner blushed instantly. "These aren't from me. I, um, just signed for these… I should have brought you some flowers too. I'm terribly sorry."

"Nothing to be sorry about, Doc, you're a busy man, and you still came to see me. That's worth more."

Embarrassed, he handed her the card that came with the arrangement. It was a funny, get-well card with a drawing of a uniformed cop with a x-shaped Band-Aid over his stomach, and it was signed by Bill McKenzie, supervisory special agent, or SSA for short.

"It's from Bill, the profiler at Quantico. I'm sure you remember him."

"The one who made you an incredible job offer that you somehow managed to refuse?" Fradella asked. "I still can't believe you didn't want to work in the Behavioral Science Unit."

"Uh-huh, I remember Bill," Michowsky replied morosely.

They'd pulled a couple of chairs closer, but there weren't enough for all of them. Melissa pushed over a lab stool on wheels, and Doc took it and rolled it next to the bed.

"We went through the preliminary autopsy results," Doc said, "and the guys said we should share this with you. I agree."

"Okay, that's my cue," Cat said, and left the room.

"The preliminary cause of death was confirmed. Lisa Trask was strangled with jute twine, about half an inch thick. It left jute fibers in the skin abrasions on her neck. But that's not all it left. This is where it gets interesting."

Doc opened a file and showed Tess some close-up shots of Lisa's throat wounds. The rope had chafed the skin raw, causing superficial bleeding.

"I swabbed these abrasions and checked for DNA. I found samples that don't match Lisa's blood type."

Tess's eyes lit up. "We got lucky. DNA test pending?"

"Yes, and it will take a while, almost a week, unfortunately. We'll discuss that later. As I said, I ran quick, blood-type tests on the samples. That's how I found two distinctive samples."

Her eyebrows shot up. "More than one DNA sample?"

Doc Rizza nodded. "That's what I found, a type O-negative, and an A-positive. Lisa was B positive. But there's more. I got intrigued, so I ran a simple, qualitative, blood test to establish gender, and that's where the surprise came. One of the samples is female."

"Oh…" Tess reacted. "So the rope left female transfer DNA in Lisa's abrasions?"

"Uh-huh, that's exactly it," Doc replied.

"You know what that means, Gary," she said, turning toward Michowsky and Fradella.

"Yeah, I do," Michowsky replied morosely. "I came to the same conclusion, but started from a different point. There have been other reports of creepy-man-with-a-rope sightings. Three more. We have a serial killer on our hands."

"Or two," Doc Rizza intervened. "If we could return to the autopsy findings, please?"

Tess frowned and propped herself against the pillows. "I'm guessing there's more."

"More DNA, for starters. There was a third DNA sample, male, in the semen I found inside Lisa's body. She was forcefully raped, multiple times. Some vaginal tearings had started to heal, while others were fresh, perimortem. Plenty of bruising on her thighs, arms, buttocks, and abdomen. She was tied up repeatedly, and there were abrasions on her wrists and ankles, some starting to heal. See here," Doc added, and pushed detailed photos toward Tess.

She picked them up, one by one, and studied them carefully.

"This is the ring you were talking about?"

Fradella leaned to look. "Yes, that's the one the husband said doesn't match."

"Looks really cheap."

"I had someone look into it. It's dollar-store grade, widely available. We couldn't lift any prints though."

"What do you think it means?" Fradella asked. "Changing her ring?"

"I'm not entirely sure," Tess replied, rubbing the back of her head. "Taking her wedding ring, that's rather common in serial-killer signature, to take memorabilia, tokens to remind him of his victims. By taking a wedding ring specifically, the killer annihilates the victim's marriage, nullifies it, erases the other man from the picture. To put another ring in place, and such a cheap one, that's the part I'm not sure about, but I'm positive it means something. Could be his way to express disdain or contempt for the institution of matrimony, or for that particular victim's marriage. We need more information about the other rope-creep sightings."

"As soon as Doc's done." Michowsky gestured an apology.

Doc Rizza checked his notes quickly. "Let's go back to Lisa Trask's throat abrasions, and what they mean. The findings are consistent with ligature strangulation, down to the very last detail. See here, we have subcutaneous hemorrhage, blistering, exfoliation. Again, some of it starting to heal. These are all antemortem or perimortem injuries."

Tess ran her hand through her hair. She still felt the fog of painkillers in her brain, and wished it gone. "Meaning she was strangled before?"

"Meaning it could have been some sort of rape and sexual asphyxia combo going on, at the hands of two assailants. Consistent with the two male DNA samples we found. One was found only in the semen; we'll call that donor 'the rapist.' The other one, probably through transferred epithelials, while the killer grabbed and pulled the rope without gloves. Simply put, rope burn. His skin exfoliated due to the rope's abrasive characteristics, leaving marks on his hands, and transferrable skin cells on the murder weapon. We'll call this man 'the strangler.'"

"Whoa…" Tess reacted. "You're saying the strangler never raped her, and the rapist never touched the rope?"

"Seems that way."

Her frown deepened. Serial offender couples or teams weren't new; just rare, and more challenging to profile.

"See here," Doc Rizza showed her another close-up image of Lisa's throat, right under her chin. "This particular abrasion that looks like pinched skin, right there, is where the rope ends crossed. The strangler stood in front of her, pulling the rope ends to the sides and upward."

"I see," Tess replied, not taking her eyes off the close-up of the victim's throat.

"There were hemorrhagic spots on her scalp. My guess is the rapist was pulling her hair, forcing her head back, and opening access to her throat for the strangler. These other images, taken at the crime scene, will show you the telltale livor mortis signs. You can easily visualize how she was placed and immobilized for her ordeal."

"Can I keep these?"

"Sure, that's why I brought them."

"Anything else, Doc? Tox screen?"

"Negative on preliminary, still waiting on the advanced. Another interesting finding is that she was perfectly groomed, for someone kept in captivity for more than a week. Fingernails and toenails perfectly manicured, freshly applied nail polish and makeup. All unwanted hair was waxed, and I mean all of it. Recently; it didn't have enough time to start growing back."

"Okay, that's unusual," Tess mumbled, then turned to Michowsky and Fradella. "Let's hear about the other rope-creep sightings."

"Database returned two other missing persons who had previously reported a man holding a rope, close to their places of employment or homes. Sarah Thomas, twenty-seven, a human resources manager for a services company, has been missing since February 10. She disappeared from a mall parking lot. She'd seen the man with the rope a few days before being taken, but didn't file a complaint because she didn't really see his face. The husband mentioned the incident in the missing person's report."

"If he's killing them after keeping them for fewer than ten days, we don't have a lot of time," Tess said. "Ten days means today. Sarah might already be dead, or they might kill her very soon. Who's next?"

"Dr. Katherine Nelson, also twenty-seven, third-year medical resident here, at University of Miami Hospital. She was taken two days ago; she vanished from the hospital parking lot."

"Oh, my God," Melissa gasped, and promptly covered her mouth with her hands.

They'd forgotten about her, and stopped noticing when she came in and out of the room, probably tending to other patients when she was absent.

"Did you know Dr. Nelson?" Tess asked her.

"A little. She's doing her pediatrics rotation. We don't cross paths that often. She's smart and decisive, just like a good doctor should be. She's also a bit snappy, even irate at times; that's not that great."

"Melissa, you know you cannot talk to anyone about anything you hear us discuss in here, right?"

"Mum's the word, I swear," she said, forcing herself to sound cheerful, but her eyes were still wide with fear. "In our parking lot? I can't believe it."

Tess and the detectives exchanged concerned looks. They didn't want any leaks to the media.

"Just be careful, and you should be fine. We'll add security to the parking lot, to make sure everyone's safe. That will make you feel better about not being able to warn your friends."

"Yeah, got it," she replied. "I know how this works, Tess. You'll land me in jail if I say anything."

Tess nodded once and smiled, almost apologetically.

"Yeah, that's exactly what will happen," Michowsky reinforced the point in a harsh voice. Tess frowned at him and he let it drop.

"Maybe it's best if I leave for now," Melissa offered. "You have enough IV drip for another hour or so, and I can work on my charts from someplace else. Buzz me if you need me," she added, gesturing toward the bed controls.

As soon as she closed the door behind her, Michowsky groaned. "Ahh, damn it. You think she'll keep her mouth shut?"

"She's a smart woman," Tess replied. "Give her some credit."

"All right," Michowsky replied. "Back to Dr. Nelson. She saw the man with the rope here first, in the hospital parking lot, a couple of days before she went missing. Then at home, that same evening. That's when she called it in. Two days later, she vanished."

"So he takes two at a time? Or maybe Sarah's dead already, and we haven't found her body yet?" Tess asked.

"*They*," Doc Rizza said. "They take two at a time."

"Yeah, you're right... Who's the third case of rope sighting?"

"An older case, a cold one from last year. Vic was found in the water, all trace evidence compromised. During the investigation, it was revealed that the victim had shared with friends she'd been spooked by the rope man, but never reported it. End of story... case went cold from there. The rest fits; strangled and raped, wedding ring replaced. No DNA though, not a trace. Water is a great forensic countermeasure."

Tess stayed silent for a minute or so, processing everything she'd learned. She needed to get involved, and she needed help. Those DNA tests couldn't take a week, not when lives were at stake. She was going to call Pearson, to have the samples moved to the FBI lab by courier, and the results delivered in a day, tops. Pearson was going to give her an earful, but she'd have to take his scolding and get the lab work approved. She needed Donovan too, her FBI analyst. The man was amazing; there wasn't a piece of data buried anywhere, in any system or database, that he couldn't dig up and cross reference.

"I know what the rope man is doing," she finally said.

The three men watched her with interest, without saying a word.

"He's giving these women warnings. He shows them what's waiting for them, and somehow they fail to heed. That's why none of them see his face... they only see the rope, coiled tightly on his fists, ready to kill. They see death; he shows them a glimpse of death."

Sarah

16

Katherine angrily paced the small room, shooting venomous glares at the dark window. She'd defied them some time ago, had yelled rants at the dark window, filled with loathing and desperation, and nothing happened. Did they not hear her? Or did they choose to ignore her for now, and save their punishment for later?

Sarah still sniffled, curled up in the armchair, turned away from the window. She must have been terrified of the potential consequences following Katherine's defiance. She'd told her the punishment had been severe for the girls who tried to disobey in one form or another, but she didn't share what she meant by that. How severe? Was it worth trying? Maybe she should just comply, trust the other woman's judgment and experience, and make sure she didn't have to suffer more than was strictly necessary.

Katherine felt her willpower erode, destroyed by hopelessness and despair. Why did it matter? Clothes on or off, who cared, if they were never going to see the light of day again? Same for the makeup and grooming masquerade those freaks imposed. A pang of guilt stabbed her weary mind when she realized she'd been gambling with Sarah's life too, by not allowing her to do as she'd been told.

She considered her options one last time, then approached Sarah and gently touched her shoulder. "Listen, Sarah, I'm sorry if I—"

She froze, hearing the clacking noise of the deadbolt being pulled. Sarah jumped off the armchair and almost hid behind her, clasping her hand. The door opened and the bastard who'd kidnapped her took a couple of steps inside the room, then stopped.

"You, let's go," he gestured toward Sarah.

She whimpered and hugged herself, half-bent forward, as if almost ready to collapse. "No, please, no." Her whimpers turned to loud, uncontrollable sobs, but the man didn't care.

"Leave her alone," Katherine said fiercely, and took a step forward, inserting herself between Sarah and the man. Maybe she could overpower him… maybe.

The man laughed, the aroused laugh of a pervert. "Wait your turn, little beauty, don't be so eager. There's plenty down here to satisfy both you bitches." He ended his phrase with a terrifying grin and a pat on his groin.

Then he shoved Katherine out of the way and slapped Sarah hard, sending her to the ground. He grabbed her arm and started dragging her away, but Katherine jumped him from behind, trying to grab his neck with both hands and pinch his carotid arteries long enough to cut the blood flow to his brain and take him down. He shook her off without much effort, then punched her in the jaw, slamming her against the wall. She heard her teeth crack and fell into a heap, seeing stars.

The man dragged Sarah away and bolted the door. Seconds later, something unusual made Katherine get back on her feet, despite feeling dizzy and nauseated.

Muffled noises came from behind that dreaded window, and the light had been turned on. In shock, Katherine watched the man drag Sarah to a tall, wooden bench. It was the only piece of furniture in the room, with the exception of a massive, leather recliner. The floor was graded cement, and had a drain at the center, where dried blood stained the dirty surface. The bench was riveted to the floor, only a few feet away from the window.

Sarah cried and begged, but the man didn't hesitate. He manhandled her brutally, and tied her ankles to the bench legs, then he cuffed her wrists and chained those cuffs across the bench, to the other two wooden legs.

Katherine cried and gasped in horror, then forced a deep breath of air into her lungs and screamed as hard as she could. "No! Let her go!" She pounded on the window with both her fists, but the man only grinned as he positioned himself behind Sarah, and grabbed a fistful of her hair, yanking hard.

Sarah's eyes turned toward the window as she endured the assault. Katherine locked eyes with her, pounding on that glass, screaming, crying, wishing she could help her with more than just a look. Then Sarah closed her eyes, taking refuge inside herself.

That's when the second man came in, the taller, stronger one, the one with dark hair. Or so Katherine thought, because from her vantage point she couldn't see his face. But she saw enough to start screaming again.

The man stopped in front of Sarah, and watched for a few minutes what the other man was doing to her. Then he slid his hand into his pocket and took out a piece of thick twine, and slowly coiled it around his fists. He tugged at it, to make sure he had a good, strong grip, then waited in front of Sarah for a few minutes more.

She'd seen that rope before. She'd seen those fists before.

"No! Please, no!" Katherine yelled, pounding some more. Neither man seemed to hear her.

She looked around the room, desperately looking for something she could use to break that window. She grabbed the chair and slammed it against the window as hard as she could, but didn't even scratch it. She tried again and again, then let it drop to the floor, breathless.

Tears ran freely on her cheeks. Her hands touched the window where she saw Sarah's face, and she screamed when the rapist grabbed a handful of Sarah's hair again and pulled hard, forcing her head up. The other man quickly wrapped the rope around her neck, and started pulling. Sarah writhed and struggled against her restraints, gasping for air, her eyes wide open and agonizing. Then her body fell onto the bench, inert, no longer moving or drawing breath.

She was gone.

The light turned off in that abhorrent room, and Katherine couldn't see anything anymore. She let herself slide to the floor, sobbing hard and hugging her knees.

There was no hope left, not even a trace. She was going to die in there. Soon.

Memories

17

He took his seat on the recliner, moving in the darkness with ease, like a feline. He closed his eyes for a second and breathed deeply, feeling sated, fulfilled. He enjoyed those moments deeply, the moments of perfect, complete gratification that came immediately after taking a life.

Slowly, he coiled the rope and slid it into his pocket. Then he opened his eyes and looked at Katherine.

She was still on the floor, under the windowsill, sobbing and hugging her knees. He could still see her, not directly, but through the reflection in the mirror hanging on the opposite wall. Her entire body heaved, and her hands trembled, clasped together, held tightly at her chest. She'd withdrawn into the corner and looked small, fragile. Not an ounce of her earlier arrogance was left.

"Whore," he whispered, "this is your lesson. Learn it well."

He leaned farther back into the recliner and closed his eyes. Against the blackness of his closed eyelids, images started to form and dance, blurry at first, almost as wisps of gray clouds against a black sky. Then the images came into focus and fell into place, countless pieces of an ephemeral puzzle, painting the picture he could never forget.

He saw his mother, naked on the floor of her own bedroom, in front of a man who pulled her hair rhythmically as he thrust his hips and groaned. He recalled the little boy running away scared, terrified she was going to die.

He squeezed his eyelids, forcing that image to go away, and the memories to fast forward a few months. There he was, on a day like many others around that time, coming home from school, wandering as slowly as he possibly could. He was in no rush to get home; nothing good waited there anyway. He examined the leaves in a neighbor's hedge for a few minutes, then played with the pastor's dog until the old mutt was out of breath and went away to cool off under a big magnolia tree.

His stomach growled, reminding him he hadn't had anything to eat that day. No one packed his lunch anymore, and there was no lunch money his father could spare. He braved it out, day after endless, hungry day.

He made a quick detour and stopped at Mrs. Kingston's. She always had something good to eat, and she shared generously, without asking questions.

She wanted little in return; just for him to wash his hands before eating, and rinse his plate after he was done.

Mrs. Kingston's car wasn't in her driveway, and he suddenly felt overwhelmingly sad, as if he'd lost a friend. He knocked on the door anyway, waited, listened, but no one responded. Resigned, he dragged his feet the remaining distance, and finally arrived home.

His father was already there, looking the same, doing the same, wearing the same dirty undershirt and shorts, and holding the same half-empty bottle of liquor. It must have been a different bottle though, because he didn't take too long to empty one, and every time the little boy took the trash out, the clinking sound of empty booze bottles resounded and made a statement.

The man barely acknowledged the boy's presence. He stared into emptiness, and didn't say anything when his son dropped his backpack near the door and went straight for the fridge. The little boy opened the door, looked inside for a second, then closed it. With his shoulders hunched and his head hanging low, he passed by his father, heading toward the back of the house.

His father grabbed his arm. "Hey, kid," he said in a coarse voice, breathing the smell of alcohol into the air, where it hung around him like a shroud. "Aren't you hungry?"

The boy shifted his weight from one skinny leg to the other, and tried to free himself from his father's grip. "There's no food, Daddy."

"There's some cheese in there, son. You like cheese." The man took another gulp of liquor, then coughed a couple of times.

"It smells funny," the boy replied, finally able to yank his arm free. He immediately took two steps back, putting more distance between the two of them. "It's got green spots on it, and it stinks."

The man didn't say anything for a while, continuing to stare into nothingness, and every now and then swishing the remainder of bourbon in the bottle with quick, round gestures.

"It's the whore's fault, son, you know that, don't you?"

The boy looked at his father, then his eyes circled the once-beautiful room, now littered with trash and dirt, and forever sunk in semi-darkness, from the blinds that never went up. The man had hardly moved since the night of the storm; something inside him had died the night he tried to kill his cheating wife. Yes, it was the whore's fault.

"That's what whores will make you do, son," he suddenly said in a forceful, angry voice. "They'll make you a killer. They'll ruin your life, snatch it from underneath you, and stop your heart." He looked at his son with bloodshot, watery eyes.

The little boy held his gaze for a while, then looked away. His stomach growled louder, and he found himself planning to wait for Mrs. Kingston to come home, hidden in the bushes off her driveway. He didn't have much longer to endure until he could run to Mrs. Kingston's; when his dad got like that, he just drank some more, cried a little, then passed out.

"Turn you into a dead man walking," the man continued after a while. "Yes, sir, dead man walking." He gulped some more bourbon. "Not even walking anymore... just sittin' here waiting to die, killed by a whore."

The boy felt a pang of fear. Was his father really dying? Should he call someone? That's what they learned in school, to dial 911 if anyone was in danger. But he couldn't bring himself to do it. He'd seen on TV what happens to children who lose both their parents. His old man might not be much of a dad, but if he called the cops, they'd bust him. They always busted the drunks, didn't they? Like that, at least he had a home, and maybe his dad wouldn't die after all. Maybe he's just saying that.

"Whores," the old man grumbled and spat on the dirty carpet, then took another gulp of liquor. "You'll know soon enough, son, 'cause you're a whore's son, destined to repeat my mistakes." He sniffled and wiped his nose on the back of his hand. "Every last one of them, you'll see. You'll come home one day to find your slut sucking someone else's fat cock, in your own goddamned bedroom, that's what gonna happen."

"What's a fat cock, Daddy?"

Silence engulfed the room, thick as the smelly, hot air that brought sweat beads on their skin. The boy waited for an answer for a while, curious, then gave up and looked away, keeping his mind busy with daydreams of Mrs. Kingston's omelet, cookies, and milk.

His father ran his trembling hand over his greasy, thinning hair. "You'll find out soon enough, kid. It's just something whores like to suck on."

The little boy fidgeted some more, still confused, eager to get out of there and put some distance between himself and his father's all-engulfing sorrow. The old man had slouched farther in the sofa, a good sign he was close to passing out. Any minute now.

"You'll see it comin'," he mumbled, "if you won't be as dumb as I was. You'll see the whores whispering, preening each other, giggling, and shooting sideway glances. Freezing when you walk through the door, 'cause they'd been talkin' trash when you weren't listening. Waxin' every bit of hair, painting their faces, their nails..."

He choked and coughed a few times, hard, and turned red in the face. He cleared his throat and spat on the floor again. "When your whore will do that kind of preening, that's not for you, son, don't be stupid... That's for some other guy. Ahh... I loved every hair on that body of hers... I loved her morning face, crumpled, sweaty, and without makeup, and her long, tangled hair, and... Lord, have mercy... I can't take it anymore."

Tears rolled on his drawn cheeks, then broke apart in his stubble. He let the bottle go, and the boy caught it before it rolled off the couch. It was almost empty, but he quietly put it on the coffee table, afraid he'd wake him up. He watched his dad fall into a deep sleep, getting a little reprieve from the unspeakable pain the whore had delivered.

Slowly, the images of his never-forgotten past dissipated, leaving only darkness behind, and that vacuum pulled him back to reality. He became aware he'd been unconsciously playing with the rope, rolling it around his fists and tugging at it, as to make sure he's ready. He coiled it neatly and tucked it into his pocket, then stood and watched Katherine for a few seconds.

She'd stopped sobbing; she still sat on the floor, holding her knees to her chest and keeping her eyes closed. Curled up like that, she didn't resemble the image he was looking for, the image that haunted his dreams and turned them into raw, soul-scorching nightmares.

He tapped on the glass, then pressed a button that carried his voice into the other room.

"Get naked, and *stay* naked," he bellowed.

Katherine jumped, startled. She stood and, for a second, stared at the dark window, with a look of sheer terror on her face. Then she turned sideways and started undoing the buttons of her white silk shirt, slowly, one by one, while tears fell and stained the fine fabric.

When she was down to the last one, she stopped moving, her fingers slightly trembling, still holding the button she'd undone. Just as slowly, she buttoned them back, one by one, under his consternated look. She wiped the tears off her cheeks and turned to the window, with a look of steeled resilience in her eyes.

"Screw you, motherfucker."

Night Visit

18

The TV was on mute, but Tess enjoyed the latest episode of *The Blacklist*. The hustle of the hospital had finally relented, leaving only core night crews on duty, and clearing the hallways of rushed traffic and swarming visitors.

Cat dozed in his chair, unwilling to leave her side. He said he wasn't going anywhere until she was fully able to take care of herself. She had to admit she wasn't there yet, no matter how much she wanted him to get a good night's sleep. Melissa had been a sweetheart and brought a small, beat-up, three-seater couch from one of the waiting rooms, so Cat could lie down for the night right next to her bed, although he kept his eyes open whenever she slept.

She looked at his tired, wrinkled face and her heart swelled with love and gratitude for the man who'd changed the turn of her life, for the stranger who saved her and took her in on the worst night of her life.

A quick rap on the door and Todd Fradella popped his head in. "Are you decent in there?" he whispered, and Cat opened his eyes and glared at him, visibly displeased.

"Yeah," she said, and waved him in, then paused the TV and elevated the bed's head section a couple of notches.

"I got these for you," Fradella said, a little awkward, offering her a dozen red roses.

"Thanks! You know you shouldn't have, right?" she replied with a wide, happy smile, then frowned a little, surprised to feel the way she did toward Todd Fradella. She was happy to see him, happy about the flowers. Too happy. *Nonsense*, she dismissed the thought, *I'm just bored out of my mind.*

She watched the two men shake hands without words, just nods and half smiles. She almost chuckled seeing how much these two men had in common, from the shoulder-length hair to the overall demeanor, yet neither seemed to be aware of it, and treated the other with suspicion bordering on hostility.

Fradella pulled the three-legged stool to the side of the bed and unzipped his jacket. "So, how are you feeling?"

"Getting there," she said, nodding a few times. "How about you? Why aren't you at home?"

"Getting there," he replied and chuckled. "Just made a stop to see you on my way to a shower and bed. Already had my fill of junk food for the day."

"Too bad, I had some hospital-flavored Jell-O left, if you want it."

"Thanks, I think I'll pass."

They were quiet for a while, the silence getting more awkward with each second. Then Fradella finally spoke. "I put alerts on all systems for any new rope-creep sightings. Next time he shows up, we'll know."

"Only if the women report it," she said.

"You think we should put out a press release? Get the public's awareness?"

She rubbed the nape of her head, thinking. "Maybe a generic one, encouraging people to report anything suspicious. If they don't see his face and, consequently, they don't report the incident, that alert you set up won't help us much. But if we call the public's attention to the rope sighting per se, we'll spook the unsub and he'll disappear before we can close in on him."

"Hey, I wanted to ask you something, regarding the victimology matrix. I started populating it earlier today. What do I do with the first case, the cold one from last year? It could be his first, and that would make it critical in the investigation, right? But we don't have much. Other than the rope sighting and the cause of death, we don't have anything."

"Add it to the matrix," she replied, sounding unconvinced. "We won't focus on that particular one, we'll stay on the more recent ones. But just put it there, to make sure we keep in mind what little information we have gathered."

"Uh-huh, will do. But why the change in approach?"

"Because we're dealing with a killing team. It's more difficult to profile, and more unstable over time, because the two unsubs evolve in different ways and also influence each other as they evolve. An entire year is a long time in a killing team's evolution. I don't want us to become sidetracked. The team might be newer than that. Last year it could have been only one unsub, acting alone."

Fradella nodded, but didn't say anything else. He seemed preoccupied.

"Tell me about the victimology matrix," Tess asked him. "What do you have there?"

His eyes lit up. "I built it by the book," he replied lively. "I put each victim's name as row headers, including those who are just missing for now. Then I added columns for each characteristic I could think of. I started with physical appearance, then worked my way to social, family, employment, and financial factors."

"How's it looking, so far?"

"Ugh… I don't think they had all that much in common," Todd stated. "They all look about the same. They're all mid-twenties, married, and have a young child."

Tess reached and took the case file from her bedside table and shuffled through the victims' photos. They could have been sisters. Gorgeous brunettes with long, wavy hair and flawless skin.

"Um, these perps cross racial lines, but only slightly," Fradella added.

"How do you mean, slightly?"

"Katherine Nelson, she's half-Hispanic, but her skin is light. As for the other two, they're Caucasian, but their skin is tan. It's almost like he's looking for this tanned skin appearance."

"You're absolutely right, Todd. Huh… That means he's very specific about what he wants and how his victims are supposed to look."

"He? I thought we're talking about a team, two men raping and killing together."

"That's correct, but in such teams, only one unsub has the anger-retaliatory profile, and that's normally the killer. The other one is a necessary element, an accessory if you will, someone who helps the killer unsub fulfill his fantasy. That means the woman in this killer's past, the one who's fueling all his anger, was a brunette with long, wavy hair and tan skin. She might have been a mother of a young child when the unsub's trauma took place. She might have been the unsub's own mother."

"We got to figure out where he sees them," Fradella added. "They have nothing else in common that we could find, although I'm not done searching yet. Gary's still working on backgrounds."

"Look at everything: friends, family, vendors, clients, where they shop, where they spend any amount of time. Financials will help with that."

"Yeah, yeah, we're on it. It just takes a lot of time, especially when you have two more women out there, missing, and you're stalled at every warrant you need to get. It's already been ten days for Sarah Thomas. I don't know how much time she has left." He stood and paced the room, keeping his hands buried inside his leather jacket pockets. "I guess I was hoping for a miracle, and you sometimes—"

"Deliver miracles?" Tess laughed bitterly. "Not tonight, I'm afraid. Just work the case, and we'll find them. We have to. I've asked my boss for analyst time and some help. If anyone can deliver any miracles these days, it's him. We need someone to look into the victims' social media profiles, someone who can access everything without any delay."

Fradella stood and stared out the window at the myriad lights adorning the Miami cityscape.

"Listen," Tess said, "you're a good cop. Trust yourself to do the good job you normally do, and I'll help as much as I can. Believe it or not, I'd rather be out there chasing those creeps than stuck here, in a hospital bed. We'll catch them, I promise." She felt her jaws clench. She hated being powerless, forced to accept the unacceptable.

Fradella nodded, then looked at his watch. "I'm so sorry, I didn't realize how late it was. You need your rest."

Cat shot him a quick, sardonic glance, but Fradella pretended not to see it.

"When you leave, please take that guy with you," Tess said, pointing at the uniform cop who sat by her door. "There's absolutely no reason for him to be here. My life's not in danger, I promise you."

Fradella's phone buzzed, and he took the call with a quiet voice. "What's up, Gary?" He listened for a second, then added, "I'll be right there."

He sunk the phone into his pocket and stopped at the foot of her bed. He suddenly looked tired, and his shoulders hunched forward. "They found a new body. They believe it's Sarah Thomas."

After the Party

19

She let a long breath of air out of her lungs and started the engine, as soon as Derek pulled the car door shut. The peaceful darkness of the car was a welcome reprieve from the office party's noisy, overwhelming clamor.

Yet Melissa had welcomed the lavish office party Derek's company put on every quarter. It was a good change from the routine, that estranging routine where the two of them passed each other in the kitchen, in the hallways, barely speaking, almost never touching. When they went out together, that changed; Derek was the perfect gentleman, treating her with deference and making her feel like he had in the old times—wanted, beautiful, and happy.

That night she'd kept her head on a swivel, checking each female employee for signs of whatever signs there would be if Derek were cheating on her with one of them. She'd personally greeted them with a handshake and a compliment, making Derek raise an eyebrow, but using the opportunity to seek the trail of that abhorrent jasmine perfume she'd smelled on his collar two days ago.

He didn't seem to mind; because he was entirely focused on his career, his wife's behavior only helped his interests. It had been a good evening for him, considering they'd bestowed on him the top performance award given at those quarterly pow wows. He was still gleaming, and he handled the crystal award with care, mindful not to put a scratch on it. He deserved the award, considering all the long hours he put into his work.

Or did he?

There she went, plunging down that rabbit hole again, although none of the female employees smelled of jasmine, or of any perfume for that matter. Unfortunately, not even the overweight, menopausal ones with thick-rimmed, jar-bottomed glasses, so the mystery remained unsolved, fodder for her unrelenting anxieties.

He'd even danced with her, twice, although no one made him. He didn't make much eye contact while at it, being too busy watching what others were doing, but she understood that. She understood the evening was a business function they attended, not an opportunity to have fun and feel good. It felt great though, to sway in his arms, and at times she'd caught their reflection in the ballroom mirrors. They made a lovely couple. He looked breathtaking in his black tux, and she'd taken a break from her typical grass-roots, practical attire. She wore a plunging neckline dress in midnight-blue silk, styled her hair, and put on a touch of makeup.

The engine idled quietly, and she took her time buckling her seatbelt, enough time to study his face discreetly. Tension lines were back, digging trenches on his forehead and marking the corners of his mouth with deep, vertical ridges. It was as if he'd worn a mask all through the evening in there, and here, with her, he let that mask drop. He kept his eyes straight ahead, waiting for her to get going, without saying a word. He managed to convey his impatience clearly though, filling the air inside the car with a crackling tension she didn't welcome.

She shifted into gear and rolled out of the parking lot. "Here we go," she said, trying to start a conversation.

Silence ensued, and his only reaction was to lean forward and adjust the air conditioning setting. The fan picked up, sending a wave of freezing air into the car. She felt the chill hit her bare shoulders but didn't complain. Instead, she forced a smile in her voice, and asked casually, "So? How do you think it went?"

A long minute with no answer. She took the on-ramp and shot him a glance as soon as she hit the highway.

"Okay, I guess," he mumbled.

She frowned a little, but then decided to kindle the conversation herself, to try to reconnect with him, to entertain and show him the two of them could still have fun.

"I have some interesting work these days," she said, forcing a smile. "There's a fed in post-op, she was stabbed in the line of duty. She's something else, that woman!"

He showed a faint glimmer of interest, so she continued.

"She's a high-priority case, and I can see why. She'd been out of surgery for two days, and cops are already lining up at her door with questions about serial killers and rapists and such."

She focused on the eighteen-wheeler she was passing, and waited for a reaction from Derek, but none came.

"This woman works on stuff that makes your skin crawl, and she's not much older than I am. You won't believe the things they can do these days. DNA, all sorts of evidence, even the rope the killer used—they know everything about it, just like that TV show you liked to watch, *CSI*."

Derek shot her a quick glance, then resumed staring at the road ahead. She fell silent, and sadness crept up on her brought by his indifference, his disengagement. She repressed a long, pained sigh that fought to escape her chest and focused on driving. A few more minutes and they'd be home, where they could both resume their barely shared routine and she could go back to feeling numb.

Unyielding memories still troubled her, reminding her of how it used to be, not so long ago when she'd drive them back home from a night out and he'd had a couple of drinks. He'd sit half-turned toward her, with a loaded grin on his face, while his hand caressed her knee. Then, inch after painfully slow inch, that warm, promising hand traveled north, seeding fire in her body. Sometimes they didn't even make it to the bedroom, scattering their clothing all over the floors and landing on the soft carpet in front of the fireplace or on the couch, for spells of passionate lovemaking. That was the man she loved and missed terribly. The quiet, dark figure riding in the car with her was but a ghost of that man, a distant stranger who no longer wanted her.

She pressed the garage door opener and pulled inside, grateful that it was over. They entered the house without a single word spoken, and just as silently prepared for bed. She let him go first, and then took her time in the bathroom, looking at herself in the mirror and wondering about the future, about the present.

She straightened her back and braced herself. She'd promised herself she'd give it one last chance, and she was going to do that all the way, no matter how painful rejection might end up being. She slipped on a silk nightgown and found her way under the covers, at a distance at first. Then she gently touched his back, as it was turned toward her, and caressed it slowly, holding her breath. She felt him getting tense under her touch, his breathing now heavier. She pulled herself closer to him and wrapped her arm around his body, feeling him get hard in her hand.

Without warning, he turned and grabbed her, landing her roughly on her stomach, with her face buried in the pillows. He shoved the covers out of the way and pulled her nightgown up, then grabbed her hips and lifted, forcing her legs apart with his knee.

"Is this what you want, huh?" he grunted as he penetrated her mercilessly. The pillow stifled her screams, and she clenched her fists on the sheets, reaching, grabbing, trying to pull away from him. His grip was strong, burning painfully where he'd grabbed the flesh on her hips.

Several minutes later it was over, and he pulled away from her without a word. He turned his back to her again, and quickly fell asleep. She tiptoed to the hallway bathroom, closing the door behind her, and sought refuge in the shower, to let the running water cleanse her aching body and hide the sound of her sobs.

Another Crime Scene

20

The upper, uncovered level of the mall parking lot was flooded with light, coming from countless powerful generators, spread throughout the concrete-paved space. Crime Scene Unit techs scrambled in all directions, examining the area in detail, and snapping photo after photo of every piece of evidence, every pebble, and every speck of dust that seemed out of place.

Detective Michowsky crouched next to the victim and looked around, using the palm of his hand to shield his eyes from the blinding lights. Toward the south, a high-rise had a prime view of the crime scene, and numerous balconies were crowded with onlookers, some equipped with powerful telephoto lenses. Distant camera flashes constantly flickered in the dark, representing the morbid interest that people have for capturing and collecting morsels of other people's suffering.

He beckoned a couple of CSU techs. "You finished here?"

They briefly looked at each other, then nodded. "Yes, we're done with this area," one of them confirmed.

"All right, then pull up a couple of your vans right here, to block the view." He pointed toward the high-rise, and the two techs acknowledged, then trotted away.

Michowsky watched them pull the vans forward and obstruct the line of sight, then saw Fradella just as he was getting out of his car.

"Good, you made it," he said, and led the way back to the body. "We need to hurry. Rain's about to start, any minute now."

"It's Sarah Thomas, right?" Fradella asked.

"Yeah." Michowsky's voice was filled with sadness and frustration. Up until receiving the call earlier that night, he thought they stood a chance to find the young woman alive, to save her. They'd been defeated.

The woman's body lay under one of the parking lot light poles, and, even without the crime scene projectors, would have been very well lit. She was completely naked and posed, this time with her arms and legs spread apart and straight, in a posture that reminded Michowsky of da Vinci's *Vitruvian Man*.

Thunder crashed nearby just as a big drop of water splashed onto Michowsky's forehead. "Let's bring a piece of tarp over here, make sure the rain doesn't wash away any evidence," he said, raising his voice to cover the blowing wind.

The techs hustled and extended a foldable canopy over the body.

"Not only did he kill her," Doc Rizza said, appearing out of nowhere, "but he wanted her humiliated after death. Exposed like that, for everyone to see... how despicable. The human race never fails to impress, in both directions. For each act of such gruesome cruelty, fortunately, we see daily wonders, acts of kindness that people bring to other people, and that helps preserve whatever faith I still have in humankind. Although, on a day like this, I must confess I struggle with that very concept."

"Doc, no offense, can we please focus?"

Doc Rizza smiled. "You mean to tell me to shut up, because *I am* working, quite focused, as fast as I can, you know. Liver temp is 30.7 degrees Celsius; that puts time of death between four and five hours ago."

Michowsky checked his watch, then wrote down the time of death as 6:00 to 7:00PM, on February 20.

"Preliminary cause of death is ligature strangulation; I see the same markers as on Lisa Trask," Doc Rizza continued. "See here, the pinched skin on her throat, right under her chin? The strangler pulled the rope sideways and upward. We have the same imprint abrasions, and I'll swab for transfer DNA."

Doc Rizza's fingers danced on Sarah's throat, following the shape of her trachea. "The rigor's starting to set, so it's difficult to feel in depth, but I can tell you this strangulation was executed with greater, more abrupt force than in Lisa's case. The right superior horn of the thyroid cartilage is fractured, and several tracheal rings were also fractured. Probably the hyoid bone too."

"He was angrier than before," Fradella commented. "That means his timeline might collapse."

"Katherine might not have ten days, like Lisa and Sarah did. She's been gone two days already," Michowsky added, then mumbled a long, detailed curse under his breath.

"Ah, and there's the cheap ring," Doc Rizza added, holding the evidence bag in the air for Michowsky to take a photo. "When you see her husband, if you please, check to make sure this isn't hers."

"I will, don't worry," Michowsky replied, as he snapped the photo with his phone.

"We see ligature marks, more pronounced than on Lisa," Doc continued. "Same livor mortis pattern as before, indicative of her being tied up on some high table or bench. I'd venture to say she was raped repeatedly during the past ten days, considering what I see in terms of bruising. Some of the bruising is almost completely healed, showing those yellowish discolored edges."

Doc Rizza hailed his assistant. "Time to move her to the morgue. I'll start her postmortem tonight. Let's step on it, it's pouring already," he nudged AJ, although the young man was moving as quickly as he could.

Fradella looked around, making note of surveillance camera locations.

"This one was disabled," Michowsky said. "It can't be a coincidence. Mall security told us it went down at 9:02PM, just as the mall was closing and all their people were sweeping every corridor to make sure no customers got locked inside."

"It's convenient," Fradella agreed. "I'm guessing not many cars came all the way up here at that time. We'll catch him on the other cameras."

"No, we won't," Michowsky said, and kicked the curb in a gesture of frustration. "Security office already screened the videos going back half an hour before closing time. No one came up here, not a single car. They're going back further, but then it could be anyone."

"You're saying this unsub brought the body with him earlier, and waited in the car until everyone left?"

"Yeah, that's right. If it had been a quick body drop, he would've come here right before posing her, and we know he did that as soon as the last car on this level pulled away. But if he was here earlier, there's no way to tell when he arrived," Michowsky said, and rubbed his wrinkled forehead forcefully, then ran his hand over his buzz-cut hair.

"Maybe there is," Fradella said. "I have an idea," he added, and rushed toward the ME's van. "Doc, can you measure the livor mortis somehow, to estimate how much time she spent tied to that bench, and then how much time she spent in the car?"

"I've seen it done," Doc replied, seemingly a little unsure of himself. "It's done through photometric measurement of color changes in livor mortis," he added, rubbing his chin. "It's not all that precise, you know. Livor mortis is the blood pooling in the tissues after death, and if the body is moved several times before the final location, some of that pooled blood shifts, and it becomes even harder to estimate."

"We need ballpark, Doc," Fradella insisted. "We need to know the time frame when the killer drove his car here, going through the areas covered by surveillance cameras. It wasn't right before he dumped her; we already know that. But this is a mall; there are hundreds of vehicles coming and going. We have to narrow it down somehow."

"I'll see what I can do," Doc Rizza replied.

"Let's get going," Michowsky said. "Chances are some of those rubber-neckers over there might have taken photos of the body, and that means soon they'll be online. We have to notify next of kin tonight. Now."

Forty-five minutes later, they watched Matthew Thomas, a thirty-year-old dental hygienist and Sarah's husband, as he broke to pieces when he heard the news. It was the worst part of the job, delivering such devastation to families, and Michowsky hated doing it, probably just as much as every other law enforcement officer out there who cared about people.

He rushed to the kitchen and brought the sobbing man a glass of cold water, and helped him to the couch. Then he sat next to him and gave him a few more minutes to regain his composure.

"I'm deeply sorry for your loss, Mr. Thomas," Michowsky repeated. "What can you tell us about Sarah? Anything you were holding back, and haven't told Detective Buchanan when she spoke with you last week?"

"She... was sad, depressed after Chelsea was born. I didn't think it was relevant."

Fradella frowned, and Matthew quickly clarified. "Our four-year-old daughter. My wife was never the same after she had her. I don't know why, and she said she didn't either. She kept saying her life was over. Then she took to drinking for a while," he added hesitantly, probably embarrassed for having to disclose that fact about his wife. "But she's strong; she battled that for a few months and got sober, stayed sober since."

"Any problems at work?"

"No, she liked her job. She helped people, and it was important to her. She was a human resources manager, working on outsourced recruiting, so she found jobs for people." He looked away, averting his eyes. "It was here, at home, where she was hurting, and I tried my best to fix that, to help her. I... couldn't." He hesitated a little, then continued. "Don't get me wrong, she loved Chelsea, but... she wasn't happy anymore."

"Was she wearing her wedding ring when she disappeared?" Michowsky asked.

"She never took that off her finger."

"What did it look like?"

"It's a swirl with two diamonds mounted in platinum, like a yin-yang symbol. It was way above my means, but I never regretted it, and she never took it off since the day I proposed to her, six years ago."

"Any personal enemies you can think of, feuds with girlfriends, maybe?" Fradella asked.

"No, nothing comes to mind." He cleared his throat and drank a sip of water. "How did she die?"

The two detectives looked at each other for a split second. There wasn't anything they could say to make it easier for the grieving man. Anything, except maybe one merciful lie.

"She died quickly, Mr. Thomas."

He nodded a couple of times in lieu of a thank you, keeping his tearful eyes riveted to the floor. Then he looked at Michowsky, letting him see the depths of his pain.

"How will I tell my daughter her mother's never coming home?"

Alone

21

Katherine kept her eyes closed, afraid to look at that dreaded window. She hadn't moved since they'd killed Sarah. Backed into the corner of the room, she still hugged her knees, and felt completely numb, except for the throbbing in her jaw where the man's fist had left its mark.

The rational part of her brain told her repeatedly this wasn't any of her fault. They'd been abducted by killers, and killers kill. It wasn't her doing. It couldn't have been. And yet it haunted her, the thought that Sarah's death could have been a punishment for her unwillingness to comply, for her stubborn and reckless defiance.

That was the thought she couldn't bear; it ripped her heart open, as if taking a knife to her chest. She couldn't erase from her mind the image of Sarah drawing her last breath, and she was terrified of looking through that window again. Would her body still be there? Would the light still be on? Would she be able to see her again?

Slowly, she pushed herself to open her swollen eyes, and squinted against the intense fluorescent light. The sight of that empty room made Sarah's absence feel more palpable, more unbearable.

She summoned her courage and stood, dizzy and unsure on her feet, then ventured a glance toward the window. It was dark again, and the absence of light obliterated all evidence of what had taken place in there. Was Sarah's body still in there? The obsessive question wouldn't leave her weary mind, although there was no answer.

Katherine felt as if she was losing her mind. Under the circumstances, her clinical judgment told her it could be expected. Everyone had their tipping point, that point of no return beyond which changes cannot ever be reverted, beyond which trauma becomes irreparable. She knew that all too well, but before letting that different kind of darkness engulf her, she wanted to see one more thing.

She slowly walked the few steps to the wall, holding on to objects, trying to stabilize her nauseating dizziness. When she finally got next to the bedpost, she kneeled on the floor in front of the wall, and looked at the scribbled names behind that bedpost. She looked for Sarah's, and there it was. *Sarah Thomas, 27,* she'd etched it sometime, unseen and unheard, probably when Katherine was sleeping.

She touched the name with trembling fingers, and a burning tear made its way down her cheek. They were the same age... but how little she knew about Sarah! She'd been so absorbed in her own despair she didn't stop to get to know her companion. That opportunity was forever gone.

She looked around and found a penny on the floor. She picked it up and saw traces of drywall on its edge, confirming it was the tool Sarah, and probably many others before her, had used to leave their names on that wall for posterity. It made sense to write her name there. At some point in the future, the bastards who took them would be caught, and that very room would be swarming with cops, looking for evidence. At least then she'd want her family to have some closure, in case they never found her body.

It felt strange to think of herself as a dead body. Surreal. Petrifying.

Yes, one last thing left to do before they killed her.

A shudder brought chills to her blood, and her hand trembled slightly as she began to write, scratching letter after letter in that grayish drywall, right under Sarah's name.

Katherine Nelson, 27.

Battle Plans

22

Melissa woke with a start when Derek barged into the room. She'd fallen asleep on the downstairs sofa, unwilling to return to their conjugal bed. She couldn't find the strength to go back there, not after what happened. She doubted she'd ever be able to sleep in that bed again.

"There you are," Derek said in place of a greeting, and gave her a disapproving look.

"I couldn't sleep," she said in her normal voice. "I kept tossing and turning, and didn't want to wake you."

He didn't reply, leaving her time to wonder when she'd learned to lie that well, unfaltering and looking him straight in the eye.

He grabbed his travel mug, filled to the brim with fresh coffee, and left, muttering something indiscernible right before closing the door behind him.

She breathed.

It was still early, plenty of time before she had to head to the hospital. She delayed leaving the couch, and thought about the next night, and the one after that. She'd lied her way out for sleeping on the couch that one time, but how about the following nights? Maybe she could change shifts, grab herself the graveyard for a few nights, until things... until what? What was she hoping for?

Resigned with not finding an easy answer, she went upstairs into the master bathroom, to take a quick shower before leaving for work. She undressed in front of the well-lit mirror, and gasped. Black-and-blue bruises marked her hips on both sides, where he'd grabbed her flesh the night before, to hold her in place. Her inner thighs were bruised and painful, where he'd forced her legs apart with his knee. Ashamed and heartbroken, she closed her eyes, unable to stand looking at the image reflected in that mirror.

There was nothing left to hope for. It was over. Her marriage was over.

She went through the motions without realizing, her mind occupied with various scenarios of how this divorce could go wrong. How would he react, when she'd tell him she wanted a divorce? He'd obviously become a violent man, and she had no idea when that crept up on them. What could she expect?

She'd heard about cases when men struggle for custody just to get even at their wives for leaving them, and she was terrified of losing Charlie. Derek made more money than she did, and was adept at winning everything he set his mind to win. He was merciless, in more ways than one. He was a wild card, and a dangerous one.

Suddenly, with the clarity only a cold shower brings to one's troubled mind, she decided to not say a word about anything, and pretend everything was all right. She'd even sleep in that bed with him, for as long as she needed to, but she wouldn't tip her hand before she'd be ready to win that custody battle, hands down and without dispute.

She grabbed her purse and car keys, and stepped out to the driveway, where she froze with embarrassment. Her next-door neighbor was picking up her garbage, scattered on the driveway and both their lawns.

"Good morning," he greeted her cheerfully, waving an empty pizza box at her. "The storm tipped these over, and the trucks haven't been here yet."

She rushed to the car and dropped her purse on the driver's seat. "Let me help you," she offered, grabbing the pizza box from his hands. "Better even, why don't you let me do it?" she asked, averting her eyes.

"Nah, no need. You're on your way to work, and I have nothing better to do," he said.

He had a gentle, soothing voice, and he smiled at her with kindness. He was good looking in a reserved, well-mannered way.

"Um, thank you so much, Brian, but I should do this. It's my trash, after all."

He laughed. "Well, unless you're going to charge me with larceny, I plan on carrying on what I've already started. And it's Ryan, by the way. Ryan Stafford."

She felt blood rush to her cheeks. "So sorry, I—" Stumped, she extended her hand.

"It's all right," he said, and shook her hand with warmth. "You're Melissa, right?"

"Yes, Melissa Henderson, but friends call me Mel."

"It's a pleasure to formally meet you, Melissa. I'm sure I can make the effort to pronounce all three syllables of your wonderful name, Melissa. Now that we've shook our soiled hands," he chuckled, "please accept my offer of assistance."

She frowned, a little confused, feeling heat flush her face.

"For what? For this?"

"For whatever you need," he replied, suddenly serious, and with a touch of sadness in his eyes. "If ever there's anything, please don't hesitate. I'm right next door."

She struggled to maintain her smile, and averted her eyes. She felt exposed, as if Ryan knew everything that was going on in her life. He couldn't have known; there was no way.

Her drive to work seemed shorter than usual that morning. Her mind was in turmoil over the impending conflict with Derek and the issue of divorce, her grim thoughts soon stifling all memory of the encounter with the kind and helpful neighbor.

She struggled to remember her last happy day with Derek, to try to pinpoint when things had started to fall apart in their marriage. When did that happen? About a year and a half before, Derek's father had died of cancer after a long agony, and Derek was never the same. He and his father had been close. At first, she'd given him time and space to mourn his loss, and was there for him, but he never reached out to her. He isolated himself more and more, and became taciturn and morose. Then he found increasing refuge in his work, or so she was supposed to believe, but he'd always been career driven, even before his father's passing.

Before her father-in-law's death, she remembered a weekend in Tampa when they'd been happy and had lots of fun. Charlie was about four years old back then, and they both enjoyed playing with him, telling him stories, making him laugh, then watching him fall asleep so they could rush and make love quietly under the covers, so he wouldn't wake up. That distant memory was almost two years old. Since then, not a single memorable moment of happiness; not one.

Two years? Where did they go?

Morning Rounds

23

Tess sat upright in her bed and watched the nurse move around, going about her business. She followed a simple routine. In the morning, she checked Tess's vitals and recorded the readings on her chart. She took her temperature, and checked her pulse manually, despite having it displayed on the monitor above her head. Then she measured her blood pressure using an analog device with a manual pump and stethoscope, rather than a digital readout. Finally, she read the night shift's annotations and took note of any medication changes, then prepared for the morning rounds that started about 9:00AM.

Tess felt better, and her head was clear that morning, most likely because she managed to skip her painkillers the night before, against medical advice. She needed her reality to be real, not distorted by some temporary high; she also needed her mind to be perceptive and fast.

She'd watched Melissa work the same routine for a few days, but lately something was off. She watched her carefully, noticing minute changes. The angle of her neck was more pronounced; her head hung lower than usual. Dark circles had appeared under her eyes, and her eyelids seemed puffy and somewhat reddish. Melissa's fingers were frozen when she touched her arm to take her blood pressure. She didn't recall them being so frozen before.

"Come," Tess whispered, careful not to wake up Cat, "sit here for a minute." She patted the bed, right next to her.

Melissa smiled shyly. "I can't sit on the bed, it's against hospital policy."

"Then pull up a chair and talk to me," Tess pleaded.

Melissa complied, appearing a little worried. "What is it? What can I do for you?"

"It's the other way around," Tess replied, "it's about what I can do for you."

"I—I don't understand what you mean," the nurse replied, blushing.

She was a bad liar too, on top of whatever else was going on with her.

"You know what I do for a living, right?"

Melissa nodded, and her pupils dilated some more.

"Then believe me when I say I can see something's off about you. I'm offering my help. What's going on?"

Melissa lowered her head. "Nothing," she whispered. "Just... family stuff."

"Then there's nothing I can do for you," Tess admitted, "except for one thing. I'll teach you how to hide it better, so others won't see what I see. It might help a little with your... family stuff."

Melissa looked her in the eye with a timid smile of gratitude.

"It's all in the neck alignment and the shoulders. Keep your neck upright, and your shoulders relaxed and lowered, and you'll appear strong and in control, regardless of how puffy-red your eyes might be."

The hint of a smile on Melissa's lips blossomed. "Thank you. Really." She stood and rolled the chair out of the way, closer to the wall. "It's almost time for rounds; I have to get you ready, and change your dressing."

A rap on the window announced SAC Pearson, Tess's boss and FBI Special Agent in Charge. She waved him in and quickly tugged a rebel strand of blonde hair behind her ear, then pulled her covers a few inches higher, to cover her chest. That was going to be as professional as she could possibly look, under her current circumstances.

"Good morning, sir," she said in a normal voice.

Cat woke up, blinked a couple of times, then stood and shook Pearson's hand.

"Good morning, Winnett," Pearson said, and remained standing at the foot of her bed. "You're feeling better, I see."

"Yes, I am," she replied, and wondered how much trouble she really was in, to warrant a personal visit from her boss.

"I received an interesting voicemail from you last night, requesting all sorts of things. Analyst time, dedicated lab time, credentials reinstated, your service weapon returned, and the list goes on, but you already know what you've asked me for."

"Yes, I do," she acknowledged, her smile now vanished and replaced by a frown.

"I wanted to ask you in person, Winnett, are you out of your mind? You've come out of surgery two days ago—"

"Four days, sir."

Pearson's chin thrust forward. "What did I tell you about not interrupting people?"

She knew better than to respond. She had an uncanny gift for reacting the wrong way and saying the wrong things to the man who could damage her career the most, her boss. The more she tried to impress him, the more she aggravated him. He did have his numbers wrong though, and she was a stickler for accurate facts. In her line of work, factual accuracy was paramount.

Cat headed toward the door, getting ready to leave. "I think I better be heading out. Same order for lunch, kiddo?"

"Uh-huh," she replied, with a flicker of excitement in her eyes, and almost chuckled when she saw Melissa roll her eyes.

Cat left the room, and Melissa followed behind him, then closed the door, leaving her alone with a grim-looking SAC Pearson.

Tess turned her attention to him, making eye contact but not saying a word. She wanted him to understand she was ready and willing to listen.

"What is this request about?" he eventually asked.

"They have a serial killing team," she replied. "Palm Beach County is working it."

His bushy eyebrows furrowed. "I haven't been made aware of a formal request to involve the bureau in this local investigation. Did they voice such a request to you?"

"No, but they're in here more often than the doctor, and it's not just because they miss me all that much."

"I see," he replied, pacing the room with a slow, measured stride. "You need to focus on your recovery, Agent Winnett. You've been injured badly, you nearly died. You can't work until the doctor says you can. Period. If they need help, I'd be happy to assign them someone else."

"No, I can do this," she blurted. "I've worked with these guys before; I've studied the case—"

"What do you mean you've studied the case?"

She reached out to her bedside table and grabbed a small stack of file folders. "I have the crime scene information—"

"You've got to be kidding me, Winnett!" he snapped, gesturing with both his hands at the file folders. "You're on medical leave, in a damn hospital no less! You *can't* be working, and I can't reinstate you. If for no other reason, then at least because legal will be on my case faster than I can say lawsuit."

"I'd never sue the bureau, that's insane!" she reacted, raising her voice.

"It's not about you suing the bureau, Winnett. It's about protocols, it's about rules and following them, and some of those rules ensure we don't open up the bureau for liability. You're not the only one who could sue if… things go wrong."

She fell silent, unable to think about anything else to say that wouldn't make things worse.

"Rules and procedures, remember those?" Pearson continued, his tone still elevated. "Pesky little things you normally choose to ignore, but the rest of us must follow."

"Yes, sir," she whispered, lowering her head for a second, then looking him in the eye again. "It's not like I can send that serial killer a doctor's note, so he can stop killing until I'm back from leave, now can I?"

"Winnett! Don't patronize me. You're not the only agent in this regional bureau. There are others, and good ones. Take some goddamned time off for a change, and stop arguing with me! No case work, no files at your bedside, no crime scene photos in your hospital room, understood?"

She nodded a couple of times, and clenched her fists. Her jaw tensed, as she made desperate efforts to keep her mouth shut and not plunge deeper into the pitfall of Pearson's increasing exasperation. The heart rate monitor above her head started beeping quietly, an alert that some of her vitals were elevated.

"Great," Pearson muttered, "just great. I can't win with you, can I?" he grumbled.

A tiny smile tugged at her lips. "I'll take the fifth on that, sir."

"Ah, wipe that smirk off your face, if you know what's good for you, Winnett."

Melissa rushed into the room and went straight to the monitors. "We need to lower your blood pressure, sweetie. Let me give you a shot of—"

"Nope, no shots. It'll come down on its own, I promise."

Melissa looked almost insulted, but caved under Tess's burning glare. "I'll give you ten minutes to get that monitor to shut up on its own, after which I'll get Dr. DePaolo."

"It's a deal," she replied, then turned toward Pearson, in time to see he could barely contain a smile. His eyes were still intense though, and his gaze carried glints of frustration.

"Glad to see you're driving everyone crazy, Winnett, not just me." He cleared his throat quietly. "I'll give your request some thought, but don't get your hopes up. There's no way I can justify any of it."

"I understand," she replied. "One more thing, what's going on with my committee hearing?"

"It's been delayed until you can return to duty. Until then, they're auditing all your recent work."

She couldn't help but feel worried. Committee hearings were career killers, regardless of how the committee ruled; such events stayed in her personnel record for the duration of her employment with the Federal Bureau of Investigation, complete with the reason why the committee had been asked to look at her record, and its findings and recommendations. Having a kill rate above everyone's average, high enough to trigger a performance review, was not going to help her career one bit. Probably not even her perfect case-solving score would mitigate that.

"Stop fussing about it, Winnett, you'll do fine," Pearson said, correctly reading her facial expression. "All your shootings were cleared, there was no dispute. It's just a formality."

She looked him in the eye, not even trying to hide her anguish. "It better be."

The door whooshed open and Detective Michowsky stepped in, carrying a large box of honey crullers.

"Hey," he said, "anyone up for donuts? How about you, Nurse Henderson?"

"I wonder why you law enforcement types have such a hard time following a simple rule. It's posted on every wall. No outside food on the post-op floor."

Michowsky shrugged, a little uncomfortable, but offered the open box to Pearson, who took a donut.

"So, tell me," Tess asked, "was it Sarah?"

"Yeah, it's confirmed. Same MO, same ring-swapping deal, same cause of death."

"We weren't fast enough," Tess said. "We need to be faster. Where was she found?"

"On the upper level of the mall's parking lot."

"Just… a mall? A random one? No correlation with anything?"

"No, in the same mall where she saw the man with the rope, and the same mall parking lot where she was taken from. We have a pattern."

"We have two," Tess replied. She adjusted the bed to sit up higher, and winced a little when the backrest moved.

"You in pain?" Michowsky asked.

"I'm off my pain meds. I'll be fine. Stop worrying about me, and let's worry about Katherine Nelson. Maybe it's not too late for her."

"You said two patterns?"

"One pattern is he takes them back where he took them from. The second is he takes them where he shows them the glimpse of death; one of the locations, anyway. Some victims had multiple sightings, right?"

Michowsky frowned and checked his notes quickly. "Yeah, Lisa Trask first saw a glimpse in the office parking lot, then at her own home. But she vanished after she went to the hairdresser, not from either of those places."

Tess rested her chin on her fist and bit her upper lip, thoughtful. "I still think the location *where* they see the glimpse of death is relevant. It's the key to this unsub's motive. Even if Lisa vanished from a different location." She bit her fingernail, then continued. "But… are we sure she did? What if she returned to her office parking lot after the hairdresser's? It's just a hunch, but I'd like to be certain."

"You're definitely feeling better. You're back to not trusting a single ounce of the work we're doing." Michowsky sighed, then continued. "I'll have her employer pull their security footage."

"Thanks," Tess replied. "I might be wrong, you know."

"We're working victim background; we talked to Sarah's family, some of her friends," Michowsky continued. "Got nothing. Fradella's working on extended backgrounds, poring over every bank statement and credit card charge for all known victims, looking for things they might have had in common."

"Include the husbands too. They must have crossed paths somewhere in the past, I agree, and the husbands might have been the ones paying for wherever that was."

"Will do. When's DNA back?"

"Later today. Maybe we get lucky, who knows. Wouldn't it be nice? To find both donors in CODIS and just go pick them up, end of story? While Katherine's still alive?"

"Right," Michowsky replied. "Has it ever happened to you before? To get that lucky?"

"No, never," she admitted with a groan. "You're right, let's stop dreaming. Better include Katherine in the background checks. Let's get ahead of this game for once."

"All right," Michowsky said, getting ready to leave. "See you later, Winnett."

"I'll call you when DNA comes back," she said, and waved at him as he left the room.

Then she looked at Pearson, who'd observed the entire interaction without saying a word.

"We have two victims, and one missing woman, Katherine Nelson, coincidentally a medical resident in this hospital," she explained. "Two sets of DNA on the victims, two unsubs, a strangler and a rapist. By the way, thanks for the lab approval. If we move fast, we might be able to save her. We were too late for Sarah, but we might not be too late for Katherine."

Pearson nodded a couple of times but didn't say a word. Then he pulled open the sliding door.

"Take care of yourself, Winnett, all right?"

Breakfast

24

Stacy Rodriguez liked to prop herself up on a bar stool in front of the kitchen island, holding a cup of freshly brewed java in her hands, and inhale the powerful aroma while watching her wife, Renata, fuss over their little girls. Renata was much better at being a mother than she'd ever hope to be; she'd been the one carrying the twins to term after the in vitro, and learning she was carrying twins in her seventh week of pregnancy brought tears of joy to her eyes. Stacy had been okay with it, but not thrilled, and that also included the in vitro fertilization. Renata wanted children, and thankfully, she wanted to be a full-scope mother, and get the IVF instead of adopting, like many homosexual couples did.

Thankfully, because Stacy had no interest whatsoever to let her body be used as a vessel for procreation, with all the side effects that followed, from weight gain to postpartum depression. She didn't even have to argue, because Renata wanted to be pregnant, wanted the "real mother experience," as she liked to call it. That was more than two years ago, and she still looked her fabulous self, no weight gain, no depression, just a maternal glow surrounding her all the time. Renata was made to be a mother.

Stacy liked to watch the acts of parenthood from a distance. She pulled her weight in the family, but she didn't feel the enthusiasm her wife did when changing a diaper or preparing a meal. Chores were chores, and sometimes she wished the time would fly faster so she'd get back to work, where she could be working with data and computer code, instead of poop and drool.

Through some strange workings of nature, Renata had carried the twins to term, but it was Stacy who struggled with the postpartum depression. In her case, because no actual baby had left her body, she secretly referred to her condition as "post-arrival blues," and kept it a secret because Renata deserved all the joys of motherhood, without having to worry about her.

She loved watching her care for the twins, though. There was this blissful peace that Renata's love spread around with every wipe, every diaper, and every kind word she whispered to the girls. The three of them together were the image of harmony, of serenity in family life. She couldn't help but smile.

"What're you grinning at?" Renata asked playfully. "Like to watch, huh?"

Stacy chuckled. Renata's mind wasn't all maternal; there was a streak of sexual impulse running through that brain of hers, hot as hell, flowing slowly like molten lava.

"Last night was nice, wasn't it?" Renata asked. "I love that patio."

"Uh-huh," Stacy replied. "They make excellent cheese sticks."

"It's good we can take the girls there, and don't have to put up with the glares from people inside the restaurant. I'd rather deal with the heat than the 'why'd you bring your kids here, they better not cry,' attitude."

"It's not so bad, Renata, really."

"Yes, it is. Maybe you're not noticing it, or maybe you're smart enough not to care, but I can feel it, their disdain, their scorned superiority, as if they weren't children themselves at some point in their lives, annoying others."

Stacy took another sip of coffee and refrained from voicing another comment. Renata was sensitive, she cared about what other people thought. Maybe it was her line of work as a travel agent booking flights for a large corporation, or maybe she'd lost the habit of not caring, after she started working from home, to be with the twins. Daily exposure to office shenanigans toughens one's skin.

"Have you thought about it some more?" Renata asked, making reference to her idea to get a minivan. Over dessert, the night before, when Stacy was most likely to say yes, Renata had listed several reasons why their small Nissan crossover wouldn't cut it anymore, and why they needed to trade that in for a full-size minivan.

Stacy looked at her, trying to gauge how badly she'd react to the "hell, no," she was dying to say. "I struggle with it, you know. I hate the damn things, and I don't see any reason why a full-size SUV couldn't be good enough. If size is the issue, then we'll upgrade the car."

"Those sliding doors are—"

"Once you have the child seats in place, you don't really need them," Stacy interrupted her, sounding a bit more dismissive than she'd intended.

"It would be easier to clean," she insisted. "Think of all the spilled liquids, all the food dropped on the floor—"

"What's with all the food and drink in the car, anyway?" Stacy blurted out, frustrated. "Why can't these kids do something else with their time in the car other than eat? What's the deal with that, huh?"

Renata dropped the diaper she was holding, and came to her quickly, wearing an expression of concern on her face. She touched her arm gently, then gave her a side hug, and Stacy didn't shun it. Instead, she lowered her eyes and stared at the marble counter's random pattern for a while.

"You're upset," Renata whispered. "I would be too. I'm scared, probably more scared than you are. What are you going to do about it?" She caressed

Stacy's long hair for a while, waiting for an answer, but none came. "I still think you should call the cops."

"Not calling any cops," Stacy replied morosely. "There's nothing to report. Maybe I just imagined the damn thing."

"I'm sure you didn't," Renata encouraged her, throwing a quick glance toward one of the twins, who started fussing. "Please call them, see what they say. Maybe it's happened before."

"No. I don't need that circus in my life. Maybe it was… I don't know, something benign. Maybe it wasn't meant for me."

"You said you were alone in that parking lot, right? No one else was there?"

"Yeah, that's what I thought. But he must have been there for someone else, not me. There's nothing special about me."

"I can think of a few things," Renata whispered in her ear, sliding behind her and wrapping her arms around her. "Beautiful, sexy, hot lady, setting my heart on fire."

Stacy turned her head and accepted Renata's kiss on her lips. "Still not calling them," she mumbled.

"So, I can't gain your favors with sex… that's disheartening," Renata laughed. "Any idea what else would work?"

"Nothing, at this time. If I see him again, maybe then I'll call them. But I'm not even sure what I saw. Just his hands, holding something. It was too far and too dark, and my eyes are shot after a day's worth of staring at a computer screen, deciphering code. Let's drop this, all right?"

She stood and grabbed her car keys, getting ready to leave for work. From the door, she turned and shot the three girls in her life a loving look. If a mini-van would make Renata happy, maybe she could learn to live with it.

Remote Office

25

"You don't know when to quit, do you?" Cat asked, slowing his pace even more, to keep up with her faltering gait. "You could give it another day or two."

"Can't do that, Cat, I'm sorry. There isn't any time, you heard for yourself. That unsub's not waiting for me to feel better. He's going to keep on strangling more innocent women, and it has to stop."

She pushed herself to keep on walking, taking step after step while clinging to Cat's arm, and felt drained and dizzy. The post-op hallway was a generous length to walk back and forth, and she didn't want to cut it short. Dr. DePaolo had said she needed to start walking, to prevent postoperative tissue adherence, and that's what she was doing. He didn't say she had to walk for an hour; that was her own challenge quota for the day.

"I can't be wobbly on my feet when they finally discharge me," she added, feeling out of breath, as if she'd been running. "They'll let me go in a day or two, you know. Then what?"

"Then come live with me," Cat offered, "and let me take care of you."

"Huh… like old times," she said, letting a wave of sadness wash over her pale features. "You put Humpty Dumpty back together once before; I think you're trustworthy enough."

"Coming from you, that's a huge compliment." Cat slowed his pace even more, and gave her a worried glance. "Time to go back to bed, kiddo, and I'm serious this time."

She nodded, letting a long sigh escape her chest.

"How about I wheel you back to your room?"

"No. It's just around the corner. Not worth the trouble."

She didn't want to end the day's challenge feeling defeated. She hated to admit it, but every time she dozed off in bed, she woke up feeling guilty, ashamed she'd stop thinking about Katherine, about how to get her back. Those weren't rational thoughts, she knew that, but it didn't help her feel any differently. Earlier that day, she'd endured through a long, detailed scolding from Dr. DePaolo, who'd mentioned a hero complex and other such nonsense. She didn't have a hero complex; she was the one who held the knowledge and skills to help get Katherine back. For Sarah, they'd been too late. She wasn't going to let history repeat itself with Katherine. It would be unforgivable.

They turned the corner, moving slower than she'd ever thought possible, and stopped in their tracks a few yards short of her door. There was a cart filled with all sorts of boxes, parked right in front of her room. She walked the final stretch no longer feeling tired and entered the room. The first thing she noticed was Melissa's disapproving glance; her arms were crossed at her chest and she stood there, watching, not saying a word. Then Tess noticed the two wide-screen monitors mounted on the foot rail of her bed.

"Who's turning my room into a scene from *The Bone Collector*?" she asked, looking at Melissa, but she just pursed her lips and remained quiet. Tess couldn't help but smile, anticipating the answer to that question.

"That would be me," she heard Donovan's voice behind her.

She turned, still holding on to Cat's arm. "Hey, Donovan. I know it's hard to believe, but I'm actually glad to see you."

"I'm not," he quipped, "not when you look like shit on death's door."

Cat grunted and frowned, and she thought she heard him mutter a curse under his breath.

"Seems you haven't lost your charm," she replied solemnly. Nevertheless, she smiled, and felt Cat's arm relax. "What goodies have you, and how did Pearson pull this off?"

"He filed a request to reinstate you as a remote consultant; he deemed you necessary, not in person, but in wit."

"My wit's damaged," she replied, "foggy and drugged. Coming off that oxy high these days. My creds are up and running?"

"Yep, on all systems," Donovan confirmed. "Since this isn't the bureau's network, I've set you up with encrypted cellular data. Make sure this data card is plugged into your laptop, or you won't be able to connect. Then use the security token whenever you start a new remote work session."

"All right," she replied, feeling excited, as if it were Christmas morning. "My weapon?"

"Strangely enough, yeah, it's here," Donovan replied, and pointed at a small, fingerprint access gun vault on Tess's bedside table.

"Um, excuse me," Melissa intervened, "this is where I draw the line. We're in a hospital. Guns are strictly prohibited in here."

"She's an active-duty, law enforcement officer," Donovan replied, "and that's the only exception to the rule allowed in your book."

"She's a patient in this hospital," Melissa replied, holding her ground.

"You didn't mind the gun on the uniformed cop," Tess intervened. "Remember the guy who was stationed at my door, up until yesterday? Newsflash: he was packing. He probably had a spare too."

"He was lucid and healthy. He wasn't on IV drugs, and he could tie his own shoelaces if he tried," Melissa replied. "This is not negotiable. If you can't see my point of view, I'll get Dr. DePaolo to explain it better. He'll throw a fit anyway, when he sees all this mess at rounds tonight."

Tess lowered her eyes and breathed deeply. Melissa was probably right. She didn't feel up to it, and her life wasn't in any danger. It wasn't as if the unsub could drop by one day, just to strangle her.

"All right," she conceded, "Donovan will hold on to my weapon until I'm discharged. But the rest of the stuff is staying."

Melissa relaxed a little. "Thank you," she said, "I'm probably going to get written up for this anyway. There are limits, you know, and you're breaking every one of them."

Donovan laughed. "Yeah, that's Special Agent Winnett for you. Glad that knife didn't cut any of your charming personality, Winnett. It would have been a disaster; the local community would have never recovered."

"Ah, screw you, Donovan. What other good stuff did you bring? Some of us have a job to do."

"You have a videoconferencing console here, on this mobile table. Wireless. The Palm Beach detectives can conference you in when they're out in the field, talking to witnesses. Then this is your camera, a simple Web cam, if you want to participate actively."

"Take that Web cam and shove it where the sun don't shine," she snapped. "Do I look camera ready to you right now?" She gestured loosely at her wrinkled hospital garb and fuzzy slippers.

"I'm going to let that question go unanswered," Donovan said, but took the webcam and put it back in its box.

"All I need now is a case board, but that's going to pose issues," Tess added. "I wonder if we could—"

"Please log in to your system for me," Donovan interrupted. "Let's see you get online."

She typed her password, then started her virtual private network application and entered the random security code generated by her token.

"I'm online, VPN's connected," she confirmed.

"See that new icon on your desktop, marked PB? Double-click it to open a feed from a camera installed in the Palm Beach County Sheriff's Office, in the conference room. It shows a direct view of the case board in there, the one they've already been working on. Zoom in, like any Web page, with control plus."

She clapped her hands. "You're awesome, Donovan."

"Pearson was clear that we can't have confidential case information displayed on the walls here, at the hospital. Rules are simple; when you're not here, the laptop is closed and all conferencing is terminated. Not paused or muted, terminated."

"Understood," she said, eager to lie down. Her knees were starting to shake, and she leaned against Cat more and more.

"You could have delayed this by a day or two," Cat said, turning toward Donovan with a grim look in his eyes.

"Sorry, man, just doing as I'm told. Her boss said he wants her to stay in bed, and apparently, this is what it takes."

"Thanks, Donovan, I appreciate it," Tess replied.

"One more thing," he said, getting ready to leave. "I'm assigned to you, full time. Please don't abuse that. Please."

She grinned widely, and he turned toward the door without a word and left the room with a spring in his step. Right before disappearing from view, he waved without looking back.

She crawled into bed and Melissa immediately checked her vitals, connected all the machines, and hooked up the IV drip.

"You know you're shooting yourself in the foot, don't you?" Melissa asked. "You're not giving your body time to heal. This is all wrong, and Dr. DePaolo will chew us both a new one for it."

"I know, and I'm sorry if I ruined your day," Tess replied, a little irritated at the thought of another scolding from Dr. DePaolo.

"You didn't ruin my day," she blurted, sounding offended. "This hospital is littered with know-it-all pricks who make a health professional's life hell." She used a small file and popped open a glass vial, then extracted the fluid inside with a syringe and transferred it into the IV bag. "Thanks for the gun part, though."

"Uh-huh," Tess muttered, wondering what was in that vial, waiting for a good time to ask.

"I wonder how much of your handiwork keeps us busy here, in the ER," Melissa added, with an almost irate undertone. "For those of us who are in the business of putting people back together again, guns are a hard pill to swallow," she said, sounding somewhat apologetic.

"None," Tess replied, a little colder than she would've liked. "I never miss."

Melissa took a step back, surprised. Her jaw dropped, and Tess couldn't tell if it was from hearing the statement of fact, or from processing what that meant.

"Never? You're saying you never shot anyone who survived?"

"Nope. I can put a bullet dead center through a perp's forehead from 20 yards, even if it's a rainy night. I don't know whose handiwork kept you busy in the ER, but it wasn't mine, I promise you that."

Melissa disposed of the used syringe and the empty vial in a biohazard container, then peeled off her nitrile gloves.

"You're something else, Special Agent Tess Winnett, I'll give you that, but you should take the doctor's recommendations more seriously. You need rest, not a remote office. Why do you think we keep you here?"

Tess didn't have the chance to reply. A quick tap on the door, and Fradella entered, followed closely by Doc Rizza. Melissa rolled her eyes and let her arms fall and slap her hips, in a gesture of both abandonment and despair.

"Whoa, look at all this stuff," Fradella reacted. "Does this mean you can work with us now, for real?"

"Yeah, that's what it means," she replied. "You finally admit you need my help?"

Fradella scoffed. "We know how to do our jobs, but the more the merrier with this case."

"Unsubs' DNAs are not in CODIS, neither strand," Doc Rizza said.

"What, the results are back? Why don't I know about it?"

"Because the lab thought it needed to communicate those results to an active law enforcement officer, not to a patient in a hospital," Doc Rizza said.

She frowned. "So much for being lucky this time. We got nothing."

"There's more," Fradella intervened. "You were right about Lisa Trask. She was taken from the place where she saw the glimpse of death. How did you know? She was last seen leaving her hairdresser, at almost 7:00PM."

"It was a hunch," Tess replied. "How did you confirm it?"

"There's 24/7 video surveillance at the bank where she worked. She must have carpooled with someone, because her car was at the bank, the last one in that parking lot after closing time. She came back for it after the hairdresser appointment; the recording shows her unlock her car at 7:49PM, but then she walked away from it and fell out of camera range. That's precisely when she disappeared. A minute later, the car self-locked automatically. Detective Buchanan found it locked the next day, when she was working the missing persons case; that's how we missed it, not that there's any excuse."

"No, there isn't," Tess snapped, feeling a wave of anger swell her chest. "Do you realize how much further ahead you could have been by now? Call Donovan, ask him to work with the Real Time Crime Center—the RTCC, pull all street cam feeds and look for cars that stopped near the bank that night. You have the precise time code; work from there. Maybe we can see him, catch a plate or something."

Fradella frowned, taken aback by her reaction. "There was no way of knowing—"

"Yes, there was, damn it, it's called diligence. You check. You don't assume, you check, especially when lives are at stake. Who did she leave the bank with, and how did she get to the hairdresser? Did she take a cab, or did she leave with someone? Girlfriend, or secret lover?"

Silence fell heavy in the room, making the low hum of the medical equipment sound almost loud.

"Listen," Tess said in a pacifying tone, "I guess I'm tired or—"

"No, you're right. We fouled up on this one. I took everything in the missing persons case at face value and didn't verify."

She shook her head slowly, angry at herself for her reaction. No matter what the case, she should have conveyed her feedback in a more professional manner. Like that, she'd bruised a colleague's self-esteem and upset a friend.

"I'll get going," Fradella said. "Michowsky's meeting me at Katherine Nelson's home. We're interviewing her husband."

"Will you dial me in when you get there?" she asked, and Fradella just nodded, then left.

Doc Rizza pulled a chair next to the bed and looked at her. She turned away from his scrutinizing glance, but Doc was not the kind of man she could keep many secrets from.

"He'll be fine, Tess, he's a big boy. He needed to hear it."

She nodded once, unconvinced.

"How about we talk autopsy results for Sarah Thomas, and you tell me what you think?"

At the Mall

26

Melissa finished her lunch early, rushed by a call to tend to an assault victim, a young woman who'd just been admitted to University of Miami Hospital. She didn't have an issue wrapping up her meal in a hurry, as she could barely force herself to swallow her food. She'd looked for Sophie everywhere in the cafeteria but couldn't find her. Sophie must have been unable to take her lunch at her regularly scheduled time, so her boss's request to help out with the rape victim didn't interrupt anything much.

She took the elevator two stories up and found the room where the assault victim waited for an examination and a rape-kit evidence collection. With her specialty and seniority, Melissa was one of the few nurses authorized to collect forensic evidence in the aftermath of an assault, and she'd done it many times. That didn't make it any easier though, and she cringed when she stepped into the room.

The young woman lay in bed with her eyes closed, but Melissa watched her breathing for a couple of seconds and knew she wasn't sleeping. An IV drip was attached to her hand, and she looked pale and vulnerable under the white sheets. Melissa gave her chart a quick look: Virginia Mayer was only twenty-three, and still attended college. Luckily, her wounds were not too severe.

Melissa cleared her throat quietly, and the young woman opened her eyes.

"Hello, Virginia, my name is Melissa Henderson, I'm your nurse. I'll be taking care of you," she said, as gently as possible. "We have to collect evidence from your body, you know that."

Virginia nodded, and a look of fear touched her eyes.

"There's nothing to be afraid of," Melissa continued. "We'll take this as easily as you're comfortable with, and take breaks if you need them."

Virginia nodded, and a tear welled at the corner of her eye. She sat on the side of the bed, and watched Melissa's every move with the eyes of a scared child.

"Let's get started," Melissa added. "I'm sure you'd like to go home as soon as possible." She took a camera out of the mobile equipment cart, labeled discreetly SAK for sexual assault kit, and took off the lens cover.

"Oh, no," Virginia whimpered.

"Only a few close-ups of any bruises you might have, that's all. I promise. Let's get you standing on this paper mat, over here."

Virginia obliged, and stepped with hesitation onto a large sheet of paper. She stood quietly, shivering at times, while Melissa disrobed her, carefully packing all her garments into paper evidence bags and quickly labeling them. When she pulled Virginia's dress over her head, revealing her bruised skin, she almost gasped. Virginia's bruises were a close match to her own, not at all that uncommon in rape cases. She'd seen those bruises before, on other rape victims. The truth about her own life was staring her in the face, as tangible as it could get. Earlier that morning, while looking at herself in the mirror, she'd closed her eyes and avoided reality; now she couldn't, not anymore. It was time for a decision to be made, no matter the cost.

With trembling hands, she combed Virginia's hair, slowly, careful to catch any bit of evidence that could have been entangled in her long, blonde hair. She took scrapings from under her fingernails, and numerous biological samples, moving as quickly and as gently as she could through the invasive exam. By the time she was finished, Melissa struggled to control her own tears. Her heart broke for young Virginia, for what she was going through, and for herself.

She wrapped up the rape kit and sealed the evidence bag, then handed it to the law enforcement officer who waited outside the exam room. Then she helped Virginia get ready to leave, as soon as a doctor signed her discharge papers.

As soon as her patient left, she went straight to the restroom and washed her hands thoroughly, looking at herself in the mirror. As she did, her tears dried up and her irises caught a steel shade of color.

She didn't return to her assigned case, the recovering federal agent with too many visitors and lots of spunk. Instead, she asked a colleague to cover for her and check in on Agent Winnett occasionally, then went upstairs and found Sophie. A few minutes later, armed with the keys to Sophie's blue Subaru and a small camera Sophie deemed absolutely necessary, she went by her boss's work station. He wasn't there; that could end up posing problems, but she'd made up her mind. She scribbled a few words on a sticky note and affixed it to his computer screen, advising him she wasn't feeling well and was leaving early. She time-stamped the note; it was 4:17PM. If she hurried, she could still make it on time.

She rushed into the nurses' locker room and looked around. Most of her colleagues were as predictable as they came, and for once she was grateful for that tiny bit of help from fate. One of the younger male nurses had just pulled a forty-eight-hour shift, and he wasn't going to be back for a while. His Miami Hurricanes jersey still hung from the locker door, sour with perspiration, as one would expect after being worn for two days. His baseball cap was also there, and Melissa put on both items, then gave her appearance a critical look in the mirror. The jersey was at least three sizes too big, but she was unrecognizable, even from up-close.

It took her ten more precious minutes to get to Sophie's car, and she hit a bit of traffic on the Interstate, but through sheer luck, she managed to arrive at Derek's office building a few minutes shy of 5:00PM. She parked in a visitor spot that was remote enough, but had a direct line of sight with the employee entrance, and waited, camera in hand, ready to zoom in and observe any details.

Her hands trembled and she forced herself to breathe slowly, to calm her nerves and come to terms with the monstrosity of what she was doing. She was crossing a line, one of probably many more she'd have to cross until she could feel safe again. Yet she felt guilty for spying on her husband, for her endless suspicions, for her lack of courage to start an honest conversation with him. Was she being a coward? Or was she, in fact, being smart? Sophie would have voted for smart. She was inclined to believe her, but still felt ashamed.

At precisely 5:01PM, she saw Derek leave the office building and walk toward his car, alone.

"Not that much overtime today," she mumbled to herself, surprised. "Let's see where you're going."

She put on a pair of oversized shades and followed Derek's car from two cars behind, an easy endeavor considering the rush hour. She drove for many minutes like that, feeling her palms sweat with anticipation anxiety, dreading the moment she'd uncover the truth about her husband. But soon she realized he'd been driving in circles, aimlessly wandering through the Coral Gables, slow-moving traffic.

She continued on his tail for another thirty minutes or so, grateful for Sophie's full tank of gas, and wondering where Derek was headed, what he was up to. Was he just killing time, avoiding going home until late at night? What the hell was going on with her husband?

Suddenly, he pulled into a gas station, and she sank into her seat as she passed only a few feet by him, desperately looking for a place to stop. She pulled into the next-door convenience store parking lot, and turned the car around, getting ready to exit as soon as he filled up.

Melissa watched him from a distance through the camera's zoom lens, and almost didn't recognize him. Derek seemed serene, relaxed, almost happy. He took his time gassing the car, then strolled inside, probably to use the restroom. A few minutes later he emerged and stopped near his car to unwrap an ice-cream bar, then savored it with his eyes half closed.

He wiped his mouth with a small tissue and threw everything in the trash. Then he looked at his watch, and his entire demeanor changed. Suddenly hurried, he started his engine and left the gas station, forcing his way into the solid traffic, causing her to do the same.

She breathed with ease when she managed to slide in two cars behind him. Soon she realized he was going somewhere this time, no more driving around in circles. A few minutes later, he slowed and pulled into a corporate building parking lot, and parked on the last lane, backing the car in against the shrubs that marked the property line. Then he lowered his window and stopped the engine.

She parked on the street, behind a row of thick bushes, ready to pull out quickly and disappear. She looked at the building, surprised she'd never noticed it before. It was a seven-story high-rise wearing a stylized logo with the letters SOSO, and the name Something Software written cursively under the logo, in brushed metal font. It was getting close to 6:00PM and numerous employees started to leave the building. They probably worked different hours, like many companies offered, to ease the burden of the rush-hour traffic for workers.

Focused on the building's entrance, Melissa almost missed Derek's change in demeanor. He was tense now, clutching the steering wheel with both hands and squinting to see from that distance. Within fifteen minutes or so, the flow of employees leaving the building had thinned, and only the occasional individual was visible. Then nothing, no one came out of the building for a few long minutes, but Derek's attention didn't waver, and neither did hers.

The door opened one more time and a gorgeous, young woman stepped out. She was breathtaking; she must have been 5 foot 8, or so, walking proudly on 3-inch heels and donning a tight-fitting dress that hugged every curve on her perfect body. She had long, wavy, brown hair and her skin glowed with a healthy tan, making her legs seem almost too perfect.

Melissa turned her focus toward Derek, and felt a pang of sharp pain in her chest when she realized that the beautiful woman was the reason for her husband's presence in that particular place. His eyes were fixed on that stranger's face, and the camera viewer allowed Melissa to discern the intensity in his hungry look.

"Oh, no," she whispered, struggling to breathe. Suddenly, the air was too thick and she couldn't fill her lungs anymore.

The woman didn't go to Derek's car, and he didn't make a move to meet her. Instead, the woman sat behind the wheel of a white Mustang convertible and drove away, oblivious to Derek's attention. Derek followed her from a distance, and Melissa followed Derek, wondering where the entire situation was going. Was her husband a stalker? Or was he doing exactly what she was, suspecting a loved one of infidelity?

Twenty minutes later, the woman pulled into the parking lot at the elegant Dadeland Mall, and Derek drove in right behind her white convertible. Melissa followed Derek from a safe distance, and had to pass right in front of him, as he suddenly came to a stop. She held her breath, but his eyes were focused on the stranger, who was already clacking her heels quickly on her way to the mall entrance.

Derek stayed in the car again, but his eyes were intently watching the mall entrance. Melissa braced herself for what could be a long evening, knowing how much time a mall visit could take for a woman who looked like that. She suddenly felt the urge to know more about that woman. Who was she? Where had Derek met her, and why was he following her?

The stranger took less than an hour to finish her shopping, and came out of the mall carrying only one small bag. It was almost entirely dark, but in the powerful parking lot LED lights, Melissa could see her clearly, every single detail. She stared at the woman's incredible figure again, and almost forgot to take pictures. She eventually trained her camera on her face and snapped a few photos. Then she turned to see what Derek was doing He was gone, but his car was still there.

She looked for him everywhere, and eventually she saw him standing near a shrub, at the edge of the parking lane where the woman had left her car. She'd have to pass by him, within 20 feet at the most. Melissa watched the interaction that was about to happen with her hand over her mouth, holding her breath.

The stranger walked toward her car, seeming carefree and relaxed, then froze. She stared at Derek for a quick second, then took a detour, avoiding him by quite a distance and almost running toward her car. She threw her shopping bag into the car and sped out of there, flooring the gas pedal and leaving the smell of burned rubber behind her skidding Mustang.

Derek didn't rush to follow her this time. He continued to stand for another minute or so, then he put something in his pocket and slowly walked to his car. She couldn't see what that object was; the spot where he stood was almost completely dark, hidden from the parking lot lights by the foliage of a massive, magnolia tree.

She watched Derek leave eventually, but she didn't follow him anymore. Drained and petrified, she drove by the hospital to swap cars and clothing, then drove home, dreading her arrival, postponing it as long as she could.

When she finally pulled into her driveway, Derek's car wasn't there, and she breathed with ease. Somehow, she didn't even want to know where he was anymore, or what he was doing; she was too afraid to learn the truth.

Her neighbor, Ryan, stopped unloading groceries from his car and greeted her warmly, then commented on what he thought was a rough day, considering how tired she looked and how late she'd managed to get home.

He had no idea just how tired she really was. And desperate.

DNA

27

Tess angrily bit her fingernail, racking her brain to find something she could use. She felt better since she'd made it back to bed, and she could focus on the case instead of her precarious balance. At least she didn't have to force herself to support her own weight on wobbly, weak knees. She still felt weak, exhausted, and Melissa swore she wasn't secretly drugging her. "No painkillers, no sedatives," she'd told Melissa, and the nurse seemed willing to honor her directive. After all, it was the law; medical personnel can't force patients to accept a drug against their will.

She looked at Doc Rizza, who sat on the small couch Cat used at night, just as quiet and as grim. "Let's go over everything we have, again."

Doc Rizza nodded slowly, and ran his fingers through the few remaining strands of thinning, disheveled hair on his balding head.

"What did you think of the interview with Craig Nelson, Katherine's husband?" she asked.

"He mentioned she was depressed after childbirth," Doc replied. "Postpartum depression is not that uncommon, you know. What puzzles me is that Katherine was a medical doctor who should have recognized the symptoms and treated herself, or sought treatment. She knew better; why didn't she deal with her depression?"

"True, but never mind that, what else did you notice?"

"Craig, her husband, was the parent who was most bonded with the baby. He took time off from work to stay with his one-year-old son and allow Katherine to return to her job. Also, not uncommon in postpartum depression, when the mother struggles with hormonal and metabolic imbalances, and cannot fully bond—"

"You know what I see?" Tess's excitement brought an inquisitive glance from Doc Rizza. "I see another pattern."

Doc Rizza frowned. "Tell me."

"Lisa Trask's hairdresser told us Lisa felt trapped in her marriage. Sarah Thomas's husband told us Sarah had struggled after birth, including a battle with alcoholism. Now Katherine, we hear she was also depressed, and, to your point, has done nothing to pull herself out of it."

"I think it's a stretch to call Lisa Trask depressed, Tess. You're reaching, or maybe I don't have all the facts."

"All right, no one really told us Lisa was depressed, and the hairdresser mentioned she was upset with family issues and her parents' hate of her husband's ethnicity, not depressed. But Lisa was letting her eyes wander a little. Now you tell me, Doc, what does constant family hardship do to people?"

Doc Rizza sighed. "Yeah… it gets them depressed."

Tess smiled widely. "So, we have young, married mothers who are depressed and not too happy to be mothers, right?"

"Appears to be that way, yes."

"I think we're getting ready to formulate a preliminary profile, wouldn't you say?"

"That's entirely your ballgame," Doc replied.

"The ring swap fits with this scenario," she added. "The replacement of the expensive wedding rings with the cheap ones is nothing if not a statement of value. The unsubs want everyone to know the victims didn't place too much value on their marriages."

Doc Rizza tilted his head a little. "You're right, it could fit. I'm still not sure about Lisa's depression. Why didn't her husband mention it as such?"

Tess resumed biting her index fingernail, and stared at the white ceiling tiles for a while.

"Universal blame, that's why," she eventually said.

"What do you mean?"

"Lisa's husband suffered directly because of his wife's parents, and he knew she also suffered. She could have been depressed, but he failed to identify it because he's used to blaming every shred of sadness and despair that entered their household on the hateful parents. He's so used to blaming them, he doesn't notice things anymore."

Doc Rizza stood and stretched his back with a groan. "It could work," he eventually said. "We could still be reaching, though."

"I'll take my chances," Tess replied. "The ring swap substantiates this theory and minimizes the risk in making this assumption. Yes, I don't absolutely know for sure that Lisa Trask was depressed, but it's a strong possibility. For our purpose, it's enough for her to have *seemed* depressed, and that could have easily happened just because she was upset about her family issues."

"Because the unsub observed them?"

"Because somehow their depression, or apparent depression, seemed to have been a factor in the unsub's decision to choose them as targets for his displaced anger, in addition to their physical appearances. We don't know that yet, but it seems plausible, and for now, I'll take that and chalk it down on that case board."

"Do you think they saw the same shrink, or something similar?"

Tess frowned. "Maybe. I'll ask Donovan to dig deeper into their backgrounds, including cash transactions if he can correlate bank withdrawals with geolocations of the victims' cars and phones. Many patients who see a shrink don't want to leave traces in the system."

"Some therapists are willing to bend the rules, yes," Doc confirmed. "Especially talk therapists, who don't write scripts, will sometimes accept patients who pay in cash and use potentially fake names."

"Yeah, Doc, I got that, but the unsub could have seen them anywhere. They could have filled drug prescriptions at the same pharmacy, or could have attended support groups online, chat rooms. AA is a likelihood in Sarah's case, but we have to check the other two victims to determine if they had addictions."

"Neither Lisa nor Sarah had any signs of addictions," Doc replied. "Tox screens came back clean, no needle marks, zero blood alcohol. They'd been gone for ten days, and that could be a factor."

"Expanded tox screen?"

"I haven't run it; there wasn't any reason to. Anything specific you're looking for?"

"We still need to figure out how he's snatching them. There's the obvious way, hit them in the head with something and haul them out of there, but Katherine was taken in broad daylight."

"I'll run the expanded tox screen, with focus on any narcotics and anesthetics. I'll run a hair analysis for drug detection; it will show more history, older drug use. By the way, neither victim had signs of blunt force trauma to the head, dating more than a week antemortem."

"Huh?"

"The unsub didn't hit them on the head when he abducted them."

"Ah, yes, I see. There goes that theory."

Tess propped herself better against the pillows, and took a sip of tea from a tall cup. "I wish Cat would get here already, I'm starving. My stomach's growling so loudly, it's... ugh."

"That's a great sign, Tess, don't be embarrassed. Let me get you something from the cafeteria," Doc offered, ready to storm out of the door.

She smiled and allowed herself to relish the heart swell she felt. She didn't feel she deserved any affection from these people, yet there they were, ready to help. Doc Rizza, Gary, Todd, even Donovan. The thought of having friends was new to her, and a little scary. She didn't feel she'd done much to deserve their friendships, and that thought humbled her. Maybe Cat was right; it was time to let people get close again. It was time to trust and share.

"What's so funny?" Doc asked, still waiting for an answer.

"Nothing, Doc, really. Let's talk DNA instead. Cat will get here eventually."

"I found two DNA samples on both victims, none of which were found in CODIS, not even familial matches. We got nothing, other than the confirmation that one sample was present only in the semen, and the other sample only on the skin abrasions on the victims' necks, from rope transfer. The strangler must have some calluses on his palms, maybe some partially healed abrasions."

Tess grinned and chuckled. Her voice sounded a little hoarse, and she cleared her voice before speaking. "How can you say we have nothing, when we have DNA, Doc?"

He shrugged, looking confused. "We got nothing to match it against. When we have a suspect, we'll be able to eliminate or inculpate, but until then…"

"Everything we are is in our DNA, right?"

"Um… yes," he replied, and his eyebrows shot up as far as they could.

"What if we ask the lab to run a full profile on those two DNA samples, and give us everything they can extract. Race, skin color, hair color, any genetically identifiable physical features, even health predispositions."

"It's never been done before as a criminal investigation tool," he objected, sounding somewhat unconvinced. "Not that I know of, anyway. I don't think it's admissible as probable cause to get a warrant for a DNA sample from a suspect."

"But it could work, right?"

"To some extent," Doc admitted, "but how will knowing the unsub has green eyes help you identify him?"

"I'm not sure yet," she replied reluctantly, and a frown ridged her forehead. She tucked a strand of hair behind her ear and nervously rubbed the back of her neck. "We could use the DNA analysis results to narrow the suspect lists, and go from there."

"Do you have a suspect list?"

"No, not yet, but we will have one, soon. How about behavioral issues, are those genetically transmitted?"

"Some are," Doc replied, starting to sound more excited. "There are numerous studies on behavioral genomics, conducted on twins mostly, and yes, it's something we could try. But this type of DNA analysis will take weeks, if not months, to complete."

Tess winked and grinned, but didn't address his concern. "How about height? Is that something that's written in our DNA?"

"Only to some extent," he confirmed, "I think there's a certain percentage of genetic predetermination of height, and that percent varies by race. The rest depends on environmental and nutritional factors."

"Okay, I get it, it's not that accurate, but we'll at least know if he's medium height or Mr. Big and Tall, right?"

"Yes, we should be able to determine height within certain limits. It would help if we knew the parental heights, then we could calculate—"

"If we had a way to find their parents, we'd find them, Doc. End of investigation."

"You could also run polygenic risk scores," Doc added, "for various mental disorders most commonly associated with convicted serial killers and rapists. It will give you the unsubs' predispositions to certain mental disorders. Typically, such disorders leave a trail of records, juvie arrests, petty crime, you know, all that."

"Where are the DNA samples now, Doc?"

"At the FBI lab, here in Miami."

"Awesome," she replied, then dialed Donovan's direct line on her conferencing phone.

He picked up immediately. "Oh, no, I just got here," he said, then sighed noisily.

"I need you to work some wonders for me, please," Tess asked in a pleasant voice.

"Shoot."

"Let's get the lab to run full DNA profiles on my two unsubs. I want to know everything there is to know about their physical appearance, and their predisposition to diseases, both physical and mental."

"Polygenic risk scores," Doc said. "Relevant chromosomal mutations too."

There was a brief moment of silence on the line.

"Okay, that's interesting," Donovan said. "It will take them forever, I guess."

"They got twenty-four hours, how's that?"

"Open the window and you'll hear them scream," Donovan replied dryly. "They have other cases ahead of yours. I'll let you know what they say. Talk to you soon."

"Uh-uh, not so fast," Tess reacted. "We need you to run full background on the three victims. We can't establish where the unsub saw them, or how they were chosen with the tools Palm Beach has been using. Anything and everything in their background you can dig up. Go deep; geophysical locations, bank withdrawals, indirect spending, online activity, and social media, the works."

They could hear Donovan typing quickly, probably taking notes.

"Remember you promised you wouldn't abuse your only dedicated analyst, right?"

"I never promised," Tess blurted. "You asked, but I never promised."

"Ahh… so that's the way the game is played, huh?"

"No, but I'm desperate, and I appreciate your help."

"Sweet talker," Donovan replied, then they heard the dial tone.

Tess breathed a little bit easier, thinking they finally had a strategy. It was hard to tell what she'd be able to derive from all the information extracted from the unsubs DNA, but it sure as hell beat having nothing.

"Do you think it's going to work?" she asked.

Doc Rizza shook his head once, smiling. "That's why, my dear, you can't convalesce like the rest of them."

Temptation

28

Stacy Rodriguez flipped her long, silky hair over her shoulder and leaned forward, to get closer to the phone. She still couldn't hear clearly. She grunted quietly and closed the door to her minuscule office, then pushed the phone's speaker volume to the max. It was better, but she still couldn't make out everything the man was saying. The connection was bad, just like it normally was, leaving a portion of the weekly interdisciplinary conference call to be inferred rather than listened to.

The speaker went on and on about some discrepancies in the documentation for a new software module, but she only needed a couple of questions answered to do her part. She was a database developer and architect, a rather unusual profession for a woman, yet it matched her organized style and her analytical mind, and allowed her to function by her own rules, while making a significant amount of money. Database architects created the backbone of software applications, and built the skeleton that supported the entire system. As such, she qualified for her own office instead of a cubicle, and countless perks, some unofficial, like gas mileage and car allowance, and others official, like flex time and remote work.

These days she preferred to come to the office though, running away from the smell of formula and the constant baby fussing. It numbed her brain, and even if her wonderful Renata was the dedicated mother that she was, she just couldn't focus on anything while they were there.

Stacy was constantly conflicted about her feelings lately. When she was at home, with her wife and two lovely daughters, she was annoyed, bored, even irritated sometimes. When she was away from home, she missed them terribly. It made no sense.

She turned her swivel chair with the back toward the glass door and continued to listen to the endless conference call, but discreetly removed a manicure set from her purse and tended to her fingernails without anyone seeing her. Her nails were somewhat too long for a professional who could type sixty words per minute, but a carefully chosen keyboard helped prevent the long-nail typos. Renata didn't like her impeccably polished nails either, saying they could scratch the girls. But Stacy liked them just the way they were, oval-shaped, painted a deep burgundy, and covered with a thick, clear, finish coat that made them shine like rubies.

A chime covered the monotone of the conference call, and she welcomed the interruption. She opened her messenger and read the text that brought an enigmatic smile to her lips.

"I think it's time we met. I think you and I should have a cup of coffee today instead of lunch," the message said, and there was no signature at the end of the text, but Stacy didn't need one. Should she dare to have that coffee? It was the first step on a road that led to nothing good, or to an amazing experience. Her feelings of guilt clashed with excitement and made her giddy. She waited for the end of the conference call, tapping her foot impatiently, and when it was finally over, she scuttled to the kitchenette.

She paced the tiled floor with a loud clack of her 3-inch heels accompanying every step, while a couple of coworkers stared at her, then at each other. She ignored them for a while, then stopped abruptly in front of them.

"Tell me, please, if you were on a diet, but you could dip your fingers into a melting pot filled with fudge, would you do it? I'm not saying eat the whole thing, just... get a taste?"

The two colleagues glanced quickly at each other, then one of them answered hesitantly, "Sure, why not? If no one was watching, I'd go for it. Life's short." The young woman laughed, and her colleague joined in.

"That's what I thought," Stacy replied, feeling better about her guilt. She thanked them with a quick nod and left the kitchenette, not before hearing chuckles erupt behind her, and one of the two saying, "Enjoy your molten fudge, Stace!"

She grinned as she walked the hallway to her office with a determined stride. As soon as she closed the office door behind her, she opened her messenger and typed, "You're on. Make mine a double cappuccino, if you please."

Entangled Leads

29

Tess felt very proud of herself, walking the entire distance from the MRI lab back to her room. She walked a little faster than the day before, and, while still clutching Cat's arm, she felt her knees grow stronger, firmer. She'd insisted to walk all the way there and back, before she even knew where the lab was, and to her it seemed as if they'd put that MRI machine at the other end of the earth. Now she welcomed the proximity of her room. For some reason, she still tired easily; somewhat to be expected after losing so much blood. "Two more days, three at the most," Dr. DePaolo had promised, and she wanted it to be two, not three before she could finally leave the hospital.

The two of them turned the corner and soon her room was within sight. Her step faltered and her grasp of Cat's arm tightened, when she saw someone she didn't recognize looking around in her room, shuffling through her things.

"Cat," she whispered, but he'd already stopped in place, his wiry muscles tense and his breathing shallow.

They watched the man, dressed in a white lab coat and wearing a surgical mask, as he approached her IV stand where an almost full bag hung in place. It was ready to be connected to her line, as soon as she returned to bed. The man checked the IV bag, then removed a syringe from his pocket and injected the contents into the bag. He tapped on the bag a couple of times, so the fluids would mix. He moved swiftly, demonstrating dexterity in handling medical instruments.

"Wait here," Cat said, in a tone that didn't accept any argument. She wasn't ready to argue, or challenge the intruder on her own, so she nodded and let go of his arm.

Cat took a few quick steps and intercepted the man as he was leaving her room.

"Hey, you, stop right there," Cat shouted, but the man shoved him forcefully against the wall and ran past him. In a second, he was gone.

Cat watched him disappear with a frustrated glare. "Ain't no spring chicken anymore," he mumbled, breathing hard. "Ain't no summer one, either. Sorry, kiddo, I know you'd've wanted that bastard nailed," he added, then helped Tess get back into her room.

"Are you okay?"

"I'll live, don't worry about me."

As soon as she sat on the bed, she pressed the button that paged Melissa. It took her nurse a few seconds to show up, then she confirmed what they already suspected. No surgical masks were worn on that floor, no one wore white garb, and no one injected anything into the IV bag's injection port before wiping it with disinfectant wipes.

"What do you want to do?" Melissa asked her in a faint voice. "Normally we'd call the police, but—"

"He wore latex gloves, the blue kind, like the ones you're wearing, so prints are off the table," Tess replied. "I'll ask someone to get the IV bag over to the FBI lab to see what he put in it for me." As she said the words, she felt a shiver down her spine. Someone wanted her dead, and, by sheer luck, had failed. Being helpless like that, depending on other people, and being an easy, lame target was something she couldn't deal with.

"What's going on?" Fradella asked, the moment he made his way inside the room through the cluster of people already huddled at Tess's door. News apparently traveled fast on the post-op floor. A couple of hospital security officers were also there, and Dr. DePaolo was giving them orders in short, muffled phrases.

"Uh, nothing much," Tess replied with a sad smile. "Someone spiced my IV, but we caught him. Well, sort of caught him. 'Saw him' is a better statement."

"Did you see his face?"

"No, nothing useful," Cat replied, seeming embarrassed. "His head was covered with one of those blue thingies that doctors wear on their heads, and he wore a mask on his snout. He seemed young, but they all seem young when you're pushing seventy, you know."

Fradella made a quick phone call, then asked, "What are we missing?"

"That's the perfect question, Todd," Tess replied. "Why me? How am I relevant, and to whom? The old case we worked on is done, finished, and the perp's dead. This new case, I'm barely even working it, and no one knows that I am on it. So, why me?"

"I trust you'll post a police officer at the door?" Dr. DePaolo asked.

"He's already on his way."

"These are the only people authorized to be in here, except you two and the other federal agents," he said, handing Fradella a short list of names on a yellow sticky note. "No one else belongs in there." He gave Tess a worried look, then went away in his hastened yet completely silent step.

Tess watched the interaction without saying a word, but then sat on her bed with a look of annoyance on her face.

"I can't wrap my head around this... why the hell me?"

"Don't worry, we'll figure it out, like we normally do," Fradella replied, then gently touched her shoulder. She pulled away abruptly; the sudden move tugged at her sutures and made her yelp in pain.

Shocked, Fradella took a step back, holding both his hands in the air in a pacifying gesture. "Whoa," he said, "It's okay. I'm sorry, I didn't mean to—"

"It's all right," Tess replied, averting her eyes. "It's not your fault."

Fradella tilted his head just a little, and scrutinized her with a puzzled look.

"Should I be chasing another perp, Tess? Maybe one who's not on any case paperwork?"

Cat glared at Fradella, but he didn't seem to notice it. His eyes remained locked on hers, and she couldn't turn away. She almost bit her lip in frustration.

"No, Todd, why would you say that?" she managed to articulate with just the right amount of annoyance in her voice.

"It's something you said right after surgery, when they wheeled you into this room."

"I don't know what you're talking about. Let's just drop it, will you?" Tess pleaded.

"I'm a cop, goddamn it, don't insult me!"

"The things people say while still under anesthesia are, most times, blatantly wrong," Melissa intervened. "People think they stand to hear all kinds of truths from their loved ones, but all they hear is chemically induced gibberish. Things that don't exist. Old memories messing with their minds and things like that."

Tess looked briefly in Melissa's direction, thinking it was the first time she'd actually been grateful to someone for lying to a law enforcement officer. Her nurse was full of surprises. Perceptive, sensitive, smart, and brave too. Melissa lied to Fradella without batting an eyelash, and she was a natural. Too bad she had such a hard time lately, leaving dark circles under her eyes and bringing a look of desperation to her face when she thought no one was looking.

"That's not what I heard," Fradella pushed back, but in a less combative voice.

"Listen, the only thing I need is to see these two unsubs locked up. I need to see Katherine out of harm's way, alive and well. How about we focus on that?"

Fradella sighed and sat on the chair closest to Tess, then opened his bag and took out his laptop.

"We made progress while you were busy getting yourself almost killed," he said, sounding more bitter than she expected to hear. "Your guy, Donovan, called with access credentials to the victims' social media accounts. I logged in to Sarah's Facebook account and found an interesting thread of conversations with a friend of hers, a chick by the name of Anita Salas."

Tess chuckled when she heard Fradella's choice of words. "Why does this *chick* stand out?"

"Read for yourself," he replied, then handed her the laptop.

She read quickly through a dozen or so intimate exchanges between the two women, then dialed a number and Donovan picked up immediately.

"Ask," he quipped instead of a greeting.

"Hey, D, if I give you someone's Facebook page, can you get me their real name and address?"

"Yep, can do."

She read the page link to him and he took less than thirty seconds to respond.

"Her legal name is, indeed, Anita Salas. I'll text you her address."

"Text it to Gary too. Thanks much!"

Tess immersed herself into the review of Sarah's social media accounts, while Fradella examined all the photos the three victims had posted over time, looking for people who didn't belong, people who might appear in more than one person's photo stream, a common face.

Michowsky conferenced them in as soon as he arrived at Anita Salas's place, and they were resigned to only listen to the conversation. The video feed left a lot to be desired.

Fradella muted the conference line for a few seconds. "Remind me to tell Gary we don't really care to see the color of the ceiling," he said. "He's such a klutz. What'd he do? Turned on the camera, then put the phone on the table, flat down?"

"Probably," Tess replied, looking at an image of Anita's living room ceiling fan.

"I'm very sorry for your loss," Michowsky was saying, over the conference system. "I understand you two were close?"

Anita sniffled and didn't respond. She'd probably replied with a gesture they couldn't see.

"What can you tell me about Sarah's recent state of mind? You two shared a lot, didn't you?"

"We were best friends," Anita said. "We grew up together, since we were six. Like sisters. She had made it in life, you know. Beautiful little daughter; a good, loving husband; a good job. She had a good life ahead of her. She met the love of her life in college, while I'm still looking. She was always ahead of me somehow, but it never bothered me. She deserved to be happy."

"Was she?" Michowsky asked, then continued. "Happy?"

A brief moment of silence took over, and the conference system hummed a little louder.

"She was," Anita replied hesitantly. "She had everything she'd dreamed of, so she had to be."

"Had to be?" Michowsky pushed back. "Based on your Facebook messages, you two shared your most intimate thoughts, yet you don't know if she was happy or not?"

"She'd never told me otherwise, but I don't think she'd been that happy lately. I think she got bored with a life most women would consider a dream come true."

"What did she say?"

"It's more like what she didn't say, or how she said what little she said. She never openly admitted it, but I think she was bored with her life. Bored to go home every day, make dinner, do laundry, you know, live the life of a young wife and mother."

"Was she depressed?"

"Maybe a little," Anita said. "Since the baby was born. I kept telling her that once Chelsea had entered her life, everything had changed, and that little girl came first. She kept saying that she knew that, but she wanted more out of life."

"More, like what? Was money an issue?"

"I don't think so. They made good money, both of them. She wasn't a bad person, you know," Anita whispered.

"I didn't say she was," Michowsky replied in a gentle voice.

"She told me once she wanted to feel in love again. To feel the blood rush through her veins when a man kissed her. She loved Matthew, but they'd been married for six years, and that does things to a couple."

"Tell me about it," Michowsky replied, "I've been married twenty-seven. We're merely friends now, and the kids are all grown and gone."

"I don't think Sarah was ready for just friends. I think something was missing from her life, something that made her sad, depressed."

"Do you think she was having an affair?"

"N–no," Anita replied with a little stutter, "I would've known about it. Those things, she always shared. The look a guy gave her at work, someone who checked her out at the store, I always knew about those things."

"But no affair," Michowsky added.

"No," she replied thoughtfully. "Um, maybe not yet. I think she was getting there."

"Any enemies, disgruntled customers, or anything out of the ordinary?"

"Lately, she felt she was being followed, or so she thought. She was afraid to tell anyone, afraid they'd laugh at her. Not even Matthew knew about it."

The conference call ended with Michowsky thanking Anita for her time. Tess opened her laptop and connected the private network, then turned on the webcam in the Palm Beach conference room, displaying the case board on the wide screen at the foot of her bed.

"Some déjà vu," Fradella commented. "Almost verbatim the interview we had with Lisa's hairdresser. These women had a lot in common."

"Yes, they did. Let's look at the victimology matrix," she said. "By the way, nice work so far. I see you added a line for depressed, that's good. All victims were or seemed depressed. But were they cheating, or thinking of cheating? Let's try to confirm that."

"I'll add a new line to the matrix. We need to talk to more people though. Husbands might not know, and we'd—"

"Hurt them if we asked? Yes, we would. Let's try a different path. If these women were starting to consider an affair, maybe someone close to them knew about it."

"Women always talk about this sort of thing, don't they?" Fradella asked, smiling awkwardly.

"Not always. We might not be able to confirm it, but it's worth adding the line anyway." She zoomed in and took a closer look at the photos of Lisa, Sarah, and Katherine. "Women who look like that, all they have to do is stop saying no."

"You think the unsub is their secret lover?"

"The profile is starting to take shape in my mind," Tess replied. "These things, they're all interconnected somehow. You have unhappiness in the marriage, the craving for excitement, for male attention, the cheapened ring, they all must tie together somehow. But the killer who strangles them isn't the one who rapes them... how does that make sense? Why is he interested in such a precise, detailed profile? How is he finding them?"

A call from Donovan disrupted her chain of thought.

"Shoot," she said, putting the call on speaker.

"We struck out with the vehicles stopped near the bank at the time of Lisa Trask's disappearance. None on video, nothing we can use."

Tess crinkled her nose. "Damn."

"There were several vehicles passing by at that time, including an unmarked police car, a black Crown Victoria. The plate doesn't show. The only view we have comes from the ATM across the street, and the image is distant and grainy."

"Can we trace it? That cop might have seen something."

"We're pushing the photo to all precincts, to see if anyone recognizes the vehicle or its driver."

"How long will that take?" Tess asked.

"A few hours, at least. There's one thing, though. This Crown Vic seems older than the squad cars I've seen roaming the streets lately. We need to con-firm if it's still in active police use. RTCC will confirm, and that won't take long."

Facts of Life

30

Melissa sneaked out of Tess Winnett's room unnoticed. She was a bit overwhelmed with the constant coming and going of people, and surprised the fed had managed to stay on her recovery schedule with so much disruption. Patients rarely understood how important rest can be for healing, and visitors understood even less. They come to see their loved ones and feel guilty for wanting to leave too soon, to go back to their normal, healthy lives. In doing so, they keep the patient from getting much-needed rest.

She began to understand why Dr. DePaolo had assigned her to this particular patient. Probably, if left unsupervised, she would have turned the entire hospital floor into a police precinct, chasing the serial killing team she'd heard Tess talking about. Melissa had paid limited attention to their conversations; for the most part it was just background noise to her. All her paperwork required attention to detail and focus, and she had to fulfill that task from Tess's room. Yet she stopped updating charts every now and then and perked her ears, when certain things sounded particularly interesting. The autopsy findings shared by the ME were quite fascinating. Tess and the other cops talking about who the killer might be and his motivations, also intriguing. Tess's aversion to being touched, and the secrets she seemed to hide from her closest friends, that was yet another mystery.

Melissa loved suspense, and read a good crime novel when she had the time. Hearing bits and pieces of a real crime story was an exciting way to pass her day, and it took her mind off her personal life falling apart. That didn't last too long, and whenever she remembered what was going on with Derek and her, what her marriage had ended up becoming, she felt sick at her stomach, as if someone had punched her hard, leaving her breathless and writhing in pain.

She'd slept poorly the night before, true to her decision to pretend everything was fine and share the bed with her husband. She found herself trying to take as little space as possible at the far edge of the bed, careful not to touch him by accident, still nauseous and frightened after what had happened between those sheets. He'd slept soundly the entire night, and that had been a relief, but she started her day exhausted and in desperate need of answers. Who was the woman he'd followed the day before yesterday? Was she his lover, or someone he couldn't stop thinking about, wanting her, craving her body like an addict craves his fix? Or was she his former mistress, one who'd dumped him and now feared his vengeance?

She'd tried coming to terms with what she'd witnessed, and had spent an entire day trying to rationalize Derek's behavior. He must have had a reason to do what he'd done, to act that way. After all, he was a financial forensics investigator; she'd always imagined him to be the typical auditor, one whose work is performed in front of computer screens scrolling through endless spreadsheets and figuring out who stole what money and from whom. But what if his duties included following targeted persons, as part of tracking their spending patterns? Maybe he was supposed to assess the lifestyle and habits of a certain suspect. Maybe that beautiful woman was nothing more than a smuggler, or a money launderer for the mob. And maybe pigs could fly.

She shook her head, disappointed with herself for trying to fabricate excuses for a man who'd become abusive, disinterested in his family, and secretive, to say the least. These few days spent in Special Agent Tess Winnett's hospital room had educated her about how real investigations were done in the modern era. No one really followed anyone anymore; it's all digital. So, whatever Derek was doing trailing that stranger through the city was probably not work related. It was time she toughened up and faced her dire reality. No more excuses, no more delays.

About lunch time, the nurses' station was at its quietest, and Melissa slid in front of a computer hooked to a laser color printer. She checked to see if anyone paid attention to what she was doing, then inserted the memory card from Sophie's camera into a media slot and sifted through the pictures she'd snapped two nights before. Most of them were quite poor, either blurry or too dark, but she found a couple that were good enough to print.

She chose a close-up of the woman's face, and a wider-angle photo, showing her approaching Derek, and her reaction when she saw him. She magnified that image, centering the view on the woman's face. Despite a grainy, yellowish hue, she was able to decipher the expression on the woman's face. Her eyes were widened and her pupils dilated, her eyebrows ruffled and raised. Her mouth was half open, as if to draw breath before screaming. Her entire demeanor proved the woman was terrified to see Derek there, in the mall parking lot. But why? Had he abused her, like she'd endured only a few nights before?

Melissa printed the few photos she'd selected, and watched the images come out of the unbearably slow printer, one by one. As soon as a print came out, she grabbed it and put it inside a clasped envelope, the type used for interdepartmental correspondence. Then she removed the memory card from the computer and rushed to the locker room, to hide from everyone and think.

Once alone, sitting on a small bench between two rows of blue lockers, she examined the photos again. This time, she took in all the details. From a distance, the woman was strikingly beautiful. Her body was perfect, and her gait was proud and self-assured. Her long fingernails were glazed and shone like glass, enhancing the stylish appearance of her hands. She wore an expensive-looking diamond ring; probably she was married.

Married... maybe that's why she was so terrified to see Derek. What if they had a fling, but Derek didn't take no for an answer when the woman told him she was going back to her husband? That made more sense than any other scenario her weary, delusional mind had conceived lately.

Nevertheless, there was no future for them together, not after what he'd done to Charlie and to her. But how could she get a divorce from a man with violent tendencies? A lawyer would make sense as a place to start. Sophie might know someone good and not very expensive.

She gathered her things and stood, ready to leave. She secured the pictures inside her locker, and, on her way out, she stopped in front of the mirror, still haunted by the image of the beautiful stranger who was at the forefront of her husband's mind.

Her hair was short, a sacrifice in the interest of easy maintenance, considering she worked in a hospital and had to wash it thoroughly every day. Her fingernails were trimmed short, and she didn't wear any nail polish. Some of the disinfectants she used quickly dulled nail polish, making it a daily exercise she didn't have time for. She preferred to spend more time with Charlie than paint her nails or style her hair. Her waist wasn't what it used to be before she'd given birth, although she still looked healthy and fit.

She sighed and gave her entire figure a critical glance in the mirror. She wore flats with soft rubber soles, the type of shoes that don't make noise and disturb the patients when she rushed through the endless hallways. She didn't wear any jewelry, also for the same reasons of practicality and hygiene while working in a hospital. Overall, she looked sensible, while the stranger looked classy and sexy. She was unfashionable, while that woman was chic. In ten years, she'd start looking shabby, while that one... she'd probably end up on the cover of some glamour magazine. She'd thought she was a loved wife, when in fact she was being replaced.

She wiped the tears pooling at the corners of her eyes, and slammed the locker room door on her way out.

"Screw that bitch," she muttered under her breath, "and screw him too. It's time to move on."

Seized

31

Stacy's heart pounded against her chest, sending waves of unspeakable fear rushing through her body. She walked as quickly as she could to keep up with the cop. Her step faltered and she nearly twisted her ankle, feeling a sharp pain in her joint. Those heels were not meant for that kind of rush, but she didn't care, worried out of her mind. What had happened to Renata? The cop wouldn't say. He'd just told her to come with him, because it was faster that way. Were the girls all right? Were they in an accident? Where was he taking her?

"Excuse me, Officer," she called out, but the man didn't slow down. He unlocked an unmarked police car and opened the passenger side door for her. She hesitated before getting in, and frowned as she processed all the details of that car. It was an unmarked, rather old and beat-up Crown Victoria, the kind all cops used to have until a few years back. The radio console had a layer of dust on it, and there were no red and blue flashers mounted behind the sun visors. Who was this man? Was he even a real cop?

He stared her down with an intense gaze. "We need to go now, ma'am," he said, still holding the door for her.

She was wasting precious time, she and her famous paranoia, instead of rushing to Renata who needed her. There was nothing to be concerned about. It was broad daylight, early afternoon, on a busy city street. The car was equipped with additional spotlights, and had a console for an onboard computer and a bunch of accessories scattered inside: a small, portable radio, a collapsible police baton, handcuffs. He seemed legit, albeit he probably wasn't at the top of his precinct's list for new equipment, or too high on the local blue force totem pole. Probably he was just a badge-carrying gofer, nothing more.

"Ma'am?" he insisted, continuing to stare her down implacably.

A little intimidated, she climbed into the passenger seat, and the cop quickly shut the door. He circled the car and sat behind the wheel, then started the engine and shifted into gear.

"What happened to Renata? Are the girls okay?"

The cop pressed his lips together and narrowed his eyes, but didn't say a word. She caught a movement and froze when she saw him take a loaded syringe out of his pocket and remove the cap with his teeth.

She pulled backward, her eyes locked on the hand that held the syringe, feeling the clasp of fear choking her.

"No... no," she said in a strangled voice, unable to breathe. "Please, no!"

She flailed her right arm, reaching blindly for the door handle, trying to free herself, but it was too late. He'd grabbed her left arm in a steeled grip and pushed her against the car seat, crushing her. She couldn't move anymore. Terrified, she watched the approaching needle, unable to fight him off. She felt a stab in her neck, then the pressure of the injected fluid as it entered her bloodstream.

"Who... are you?" she whispered, but he didn't care to answer.

He released the grip on her arm and set the car in motion. It was too late for her to try to escape. Dizzy, she tried to steady herself against the backrest while the car sped away, and struggled to stay awake as long as possible, memorizing the streets he took. Her blurry vision didn't help much with that, and soon the world darkened and became one endless fall into nothingness.

Preliminary Profile 32

Tess dried her face with a small towel, then brushed her hair. They were such routine gestures, but the ability to do them again, the simple pleasure of taking care of herself unassisted was something she'd missed during the past few days. Life was returning to normal, unnervingly slow, but it was getting there.

She was getting ready for the conference call with SSA Bill McKenzie, and she felt restless, anxious at the thought of speaking with him. He was one of the best profilers at Quantico, and could see right through her, as he'd previously demonstrated on several occasions. She appreciated his friendship, but feared him somewhat, because he'd become involved in her career in an unusual way.

He knew her deepest, darkest secrets, and that made her feel vulnerable and exposed. As a supervisory special agent, Bill held the power to make the recommendation to park her behind a desk forever; that was the standard procedure for agents suffering from PTSD. Instead, he'd made an agreement with her. She was to undergo therapy, and he'd continue to discreetly monitor her progress. He'd done more than that; he'd offered her a position on the Behavioral Science Unit, to work with him at Quantico. She shied away from that opportunity, feeling she needed a few more months of therapy before she could work on a daily basis with the worst people that humankind has to offer. Some of the cases she worked on, like the current one, still triggered her traumatic memories and gave her nightmares. Bill was patient, and nothing short of supportive and understanding, but she was still anxious at the thought of speaking with him.

She wanted to make him proud of her, to make sure he didn't regret bending the rules to keep her in the field. She'd held her end of the deal, and had to admit the therapy was working, although incredibly slow. It's strange and just plain wrong how quickly a human can be damaged, in a matter of only fractions of a second, and how difficult it is to heal the body and the mind of the injured. "Difficult, but not impossible," her off-the-books therapist would have said, and that had to be good enough for her. There was no other option.

She checked the time and went back to her room, where she stubbornly rejected Melissa's help and climbed into bed on her own, wincing, clenching her jaws, but unwilling to compromise. She propped herself against the pillows, and pulled the bedside table closer, ready to dial the conference number. Michowsky and Fradella were calling in from the precinct, and Doc Rizza from the morgue. As for Bill, he'd said he was in Montana somewhere, hunting down a serial arsonist.

She dialed the conference number and when the line connected, she heard the others already talking, clamoring excitedly and interrupting one another.

"Hello," she said, and the clamor came to a stop. "What's going on?"

"We have a new abduction," Michowsky replied. "Stacy Rodriguez, twenty-nine years old, a database developer."

Tess felt a wave of anger rise in her chest. They were never going to get ahead of these bastards, not like that. The perps moved too fast, and they were too unpredictable. "When was she taken?"

"Just a few hours ago. She didn't come back to work from lunch, and her wife got worried."

"Wait… her wife?" Tess said. "That throws a wrench in the profile."

"Stacy was gay," Michowsky confirmed.

Silence took over the conference line, and Tess felt her blood boil.

"Don't you dare, Gary," she said, speaking in a low voice between grinding teeth. "Stacy's still alive, and we'll find her. She's not a foregone conclusion, you hear me?"

Another split second of silence, then Michowsky replied dryly, "Yeah, I hear you."

"How come we learn about it so soon?"

"They weren't going to log the case as a missing person so early, but the wife mentioned the glimpse of death."

"What are you talking about?" Bill asked.

She'd managed to ignore him instead of thanking him for the flowers he'd sent. She shook her head, disappointed with herself.

"It's good to hear you, Bill," she said, fidgeting and twisting the conference phone's power cord between her fingers. "This killer shows himself to the victims, holding a piece of rope coiled around his fists, as if he's getting ready to strangle them. We believe it's a warning of sorts. When did Stacy see it?"

"Um, she saw it three times," Fradella intervened. "First time in her office parking lot, then at the mall, and finally last night, in front of her apartment building."

"And she didn't report it?" Bill asked.

"She only saw the hands holding the rope, nothing else," Fradella explained.

"Bill, would you like to take over?" Tess offered.

"No, you lead this one, and I'll just chime in as needed."

"All right, let's start with victimology," she said, and before she could continue, Stacy's photo appeared on the screen. "All victims that we know of so far are mid to late twenties, Caucasian or Hispanic, with long, brown hair. They're all beautiful, married, young mothers. A common theme we've uncovered is depression, in two cases confirmed to be related to the birth of their children. In a couple of cases we have statements from friends saying that the victims were potentially considering having an affair."

Tess paused for a while, waiting to see if anyone had any questions, then continued, "What makes this case stand out is the fact that we're dealing with two perpetrators, or what we call a killing team. Two sets of DNA were found on the victims, consistently indicating one profile as the strangler, and the other as the rapist. This is where we need your help, Bill. Typically, serial killing teams are man/woman teams, in a dominant/submissive relationship. I believe this duo is not dominant/submissive; it's almost symbiotic."

"Why do you believe that?" Bill asked.

"Both men are in positions of power. Rape is about power, and strangulation is the most personal form of power-assertive killing there is, especially when performed this way, with the killer's hands tightening the rope around the victim's neck, looking her in the eye, while she's also being raped. These two killers share equally or almost equally in the assertion of power over the victim."

"It's rare, but possible. Henry Lee Lucas and Ottis Toole have killed a lot of people together," Bill said, "in excess of six hundred. They were a team of equals, so to speak, in which neither was the dominant party, and both men killed. In this case though, only one man kills. That, inherently, gives this man, the killer, a position of implicit authority over the other man, the rapist."

"So, the questions are, why doesn't the killer rape, and why doesn't the rapist kill?" Tess asked.

"The way I see it, the two unsubs have complementing fantasies; they need each other to fulfill whatever fantasy is playing in their minds as they perform their criminal acts. They could be two matching puzzle pieces that have found each other. It's also possible that the rapist hasn't evolved to killing yet, and will do that at some point in the future, at which moment this team would disintegrate. Their balance is fragile and will not withstand devolution."

"They're not devolving. They've been very precise in their timing so far," Fradella said.

"I can think of two early signs of devolution," Tess said. "There was significantly more strength, more anger in Sarah's strangulation, and the glimpse appeared three times for Stacy. Until now, the norm was two."

"Precisely, these are signs of devolution. The anger levels are increasing for the killer unsub, which tells us his fantasies are starting to become less satisfactory."

"There are signs of repeated sexual asphyxia on both victims," Doc Rizza said, "only partially healed. That means they were strangled a few times before, using bare hands, if I had to guess. Definitely not the murder weapon twine. All skin abrasions due to rope friction were perimortem."

"That's the devolution indicator for the rapist unsub. He wants to start killing too, but he's not ready yet," Bill said.

"The killer unsub is anger retaliatory," Tess added, "one who doesn't rape, which is rare for a lust serial killer. I believe he's searching for a highly specific surrogate, and that represents a woman who has wronged him, at least in his perception. He is hateful, and his anger is increasing. But why does he show the victims the glimpse of death? Bill, what do you think?"

"You said earlier the glimpse was a warning," Bill replied, thoughtful, speaking at a slower rate.

She could picture him with his chin propped in his hand and his eyes closed, thinking, putting pieces together in his mind and seeing how they fit.

"I agree it's a warning," Bill continued, "but by the time he shows them the glimpse of death, the victims are already chosen."

"So, from that point forward, the victims don't control the outcome at all, that's what you're saying?" Michowsky asked.

"Considering the victimology findings and the ring signature, we believe that maybe he's giving them a warning to care more about their families, or maybe not to cheat," Tess added.

"I believe that every woman who sees the glimpse will be taken, regardless of what they do or don't do from that point onward," Bill confirmed.

"This is a very specific victim profile," Tess said. "How is he able to find them? There can't be that many young, beautiful, married brunettes with small children, depressed, and looking to cheat. This has us puzzled; our victimology matrix has too many lines."

"I'm assuming you ran deep background checks, and there's no common ground you can pinpoint yet?"

"Deep backgrounds are still running, and now we have one more name," Tess replied. "So far, nothing we could find. We also haven't found more than one earlier victim, dating about a year ago, but there had to have been more. These unsubs aren't beginners at their game. They're moving victims on a conveyor belt. The victims overlap; there's a period of time where two victims are held together, and we're not sure why."

There was silence on the line, except from the sounds of shuffled paper. Probably Bill was reviewing the case notes.

"Would you like to venture a guess?" Bill invited her.

"I have a theory," Tess added hesitantly. "See there, in the autopsy reports, where it says the victims were perfectly groomed, and that included having all their body hair waxed?"

Bill shuffled some papers again, then replied, "Yes, go ahead."

"I don't see these unsubs waxing the victims, and believe me, you have to have help for that level of waxing precision."

"It fits," Bill replied. "They force the experienced, subdued victim to groom the other."

"I'm guessing this could be part of the killer's fantasy, seeing women together like that," Tess said. "Getting ready to… go out, maybe?"

"To cheat," Bill replied. "The cheating woman in the killer unsub's life was grooming herself or with a girlfriend before she went astray. She was his mother or wife, but I'm betting on mother."

"May I ask why?" Fradella said.

"Because victimology shows he targets young mothers, and I don't think this unsub has children," Bill replied. "It's not a certainty, but I'm inclined to believe the woman who wounded this unsub was his cheating mother. That plays well with the dominating parent and abandonment issues that normally feed the anger-retaliatory killer's resentment."

"Ah," Tess gasped, "I see it now. That's why the killer unsub needs some-one else to perform the sexual acts. He's reenacting. Bill, you're a genius."

"We repeat to remember; it's that simple. You would have gotten there on your own," Bill said. "You just needed a little more time."

"We don't have time," Tess replied grimly. "He just took Stacy, and that means he's going to kill Katherine in the next two days. We can't let that hap-pen." No one replied; there wasn't anything they could say. "Let's discuss victim acquisition. How do these unsubs find them?"

"It has to be something in the victims' common background," Bill replied. "Keep digging, and you'll find it."

"We're doing that. But how would you start?" Tess replied.

"Let's talk about the rapist unsub. What's his profile?"

"I'd say he's an immature, anger-excitation killer, immature because he hasn't killed yet. A lust predator on the verge of becoming a lust murderer," Tess replied.

"Correct," Bill said. "I believe these two unsubs are sharing in the task of finding new victims."

"Division of labor, you're saying?" Michowsky asked, surprised.

"It makes sense," Bill replied. "However, we don't know much about the rapist unsub; it's next to impossible to generate a profile based solely on the act of rape. He's not torturing the victims, he's not mutilating their genitals, and, while there certainly are distressing psychopathological processes going on in his mind, we can't estimate what those are. That leads me to believe he's the one finding the victims, not the killer. He might follow the killer's direction with respect to the general victim profile, but the rapist unsub is the one who's lusting."

"That still doesn't tell us how they find them," Tess replied, disappointed.

"This profile won't give you that, unfortunately. From social media stalking to a certain background item all victims have in common, everything is possible. Do you know why crime-solving rates have dropped so much in the past decade?"

"The personal factor disappeared?" Tess replied.

"Decreased, not completely disappeared. Random happens more and more often, from drive-by shootings to completely random attacks on strangers, culminating in random targeting via the Internet, which remains the hardest one to trace," Bill added, and let escape a sigh loaded with frustration. "Let's hope the profile is accurate, because lust murderers are statistically more likely to acquire victims they have seen and lusted for. Tess, are you ready to give the profile?"

"I think so. Let's get Dade and Broward counties on the call."

"On it," Fradella replied.

Tess heard a chime on the conference line, and asked, "Who just joined the call?"

"Yours truly, Donovan," she heard a familiar voice reply.

"How did you have this number?"

"Your Outlook calendar. You were ignoring my calls, and so was everyone else. Instead of thinking it's a conspiracy against dear old me, I assumed conference call. Hey, what do you know, I was right!"

Michowsky and Bill chuckled.

"What's up?" Tess asked, trying to come to terms with the fact that he'd remotely hacked into her laptop, without her even knowing. Analysts were a terrible pain to deal with, but too useful to annoy with a well-deserved scolding.

"I got some news on the black Crown Vic. Four precincts still use that model, unmarked, mostly for court errands and low-key assignments, that kind of thing. None of the precincts recognize that particular car, but they can't eliminate it either, because the photo's too grainy. Two of those precincts don't keep a log for that vehicle, so they need to look at their own surveillance video to figure out who took it out the night Lisa Trask vanished."

"Okay, that's good work, Donovan," she replied. "That's a solid lead."

"Not really, no. More than a thousand Crown Victoria cars of that generation were auctioned to the public in southern Florida during the past five years, as they were replaced as active-duty police vehicles. Quite a few of them were black, 187 to be precise, and that's a lot for sunny Florida. More could have been painted black since they were auctioned. Truth is, we got nothing."

She let out a long, frustrated breath of air and rubbed the nape of her neck with frozen fingers. Wherever they went and whatever they tried, they hit a wall. Killing teams meant double the chances for mistakes being made, yet these unsubs didn't make any. No mistakes whatsoever, except for leaving DNA evidence on the bodies.

"Please follow up on the DNA analysis. Light a fire if need be, or tell me if you need me to call them myself."

"Done already," Donovan replied. "They're swamped, and calling yours 'a monstrous order,' and that means it will take a while."

"I don't have a goddamned while," Tess snapped. "Katherine Nelson doesn't have a while, and neither does Stacy Rodriguez. Find a way to rush that, please."

"That wouldn't be a complete genome sequencing order for two DNA samples?" Bill asked. "The lab called me earlier today, hoping the order was ours, to beg for some leniency on turnaround time."

"Yes, that's mine, and now you know there can't be any leniency. It's a damn computer running it, so watch me how I don't give a shit if a machine gets overworked."

She bit her lip the moment she let the profanity escape. A conference call was the wrong place to do that, and one with Bill in attendance was even worse.

"Glad to see you're feeling better, Tess," Bill laughed. "It's not really that simple to run a full DNA profile, but I see what you mean. I'll make a call right after this, and fuel that fire under the lab's rear. If you pull this off, if you close this case based on DNA sequencing, my hat's off to you. It's never been done before, you know."

Two chimes announced two more participants on the call.

"This is Miami Dade, Detective Rivera here," a woman's melodious voice announced.

"Broward County, Detective Greene," a man added.

"Thanks for joining, everyone," Tess started. "SSA Bill McKenzie and I are ready to release the preliminary profile in the glimpse of death killings. We're looking at two different unsubs, both upper twenties to mid-thirties, both Caucasian or Hispanic. DNA will confirm their ethnicity shortly, and we'll communicate with you as soon as we have it. These two men are a highly organized and methodical killing team. They're precise in execution, and carefully plan each abduction, including layers of preliminary work that is part of their complex signature. That makes them highly intelligent, and demonstrates a high level of self-control in both individuals."

Tess stopped talking, waiting for questions. None came, but Bill took over and continued.

"We believe the killer unsub has a history of personal trauma that motivates the narrow victimology. In addition to that history, there must have been a relatively recent trigger event, which started him on the path of killing. He's an anger-retaliatory killer who makes a statement with each victim. He takes their expensive wedding rings and replaces them with low-priced, mass-market ones, delivering the message that the victim has somehow cheapened the value of marriage. The victims they target are young wives and mothers who cheated, or were inclined to cheat at some time. Their choice of victim appearance is also very precise. This will help you narrow the list of missing persons and cold cases that fit, because this killer has taken many other lives before killing Lisa Trask."

Tess picked up from Bill, and continued delivering the profile. While she spoke, she couldn't help but notice how well the two of them worked together.

"These killers are highly prolific, and they take a life every eight to ten days," she said. "This pace might escalate; we're already seeing signs of accelerating rage. They have abducted one more victim this afternoon, and that puts the life of Katherine Nelson, the young doctor who was kidnapped on February 18, in immediate danger."

"This is Dade," Rivera said. "You haven't given us much. How can we find them?"

"They most likely hold steady jobs, because all the rope sightings happened after business hours," Tess added, "and they must have access to a secure, isolated place where they keep victims locked up for so many days. Check suspicious warehouses, abandoned buildings, construction sites, remote Glades dwellings. Since the killer unsub has had a traumatic past, that's likely to manifest in adulthood as one or more of many psychological conditions, such as personality disorders, compulsions, PTSD."

"They're very bold," Bill added. "They return the victim to the site of the glimpse of death sighting. As of right now, we have plainclothes people watching all those locations for Katherine Nelson, and we'll deploy more for the three locations where Stacy Rodriguez saw the man with the rope."

"Doesn't that mean Katherine has to die for the plainclothes to catch him?"

"Yes, and hence lies the problem. We need to move faster than that. Your best shot is if you hear about any sightings whatsoever and follow those leads. Pull video surveillance, engage RTCC, work that rope sighting like you've never worked a case before. Take this message to your teams; they need to hear the urgency and the importance of it."

"How about that rope?" Greene asked. "Anything special about it?"

"Unfortunately, no. It's just plain jute, the type any hardware store carries; nothing we could trace," Doc Rizza replied.

"Can we put out a press release?" Rivera asked. "There are millions of people in the Miami-Fort Lauderdale area. Thousands could be potential victims, and thousands more could be the killer."

"We believe the press release could potentially spook the killing team, and make them change their MO, leaving us in the dark. We will coordinate with the bureau's press office to put out a generic message advising people to report anything unusual," Tess replied. "Speaking of press, so far the rope sighting aspect of the killings hasn't been leaked to the media. This is nothing short of a miracle, considering how many civilians were involved. Please keep it that way, and direct all inquiries to the FBI media desk."

"One of these two unsubs could be driving a black, older model, unmarked Crown Victoria, either an active or former police car. This has not yet been confirmed, but keep the detail in mind," Bill said. "The kidnapper could be using real or fake police credentials to kidnap the victims. Stacy was taken from a high-traffic street in broad daylight. Fibers found on the two victims, Lisa Trask and Sarah Thomas, are consistent with that vehicle."

No one had any more questions. They hadn't given them much to go on. A needle in a haystack was an understatement. Tess rubbed her neck again, feeling tired and frustrated. It was hard to admit they had detailed behavioral profiles and even DNA evidence, but still had no leads. They had nothing, and Katherine Nelson had fewer than two days left to live.

Evidence

33

Melissa waited for her husband to come home, jumping to her feet with every passing car that slowed on the street, with every squealing brake. She had the TV on a movie channel with the sound on low, and a glass with some wine on the small table in front of the couch. Carefully planned, the setting was meant to relax and entice him to share a glass or two with her.

She saw the lights go off in the neighbor's living room, and checked the time. It was late, almost ten o'clock. She slowly paced the living room, every now and then taking a small sip of already warm wine. She found herself thinking a little too much about Ryan, wondering what it was about him that she liked. Maybe the kindness in his eyes, at contrast with Derek's fierceness of late, or maybe his willingness to help her even with the smallest of things, the simple gestures of camaraderie she missed in her family life.

She heard a car in the driveway screech to a stop on the loose pebbles at the edge of the asphalt. She went to the window and watched Derek climb out of his car and approach the door. She rushed back to the couch and threw herself onto her favorite spot, picking up the wine glass in one hand, and the TV remote in the other.

Derek unlocked the door and walked in. He looked a little tired, but not more than usual. She swallowed hard and cleared her throat, turned dry all of a sudden.

"Hey, want some wine? I just opened it," she asked, in what she wanted to sound like her normal voice.

What did normal sound like? She didn't know anymore, and she cringed thinking Derek would see through her transparent intentions.

He didn't; he kicked his shoes off and loosened his tie, then took off his jacket and hung it on the back of a chair. Next, he dropped on the couch and promptly put his feet up on the coffee table, inches away from her wine glass.

"Uh-huh," he replied, and closed his eyes.

"Want something to eat? I have some pastries, and I can make you a grilled cheese sandwich if you'd like."

"I ate at work. They gave us some pizza."

She brought another glass and the wine bottle, and filled his almost to the brim, then handed it to him.

"Cheers," she said, and clinked her glass against his. "How was your day?"

He gulped more than half the wine and set the glass on the table. She filled it again, and he didn't object.

"Boring... How come you're drinking?"

Her breath caught; she needed to tread carefully.

"Ah, just a lousy, miserable day at work, that's all. I just got home myself."

"Your mysterious federal agent causing you trouble?" he asked, and shot her a quick glance between half-closed eyelids. Even so, she could see the derision in his eyes, but she was also surprised he still remembered what she'd shared about her work on the way back from the office party.

"No, she's fine. I wish I could spend all my day with her, but I also work in the ER. Today it was crazy busy. Heart attacks rolled in one after another, a couple of car crashes, and bad ones too. Two ended up dead, one in a coma. Ugh..."

Melissa took another sip of wine, and soon enough, Derek followed her example and drank some more. As soon as he closed his eyes, she filled his glass again and topped her own with just a few drops.

"What's she up to these days? Keeping you entertained?" he asked. He was slurring a little, probably the effect of the wine on an empty stomach and a tired brain.

"Who? The fed?"

"Uh-huh," he replied, without opening his eyes. "You work on something interesting for a change."

She frowned, intrigued by his interest, but stayed true to her plan and replied almost cheerfully.

"She's something else, this gal. It's like being on the set of *Criminal Minds*, you know. I love it. People come and go, all kinds of people, other feds, cops, they all talk about all these murders, sheesh... scary!"

"What's she saying?"

"Oh, I don't really know. I'm in and out of there, between her room and the ER. I can't really keep track of what they say. Just like TV," she added, gesturing toward the screen displaying the latest episode of *CSI*. "Can you recall what these guys just said? Just that it was some guy who stabbed his brother; that's all I remember."

She shrugged, and waited patiently for Derek to want another sip of wine. As soon as he did, she poured the rest of the bottle in his glass.

"Okay, one last swig and it's off to bed with you. They work you hard, these guys."

Just like Sophie had said he would, Derek listened to her and did as he was told. He drank the rest of the wine with thirsty gulps, then followed her upstairs to the master bedroom, where she helped him get undressed. Her fingers trembled when she reached out to touch his clothes, so close to his skin.

She held her breath the entire time, and soon it was all over. Then she waited for him to brush his teeth and get into bed. Before she could tell him that she'd be joining him soon, he was fast asleep, snoring something fierce, with his mouth open.

She watched him sleep for a few minutes, her forced smile long gone, replaced with a look of intense concentration. She had all the steps planned in detail, so she didn't hesitate.

First, she took out Charlie's old baby monitor, the one with a small camera that hooked to her tablet. She connected it, made sure it was positioned to capture the bed, and covered it with a couple of clothing items, to hide it from view in case he woke up unexpectedly.

Then she went downstairs, taking the tablet with her, and passed through the kitchen, where she found a small LED flashlight and a handful of Ziploc bags. Armed with those items, she proceeded to the driveway, where she unlocked his car using his keys, not the remote.

It was dark and quiet outside, and she was in her own driveway, yet she felt uncomfortable doing what she was about to do. She rarely missed having a garage, but now it was one of those times.

She sat behind the wheel and quietly closed the door. The ceiling light went off, and she lit the flashlight. Carefully, she examined the passenger seat, inch by inch, working her way up the seat to the headrest. Right there, clinging from the headrest, was a long hair fiber, barely visible in the flashlight beam. She grabbed it with one hand, and examined it closely. It was long, much longer than her hair had ever been. It was almost black and shiny, wavy yet smooth. She reached into her pocket and pulled a Ziploc bag, then opened it with her teeth, afraid she'd lose the hair if she let it out of her hand.

A quick tap on the window almost made her scream. She dropped the flashlight and its light went off. She threw a quick glance at the tablet screen, and saw Derek was still sleeping. Then she looked at the man who waited outside her car window with a familiar smile, and breathed more at ease. She lowered the window.

"So sorry, Melissa, I didn't mean to startle you," Ryan said. "Can I help you find what you're looking for?"

She felt a rush of blood color her face. How could she tell him what she was looking for? "No, no, I'm fine." She shifted in her seat, trying to prevent him from seeing the tablet, left open on the passenger seat.

He gave her face a quick, understanding look, and nodded once, slowly. "All right, I understand," he replied, and his eyes wandered from the tablet's screen to the Ziploc bag she was holding. "I'm here if you need anything. At least let me give you my flashlight, while I fix yours."

She accepted the flashlight from his hand, and handed him her own. "No rush," she whispered. "We can trade them back tomorrow. Please."

He held her gaze for a second, then nodded again. "Good night, Melissa."
Then he walked slowly to his house and disappeared, closing the front door
behind him without a sound.

Relieved, she closed the car window and resumed her search. She put
the incriminating hair fiber in the plastic bag, then continued searching the car
for anything else that could help her prove her husband's infidelity. She found
nothing more, and, an hour later, after going through all his pockets and his
briefcase just as thoroughly, she finally went upstairs, to bed.

She washed her face and brushed her teeth, feeling numb. Yes, Derek was
cheating on her, and that was now a certainty, even though a single hair fiber
proved nothing. Locked inside the bathroom, under the bright vanity lights, she
examined the hair again. Could it be from the mysterious, young woman he was
following a few days earlier? It appeared to be the right length, color, and type,
but she couldn't be sure.

One thing was certain, though. Even when he'd asked about her day, a
rare occurrence she hadn't seen in months, he seemed more interested in what
another woman was doing, not her. Even if that fed was a woman he'd never
even met, he cared more about *her*. Melissa simply didn't exist anymore.

She snuck under the covers, careful not to wake him up, trying to take
up as little space as possible. She settled in a comfortable position and almost
dozed off, when he turned around and put his hand on her hip, mumbling
something, reaching lower.

She froze, afraid to breathe, her eyes wide open in the darkness of the
bedroom.

Dance of Chromosomes

34

Tess was still sleeping when the conference terminal chimed, and she pressed the green button before Cat made it around the bed, probably with the intention of silencing the ringer, considering the look on his face. She smiled at him and he sat on the couch, resigned.

"Wouldn't have it any other way," she whispered, then unmuted the phone call.

Cat shook his head, smiling. "Yeah, kiddo, I know."

"Hello," she said in a raspy whisper, speaking close to the phone. It was early morning; people were still sleeping in that hospital, and the glass door, although shut, only gave them limited soundproofing. If she could hear the man next door coughing in the middle of the night, probably he could hear her speak on the conference IP phone.

"Rise and shine, beautiful, it's a brand-new day," Donovan said loudly, and Tess was quick to adjust the sound volume. "DNA's back, with the lab's many, unquotable compliments. In your inbox, if you please."

"Uh-huh, one second," she said, then fired up her laptop and adjusted her bed while it was starting. She still struggled to find a comfortable position, and had to sit more on her right side to avoid putting pressure on her sutures, but with the help of a couple of pillows, she was all set.

She opened the email attachment and scanned quickly through the first few paragraphs.

"What is this, the revenge of the lab nerds?" she asked, staring at what appeared to be a mumbo-jumbo of English-sounding words mixed together by an angry tornado. "I can read it, but I don't really... You know what? Get me Doc Rizza on the line. I bet he'll make some sense out of this report."

"I'll ping him with the conference call number," Donovan replied, laughing. "They said you were going to say that, you know."

"Yeah? What else did *they* say?"

"They said you're crazy, if you're thinking that DNA will give you the portraits of the men you're looking for. They actually said, 'bat-shit crazy,' to be exact." Donovan was still grinning; she could hear the amusement in his voice.

"Well, if anyone knows about bat shit, it's those guys," she replied, not in the mood to let that kind of attitude ruin her day.

"They said the technology is decades away from being able to give you the physical appearance of a person, based solely on DNA."

"Tough luck; I'm not willing to wait a few decades. Any other pearls of wisdom you need to convey? Maybe something useful for a change?"

"No, not really," Donovan replied, but the amusement in his voice was gone.

"I'm listening," she insisted.

"They said that, um, being how understanding you were of their work-load and priorities, they don't mind if you hang yourself professionally with this aberrant use of science, the worst they've seen since the medieval inquisition used the swim test to prove witchcraft."

"Why do they consider this a foregone conclusion test?" she asked, feeling more intrigued than insulted.

"What do you mean?"

"Back in the medieval days, they used to throw suspected witches into the water, with their hands and feet bound. If the women were innocent, they'd sink and drown, while witches would float. Everyone sunk and drowned, for obvious reasons having to do with physics, not wizardry, but all tests returned the same result. Foregone conclusion. Is that what they think will happen here?"

"Don't take it up with me, take it up with them instead. I'm just the unwilling messenger."

As he spoke, she felt the grip of anxiety churn her stomach. What if they were right? She knew close to nothing about DNA, and she'd demanded test results instead of consulting with them first. What if she was wasting valuable time chasing the DNA evidence, when there was little to be gained from it? The FBI lab had an impressive line-up of scientists and forensic experts; maybe she should ask their opinions before forging ahead on her own.

"Oh, by the way," Donovan interrupted her introspection, "the lab returned the results of your spiked-up IV bag. Propofol and potassium chloride, enough to put out ten like you."

"Oh." She couldn't think of anything to say. Propofol would have put her into a deep sleep, while potassium chloride would have stopped her heart. Perfect recipe for taking someone out quietly, without them even knowing it. She felt her throat constrict and swallowed with difficulty, then gulped some tea to wash away the chill that had crept up her spine.

"Good morning," she heard Doc Rizza's voice on the call. "I heard you want to talk DNA."

"Hey, Doc," she replied, thankful to be pulled away from her morbid thoughts. She immediately noticed her voice sounded deflated. She closed her eyes for a second, and called on her instincts to give her some direction. No matter what the lab had said, she was going ahead with her plan, at least until they had a better way. It wouldn't be the first time someone did something they didn't know it was impossible to do. "Can you please translate the DNA results into actionable information? I want to organize the two profiles with every bit of physical details we can derive from these tests."

"Let's start with the killer unsub," Doc replied. "But first, let me tell you that we can't translate DNA into firm, physical characteristics, not for every facial feature."

"What do you mean?" Tess asked.

"Call it scientific guesswork, because that's as good as it's going to get. You'll understand more as we go along."

"Okay," she replied, more confused than she cared to admit.

"So, our killer unsub is a Caucasian male of European descent. That doesn't mean he wasn't born in the United States," Doc added quickly. "It just means his genetic heritage stems from European Caucasians. In short, he's white, and we got a little lucky."

"Why?"

"There has been significantly more phenotype study done on whites than on any other race. Simply put, it's better understood how and in what measure genetics influence the physical appearance of whites. Our portrait will be a little more precise. Then, we got lucky again, because your killer has a cleft chin."

"That's genetic?"

"Yes, absolutely. We can't tell how prominent, but he's got a dimple on his mental region."

"They call the chin, the mental region? Really?"

"Yup. Comes from the Latin word for chin, *mentum*. We did a poor job translating into English, because the Latins used *mentalis* or *mens* for mind, but we use mental for both terms."

Tess repressed a sigh, eager to move along. "What else can you tell me?"

"Earlobes are next. They can be attached or non-attached, and your killer's got them attached. That doesn't say anything about how pointy or floppy they are, or if they're sticking out. You see, that's the real challenge with this type of profiling. You know a few things, but—"

"But you have to assume for the rest, I know that, and I can live with it. Attached lobes, I got it."

"He's probably got blue eyes, and, most likely, brown hair."

"Why probably and most likely? Aren't these traits genetic?"

"They are, but they're not fully understood, or are too complex to predict accurately."

"I was counting on this, you know. I was counting on at least this much to know with some degree of certainty," she said, having a hard time swallowing her disappointment. Maybe she was crazy after all. "Why can't we be sure? Help me understand."

"Okay," Doc replied and shuffled quickly through some papers. "I'll explain it as well as I can, and you stop me if I'm getting too technical."

"All right."

"Eye color is determined by variations in the HERC2 and OCA2 genes, but also variations in at least ten other genes. These other variations, and the *interactions* between variations are not fully understood yet. The degree of confidence for the phenotype characteristic 'blue eyes' is 89.74 percent. That means they have established that 89.74 percent of people with the same variations in genes HERC2 and OCA2 have blue eyes. They can't ascertain what the other variations and their combinations might generate."

"I'll take 89.74 percent gladly. I feared it was worse. What about hair?"

"The genetics of hair color are not fully understood yet," Doc said. "Genetics is a relatively young science, one that evolves with new technologies and with every single human whose DNA is mapped, compared, and analyzed by itself or in reference to others."

"Okay," Tess replied, sounding a little impatient.

"Without getting too technical, hair color is mostly dictated by two gene pairs. One is brown/blond, where brown is dominant, and blond is recessive. The other pair is non-red/red, with non-red dominant. Our unsub has the dominant brown hair, but there's no telling what shade of brown that is. I don't think genetics has fully established how shades of hair color are determined, or why some people's hair color darkens with age. These shades of color are given by two pigments found in human hair. One is eumelanin and will determine how dark the hair is. The other, pheomelanin, will give hair the reddish orange hues. Genetically, we don't know how to predict the concentrations of these hair pigments; we don't know which gene variations will decrease eumelanin, for example, making your killer's hair a lighter shade of brown hair, or almost blond. "

"Ugh, Doc, so he could have any hair color, from light brown to black?"

"Yes, I'm afraid so, not to mention hair color can be so easily altered."

She let a long breath of air leave her lungs. "I see."

"But here's a trade-off," Doc added, "he's got the Cs combination of the hair-type gene, what they call incomplete dominance, and that means wavy hair. Not curly, not straight, but wavy."

"That's precise," she commented. "I wish we knew his hair color with that amount of accuracy."

"Nose shape is next," Doc continued undisturbed. "Several face-shaping genes have given us some insight into how his nose is shaped. Another incomplete dominance gives us a medium-sized nose; actually, this man's nose is average from all points of view: width, pointiness, bridge, nostril size. Completely average nose, with slightly wider nostrils than the norm. Also average is the chin protrusion, per the incomplete dominance found in the EDAR gene."

"That's it? That's all we have?"

"Height is the only physical trait we have left, and it's the most uncertain of them all."

"Great," she muttered under her breath.

"In Caucasians, the heritability of height is 80 percent, and this man's variants place him at above-average height. The lab recommended unofficially, under a pile of disclaimers, that we should add 5 centimeters, not more, on top of the average height for men of his genetic background."

"Which is what?"

"Um, 183 centimeters, plus 5 more, that's 188 centimeters."

She rolled her eyes, and reached for her phone, to calculate what that meant.

"That's 6 foot 2," Doc added, before she could finish her calculation.

"Fairly accurate," she said, with a smile in her voice.

"Everything is under a big caution flag," Doc replied, "but we're not done yet. We have some other interesting data, in the polygenic risk scores."

"That's diseases, right?"

"It's more than that, and it's less. These are predictors that speak to the likelihood of the individual to have a certain ailment, whether physical or psychological. These are predictors though, nothing more. The individual might or might not get the disease, depending on socioenvironmental factors, lifestyle, and so on. However, your killer stands out with a very high likelihood to have schizophrenia, even if undiagnosed."

"That's not going to help much," Tess replied, thinking hard. If he wasn't diagnosed, how could she trace him?

"It could help though. Those with genetic predisposition to psychoses have an array of other ailments. Anxiety, major depression, addictions. This is a marker that could be useful; chances are this man is on some kind of anti-psychotic or anti-depressive medication, or has been at some point in his life."

"Huh… very useful, Doc, so has the rest of America."

Doc Rizza laughed. "Every itty-bitty morsel counts, that's what you once told me, *ad literam*."

"Very true. What other morsels can you share?"

"Um, nothing much. His other genetic health predispositions are incredibly average, except this one: he's almost twelve times more likely to get severe migraines than the average individual."

"Migraines?"

"Severe ones, yes."

"Okay, thanks for that profile. Now, how about the rapist, Doc?"

"Male, Caucasian, blond hair, and, if you recall, with blond hair there's less room for error. Straight and fine, with strong markers for balding on chromosome 20. Attached earlobes, but no cleft chin in this unsub. A slightly aquiline nose and a stubborn, protruding chin. Brown eyes, or better said, non-blue. They could be any color from hazel to black."

Tess took notes on her laptop as fast as she could, grumbling quietly on occasions when she didn't like what she was hearing.

"Average height, so 183 centimeters is the best guess in height. That's 6 feet even."

"Got it. Diseases?"

"We might have some luck with your rapist. He's got a genetic condition, autosomal dominant polycystic kidney disease or PKD."

"Meaning what? I've never heard of it."

"It's one of the most common genetic mutations, causing cysts to develop on one or both kidneys."

"That means there's a specific drug we could trace?"

"Unfortunately, not. Antibiotics might be prescribed, but he could also be asymptomatic. Sometimes, PKD doesn't manifest until mid-life. On the other hand, he could be on dialysis; there's no way of knowing."

"Any other— what did you call those— health predictors?"

"Health predispositions, yes. He's at risk of developing dementia in his old age, and has an 18 percent higher-than-average risk of stomach cancer. Nothing else we could use, I'm sorry."

Tess massaged her temples, trying to think. She didn't have much, but she had more than she did the day before, and that, in her book, was called progress.

"One other thing, I almost missed it," Doc added. "Their ages."

"You can tell age from DNA?"

"Yes, you can. There are four, age-associated DNA markers that can give an accurate estimate of age, based on methylation."

"On what?"

"Chemical reactions that take place in human DNA with age. This test is actually being used in Europe in routine forensics, in the Netherlands if I'm not mistaken. Anyway, the margin of error is less than four years; the younger the subject, the higher the accuracy."

"Give," she said, feeling more hopeful.

"The killer is about thirty-five, give or take three years, and the rapist is thirty-one, also give or take three years."

"It matches the behavioral profile," she concluded. "Thanks, Doc, you're amazing, like always."

"What are you going to do with all this?" Doc Rizza asked.

"I'll get portraits done," she replied. "Just like we normally do when we have a witness. This time I'll be the witness, that's all. I'll ask Donovan to send me the best sketch artist who ever lived."

"Copy that," Donovan confirmed.

"And do what?" Doc Rizza reacted. "Take the killer unsub, for instance. His face could be wide or narrow. His forehead could be tall or not. His eyes could be wide or small. He could have long hair and a beard, or be completely clean shaven."

"I know all that, but it's not going to stop me. I'll use approximations and averages for everything we don't know; that's why I need the best artist there is."

"Even so, you could get the face of no one specific, who's going to generate more errors and false leads than anything," Doc Rizza insisted, although sounding less convinced.

"It's a risk that I'm willing to take," she replied. "Otherwise, what the hell would I be doing in here all day, twiddling my thumbs?"

A moment of silence filled the conference line, and the amplifier kicked in, generating an annoying, buzzing sound.

"Look, I think I can get somewhere with this," she insisted. "I believe if we can somehow mix emotions and life experiences in the facial features of these men, we can get even closer. Emotions leave their marks on people's faces, Doc."

Another moment of silence, most likely while Doc processed her idea. "Why don't you throw in some correlations too?" he offered. "Statistical findings."

"Such as?"

"For example, there's a documented, strong correlation between the width of someone's face and their predisposition to violence. Your killer unsub is more likely to have a wide face."

"Can you dig up more of this stuff, Doc?" she asked, sounding excited for the first time since the phone had rung.

"Sure I can," he confirmed.

"Sorry to interrupt," Donovan said. "I just found a commonality point buried deep in the victims' background. Lisa Trask and Sarah Thomas had the same yoga instructor. Both women paid him in cash."

New Arrival

35

Katherine stood near the bed where the new girl lay and watched her shift in her sleep. She was curled in the fetal position, and her long, wavy hair covered most of her face. She was about to wake up, judging by the small movements she made, and that meant Katherine would have to put up with her shock, her tears, and her denial.

Katherine clenched her jaws and crossed her arms at her chest, continuing to wait. She was a doctor, one who had the calling and drive to care about other people, about their well-being. Yet she didn't feel up to it, not there in the deepest recess of hell. The new arrival forced her to relive her own despair after realizing she'd been taken away from everything she loved on earth. To make things worse, her bedside manner had vanished about the time she felt relieved that the man had brought someone else instead of coming for her.

She had mixed feelings about the new girl's abduction. She'd been relieved at first, because whenever she heard the man unlock the door that could only mean two things, and this one was the least painful option for her. Yet it was contradictory, the temporary solace she felt, knowing that she'd be killed soon, now that the new girl was there.

It had happened the same way with Sarah; shortly after Katherine was kidnapped and brought to that abhorrent detention room, Sarah was killed while she watched helplessly, and the memory of Sarah's cries of pain still haunted her weary mind. What little she knew about serial killers and rapists told her she didn't have much longer to live, and she welcomed the thought. There was no way she could escape her agony, and she'd lost hope to be rescued a long time ago. She just wished death would be quick, because she knew for sure it wasn't going to be painless.

The thought of losing her loved ones, of never seeing Craig again, of never holding her son in her arms again, that was unbearable. It broke her heart and weakened her spirit, and she'd tried anything she could think of to change the mind of the man who took her. She'd begged him, implored at his feet, offered him money, even drugs—a lifelong supply. There wasn't anything she wouldn't trade for her freedom, but the man was unimpressed and went about his routine the same way he'd done with Sarah. Resigned, at some point Katherine had to accept that the monster didn't even see her as human; only as an object, a device he used to get what he needed, every time he needed it, and nothing more. He didn't care if she was hurting, not more than he'd care if his car door made a loud sound when he slammed it shut. And with that, she couldn't deal; she just wanted everything to be over already. There was no hope.

The girl shifted again, and this time rubbed her eyes with her hands, then opened them a little, blinded by the strong, fluorescent lights. Then, as she realized what was going on, her pupils dilated, and her mouth gaped to let out a blood-curdling scream. She jumped out of bed and paced around, looking for a way out.

Katherine stood calmly, waiting for her to process her situation. The young woman sobbed uncontrollably, pounding with both her fists against the massive door. Yeah... she'd done that too, and to no avail.

She finally settled in an exhausted heap on the floor, near the door, and Katherine approached her slowly. "What's your name?" she asked, as gently as she could, although she felt nothing but an all-consuming rage against their captors, against life itself.

"Stacy... Stacy Rodriguez."

"I'm Katherine Nelson, or Dr. Nelson if you prefer."

Stacy nodded, tears flowing in rivulets down her stained cheeks. She hugged herself, right there on the floor where she'd collapsed after realizing that door wasn't going to open.

"You've been kidnapped," Katherine said sternly, "by two men. At some point in the near future, you will be raped. Don't—"

"Oh, God..." Stacy said and her sobs resumed.

"Don't fight the assault," Katherine continued. "As much as you can, don't fight it. All you're going to get is more vaginal tearing, and life here is horrible enough without that to endure. They're still going to do what they want to do, so there's no point resisting."

Stacy had buried her face in her hands and flailed her legs as if trying to run from Katherine, but her back was against the wall and there wasn't anywhere she could go. Katherine knew she wasn't really running from her; she was merely trying to escape the reality she'd been dealt.

"Think of a place that makes you happy, and send your mind there; escape this hell at least in thought," Katherine continued. "It's called dissociation, or detachment; practice it here with me, and be ready to do it in there, with them," she pointed at the dark window.

"But... how?" Stacy whimpered.

"I'll teach you," Katherine sighed. "They can do things to your body, but they won't reach your mind unless you let them."

Stacy pulled her legs under her body and clenched her hands in her lap. She tightened her lips in an effort to control her tears, but her chin still trembled. It would take her a while.

"How bad is it?" she asked in a quiet whisper. "The rape?"

How was she supposed to answer Stacy's question? Words couldn't begin to describe, unless she used the clinical terminology employed in medicolegal examinations of sexual assault victims. What good would that do, other than terrify her more? She swallowed, trying to block the memories that invaded her brain. How powerless she'd felt, the despair, the pain… and then the excruciating anguish of the endless hours waiting for the next attack, fearing every sound, every passing minute, knowing it would happen again, and again.

"They're not too bad," she managed to say, but turned away instinctively, to hide her lie. "Just do as I told you, and it will be better."

"What's with all these clothes?" Stacy asked, pointing at the pile of abandoned garments on the floor.

There was never going to be a good time to tell Stacy what she needed to hear, and there was no easy way. Might as well do it quickly and be done with it.

"I guess you should know these bastards want us to stay naked the entire time," Katherine said, "but I decided I wasn't going to do that. They're going to hurt me no matter what, so I'd rather hold on to whatever self-esteem I can. However, if you prefer to do what they—"

"No, I don't," Stacy replied firmly. "But what's with all that?"

Katherine didn't say anything for a while, and turned her face away from Stacy. A wave of sadness overwhelmed her, sadness for all the innocent girls who'd found their demise in that hellish torture chamber, leaving nothing behind except for a heap of discarded clothing.

"I'm… not the first one they took," she eventually replied, her whispered words bringing instant pallor to Stacy's tear-streaked face.

"How many?"

"Too many," Katherine replied, then invited Stacy to come with her with a quick hand gesture. She took her near to the bedpost where she could see the names scribbled on the wall.

Stacy looked at the wall with eyes rounded in shock, but didn't say a word. She just sat on the edge of the bed and took Katherine's hand, squeezing it tight.

"We're already dead, aren't we?" she whispered.

All Katherine could do was nod. There was nothing left to say.

Sketches

36

Tess hung up the conference line and immediately speed-dialed a number on her cell. It wasn't even eight o'clock yet, but he wouldn't mind.

"Gary?" she said, keeping her voice low, as soon as the call connected.

"Yeah, who else?" he replied, sounding morose, inconvenienced.

"You're picking up that yoga instructor, I hope."

"No, we were waiting for you to tell us what we need to do. Jeez, Winnett, you must think we're complete bozos or something. What the hell?"

She bit her lip, frustrated with him, with herself, with everything that kept her in that hospital bed instead of being out there, dragging that yoga instructor by the collar into an interrogation room herself.

"It's just that we're running out of time, that's all," she said by way of an apology.

"And you think we don't know that?" Michowsky replied.

"I know you do," she eventually said, after letting a second or two go by. "I'm sorry."

"Yeah," Michowsky acknowledged and promptly hung up.

She was so frustrated she could scream. Sitting idle while Katherine and now Stacy were being tortured brought a wave of rage, making her heart beat faster, flush with adrenaline. Tess still remembered what had happened to her ten years ago. Those memories would never go away, no matter how hard she tried, or how much time she spent in therapy.

"What's on your mind, kiddo?" Cat asked.

"These girls, Cat. It's just that I know what they're going through. I've been there, and sometimes it seems like yesterday. I close my eyes and I see them, I hear their screams, I feel their pain."

He gently squeezed her hand, and looked at her for a long moment. She saw understanding in his eyes, just as she was sure he could see the held-back tears in hers.

"That's your edge, Tess. That's what makes you so damn good at what you do. Hell, that's why these badge-wielding bastards won't let you sleep, not even here, in the hospital." He chuckled lightly. "Remind me to have a talk with them after this is all over, somewhere other than here, somewhere where I can express myself."

Tess smiled, feeling her heart swell with love for the man who'd rescued her ten years ago. He'd taken her in on the worst day of her life and put his entire life on hold, just to take care of her, a complete stranger. Now, a decade later, he still rushed to her side when she needed him the most.

A hesitant knock interrupted her thoughts, and she waved the stranger in, after acknowledging that the police officer guarding her door had cleared him to come in.

"See? What did I tell you?" Cat whispered, gesturing toward the door.

The man who entered the room couldn't have been more than twenty-two years old. He wore a simple, gray T-shirt and ratty jeans, and his beat-up, running shoes were unlaced with their tongues sticking out. His youth came across even more in his facial hair, the majority of which was still fuzzy, like a teenager's.

"What can I do for you?" Tess asked, using her typical replacement phrase for, "Who are you and what do you want?"

The young man shifted his weight from one foot to the other, while his eyes took in the details of the room. He seemed particularly impressed with the remote office setup, the monitors, and the conference terminal.

"Wow… how cool," he said, then cleared his throat and continued. "I'm Tyler. You need me, right?"

Tess's eyebrows shot up. Who was this guy?

"Ah," she finally said, taking in the size of his shoulder bag and the black residue on his fingers. "You're the sketch artist?"

"Yeah," he acknowledged, nodding vigorously and smiling with his entire face.

Tess repressed a frustrated sigh. She needed someone great, experienced, who could compensate for the number of facial features that DNA analysis didn't reveal.

"It's just that I was expecting someone else, that's all," she explained, seeing how he reacted to her sigh. "I have a rather unusual situation here, and I need someone—"

"You need the best, right?" Tyler asked. "The best there is? At least that's what they told me."

"They?"

"The local bureau. SAC Pearson called and had me flown in here this morning."

"Where from?" she asked, more and more intrigued.

"Quantico," he replied coolly. "I'm the best they got," he added with a hint of smugness in his grin. "For real."

She'd just learned about the DNA results two hours earlier, not more. Good old Pearson must have been keeping tabs on everything she did. As usual, he was one step ahead of her.

"The timeline doesn't make sense, Tyler. When did Pearson call?"

"Last night. I was told I have to report here and not return home until you're done with me," he added calmly. His eyes searched the room and didn't find what he was looking for. "Where can I set up?"

She felt like an idiot for being so suspicious of everyone, but it was in her nature and couldn't be helped.

"Will this bedside table on wheels do? Take the conferencing terminal and park it somewhere else. I'm not expecting any calls for at least another hour."

With her peripheral vision, she caught Cat, as he lowered his head slowly, unable to contain a smile. Then he started to leave, but stopped in the doorway.

"Same order?"

"Yup. Fries too, please," she replied and licked her lips, glad Melissa wasn't there to roll her eyes some more.

"What's going on here?" Tyler asked, as soon as Cat pulled the door shut behind him.

"We'll try something that hasn't been tried before, at least not how we're going to do it. We will build two portraits starting from some specific features and some inferences we'll make based on other nondescriptive data, such as statistical or emotional data. We will combine the results of behavioral analysis with genomics and generate a likeness; that's all there is to it."

He stared at her as if she'd been on too many drugs for too long. She could read him quite easily; he wasn't sure whether she was crazy, or onto something truly innovative. She almost chuckled.

"Emotional data? You lost me there," Tyler asked, going with the second option.

"You're going to draw emotion on top of physical detail, that's all. You can draw emotion, can't you?"

"*Can I?*" he spat the words, sounding somewhat insulted. Then he extracted a portfolio from his bag and handed her a stack of drawings. "You tell me, can I?"

She viewed the portraits one by one, and halfway through the stack she whistled appreciatively. The kid was good; the people he drew were memorable, brimming with expression, with intent. They came alive on the page. That was exactly what she was looking for.

"I guess you can, Tyler," she replied, tilting her head in appreciation. "Now I know why Pearson sent you. Let's proceed. Please treat me as you would a witness, if that makes you more comfortable."

"Uh-uh," he reacted. "If we're going to do this right, you're going to have to level with me. Don't give me that witness crap; just tell me everything you know, then we'll build the likeness together."

"Fair enough," she replied. She'd hoped for a talented artist. She got a smart, gritty, and perceptive artist who, judging by what she'd seen in his portfolio, came second to none she'd ever worked with. "We'll work the killer first."

The young man started jotting notes on a notepad, and switched from the sketch to the notepad frequently, moving very quickly. As he drew, she watched his thin fingers move as if they were dancing above the sheet of paper.

"He strangles people," Tess said, decided to portrait the unsubs by telling their stories, making them as visual as possible. "He's intense, I'm guessing, because he likes to look victims in the eye as he coils the rope around their necks and kills them. He's suffered; he was hurt badly in the past, and he's been at the whim of migraines all his life."

"Migraines, huh?"

"Yeah, why?"

"Have you noticed, migraines tend to dig two vertical ridges on the sides of the nose bridge, because we frown and rub our foreheads a certain way when the migraine hits," Tyler demonstrated. "That will create these ridges over time, here and here," he added, touching the base of his nose.

"Yes, that's exactly what I'm looking for," Tess replied excitedly. "His hair is brown and wavy, and his eyes are blue."

"Long or short?"

"No clue."

Tyler's hand hesitated above the paper for a second, then continued to draw with long, decisive lines.

"I'll go with average. Whenever you don't know, I'll go with what I typically see out there. I see a lot of these slimebuckets, and I draw a lot of them too."

"Perfect. His nose is average, but his nostrils are just a tad larger than normal. Just imagine him flaring those nostrils in rage, when he's about to kill again."

"Uh-huh," he replied, and for a minute or so, the only sound in that room was the faint scratch of the pencil touching paper.

"His face is a little wider than the average, and his eyes could appear a little hollow. These are statistical correlations found between homicidal behavior and facial measurements. He's organized, and a little OCD. You see rigor in his eyes."

"Uh-huh, go on."

One by one, they incorporated every single bit of information she had, from all sources. She hoped the puzzle she was trying to build was not going to end up looking like Mr. Nobody.

"What do you think?" he asked, and put the sketch in her lap with little warning.

She gasped. The portrait was astonishing. He'd drawn tension lines in his jaws and around his mouth, a signature of those who deal with trauma-induced anger. The result of his work was not a bland, could-be-anybody likeness; it was a haunting, memorable depiction of a killer.

"I'm speechless," Tess said. "This is amazing."

"Told you, I'm the best there is," Tyler stated matter-of-factly.

She laughed. "Let's draw us a rapist now. He's a lust murderer waiting to kill for the first time. Until he gets his guts together to take that final step, he lusts and he rapes. He's a violent man, and you can read the lewdness in his eyes, together with his deep contempt for women. They are objects to him, nothing more."

Tyler's pencil moved quickly, jumping from notepad to sketch book and back.

"His hair is blond and he has a strong baldness tendency. He might be bald already; we don't know that. As he's only in his early thirties, he might still have hair left. He's the more rudimentary of the two, the least sophisticated. He's also sick, and has been his entire life, with a painful genetic condition called polycystic kidney disease."

"Ewww," Tyler reacted.

"He might not know it yet, but his kidneys might bother him now and then."

"Keep going," Tyler encouraged her.

After a short while, Tyler put the second portrait in her hands, and she was equally impressed. The rapist unsub had strong, distinctive features, combined with an expression of lechery and contempt that was captured smartly in the tension drawn in the corners of his mouth, and the expression in his eyes.

"Now I'll scan and send these to the team, and you can go home," Tess said, smiling widely, feeling confident about the results of their work. "You have a lot of talent. When we've caught them, I'll send you a note with their photos, to compare with how you did."

He laughed quietly, packing his things. "Okay, sure, but I know I'm close, as long as you gave me the right information."

"You're also quite modest, aren't you?" Tess asked.

He waved at her and left the room with an unbelievable smirk on his face.

Her smile disappeared the second Tyler did. She spread the two portraits in front of her, studying them closely. She hoped she was right in her insane quest. People remember mostly about other people what they felt when they looked at them, even more than what they saw. They're most likely to recall that someone made them feel a certain way, and completely miss their hair color or face shape. That's why witness accounts are so unreliable. Under the pressure of intense emotions and adrenaline, little attention is given to the measurable details of one's physiognomy.

Her gut had told her she had a shot to build a true likeness of the unsubs with this method, although never tried before, and she'd bet her career and her reputation on it. Pearson's too. Regardless of that, Katherine and Stacy's lives were at stake, and it was the only thing that mattered to her.

She had her portraits. If she couldn't get to Katherine and Stacy in time, nothing else really mattered.

Sick

37

Melissa found Tess's door open when she came back from lunch, and the hallway flooded with the telltale smells of illicit foods. She locked eyes with her patient, and saw the guilty look on her face. She was recovering quickly, and that was the only thing that mattered. If burgers helped her do that, then burgers were just fine. Even Dr. DePaolo looked the other way in her case.

She entered the room carrying an armful of supplies, and rushed to the cabinet counter to drop her load. She'd brought everything needed to restock the room, and to change Tess's dressing. Opening one drawer after another, she inspected and replenished everything, while jotting notes on her notepad.

"I'm leaving tomorrow," Tess said, lifting her eyes from the file she was reading.

She'd littered her bed with case files and crime-scene photos, and Melissa averted her eyes whenever she could.

Each line of work steels the people who make a career out of it; she knew that well, but she still couldn't look at crime-scene photos the way her patient did. Probably, Tess would faint if she had to run a bowel with her hands during surgery; that was something Melissa could easily stomach, but not the crime-scene photos.

Melissa pursed her lips and put a furrow between her eyebrows, while checking Tess's chart.

"I have you staying with us for at least three more days," Melissa replied, showing Tess the chart.

Tess didn't take her eyes off Melissa; didn't even pretend to give the chart a look.

"I'm not asking; I'm telling you. I'm leaving tomorrow, and if it's against medical advice, then so be it. I've got work to do. Do what you have to do to release me tomorrow morning and please don't delay."

Melissa dropped the chart on the counter and approached the bed.

"Listen, why don't you give yourself a little more time?" she asked patiently, concern seeping through her voice. Her patient was about to do something really stupid, regardless of how smart she seemed to be. "You've got everything you want here, monitors, and computers, and phones, people come and go as they wish, and you eat burgers and fries, and who knows what else. You've got it all; why rush out of here and risk your life?"

"Mel, you and I are friends, right?"

"Yes," she replied, unsure where that was going.

"Then, as your friend, I'm asking for your help. I'm not walking out of here now, with zero warning, as I'm inclined to do. I want to give you and Dr. DePaolo time to sort this out. Believe it or not, I don't want to be in more pain than I absolutely have to, or have long-term consequences from this injury. If you want, I'll swing by every now and then to get checked out, but I need to be out there. Help me, Mel."

Melissa looked in Tess's eyes and saw determination, the kind of resolve that no one could overturn. She sighed, defeated, and took to changing her patient's IV bag.

"People are dying, Mel," Tess insisted in a softer voice. "I need to do this."

"To do what? Be one of them? You're still dehydrated, and off your pain meds AMA. How far are you willing to push this?"

She threw the words over her shoulder, not even turning to face her. Some people believed with all their hearts the world would stop turning if they didn't show up for work one day. Until she'd met Tess, she thought only doctors had this issue; but apparently, it wasn't true. Cops could develop a God complex too.

"Look," Tess said, but Mel didn't react. "No, I mean turn around and look. All these women are missing. Some of them are already dead. You know her," Tess added, putting aside Dr. Nelson's photo. "Maybe we can still save her."

Melissa looked at Katherine Nelson's photo with hesitation, almost afraid of what she'd see. It was a good photo of her, not a crime-scene photo; she was still missing, not dead. She looked happy and beautiful in that photo. But then Tess took that picture away, and revealed the image underneath Katherine's.

She gasped as her heart started pumping hard, thumping against her chest. She covered her mouth with both her hands, while her eyes, rounded in shock, stared at the photo. She took staggering steps back, as if she'd seen a ghost. By accident, she stepped on one of the IV stand wheels, and tripped that over, sending it crashing over the bedside table onto the floor, taking the phone with it. The ruckus got the attention of the uniformed officer stationed outside the door, who gawked inside with a disapproving look.

"Oh, my God…" she whispered, and rushed to pick everything from the floor. "Did I hurt you? Did the IV line—"

"No, I'm fine," Tess replied, and scrutinized her from head to toe. "Are you all right?"

She wasn't all right, and probably wouldn't be anytime soon, not after seeing the photo of that woman. How could she begin to tell her patient, none other than an FBI agent, that the woman the police were looking for was the same woman her husband had stalked, just three days ago? There was no way... no, not until she was sure.

Sure of what, exactly? With her own eyes, she'd seen her husband follow that woman, and had pictures of her, on the memory card from Sophie's camera and in her locker where she'd hid the photos she'd printed. Was it the same woman? Maybe she was wrong... maybe she'd become so obsessed with that woman that she saw her face everywhere she looked.

Yes, that must be it, she reassured herself, and breathed a little easier. The breath did little to relieve the rampant anxiety that wreaked havoc on her mind and body. It had to be a mistake, because the alternative was incomprehensible. How could Derek be involved with missing women? With dead women? No, he couldn't be, and her memory was playing tricks on her. Derek was just cheating on her, that's all there was. It had to be.

"Mel?" Tess pressed on. "Are you all right?"

"Um, yeah... I get dizzy sometimes," she said, but shifted her eyes without realizing.

"Uh-huh... Really, Mel? Remember what I do for a living?"

She closed her eyes for a second, worried sick she'd triggered the fed's endless suspicions. Law enforcement had earned a bad reputation lately, of abuse, violence, and wrongful convictions, and she didn't want her family on the receiving end of that.

"No, really, I have vertigo. I've had some problems lately."

"I know that, we talked about it. But I believe something scared you, something you saw here," she patted on the photo-littered bed cover, right next to that haunting woman's picture.

"N–no," Melissa replied, feeling her dry throat constrict. She swallowed hard and took a few steps toward the supply cabinet, putting more distance between the perceptive fed and her own worst fears. "I swear to you, it's nothing. Just vertigo."

Tess nodded sideways and pursed her lips; she seemed disappointed, and maybe she had reasons to be. Melissa's instincts told her she could trust Tess, but she was too afraid to open up her concerns to official scrutiny. She knew exactly what was going to happen if she said anything. Sworn statements. Derek interviewed, maybe even arrested, when in fact he was innocent... he was just having an affair, and everything was nothing more than a coincidence. He was her husband, and the father of her child. He deserved the benefit of the doubt, and more.

She pretended to count syringes and needles in one of the drawers, avoiding Tess's perceptive gaze, and thinking bitterly how three days ago the tragedy of her life was discovering Derek was having an affair. Now it seemed to be the best of all remaining alternatives.

Life changes from underneath you really fast, she reflected. Maybe it wasn't such a bad idea to help Tess leave the hospital as soon as possible.

"Okay," Tess replied, still gazing at her intently. "I'm not buying it for a minute, and I'm only going to say this once. If you know anything about any of these women and you don't tell me, not only would you be guilty of obstructing justice, but you'd be responsible for someone's death. You could go to jail for a very long time. Keep that in mind when you tell me it's nothing, Mel. Don't do this to yourself; no one's worth it."

Tears flooded Melissa's eyes and started running down her cheeks, and she slammed the drawer shut, angry with herself for her lack of self-control. She pounded on the counter with both hands, rattling all the scattered objects on its surface. She felt sick to her stomach and wanted to get the hell out of there before she collapsed. Somehow, she found the strength and turned to face Tess.

"I'm sick, all right? That's what's wrong… I'm sick. Don't do this to me, please!"

She rushed out of Tess's room and didn't stop until she made it to the locker room. She grabbed one of the folded towels on the counter and buried her face in it to suppress the sound of her wails.

Her courage returned and her convictions demanded truthful answers. Derek couldn't be involved in this nightmare, and the woman she'd seen in a photo on Special Agent Winnett's hospital bed wasn't the woman her husband followed three nights ago. It couldn't be, and she had proof. All she needed to do was look at the pictures she'd taken, and immediately alleviate her senseless, nightmarish fears. She'd see it was a mistake, and regain her composure immediately. Then she'd be able to deal with Special Agent Tess Winnett again, and put her mind at ease.

She opened her locker and took out the prints from Sophie's camera. She clutched them with frozen, trembling fingers, and stared at the face of the woman captured in a poorly lit, yellow-hued photo.

She heard a loud ringing in her ears, and felt the blood rush to her head. She managed to put the photos in the locker before rushing to the sink, where she dry-heaved between sobs until she couldn't stand anymore and had to sit, weak at the knees, feeling her head was about to explode.

The woman her husband had followed three nights before was the same woman the FBI was looking for.

The Yoga Instructor 38

Tess watched the suspect on the laptop screen and had the audio feed tapped into her headphones. Michowsky and Fradella wore earpieces, and she could communicate with them in real time, courtesy of the modern technology Donovan had laid at their feet. Nothing was better than her live presence in the interview room though, and she yearned to be there in person, to see the microexpressions on the suspect's face, to smell his fear, to see the beads of sweat breaking out at the roots of his hair.

The wide monitors at the foot of her bed were dark for the first time since they had been installed, and they were going to stay dark for the remainder of her hospital stay. All case photos were neatly stashed inside file folders, and no trace of case information was visible anywhere. She'd broken many rules by letting any piece of information be in plain sight, and she knew it.

She shook her head, angry with herself for breaking the one rule that should at no time be broken: never share any information about an ongoing investigation, the operative word being "any." She hadn't been sloppy about the information that could be visible to others, and had the door and blinds closed whenever she reviewed anything, whether reading from a file, speaking on the phone, or seeing something on the computer screens. Still, the one person who had, at times, overheard conversations or seen anything was Melissa, her nurse. She'd thought she was safe with her around, how she seemed to mind her own business and not pay any attention, but she'd been dead wrong.

Melissa was hiding something terribly upsetting, and was doing a remarkably poor job at it. Maybe Mel would grow a brain and talk to her openly about what that was; if she was protecting someone, Tess was her only chance of getting the kid-glove treatment about it. In any case, Tess held her cards closer to the vest now, even if Melissa wasn't in the room.

She refocused on the suspect, parked in one of the Palm Beach County interview rooms and left to fester, as Michowsky had put it. It was a common interrogation technique; suspects were locked in the interview rooms alone, to wait while building anxiety and anger, thus becoming more likely to react impulsively and start talking.

She was viewing a video feed taken from the ceiling camera, and for the longest time she couldn't see the suspect's face. Eventually, exasperated by the long wait, the suspect, a yoga instructor both Lisa Trask and Sarah Thomas had classes with, looked up at the ceiling in a silent stance of annoyance. Quickly, she captured a screenshot of the video feed and compared it to the likeness Tyler had drawn.

He was a strong match for the rapist unsub; he had blond hair and he kept it gelled generously over his head to keep it in place, despite it wanting to stand upright, like bristles on a brush. He wasn't showing signs of baldness yet, but he was younger, only twenty-nine. His eye color matched, his earlobes were attached, and there was no cleft chin that could have eliminated him. Overall, he looked compatible with the likeness, although not that close. However, without a DNA sample they couldn't be sure, and the detectives knew that very well.

Michowsky and Fradella entered the room, and the suspect leaned forward, propping his elbows on the table. "Finally," he said, "I have a business to run. How much time are you gonna waste me, huh?"

Michowsky took a seat across from the suspect, while Fradella remained standing, leaning casually against the wall with his hands buried in his pockets.

Michowsky opened the file he'd brought in and started reading, as if for the first time. "Eugene Bolton, right?"

"Gene, yeah."

"You a yoga instructor?"

"Pfft… like you didn't know."

"Yoga's about anything else but touching other people," Michowsky replied unperturbed, "so I wonder if you know that much about yoga to call yourself an instructor."

The suspect froze. "What do you mean?"

"Two complaints, right here," he said, tapping the folder he'd placed on the table. "Two complaints that never made it to court, but that doesn't mean the deeds didn't happen. What did you do to those women?"

"Nothing," he replied a little too quickly. He smiled, but he was tense, worried. "Innocent until proven guilty. Remember that part of your job, Detective?"

"You like touching women, don't you?" Michowsky continued. "You like to stare at them as they stretch their bodies in front of you, offering them for you to see and desire, then whisk away without letting you closer. You get close, but never close enough."

The suspect shook his head and pressed his lips together. "That's not—"

"It's not? Are you sure? Why, then, would you badger these women until you make them call us? Just man up and admit it: you like women a little too much."

"I didn't know there was such a thing, unless you're gay," he replied with a crinkle of his nose.

"Where were you on February 20?"

"What time?"

"All day."

He scoffed and leaned back in his chair. "You people are unbelievable. That's almost a week ago."

Michowsky waved him on with his hand, and Bolton took the hint.

"I started my day about 10:00AM, then went straight to the studio, after grabbing a cup of coffee on the way. I was at the studio, and had classes almost all day, until seven o'clock. With students, I mean, witnesses."

"All day? Really? Because you don't seem like the hard-working type to me, you know."

"I had a break or two," he admitted reluctantly, and scratched his chin. "Lunch, and then mid-afternoon. Everyone takes breaks."

"Where did you take lunch, and how long was your break?"

"Um, I was at Ronnie's Bar & Grill, from about eleven o'clock until about two-ish. My next class started at three."

Michowsky chuckled. "So how many classes did you have on the twentieth? Two?"

"No," he replied, indignant. "Three. It was a full day."

"Oh, I get it; you work hard. Why do you get paid in cash?"

The unsub flinched when he heard the question, and fidgeted nervously in his chair. "That's what people want. I don't take American Express; it's too rich for me. But it's their choice to bring cash. I can't say no."

"If we traced these cash payments, we'll find you deposited all of the money in the bank, right?"

Bolton leaned forward again, with his elbows on the table. "What do you guys want?" he asked in a grave, determined voice.

"A DNA sample. To exculpate you from a series of rape-murders you could be going down for, considering you don't really have an alibi for the twentieth."

The unsub's eyes widened, as he took in the implications of the detective's request.

"Did I mention two of the victims were your students?" Michowsky said, delivering the blow casually. "Give us a DNA sample, and you can go home in minutes. That's the deal."

"How about a lawyer? This conversation's over," Bolton said, and promptly clammed up with his arms crossed at his chest.

Tess unmuted the line. "Gary, please stay in the room for now. Todd, get outside, where you can talk to me."

Through the video feed she saw Fradella nod slightly and leave the room.

"Shoot," he said, once he'd closed the door.

"Where's the thermostat for that room?" Tess asked.

"Here in the hallway. Why?"

"Turn on the heat and crank it up to 82. Then grab a can of Coke and go back inside."

Todd laughed quietly. "Remind me to never piss you off, Agent Winnett."

She watched Todd as he entered the interview room, a can of Coca-Cola in his hand. He almost opened it, then left it on the table when Michowsky glared at him. They were smart cops, both of them, and Michowsky didn't need to see more than the sweaty can of pop to figure things out and play along.

"Okay, you lawyered up," Fradella said. "That means you don't need to say anything until your lawyer gets here. Who's your lawyer? I'll call him for you."

"You think I'm made of money, or somethin'?" Bolton reacted. "I can't afford a lawyer, but that doesn't mean I'm not getting one, right?"

"Right," Fradella replied, then he and Michowsky left the room.

"Hey, you forgot your Coke," Bolton called just as Fradella was about to shut the door.

He popped his head back into the interview room. "Did you see the look my boss gave me just now? He'll shove that down my throat if I touch it before break time. Be my guest, or just leave it there; the janitor will take it back later."

It took Bolton less than ten minutes to pop the can open and thirstily down the contents. A few minutes later, Fradella moved him to another interview room to wait for his legal counsel, then picked up the can with a glove and sent it sealed in an evidence bag to the lab, via courier.

In a few hours, they'd know if Gene Bolton was the rapist unsub, or just a lecherous low-life like many others.

Ready

39

He sank deeper in the recliner, keeping his eyes riveted on the two women. Watching through the one-sided window, he took in every detail. How they moved, and how they talked. The angle of their necks, and the straightness of their spines. The expressions on their faces, and the sounds of their sobs.

They were different, these two. The new one had a hardened mien, as if nothing could break her; she was cold and unimpressionable. She hadn't seen everything yet; she still had a lot to learn, and that cold, brave attitude would soon be washed away by tears. Be it enough of those, and all that fortitude will fade away, like sand carried away by torrents, or stone carved by rain.

The other one still made his heart skip a beat whenever he glanced at her beautiful face. She looked just like his mother. If she'd somehow mastered the passing of time, she could *be* his mother. She had his mother's beauty, her elegance. She even walked like her, and when she flipped her long hair over her shoulder, she *was* her.

He still remembered his mother well, because he'd cherished her fading image in his mind, forbidding himself to forget. He'd hidden a picture of her under his mattress, before his father destroyed all memory of her in the back-yard firepit, and still stared at it for hours sometimes, remembering all about her and the way she used to be before the storm came.

This woman was the spitting image of his mother, but not only in physical form. When he had his rope around her neck she was defiant to the point of turning self-destructive, looking him in the eye and spouting her contempt in words spoken on raspy gasps of air. A true free spirit, she'd ignored his orders and had inspired resistance in the new girl. He wanted them naked, yet they both kept their clothes on. He wanted the whores to groom each other under his hungry eyes, yet they did none of that. Every time he took her to the other room, he stripped her of her clothes and punished her for her defiance, but it didn't matter. As soon as she returned to the holding room, she dug through the pile of abandoned garments and chose something that fit. There was no breaking her, and that drove him mad. He wanted her defeated, pleading for mercy and forgiveness; she gave him none of that.

He clenched his fists and gritted his teeth. The whore was ruining it... messing everything up. He needed to go in there and teach her a lesson she wouldn't forget. What would his father have done with a bitch like that? His nostrils flared, filled with rage.

Slowly, he uncoiled the rope he'd pulled from his pocket, and felt its ruggedness between his fingers, while keeping his eyes on the woman who defied him. He was ready.

Early Morning

40

She'd been up since about four in the morning, grateful for the peace that engulfed the hospital hallways, and eager to leave that place behind her once and for all. The harsh words of Dr. DePaolo still resounded in her mind, but didn't erode her decision to be released immediately. She'd promised him she wouldn't leave until he came back for one last exam, and he'd promised her she wouldn't have to wait too long for it.

She fired up her laptop and went through emails, then connected the remote camera and examined the victimology matrix drawn by Todd on the Palm Beach County case board. There were a lot of commonalities between victims, and that normally was a good thing, because it allowed investigators to reel in suspects who intersected the lives of the victims at the points of commonality. Gene Bolton, the sleazeball who was spending his night in Palm Beach County lockup waiting for the DNA test result, was an example of how such a commonality in victimology helped. Even so, only two of the victims had been involved with yoga, and Gene Bolton looked less and less like a viable suspect.

Tess shifted a little to get more comfortable against the pillows and typed an email to Donovan, then opened the case file and studied the crime-scene photos in the dim light of her night lamp. The glimpse of death, the position-ing of the victims, and the preening ritual that was so important to the unsubs were the most disturbing aspects of the case. All serial offenders were disturb-ing to her, but this case simply gave her the creeps. She closed her eyes and cringed, imagining how Lisa and Sarah must have felt, probably Katherine too, having to endure through the killer's rituals. They were subjected to the phys-ical and psychological tortures of laborious cosmetic procedures, some quite painful, like the Brazilian waxing was, under the lecherous eyes of a lust rapist.

Tess repressed a shudder and pushed away the nightmarish images from her mind. Sometimes, when such nightmares invaded her and raised ghosts from her own past, she saw herself pulling the trigger and ridding the world of such scum. Not anymore though… she had to catch them, if she was ever going to survive the committee hearing about her kill ratios. She forced some air into her lungs and soon the darkness that had invaded her mind cleared enough to let her focus on finding the two degenerates who'd taken so many lives.

A quiet chime alerted her to a new text message from Donovan, "If you're awake, please call this line," then a link to a conference call was pasted in the text message, complete with call number and secure access code.

She checked the time; it wasn't even 5:00AM yet. She put on her headphones and dialed the number, then entered her passkey. The system connected her with the call already in progress, and she recognized Michowsky, Fradella, and Donovan on the call.

"Good morning," she said quietly.

"When do you ever sleep?" Michowsky asked.

"I don't. Not while those freaks are still out there. Not while they have Katherine and Stacy."

"If there's any consolation, neither do we," Donovan replied.

"Let's start with some bad news," Michowsky intervened. "That schmuck, Bolton, is not our doer; his DNA doesn't match. As much as it pains me to say it, I cut that perv loose."

"I was expecting that," Tess replied. "We need to find someone who had access to all victims; Bolton only had access to two of them. He was a long shot to begin with."

"And the physical appearance match?" Fradella asked.

"Just a coincidence, I guess." Tess replied, trying to ignore the pang of fear that churned in her gut. What if the portraits were useless, more of a distraction and a time waste than a useful tool? Only time would tell, but for now it didn't look too good.

"BOLO's out on the sketches anyway," Michowsky added. "And we've been busy. We've talked to every friend and close relative of the victims, and we started on Katherine's and Stacy's. Are you busy this morning, Winnett?"

"What do you think?" she scoffed. "Why?"

"There's a Constance Gilliam on staff at the hospital. She and Katherine were best friends, by her husband's account. Will you save me a trip?"

"Sure, as soon as the day shift starts, I'll get to it."

"I got some interesting stuff that popped up from searches tonight. Deeply buried data, that's why it took so long to dig it up," Donovan said. "All financials are pristine, for all the victims and their immediate families. No debt, no unusual transactions, nothing to mention. Katherine Nelson has these cash withdrawals that I can't correlate with any activities; maybe her bestie Constance Gilliam can shed some light."

"How much?" Tess asked.

"At least six or seven hundred a month, two or three hundred at a time."

"Okay, I'll look into it. What else?"

"A few commonalities, but they're partial. The Thomas family and the Nelsons used the same plumbing company recently. Lisa Trask and Katherine Nelson lived relatively close to a recently released sex offender who matches the physical description and the behavioral profile."

"Bring him in," Tess said. "Maybe it's that simple."

"Is it ever?" Michowsky replied with a hint of sarcasm. "We're on our way there now."

"We still don't have someone who had access to all of them. Keep looking, Donovan, please."

"I'm running out of ideas, what to look at and where to dig."

"Maybe it has something to do with their children," Tess offered. "All these women were young mothers; maybe that's the connection."

"I've already checked day care and nannies, pediatricians and nurses, even baby food choices. Nothing."

"Let's go back to the women, then. What about their professional backgrounds?"

"Nothing there, at least on the surface. Four victims, four different companies, and four different professions. Couldn't be more scattered."

Silence took over the line, and the usual amplified hum made itself heard.

"These women have more than a few things in common. Young mothers, we looked at that. How about their depression? Anyone self-medicating? Seeing a shrink? How about their cheating? Maybe the same man asked them out? Take another look on their social media profiles."

"They're married, Tess," Fradella said, "they're not going to post their lover's name and number on Facebook."

"You're right, Todd, I'm reaching; I'm getting desperate. It's just that... I don't know how much longer they're going to keep Katherine alive, that's all. It drives me crazy."

Silence took over the line again, except for the sounds of Michowsky's car, driving fast over the concrete slabs of a bridge.

"Listen, guys, I know it's farfetched, but I have this gut feeling, you know? I think the unsub is choosing them because they rejected him. It's something about this grooming ritual that makes no other sense."

"What do you mean?" Fradella asked, "and which unsub are you talking about?"

"The rapist. I know he's not killing them himself, but he chooses them to be killed while he rapes them. We talked about it when we built the profile. Now, see? Women spruce up before going on dates, right? In this case, and in the mind of the profoundly deranged rapist unsub, before cheating. But the lust rapist objectifies women; he doesn't care about pretending he's on a date."

"I'm confused now, what are you saying?" Michowsky asked.

"I think we should disentangle the unsubs' fantasies," Tess replied. "I think the grooming ritual supports the killer unsub's fantasy, and we've already established that the rapist unsub is most likely to be the one who chooses the victims. I think it plays like this: the rapist sees the woman, approaches her, and is rejected. That feeds both his lust and his urge to possess the woman, to get sexual gratification contingent on her death, as a form of supreme punishment. It's called erotophonophilia, or sexual arousal contingent on the death of a human. He can't kill them himself yet, so he needs the strangler unsub to do the job for him."

"Well… that puts things in a new light," Michowsky commented. "How about the strangler's fantasy? How do you see that playing?"

"He's the one who dictates the physical appearance of the victims. He has a type, because he's an anger-retaliatory killer, and he repeats something he needs to remember, just like Bill said. That something is centered on a traumatic memory involving a woman who looked a certain way. I believe the killer unsub dictates the specific physiognomy type, but the rapist goes out there and chooses the victims, and later the killer stalks them and shows them the glimpse of death. These two unsubs are completely symbiotic. Their fantasies intertwine and complete each other."

One of them whistled quietly, but Tess didn't recognize who that was.

"When did you come up with all this?" Michowsky asked.

"I had a lot of time on my hands," she replied dryly. "See why I think these women might have met the rapist unsub? I believe he approached them, and they rejected him. I have no rational evidence to support that thought; it just makes sense to me, in my gut."

"Yeah, but Stacy's gay," Fradella said. "You said these unsubs are highly organized; how did they miss that?"

"You're right. Stacy being gay is an exception in our victimology matrix, and we don't understand this exception yet. Ultimately, Stacy being gay can only mean she rejected him if he approached her. I say, go back and talk with all the girlfriends; maybe the victims shared that they met someone recently, someone who approached them and they didn't accept. Maybe it was someone creepy, or too shy, or just… not the right guy. Maybe we get lucky, and one of these girlfriends saw him."

A Shower 41

When Melissa entered Tess's room, her hands trembled slightly, holding tightly to the envelope with the prints of the photos she'd taken a few days before. She felt tired and jittery, living off coffee and adrenaline, both fueling her rampant anxiety. She'd spent the night wide awake, pacing the living room in her socks so she wouldn't disturb Derek, avoiding him.

She couldn't look him in the eye; not with the terrible suspicions that whirlpooled in her mind. She was afraid he'd see right through her in a matter of seconds, and ask her questions she didn't want to answer. She'd spent the evening curled up on the couch and wrapped in a blanket, blaming her state on nonexistent PMS and some nonexistent cramps. Later, when Derek had gone to bed, she started pacing the floor, unable to sleep, unable to rest.

A night's worth of anguish had brought no answers; only more questions, more fears. Yet, after all that time spent twisting the same hypotheses in her weary mind, she'd decided to look again, just to be more than sure. This time, she wanted to put the photos side by side, the ones she'd taken herself, and the one Tess kept in the case file. What if they were two different women, who just happened to look alike? What if her terrified mind had played an ugly trick on her?

Her palm sweat and stained the envelope. She gripped it firmly, terrified of what could happen if somehow the photos fell to the floor under the gaze of the fearsome Agent Winnett. She walked inside the room and fumbled to push the door shut, because her right hand clutched the photos, but she made it to the cabinet without incident. Then she breathed for the first time in what seemed like minutes, but it had only been seconds.

She ventured a quick glance toward Tess, who was reading something on her laptop. Tess held her hand up in the air, as if pleading for a little more time.

"One sec," she said, "let me finish this, okay?"

Melissa didn't reply; instead, she approached Tess shyly, and waited by her bed.

"Um, done," Tess said, then closed the laptop. "Good morning to you," she added, sounding cheerful.

Melissa forced a smile but quickly averted her eyes. "Good morning. How are you feeling today?"

"Great, because I'm about to leave this place," Tess replied, then stopped talking, giving her a long, scrutinizing look. "Is everything okay with you?"

"Yes, I told you," she rushed, "it's nothing. I'm fine."

She thought she saw a flicker of a frown on Tess's forehead, quick to come then disappear.

"All right, then," Tess replied. "Listen, I was too harsh on you yesterday, and I want to apologize."

Melissa's eyebrows shot up, and she put her palm in the air. "No, it's all—"

"Please, let me finish," Tess interrupted. "You've been great with me all this time; you've been amazing. You put up with all this crap, with the burgers, with everything. And still, at the first opportunity, I treated you like a murder suspect. It's in my blood, I guess, but that's no excuse. I wanted to apologize… I hope you can forgive me."

Melissa's cheeks burned and her heart beat fast. The fed seemed sincere, although one could never tell with the likes of them. This one seemed different somehow, more trustworthy, more friendship worthy. She ventured a timid smile. "It's all right. I was worried you didn't believe me, you know."

"I believe you," Tess replied. "And I need to be in your good favor to take my stitches out in a few days. I won't let anyone else touch me but you." She smiled, a little dramatic, trying to be funny, and lowered her head a bit. "Am I forgiven?"

"Yes," Melissa replied quickly, relieved she was off the hook.

The fed would be discharged before lunch, and soon she'd be gone. But until then, she had a job to do, and for that, she needed her gone from the room first, and that friend of hers too.

"Say, would you like to take a shower before leaving?" Melissa offered. "I heard you weren't going home from here."

"Great idea," Tess replied. "Can't wait to get the hospital stink off me. I've got some clean clothes here; I could change already, right? Get rid of the ass-revealing hospital garb?"

Melissa helped Tess get out of bed. She moved better, but she probably was in pain, considering she'd been off her pain meds for the past three days. She seemed reinvigorated, ready to leave, although she shuffled her feet and walked slower than a three year old.

"Would you like me to call your friend to help you?"

"Nah… I sent him home. He needs to get some rest. He's done enough. I should be fine on my own," she added, and walked into the bathroom, then closed the door.

"I'm here if you need me," Melissa said a little louder, so Tess could hear her from the bathroom.

Tess didn't respond, but Melissa soon heard the toilet flush, then the shower running.

She took a deep breath, then rushed to the cabinet and took out the photo prints. Then she opened one of the files Tess kept on her bedside table, and flipped though the photos in it, looking for the one she wanted to compare with her own.

She found it, and took it out of the file, then held it in her hand next to the dark, yellowish one she'd taken at the mall. It was the same woman; there was no doubt about it. Realization hit her in the stomach like a fist, and she almost retched.

She forced a deep breath of air into her lungs to settle her stomach, and took her photo prints back to the safety of the cabinet, then returned to flip through the case file some more. A few pages further, there were two drawings. She'd overheard enough of Tess's conversations to know exactly what she was looking at. She stared at the first sketch for a long minute. Could that be Derek? No… it couldn't be. His hair wasn't like that; it was darker, longer, completely covering his shirt collar. His eyes were smaller than this man's, and his gaze kinder. He had a nice smile, when she could still see him smile, and had fuller, more sensual lips. No, her husband didn't even look like the man in the sketch. She breathed again, relieved.

Then she looked at the second sketch, and didn't spend any time analyzing it. It was the face of a complete stranger, although the eyes… the hair… No, that was nonsense. She didn't know that man either.

She was about to close the file, when a new wave of adrenaline hit her in the gut, sending panic though her veins. What if the police had their sketches wrong? She remembered overhearing all sorts of arguments about these portraits; she couldn't remember too much detail about the arguments, but what if they were wrong? How could she be sure her husband had nothing to do with that woman's disappearance?

Another file caught her attention; it was labeled, "DNA Profiles," and as soon as she saw it, she had an idea. She knew someone who owed her a favor at the hospital lab, and she could take Charlie's DNA and compare it… to what? She needed to make copies of the DNA profiles printed in full color and stashed in that file.

She pressed her lips together and breathed deeply, trying to control the waves of fear that ran through her body. She needed to know for sure, and it was now or never. The shower was still running in the bathroom, but she needed to make it quick.

She put the case file back on the bedside table, trying to remember the exact position where she'd taken it from. Then she accessed her phone, and quickly took snapshots of the two DNA profiles in the file. Finally, she let the phone slide back into her pocket, and closed the file. She patted the sides, to make all the sheets of paper stay in place, and reached out to put it under the case file.

Then her blood turned to ice when she noticed Tess was looking at her from the bathroom doorway. Her eyes were cold, analytical, inquisitive. "Are you looking for something?"

A Promise

42

Stacy stood at the edge of the bed and rocked back and forth, with her eyes squeezed shut and her palms covering her ears. As soon as they'd taken Katherine and the lights turned on in that other room, she rushed to the window and tried to make them stop. She watched helplessly how they tied Katherine to that bench, and saw her encouraging gaze before she spaced out and her eyes glazed over.

Katherine was encouraging *her*... The very thought of that was twisted and surreal, yet minutes later she'd understood why. It was the first time she had to watch what went on in that room, and the things she'd seen those men do to Katherine would haunt her for the rest of her life. Katherine's screams soon became unbearable, and Stacy couldn't handle it anymore. She found refuge by putting as much distance between herself and that dreadful window, and hoping that Katherine would forgive her for running away.

Then she realized what she'd just seen was the sick, horrifying sneak preview of what her own future held for her, as long as she remained at the mercy of those brutes. Panic rose in her chest so violently she couldn't breathe; when she finally drew breath, it came back out as a low-pitched cry that had no beginning and no end. She rocked back and forth continuously, and her panicked mind rushed, recalled, and grabbed onto the image of Renata and the girls, how they looked when she'd last seen them from the doorway of their home. Sweet memories of their peaceful life, the life she didn't know to appreciate enough before it was all gone.

She realized Katherine's screams had quieted, and her entire being switched into high alert. Were they coming for her now? Panting and shaking, she jumped to her feet and hid behind the shower cabin the moment she heard the door unlatch.

The man who'd raped Katherine brought her back, half dragging her inert body. He let go of her, and she fell to the cold floor with a sickening thump. Then he looked at Stacy and sneered; that sneer evolved into a libidinous smirk, as he checked her out, head to toe.

She shuddered under his gaze, holding her breath, and heard herself whimper. She wasn't ready for what was going to happen to her. She wasn't ever going to be ready. *Oh, God... please, no.*

The man turned around and left, and she breathed when she heard him latch the massive door shut. Then she rushed over to where Katherine lay.

Her naked body was badly bruised and her legs were stained with blood. Some bruises were older, but most were new, reddish, swollen areas that would turn black and blue in a day or two. Her neck was discolored and swollen, where he'd tried to strangle her from behind. Her breathing was shallow and raspy; she was still alive.

Stacy tried to lift her gently, to put her on the bed, but she was too heavy. Katherine's swollen eyelids stayed closed, but her lips moved slightly.

"Don't... touch me," she whispered hoarsely. "I...can't."

"Tell me what to do," Stacy pleaded, tears running down her cheeks. "Please... You're the doctor, tell me what to do."

Katherine didn't move, or say anything. After a while, Stacy covered her with the blanket she took off the bed, and sat on the floor next to her. Gently, she took Katherine's head in her lap, and ran her fingers softly through her hair.

"They'll come for us," Stacy whispered, "you'll see. They're looking for us. They'll find us soon, I promise."

Discharged

43

And that's how you catch 'em, Tess thought, seeing how Melissa had frozen in place, blood draining from her face. For a while she'd suspected her nurse had something to hide, and a personal agenda on top of that, but she couldn't get her to talk. The folder she'd messed with had DNA profiles, nothing more. Those weren't of any use to anyone.

Maybe catch that fly with honey, and find out what was going on?

Melissa stared at her for a long second, speechless, then she shot a quick glance at the bathroom door. The shower was still running, and she probably was asking herself what the hell had just happened.

"Are you looking for something?" Tess repeated her question in a softer tone, staying true to the honey strategy.

"N–no," Melissa managed to say. "I just swatted this file by accident, and it fell. I was putting it back."

"Oh?" Tess asked, careful to put just enough worry in her voice to keep it credible. "What were you doing there?"

"Getting readouts from the machines," Melissa replied, pointing at the heart monitor installed above Tess's bed. "I turned too quickly, and... I'm sorry."

"Don't worry," Tess replied. "Can you please turn off the shower for me? I don't even have the strength to do that... it's pathetic."

Melissa went straight to the bathroom, seemingly relieved. The shower's noise subsided, and she reappeared, a little hesitant.

Tess looked at her with a smile, carefully taking in all the details. Her hands were trembling slightly, and she clasped them together, trying to hide it. Tiny beads of sweat were appearing on Melissa's forehead, and her pulse was rapid and strong, visible on her carotid, on the side of her neck. She was scared.

Tess took out a business card from her laptop bag and handed it to her.

"This is my cell phone number, if you ever need anything. I know you're under some nasty personal stress lately, and I want you to remember you can call me at any time, for anything, all right?"

Melissa nodded quickly, but didn't say a word.

"Family stress can sometimes go south really quickly, and if it does, I'll be there for you, Mel. I'd be happy to pay you back with a favor, any favor."

Melissa started to shift her weight from one foot to the other, while her eyes danced around, from Tess's face to the ceiling, walls, floor, and back. She was probably considering the implications of what she was going to say, her internal turmoil reflected in her eyes, every unanswered question and every bit of worry.

"There's, um, something that I—"

"All ready to go, against my firm recommendation?" Dr. DePaolo interrupted, appeared out of nowhere at the worst possible moment.

Tess refrained from cussing out loud and averted her steaming glare away from Dr. DePaolo, who'd done nothing to deserve it. Instead, she quickly pasted a smile on her lips, while secretly hoping she'd get Melissa talkative again.

"Yes, ready to go, Doctor. I've been ready to go since you let me off your table."

"You've ignored the majority of my recommendations, Agent Winnett, but who am I to complain when you're recovering so nicely?"

He lifted her dressing and inspected the sutures, then touched the edges of the wound with his gloved finger. "Any pain here, if I touch like this?"

"No."

"Good; no signs of infection, so you're doing great. Please don't ruin my work, Agent Winnett. Take it easy, rest a lot, keep the showers short and moderate temperature, don't make sudden moves. Same thing I've been telling you since the day we met."

"Yes, sir," she replied, smiling.

"We'll see you back here on the twenty-seventh, to remove your sutures. Then we hope to never see you again, Agent Winnett." He chuckled lightly and squeezed her shoulder.

Tess could barely wait for the doctor to pull the door shut behind him. As soon as he was gone, she turned to Melissa, smiling encouragingly. "I'm listening, Mel. What were you trying to say?"

"Oh, nothing," she replied, keeping her eyes riveted to the floor. "Nothing important."

Damn, Tess thought, but her smile didn't waver. "Call me, all right? Anytime."

"Uh-huh," Melissa replied, and helped her get dressed, without saying another word.

As she held Tess's shirt, she touched her bare skin and Tess felt the coldness of Mel's fingers. The coldness of extremities only fear puts in humans, when the flush of adrenaline and cortisol rushes blood to critical organs, to ensure survival.

Cat opened the door and pushed a wheelchair inside. "Ready, kiddo?"

"More than you'll ever know, Cat," she replied.

She turned and opened her arms. "Give me a hug?" she asked Melissa. "You're good people, Mel. Know that."

Melissa hugged her hesitantly, a little rushed to let go, still averting her eyes.

"You know you're getting out of here in a wheelchair, right?" Cat asked, holding on to the chair's handles.

"Yeah, whatever," she grunted, but sat in the wheelchair without dispute.

"I'm surprised you're not arguing with me," he said, and started pushing her down the hallway, toward the elevators.

"Not worth it," she replied with a chuckle. "I'm saving my energy for the suspect I'll be interrogating later."

"Later this week, I hope?"

"Later today, after you drop me off at Palm Beach County Sheriff's Office."

"Jeez, kiddo, you don't let those engines of yours idle, do you?"

As soon as she took the passenger seat in Cat's old Jeep, she whipped her cell phone out of her pocket and dialed a number.

"Donovan? It's Tess. Hey, listen, Constance Gilliam, Dr. Nelson's so-called best friend, wasn't her bestie after all; she was her AA sponsor. Our Dr. Nelson was a struggling addict; amphetamines. That explains the cash withdrawals she was making. Find her dealer, and let the guys know to reel him in."

"You must have me on speed-dial or something," Donovan said humorously. "Consider it done."

"Check with the ME, see if the advanced tox reports for Lisa and Sarah showed any drug use, recent or not."

"Got it."

There was silence on the line, while Tess bit her lip, then her index fingernail.

"Okay, spill it, what else?" Donovan asked. "You got something on your mind, or you can't seem to let me go? Which one is it?"

"It's… I don't know what it is, nothing more than a hunch, I guess. Run background on Melissa Henderson's husband. Tell me what you find."

"Your nurse?" Donovan sounded almost shocked.

"Yep. Don't ask… it's just my gut, that's all."

Back in the Saddle Again 44

Tess entered the Palm Beach County Sheriff's Office building and gave the stairs a long glance, then opted for the elevator instead. Despite how miserable she felt at the thought of taking the elevator for one level, it was faster, and they didn't have any time to lose.

She entered the conference room after walking through the squad room and greeting briefly the few people who were there and knew who she was. Once in the conference room, she stopped right in front of the case board, going over every detail, although she'd seen it all before. It was different when she could look at it up-close, and could write on it without asking Fradella to wield the dry-erase marker for her.

Fradella sat at the table, buried in his laptop, typing quickly.

"Good to have you back," he said, without taking his eyes from the screen.

"Thanks," she replied. "Where's Gary?"

"Downstairs, with Doc. He's got something new on the tox reports. I'll ping them," he offered, then sent Doc Rizza a quick message on the internal communicator.

"We're running out of time," Tess said, as soon as Michowsky and Doc Rizza entered the room. "I have a bad feeling about this," she said, pacing the space in front of the case board nervously, and sipping precinct coffee from a borrowed mug.

"They've only had Katherine Nelson for a week," Fradella said. "Not that we're not moving as fast as we can, but—"

"Every day she's in their hands she's being raped and tortured. Trust me, every minute counts."

"We know that," Doc Rizza said, putting his hand on her shoulder, squeezing gently. "We all do."

"I just… have a bad feeling about this," she repeated. "Serial killers sometimes escalate, and the timelines collapse. This could happen, and we can't *let* it happen."

"And we won't," Doc Rizza added. "Advanced tox screen came back with faint, metabolized traces of propofol. It's a powerful anesthetic and relaxant, injectable. I reexamined the bodies and found a needle mark on Lisa's neck, almost entirely healed. It could be how they were abducted, how they were so quickly subdued."

"How about Sarah's neck? Any injection marks?" Michowsky asked.

"None that I could find. But keep in mind Sarah's strangulation was significantly rougher than Lisa's. The abrasions and contusions on her neck might have obliterated any injection mark, especially one that was almost completely healed antemortem."

Tess bit her lip nervously. These unsubs were too smart, too organized for a killing team. They must have killed many times before; such perfect level of organization happens only when the unsubs repeat the same MO over and over again, until every detail is perfect. Then what changed? Why weren't they seeing evidence of earlier kills? Why weren't they finding earlier mistakes?

"Todd, how does our victimology play out against open missing persons cases?"

"Only two others who'd seen the glimpse of death. If we remove that condition, and apply the narrow victimology traits—small child, married, physiognomy, the count goes up to twenty-one open cases."

Tess's brow instantly furrowed. "During what period of time?"

"The past two years."

"What if you open it up to, say, ten years?"

"Nothing, or almost nothing. I'm thinking that whatever stressor triggered the unsub's killing, it must have happened roughly two years ago. Can't speak for rapes though; they're just too many."

"Yeah, that's what the data indicates. It's either that, or he was locked up somewhere, unable to do his bidding. But it's clear he's done it many times before; he's too experienced, too organized. This killing team, they have it together like none I've ever seen."

"Then why didn't we find the bodies? What changed?" Michowsky asked.

"I think this unsub buried his mistakes… I believe he's started displaying them only when they were worthy of admiration, perfect to the tiniest detail. When he was sure he'd taken all forensic countermeasures to keep us at bay."

"How can you say that, when the unsubs left heaps of DNA on the victims' bodies? How's that a forensic countermeasure?" Doc Rizza asked.

"Because DNA wasn't left by accident; case in point, Doc, you said, 'heaps.' The unsubs marked the bodies with their DNA."

"Like a brand, or something?" Fradella asked.

"Exactly. Leaving DNA behind is part of their signature. It doesn't change the profile; it just reinforces it, and adds a new dimension. The unsubs want the victims tainted, marked by semen, bearing the imprint of the carnal contact they've had."

"What does that mean?" Fradella asked, frowning.

"Combine that piece of information with the way he put the victims on display, naked, with their genitals exposed, in plain sight. These unsubs see the cheating wives as fallen women, as sluts, and make it their mission to let the world know who they really were."

"You think their motivations could be religious?" Michowsky asked.

"I doubt that, for some reason."

The conference line rang and Fradella picked it up with the press of a button.

"Conference room," he announced.

"I know that," Donovan said. "I can see you all on video, remember?"

"Ugh… remind me to flag you in DIVS as a stalker," Tess chuckled. "What's up?"

"Two things, actually. Stacy Rodriguez is openly bisexual. Not sure how that changes things, but in her social media there are plenty references to her being bi. Older photos, pre-marriage, show her with girlfriends and boyfriends, with no pattern or commitment to one gender or another."

"Okay," Tess replied, "that does change things a little. It removes the oddity in our victimology table. She might have been inclined to cheat with a man, not a woman, confirming every bit of data in the matrix. What else?"

"Your special request, is it okay to share findings on an open line?"

"Absolutely. It might be illogical, but my gut tells me it's related to this case."

"Your Mr. Henderson is squeaky clean. A forensic accountant, CMA, who's working hard and has been promoted three times in the past four years. Impeccable finances, clean and almost nonexistent social media, no reports of domestic violence, happy family photos posted online with his wife and child. No health issues, no addictions. Do I continue digging?"

"N–no," she replied hesitantly. "My gut must have been wrong on this one." Her frown deepened. "How old is the child?"

"He's six," Donovan replied promptly. "Why?"

"Ah, don't know. It's just—"

"Your gut, again?" Donovan asked. "Only time will tell."

He hung up, and no one said a word for a while. Tess's mind ran back to Melissa's unusual behavior of late; she must have had other reasons to behave the way she did, to look so distraught, and to have those growing black circles under her eyes. People's lives held all sorts of heartache, and serial killers weren't seen at every corner. *Only in my world,* Tess thought bitterly, *killers are everywhere I turn.*

"Why is the name Henderson familiar?" Michowsky asked. "I could swear I—"

"My nurse, her name is Melissa Henderson."

"How does she play in all this?" Michowsky asked, rushing his hand over his buzz-cut hair, while his eyebrows shot high up his forehead.

"She doesn't; it was a hunch I followed up on, and it was a dead end. You heard Donovan. Did you pick up the plumber?"

"Yeah, he's been slowly cooking in Interview Two. Ready?"

"Yep," she said, and followed Fradella as quickly as she could. "It was the same plumber in both Sarah and Katherine's homes? Or did you bring in the company manager?"

"The same plumber. He closely fits the rapist composite; we might have our doer. One of them, anyway," Fradella added.

She took a seat across the table from the suspect, and looked him in the eye. He didn't flinch; he just scoffed quietly, as if asking, "Really? Why do you keep me here, and why do you look at me like that?"

He was strong, muscular, but cleanly dressed and well kempt for someone in his line of work. He matched the rapist composite sketch, but Tess wasn't getting from him the lustful vibes a rapist normally puts out in the presence of an attractive woman. She opened the folder she'd brought along, and looked at the sketch again. His eyes were different; mostly because there was no evil intention in them. He was also too young, and didn't have a record, not even a parking ticket. Most likely he wasn't their guy, but she needed to be sure.

She pulled out Lisa Trask's photo from her file, and asked, "Do you know this woman?"

"No, I don't," he said, after a split-second hesitation.

"How about her?" she asked, and offered Sarah's photo.

"Yes, I think I fixed her shower faucet a few months back."

"And her?" Tess offered Stacy's photo this time.

"Um, no, I don't think so. They all look alike, you know."

He was perceptive, but open with his observations. A good indicator of innocence.

"How about her?" Katherine Nelson's image was the last in the lineup.

"I changed a toilet for her, um, maybe last December?"

"So, what, these women rejected you and you got angry?" Michowsky intervened, so out of order it was almost funny.

"What?" he said, taken aback by Michowsky's question. "What do you mean?"

"I think you got jealous of these women, being how they're successful, they didn't want to have anything to do with you, because you're nothing but a shit-stirrer, aren't you?"

Tess almost rolled her eyes. She needed to have a conversation with Michowsky. She was about to interrupt the interview, when the plumber's reaction surprised her.

He was laughing out loud, his hands clasped over his abdomen, as if to keep it in place.

"Is that what you think? Do you think there's anyone out there doing this job because they like stirring shit? Let me give you some perspective. How much money do you think I make a year? More than the two of you combined, and then some. I drive a Cadillac, and that's how I get laid. I make more money than those two women who were my clients. The other two I never met. I don't know what you guys think I did, but I didn't do it. You're so wasting your time."

"Do you want to exculpate yourself with a DNA test?" Tess asked.

The plumber frowned; he seemed concerned, and his laughter had vanished.

"How do I know you're not going to abuse this test? Cops these days... no offense, but I don't really trust you, that's all."

"The law prohibits us from storing any DNA that was taken as a voluntary, exculpatory probe," she said. "It will only go to the trash, I promise."

He looked at Tess, then at Michowsky and frowned some more. Then he sighed and looked at Tess again. "Okay, have at it."

Turmoil 45

Melissa turned on the light in the small bathroom her son used and looked around. Her eyes stuck on his toothbrush, and she stared at the familiar object for a long time, trying to breathe normally. Then her gaze lifted and met itself in the mirror, hesitantly, through a thin mist of tears; she could barely stand looking at herself. The woman in the mirror appeared just as terrified as she felt, inches away from doing the most unthinkable thing of her existence. She was about to compare her son's DNA with the DNA profile of someone the FBI had labeled, "Unsub one: killer."

It was unthinkable, but that way she'd know, once and for all. She'd know for sure, without asking that fed a single question, or sharing any bit of her husband's illicit pursuits. Cheater or not, he was her son's father, and she couldn't conceive drawing any law enforcement attention to him, not unless she was sure, positively sure, beyond any possible doubt.

Her hands trembled, as they'd done quite often lately, but she opened the Ziploc bag she'd brought with her and put her son's toothbrush inside, then sealed the zipper. She was ready… or was she?

A fleeting thought of gratitude toward Tess Winnett passed through her mind, for being so well organized. She'd labeled the sketched portraits and the DNA profiles with the same monikers, making it easy for her to choose the one she needed to use. She'd researched online the term *unsub*, and found it meant unknown subject. There were two profiles in Tess's DNA file, one for each unsub, but she only needed the one that looked most like her husband, although not even that one was a close visual match. It was probably nothing, but, as a mother, she needed to be more than sure, otherwise she couldn't bear the thought of Derek touching Charlie, or even looking at him. She'd lose her mind, waiting for that case to be closed, those evil men to be found and arrested, and for the truth to finally dissipate the wave of ominous darkness that swirled through her heart and brought a constant state of fear to her life.

Her son could be the son of a serial killer. The thought passed through her mind leaving deep ridges of terror and pain. She cringed inside, and it took all her willpower to leave that bathroom, clutching the small Ziploc bag and getting ready to leave.

She was about to put her entire existence in the helping hands of Charelle, her nursing school friend, currently a lab technician at the hospital. Charelle had laughed when she'd heard Melissa had doubts about the paternity of her son, and needed her help in the strictest of confidence. The time was right, Melissa had explained, because her husband had had a DNA profile done to look for health risks, considering his father had died of liver cancer. Once Melissa had started lying, she didn't stop; she poured them out there, one after another, until Charelle laughed again and said, "Relax, sweetie, you're not the only one who… shopped around, if you catch my drift. Just bring something of your son's to the lab later tonight, and by morning, you'll know if hubby's your baby's daddy."

It was already seven o'clock, and Charelle's night shift was starting at eight; she needed to get going. She grabbed her car keys and Charlie's toothbrush, and rushed toward the door, but stopped in her tracks when she heard a key turning in the lock.

"Ah, you're home early," she reacted without thinking, the moment Derek walked through the door.

Derek looked her in the eye for a second, then his gaze stopped on the toothbrush she was carrying.

"Going somewhere?" he asked, then gave the open door a strong shove and watched it slam shut behind him.

"Yeah," she replied, struggling to speak normally. She cleared her throat, and managed to continue. "Why? You needed something?"

"Where are you going?" he asked quietly, still staring at the toothbrush. "That Charlie's?"

"Yeah… There's a visiting specialist at the hospital; his expertise is in childhood oral health. I told him about Charlie's cavities, and he suggested we get his saliva tested to see if he's prone to cavities."

"What kind of test?" he asked.

He hadn't moved from the hallway, nor put his car keys on the rack. He just stood there, staring at her, questioning her. She felt the hairs on the back of her neck stand on end.

"Uh, acidity, bacteria, PCR, that kind of stuff." She lied badly and she knew it, yet she couldn't help it. Her mind had turned into a completely empty shell, unable to draw a single useful idea, and spewed too many details, way more than necessary.

"PCR, huh?" Derek said, smiling faintly, and looking in her eyes. "Isn't that a type of DNA test?"

"Um, uh-huh," she replied.

"I see," he said, and took a few steps toward her. "I won't keep you. I'm heading back to the office, I have a project I need to wrap up tonight. I need my laptop; I forgot it in the bedroom this morning."

"Want me to grab it for you?" she offered.

"Sure, if you will. Thanks."

She went to the bedroom and found the laptop bag leaning against the bed. She grabbed it and took it to him. He gave her one long look before grabbing hold of the bag.

"I won't be long; maybe a couple of hours at the most."

"Okay," she replied, trying to hide her relief. "I should be home before that, anyway."

Once the door closed behind him, she leaned against the wall, pressing her hands on her chest to calm the desperate beats of her heart. She breathed deeply, letting a rush of air out of her lungs. She couldn't help but think of how badly the two of them lied to each other, yet neither addressed their issues openly. She knew what *her* reasons were for accepting his lies without challenge, but she found herself wondering what were his reasons. What was *he* afraid of?

She waited until she heard his car pull out of the driveway, then waited another couple of minutes before leaving. Then she snuck to her car, almost afraid she'd be seen, feeling like she was doing something illegal.

"Hello there, beautiful Melissa."

Ryan's voice startled her. She looked at him while noticing how badly her hands and knees trembled from the scare. Too many adrenaline jolts had rushed through her body lately, turning her into a nervous wreck, a panicky mess.

"Oh, hi, Ryan," she said, smiling unwillingly, and just feeling better because her neighbor was there. For the first time in what seemed like ages, she felt safe, although there was no rational reason for it. Ryan Stafford was nothing more than a kind stranger, yet a stranger, nevertheless.

"Rushing off somewhere?" he asked, his smile lingering on his lips.

"Yeah, got to run to the hospital and drop something off at the lab."

"Why don't you let me do the honors? I wanted to talk to you about something," he added, a little hesitantly.

"What about?"

He fidgeted for a second, as if trying to find the right words for what he was going to say. "I'm worried about you; no, I really am," he added, reading her body language.

She'd lifted her hand in a denying gesture, waving the toothbrush bag with it. "No need," she replied, "I'm fine."

"I'm not buying that, you know. You're always so upset when you think no one's watching; you look grim, worried. What's on your mind?"

She looked away, unable to say anything. Deep down she desperately wished for someone to talk to, but Ryan wasn't that someone. She was also surprised at herself, at how willing she was to spend time with him, to lengthen and relish the feeling of safety, of being nurtured, cherished, and respected.

Why did a simple driveway conversation convey all that meaning? Too much adrenaline, probably. That, and prolonged exhaustion from her troubled, sleepless nights.

"Why don't you let me take you out for coffee, then take you wherever you need to go? It might do you some good," Ryan added, and his friendly smile widened.

She gave the toothbrush bag a furtive look, then made up her mind, almost. "At this time of night?"

"Tea, then?"

"Okay, if you insist," she said, then let herself be led to Ryan's car.

He opened the door for her and held it, and she appreciated the gesture, along with every other kind gesture the man made, and every word he said. She climbed into the passenger seat and felt more relaxed, able to relieve some of the tension she'd accumulated in her neck and shoulders. Somehow, just leaning against Ryan's passenger seat felt good. She shook her head almost imperceptibly, thinking critically of how tempted she was by that man, how willing she was to let him take care of her, and how few additional complications her current life needed.

The Giver

46

Tess left Interview Two with a DNA sample, but didn't hold much hope. The plumber had voluntarily offered the sample and that meant he knew he never touched those women. Dead end, and just more wasted time, when time was something they couldn't afford to waste.

She topped the cold coffee in her borrowed mug and took a swig, stopping just briefly on the way to Interview Three. Before entering, she followed Michowsky to the adjacent observation room, and looked at the next suspect in line for interrogation.

"Why is he half naked?" she asked.

The suspect, a skinny-looking street thug with light-brown hair and a three-day shadow that revealed a scar on his chin, wore a pair of faded, black jeans, and some running shoes that had seen better days. He fidgeted incessantly and glanced at the ceiling camera at least once every minute.

"This lovely young man is Gino 'The Giver' Janda, twenty-five, with an endless rap sheet for any drug-related offense known to man," Michowsky said. "He's Katherine Nelson's dealer. He didn't have a shirt on when the unis chased him for three blocks to drag his sorry ass in here."

"Any correlation with the other victims?" Tess asked, frowning at the restless man. She didn't want to waste more time with a nonviable suspect, but gaining any perspective into the secret life of Dr. Katherine Nelson could prove beneficial.

"None we could find," Michowsky replied. "Doc Rizza confirmed neither Lisa nor Sarah were using."

Tess went straight into the interview room and put Katherine's photo in front of Janda, and he flinched.

"Whoa," he said, pulling away from the table.

"We have you for distribution of a controlled substance," Tess went straight to the point. "You're pushing amphetamines to her."

"I wasn't—"

"Save your breath, Janda, we have proof. But that's not why you're here. She's missing, and we need to know where you're holding her."

"No, no, no," he said, "you can't pin that on me. I didn't sell her anything; I just saw her passing down the street. Maybe someone else was selling her stuff, but I don't know nothing of any of that."

"You know that street corner where you, um, don't sell anything? Across the street there's an ATM, you asshat," Michowsky intervened. "We have you on video, selling to her. Now spill it."

Janda's face fell apart, as if coming unglued at the seams. He ran both his hands over his face, then wiped his clammy palms against his jeans, while his eyes darted all over the room.

"You're going down hard, asshole," Michowsky continued. "This ain't your first dance."

"I want a deal," he said. "I'll tell you all I know, but I want a deal. No deal, no spill."

"Possession with intent to distribute," Michowsky offered. "Down from dealing, that's a walk in the park for you."

"I'll do too much time. Nope. Simple possession, or I keep my trap shut."

Michowsky glanced at Tess and she nodded.

"Simple possession, okay, now spill and make it worth my while."

He looked both of them in the eye, as to make sure they weren't screwing with him.

"She bought amphetamines from me," he eventually said, "once or twice a week, not more."

"For how long?"

"More than a year, I guess. The lady had her high under control."

"What do you mean?" Tess asked.

"She didn't spiral, just kept it even. Not many people can do that. But I guess someone in her position would know how to handle herself."

"What position is that?" Michowsky asked.

"You know, a doctor. Made me wonder why she didn't script for herself; there's legal highs out there you can write up and take forever, and way better than my shit."

"Why did she buy from you? Did you ever ask her?"

"Yeah, sure I did. After so long, we were almost like friends, although she wouldn't script for me, either. She said she wanted to keep things clean, not mix her work in any of that."

"But why was she using?" Tess asked.

"She said she needed the edge for work. Long hours and stuff like that. She said most young doctors are using something to put up with it. 'No one's clean,' she said."

"So why did you kidnap her?"

"What? I didn't! I swear to God." He'd become agitated again, and wanted to get off the chair.

"Sit down," Michowsky snapped at him, and he froze. "You were dealing to her, and now she's gone. She disappeared that same afternoon. Do you have any idea how much trouble you're in? I'm sure even a bonehead like you can figure out just how bad this looks."

Janda's blood drained from his face, and his knuckles turned white, as he clenched his fists on the tabletop.

"Yeah, you made a great deal. Simple possession, on top of rape and murder," Michowsky added.

"Wait, what? I ain't done any of that, I swear!"

Tess stared at him for a second and wondered if he had anything to do with their case. Most likely not, but it was worth one more question.

"Why did you rape her, Gino?" Tess asked quietly.

"Listen, I might do a lot of things," he replied, "but I don't need to rape no one."

"Why is that?"

"Let's say that I would, in theory, be selling something like breath mints that make you feel good, or some sugar. Do you know how much pussy I can get for a single hit of Oxy mints?"

Tess stood, getting ready to leave.

"Listen, you got to believe me," Janda pleaded. "When she and I finished our business last week, she said she was going out on a date. She was fired up about it."

"You're not making this up?" Michowsky said, getting in Janda's face.

"No, that's what she said. I remember joking with her 'cause she was married. I asked her if she was going to ditch that whale of a wedding ring. I'd have taken it off her hands if she insisted, you know. She said no, 'cause the dude knew she was hooked up."

"Who was this guy?"

"What, you think she showed me his driver's license? I don't know, just some dude, some doctor she worked with, that's all."

Tess left the room without another word, followed by Michowsky, just as Fradella rushed toward them.

"Got bad news," he said, "they just found Katherine Nelson's body."

Ambulance

47

The Ford Expedition swerved and weaved through the thick traffic with Fradella at the wheel, lights flashing and siren blaring. On the passenger seat, Tess winced with every pothole or change of direction, and held on tightly to the armrest to reduce the effect on her healing sutures.

"We should've had more time," she said angrily, raising her voice to cover the blaring siren.

"I know," Fradella replied, "you said it three times already."

"This was not supposed to happen," she added. "We had plainclothes cops all over that damn hospital, in the parking structure, on each floor, everywhere. I just left that place, for God's sake. How could he—"

"They said she was found in an ambulance, parked near the ER receiving area."

"Are they pulling video?"

"As we speak," Fradella replied, then took the off-ramp, driving much faster than he should have.

Tess felt how the SUV tilted to the side, almost ready to flip, and held on with both hands.

"Whoa, Todd, let's not get there in an ambulance ourselves, all right?"

He slowed down somewhat, but then floored it again as soon as he got to a straight stretch of road.

They arrived a minute later, and the first thing she saw was the commotion of police cars and vans surrounding a cordoned-off area of the hospital's ER access, centered around an ambulance with its rear doors wide open. Doc Rizza's van was parked closest to the ambulance, and AJ, his assistant, went back and forth between the two vehicles, carrying evidence collection kits.

She got out of the car and ran toward the ambulance, taking in the surroundings. This was bold, to drive in plain sight like that and leave an ambulance with a body inside, in the middle of the road under 24/7 video surveillance, and just walk out of there, unfazed. Maybe they'll see him on camera, and trace where he went. Maybe they'll finally catch a break in this deeply upsetting case, and get a lead that actually went somewhere for a change. While Stacy was still alive.

She stopped a few feet shy of the ambulance, bracing herself. She'd believed she'd find Katherine in time, while she was still alive. She never thought the day would come when she'd see the young Dr. Nelson inside a body bag, not while the team worked the case the way they'd been working it, with all their resources pooled together and enduring a slew of sleepless nights, leaving no stone unturned and no lead unfollowed. Yet Katherine's body was inside that ambulance, with Doc Rizza hovering above it with a liver temp probe in his hand, while AJ was unsealing a new body bag.

She grabbed the door handle and climbed a step onto the van's wide bumper, wincing.

"Hey, Doc," she said, letting undertones of anger and frustration color her voice.

"Ah, good, you're already here," he replied, without looking at her. "Time of death was roughly three hours ago, at about 7:30PM. I'll step aside now, let you take a look, and then AJ will take more photos. It's quite crammed in here."

"What can you tell me, Doc?" she insisted. "You have to give me something we can use."

Doc Rizza straightened his back with a sigh, propping his hands on his hips, as if to ease the pressure on his back.

"This isn't getting any easier, Tess," he replied, looking away. "Here we go. Cause of death was similar, only more brutal, so I'll probably write it down as crushed trachea, not just strangulation. I'll decide after I open her up. She was badly beaten and raped, and the ligature marks were deeper, more severe, some lacerating the skin all the way to the tendons. She fought bravely, with a lot of energy."

"Was she beaten worse than Lisa or Sarah?"

"By far," Doc replied. "I'll have to confirm it on my table, but I'll venture a guess and say the rapes were more brutal also."

"She's only been gone a week," Tess said, and as she was articulating the words, she shuddered at the thought of what that meant. Being captive and enduring that kind of repeated assault for a week... she couldn't bear to think about it anymore. It clouded her judgment, making her enraged, hence irrational, and she needed every ounce of rational thought and deductive logic she could muster to catch those monsters. "I thought we had more time," she added angrily. "I thought we were going to get to her in time."

"He's probably devolving, or, better said, *they* are probably devolving," Doc said. "The increase in the severity of the attacks surely points that direction."

"How about her ring?" Tess asked.

"Gone, and replaced with a cheap one, probably identical with Lisa and Sarah's."

"Livor mortis?"

"Same as before, only he was in a hurry to dump the body. She'd been tied up and killed in the same position as the other two victims, but the blood didn't have that much time to pool."

"Any other discrepancies? I need to understand how these bastards are escalating."

"One other thing, at first sight. She wasn't groomed that thoroughly, the way Lisa and Sarah were. She had some hair on her legs, armpits, and her pubic region. She wore no makeup, but her skin was clean and so was her hair."

"So, she took showers, but didn't do the grooming part," Tess summarized, thoughtful.

"What do you think that means?" Doc asked.

"I don't know yet. It must have enraged the killer to see his fantasies disintegrate. Maybe she disobeyed him; it could be that simple. How soon can you tell me if she'd been taking amphetamines before being abducted?"

"Right now, just give me a second." He took a test strip out of a small jar and pricked Katherine's skin with a needle. A droplet of blood appeared, and Doc quickly smeared it onto the test strip. He waited a minute, then rinsed it with distilled water and compared it against the label of the jar.

"She's still bleeding, Doc," she whispered.

"Yes, she is, poor thing," he replied. "For about ten hours after death, blood will still preserve some measure of its liquid form. However, that's more like oozing rather than bleeding. To me, bleeding presupposes a live, beating heart, while hers no longer beats." He wiped his brow with the back of his gloved hand. "You're right. She'd been taking amphetamines, and by the residual concentrations I'm seeing here, she must have been past the peak of her withdrawal."

"I see. Doc, what does amphetamine withdrawal look like? What are the symptoms?"

"Anger, irritation, fatigue, hunger, suicidal ideation... the whole shebang. Why, you have a theory?"

"I do, but I'm not sure how much it's worth."

"Share," Fradella said, appearing behind her.

"This kind of escalation in violence, when dealing with killing teams, can happen in two situations that I can think of. One is when the team dynamics are deteriorating, the team bonds are degrading, and they're on a path to a breakup. Many times, such breakups end in murder after a short burst of escalated violence. The second situation will occur in the rare cases of defiant victims who'll do everything they can to enrage the captors, to trigger a different kind of response. It's possible that Katherine provoked the killing team."

"Why would she do that?" Fradella asked.

The question brought a wave of bad memories to her, so violent she wavered under its weight.

"Um, to die faster, to end her suffering," she said, feeling choked with emotion. "Dr. Nelson was an educated woman who must have understood her situation quite well. That, combined with the rage and suicidal thoughts given by the amphetamine withdrawal, could have motivated her to taunt her attackers, to provoke them into ending her misery sooner."

"Yeah, but they still took Stacy Rodriguez before killing her. Her death wasn't just impulse," Fradella said.

"I noticed," Tess replied. "For this killing team, having the two women together for a couple of days is paramount. I had a bad feeling when they took Stacy sooner than we'd expected, and I hoped I was wrong. I hoped we still had time for Katherine."

She climbed the second step into the ambulance and slid past Doc Rizza, approaching the head of the stretcher where Katherine lay. She looked at the young woman's livid body, quietly observing all the details. The bruising and abrasions on her neck, where a half-inch rope had left its mark repeatedly, scraping and blistering the skin while she was still breathing, then crushing her windpipe and ending her life. The petechial hemorrhaging coloring the conjunctiva of her eyes, even her eyelids. The marks on her beautiful face where she'd been pummeled, and those on her arms where they'd manhandled her ruthlessly. The ligature lacerations on her wrists and ankles, some cutting deeply into her skin, a sign of the fight she'd put up for so long. Without realizing, Tess touched Katherine's hand and whispered, "I'm sorry."

She felt Doc's warm hand giving her shoulder a gentle squeeze. "You'll find them, Tess. If anyone can, you can."

She turned around, still choked, unwilling to let others see her moment of weakness. She saw Michowsky approaching the ambulance, and stepped down, meeting him halfway.

"Please tell me we have video of this bastard, Gary."

"We do, but it's no good. All we see is a man in a black hoodie getting out of the ambulance and disappearing on foot. Then we lose him on campus, when he moves out of camera range."

"The wedding rings still didn't show up anywhere, at pawn shops?"

"No, there's no sign of any rings anywhere," Michowsky replied calmly.

Tess glanced quickly in his direction. "Did you check?"

"I did, Tess. I know how to do my job."

"Well, apparently, you don't," she snapped, "and neither do I. Not as long as they're out there, killing and raping at will, with no one to stop them."

Michowsky pressed his lips together, but didn't say anything.

"It's got to stop," Tess said, grinding her teeth in anger. "It's just got to stop. How much longer? How many more women have to die before we catch these bastards?"

Doc Rizza approached her and touched her arm. "You need to get some rest, Tess. You've just been released from the hospital, and you've worked a full day, on your feet. It's too much; go home and get some rest."

"No," she replied coldly. "I'm going back to that conference room, and I'll pore over every piece of data again, and again, and then run the searches one more time, for as long as it takes. There must be something that we missed. No one's that goddamned perfect."

No one spoke for a while, but that didn't make her feel any better. If she were in better physical shape, she'd probably kick something, or drive her fist through a wall.

"I'm coming with you," Fradella offered. "We'll look at the evidence together."

"Yeah, me too," Michowsky offered.

She kept her eyes on the many lights of the hospital. Its main building towered over them and most of its windows were lit. The night was still young, and the hospital was humming with activity. She still remembered the dynamic of the place; up until earlier that same day, she'd lived there continuously for almost an entire week.

There was something that wouldn't let her leave; somehow, the hospital seemed relevant to the case, although it didn't make any sense. Yes, Katherine Nelson had been a doctor at that hospital, but none of the other victims had anything to do with that place. Her instinct to check on Melissa's husband had proven to be a complete waste of time, and the fact that the killer had dumped Katherine's body at the hospital wasn't that relevant either, considering he always dumped the bodies where he'd abducted his victims. Then, what was it in her gut that wouldn't let her be? She shrugged it off, and started walking toward the car. If it was that important, it would come to her, probably as soon as she downed another stiff coffee. They'd already looked at the hospital as a possible correlation and found nothing.

"You coming?" she asked Fradella, and he was quick to follow. Michowsky hurried along, but she stopped him.

"Hey, I need you to find me the doctor who Katherine was secretly dating, and see what you can find out."

"Will do. How much time do you think Stacy has, considering what went down with Katherine?"

There it was, a simple question summarizing all her fears.

"I don't know," she replied simply, "I just don't know."

Awake

48

Melissa opened her eyes, then closed them again. She felt dizzy and confused, and the reality she was seeing didn't make any sense. She felt the cold hardness of the floor underneath her, and she opened her eyes again, forcing them to adjust to the harsh, fluorescent lights.

Next, she noticed the young woman crouched next to her, with her legs folded underneath her. She stared at her with red, swollen eyes and an expression of immense sadness on her face. She looked somewhat familiar, despite the bruises on her face and the pallor of her skin. She kept her arms wrapped around herself, trembling.

"Who… are you?" Melissa asked, feeling her throat parchment dry. "Where the hell am I?"

The woman didn't respond; she just bit her lip and looked sideways. A tear rolled from the corner of her eye, leaving a trail in the makeup she wore.

Melissa pulled herself to her feet and looked around at the dreary room she was in. The barren walls, the massive door, the improvised shower in the corner, the dark window. A wave of deep panic grabbed her insides and twisted them hard, and breath left her chest in a quick, noisy burst. Her panic turned to nausea, as if someone had punched her in the pit of her stomach. She felt the urge to scream from the bottom of her lungs.

Melissa forced some air into her lungs, trying to overcome her paralyzing fear. She looked at the woman's familiar face and slowly she recalled where she'd seen her before. She recognized her, but that only made things worse. She remembered her beautiful, haunting face, as she'd seen it herself, walking proudly in the mall parking lot, while her own husband stared at her, fixed on her undulating form and her stunning eyes. She thought that had been the worst of it, but later, she'd seen the same unforgettable face in Special Agent Winnett's case file, with a name scribbled in black Sharpie at the top of a full-color photo printout.

"I… know how you are," she said, grabbing the young woman by the arm so strongly she whimpered and pulled away. "You're Stacy… Stacy Rodriguez."

"How did you know?" the woman asked. "How could you possibly know that?"

"The feds… they're looking for you. They're looking everywhere for you."

Stacy clasped her hands together and rocked side to side, gently, keeping her eyes closed while tears rolled on her pale face.

"They'll be too late," she whispered.

"Oh, God," Melissa said, as the next wave of realization hit her. "That means… We need to get out of here," she said, suddenly remembering what she'd overheard in Tess's room. All the women who were taken were raped and beaten, then killed, strangled with a rope. They didn't have much time.

She sprung to her feet and went to the door. She tried the handle, but the massive door wouldn't budge. Feeling desperation choking her, she banged on the door as loudly as she could, until she could barely stand. Then she moved to the dark window, and tried to break it.

"You don't want to get their attention," Stacy said pleadingly. "Please, stop. You're making it worse."

"You don't understand," Melissa replied. "If we don't get out of here, you'll…" She stopped talking, realizing what she was just about to say.

"I know," Stacy replied. "I've been here a while, since Katherine was still alive."

"You met her?"

"Yes… She's gone now. They killed her last night. I saw everything," she whispered, closing her eyes, as if to seek refuge within herself, away from the horrors of their prison. "Maybe you still have a few days, but they'll kill me today or tomorrow. I remember… that's what happened to her, to Katherine."

Melissa felt her knees weaken and sat on the edge of the bed, then covered her mouth as if to hold her screams inside. She desperately fought the urge, but the thought of never seeing her son again ripped through her heart and she let out a long, wailing sob.

After a while, spent, she silenced her sobs and opened her eyes again, feeling a second wave of panic overtake her as a troubling thought gnawed at the edges of her mind. Was Derek involved in any of this, like she'd feared in her worst nightmares? Could he really be a part of what Tess had called, "the killing team"?

She crouched next to Stacy and grabbed her hand with both of hers.

"What do they look like? Please tell me… I have to know."

Correlations

49

Tess had dozed off on the couch in the captain's office, giving in after her mind had turned to sludge and her vision became so blurry she couldn't read the report data on the wide-screen display anymore. She woke up abruptly, startled by the approaching noises, and sat on the stiff couch with a long, pained groan. The site of her wound hurt with a pulsating, dull pain, and she felt every stitch like it'd been sewn with fire, not first-rate surgical sutures.

She stood, a bit unsure on her legs, then walked into the conference room, still blinking from the lights. The clock on the wall showed twelve minutes after eight; she'd been asleep for almost four hours.

Fradella and Michowsky stopped their argument when she walked in, and Doc Rizza turned toward her with a faint, tired smile.

"What's going on?" she asked, rubbing her eyes with the back of her hands.

"It leaked," Michowsky said, letting the air escape his lungs in a frustrated sigh. "This morning, on the news."

"Damn," she muttered. "Do you have it?"

Fradella was one step ahead of her, working the remote. Soon, he'd rewound the recording to its beginning, and she heard the voice of a news reporter speak, while the screen displayed first an image of Katherine Nelson, then a poorly executed sketch of the glimpse of death, the rope coiled around a man's fists.

"We're only now learning that there is a dangerous team of serial killers on the loose in the area," the reporter said, "and this young woman, a resident at the University of Miami Hospital, is their latest victim. Our sources tell us the killers like to threaten the victims prior to their abduction, by showing them what law enforcement, including the FBI, have been secretly referring to as the Glimpse of Death. Have you seen someone like this? Call the number on the screen immediately; your life could be in danger."

"Oh, crap..." she muttered. "Although I'm surprised we lasted this long."

"Hell is going to break loose now," Fradella said grimly.

"Screw hell," Tess replied. "I'm worried the glimpse of death is gone. The unsub won't do it anymore, not after this," she pointed toward the TV frozen on a still image of the amateurish sketch. "Even for him, it will be too risky. Then, how will we know when he takes someone again?"

No one replied, and heavy silence took over the room until Tess's phone rang, resonating strangely against the glass walls. She picked it up quickly, after frowning at the name displayed on the screen.

"Sir?"

"Winnett," SAC Pearson said, and, by the tone of his voice, he didn't sound happy at all. "Why do I have a horde of newspeople on my doorstep this morning?"

She swallowed a few loaded cuss words. "It's in the news, the case we're working on. It just hit, and they know the FBI is working it with the local LEOs."

"Ah, for Chrissake, Winnett… Since *we're working* the case, would you be so kind to give me an update?"

The sarcasm in his voice was tangible and searing; she cringed and closed her eyes for a split second. "We're following multiple leads, and Donovan's—"

"Winnett, cut to the chase, will you? Do you have a suspect?"

"No, sir, we don't. Not yet. But we're—"

"Great… just great," he muttered, then ended the call without saying anything else.

She gently put the phone on the conference room table, when in fact she would've liked to smash it to bits against the wall.

"That's that," she said quietly, speaking more to herself. Then she shrugged off the mental image of her angry boss and refocused. "Moving on. Gary, did you find Katherine's secret lover?"

"Yes, just spoke to him a couple of hours ago."

"At six in the morning?"

"It worked out well, because of the time zone. The guy's in Australia. He's a cardiovascular surgeon on a three-week exchange program in Canberra. He left the day Katherine disappeared, and they'd just hooked up before she was gone."

"So, he's not our guy. Any insight from him at all?"

"Nope. They were having coffee and quickies now and then, that's all. This doctor is married too."

"How about you, Doc?" she turned to the ME. "Any new findings?"

"Nothing I haven't already mentioned," Rizza replied, then cleared his throat and wiped his mouth with the back of his hand. He looked tired and his eyes were bloodshot, a common trait they all shared after the past few days had started taking their toll. "Cause of death is a crushed trachea, just as I anticipated. Same fiber traces on her body, same DNA smudging."

"Smudging? So, you agree they left their mark on purpose?"

"Looks that way, at least the rapist," he said. "I have an advanced tox report on expedited order with your lab, and, because Katherine died so soon after her abduction, I have a much clearer mark of the needle he used to subdue her. He poked her with a medium-bore needle, nothing unusual about it, and injected her in the neck with propofol, just like before."

"And used the same Crown Vic for the body dump?" Fradella asked.

"That I can't answer," Doc Rizza replied. "All I can say is that I found the same carpet fibers on her body like we found on Lisa Trask and Sarah Thomas, and those fibers are consistent with the Crown Vic model you have on video. But she was found inside an ambulance, and I have no way of telling, not for sure—"

"Yeah, Doc, we get it," Tess replied gently, and touched his elbow. "You should get some rest."

Doc Rizza shook his head slowly and stayed in his seat.

Tess pulled out a chair and sat slowly, then leaned against the back, while her eyes stayed focused on the ceiling tiles. For some reason, staring at the ceiling helped her concentrate.

"The timeline's collapsing," she eventually said, speaking slowly, thinking out loud. "They're devolving; we've already established that. Stacy was taken only five days after Katherine disappeared, boldly snatched from a high-traffic area in broad daylight. What does that mean?"

"Huh?" Fradella asked. "Not sure I follow."

"It means that regardless of how they're devolving, or how much Katherine might have provoked them, they don't budge from their set overlap of two days between victims, and from the bold abductions. Not to mention the glimpse sightings, three, not two, in Stacy's case. That's their core fantasy, guys, not the timeline. We're totally screwed." She looked at each of them intently, to see if they followed her chain of thought. "They could kill Stacy anytime, especially if they already took someone else we don't know about. This is the third day they've had her. But the glimpse and the overlap are critical components. Let's hope with the news coverage they'll still feel compelled to show the glimpse."

She stood and went to the door. "Are you coming?"

"Where?" Fradella asked, but grabbed his car keys and walked behind her.

"Let's trail Stacy's glimpse of death. I think we have the killer's message all wrong."

"Wait, what?" Michowsky said, while Fradella stopped in his tracks and turned toward her.

"We assumed he shows them the glimpse, then abducts them from one of the sites where the sightings take place. That's what we thought happened with Lisa Trask. She saw the glimpse at work and at home, and she was taken from the office parking lot, the precise spot where she'd seen the glimpse. Then she was dumped at the second site of a glimpse sighting, her backyard. Almost the same happened with Sarah, who was taken from and dumped at the mall, where she saw the glimpse both times. That's why we assumed he takes them and dumps them at the places of the sightings."

"Precisely," Fradella said. "Why are you saying we got it wrong?"

"Because Katherine was not taken from work, where she saw the glimpse, but from a busy street downtown. So was Stacy. She was taken from the street, during her lunch break, downtown, not at the office. We were wrong, guys; we jumped to conclusions."

"I still don't follow," Michowsky said.

"It's something you said, about coffee and quickies, that made me think about it. We profiled that the glimpse is a warning of sorts, but then what if he takes them from the place where they're cheating? Katherine's car was found in front of a coffee shop, and you just told me she had coffee and probably a quickie with the surgeon, right there where she was taken."

"A quickie in a coffee shop? Really?" Fradella asked, with an incredulous grin on his face.

"Not in the coffee shop per se, but that time, that day, somewhere around there. Have a uniform show their pictures at the motels nearby; see what pops up. Then let's find out where Stacy was going on that lunch break of hers. What if she was doing the same thing, only we don't know with whom and where? No big surprise, Stacy's car was found right in front of another coffee shop, and, if I remember correctly, the preliminary fact finding shows her at that same shop having coffee with a man. You guys pulled the video."

"If he takes them from the place of their cheating," Fradella said, "does that means Lisa was involved with someone in her office?"

"It's a possibility," Tess replied. "I don't know what the mall location meant for Sarah. All surveillance video showed her browsing around that mall alone. I'll ask Donovan to take another look, find out more about Lisa's office life. Maybe he can look into Sarah's life some more too."

"Maybe the unsub was wrong? This victim profile is incredibly precise and detailed; he could've made a mistake. Maybe Sarah wasn't cheating."

"Then, what's the meaning of the dump site?"

Tess bit her upper lip and resumed her walk toward the car.

"I think it's maximum exposure to the people who needed to know about the cheating."

"How is dumping someone in their own backyard maximum exposure?" Fradella asked, and unlocked his car.

"Lisa was the most reclusive of all; no one really knew her. Her family was targeted in Lisa's case, just like the University of Miami Hospital employees were the audience in Katherine's case. Everyone knew Katherine, and the unsub wanted to make sure they knew the real Katherine, by his standards. Now let's trace Stacy's sightings of the glimpse."

"This profile is too damn precise," Fradella muttered. "I don't think we have the big picture yet."

Tess repressed a long sigh. "Yeah, you're right. Where on earth could the unsub see hordes of women, know that they're depressed, and that they're on the market, so to speak? Where?"

"Well, the market thing you can tell," Fradella said, turning a little red and clearing his throat quietly. "The way they look at you, you know. They, um, size you up, if you know what I mean."

"Huh, maybe they size *you* up," Michowsky said, laughing. "Their eyes don't even stop on me anymore, not even for a split second. Jeez, I'm old."

Tess didn't laugh with them, her mind barely registering the exchange. Where? Where could he see them, *and* have access to so much information about them? Do they know him? Do they meet somewhere, and that's why later, when he abducts them, they fall prey so easily?

Michowsky took the back seat, leaving Fradella behind the wheel. In his typical driving style, he took them to Stacy's residence in just a few minutes.

They rang the bell and immediately heard footsteps behind the door, rushing to open. A young, pale woman gave them a long look, then recognizing Fradella and Michowsky, opened the door widely to let them in.

"Please tell me you found her," she said, clasping her hands together in silent imploration.

Vantage Point

50

Stacy's wife sobbed hard, her thin shoulders shuddering convulsively with every gasp of air she took. In the neighboring room, the two little girls had started to whimper and fuss, while the detectives exchanged worried glances.

Tess stood and touched Renata's arm. "We need to go now; we're pressed for time. I'm sorry I don't have—"

Renata grabbed Tess's arms with both her hands. "Please! A serial killer has my Stacy; I've seen it on TV. If only she had listened… I begged her to report the man with the rope, but she wouldn't listen. Please don't give up on us. She's all we have in this world."

There was nothing more they could say, no guarantees they could offer, and very little solace. Whether Tess wanted to admit it or not, Stacy's odds didn't look too good.

Once outside, they huddled together in front of the building, and Tess looked up at the apartment complex, then at the surrounding areas.

"So, she'd seen the glimpse over there," Tess pointed toward the building across the street. "He was standing right there, under that tree. I wonder who else saw it. Didn't Renata say that Stacy screamed?"

"Yeah, she screamed and he vanished," Fradella replied.

"Then maybe someone else saw him. Let's try that apartment over there, the corner one, left of Stacy's. I just saw the curtains move."

They rang the bell on that apartment door, and heard someone's guttural, raspy voice shout, "Just a sec." It took more than that, but eventually a man opened the door and welcomed them inside, albeit struggling somewhat in the process. He used a wheelchair, and every time he moved around, he banged into a wall or a piece of furniture. The apartment was small and smelly, but he didn't seem to care.

"I was wondering when you'd show up," he said. "That girl, such a shame."

"Did you see the man with the rope?"

"Yes, I did. I couldn't see anything else, didn't see his face; it was dark already. Days are short this time of year. But that Stacy, she's one hell of a dyke. She screamed fire, like you're supposed to, if you want anyone to give a shit. But he was quick to disappear, and I didn't see where."

Tess frowned and looked at the man, observing lots of details. Unshaven, with a poorly kempt head of thinning hair, and pale, with scorched lips, probably from too much vaping. Paraphernalia scattered everywhere was a testimony to his habit, just the icing on the overall caked mess of dirty dishes, clothing, and food wrappers. He probably didn't get out much, resigned to spend all his days behind that curtain, looking at strangers.

"How come you saw him? Were you looking out the window at that time?"

"At *all* times," he laughed bitterly. "I'm sick and tired of shitty TV, and I can't afford HBO. Look at me, what the hell else can I do?"

Tess could think of many things, but this wasn't the place nor the time. There was nothing there that could help with their investigation, no new information, no leads. Again, nothing.

"You know what I wish for?" the man said, keeping his eyes riveted on the thin traffic on his quiet street as Tess was getting ready to leave. "I wish this goddamned window would face a really crowded place, where I could see people all day long, not just have to wait for my five neighbors to come home." He pulled an e-cig out of his pocket and, with one drag, filled the room with a cloud of vanilla-scented fog. "If my window would face a boardwalk, or a mall food court, that would be something, wouldn't it? I could see people, real people, like you guys get to see. And I know how to read people too; one look, and I can tell you everything there is to know about them. Who's happy or sad, who's getting married and who's getting divorced. Can you make that happen, Agent Winnett? Can you get me such a view?"

Tess didn't recall how she got back to the car. Something that man said made a lot of sense. A boardwalk, a mall food court, where people would pass by and be seen by the unsub, without leaving any trace in any system. No credit card transactions, no cash payments, lost among thousands of anonymous faces in the crowd, yet registering on the rapist's keen radar.

She speed-dialed Donovan and put him on speaker.

"Shoot, and make it quick and painless," he said, sounding serious.

"Hey, D, I need a big favor."

"Oh, no," he quipped.

"I need to know what are the areas of this metro with the highest foot traffic, where our unsub could have seen the victims. I'm talking about places where the women didn't need to use a credit card or a form of identification. No paper trail, got it?"

"Like the airport and such?"

"Yeah. Look at shopping areas, downtown streets, boardwalks, areas where the unsub could have spent inordinate amounts of time without getting noticed. Once you have these locations, can you look at the victims' cell phone histories, see if they've spent any time in one of those areas recently?"

"You're kidding, right?"

"Not at all, D. You're our last chance, and Stacy's. Don't let us down."

She ended the call and leaned back, letting a loud breath of air leave her lungs. Maybe there was some hope. Maybe they needed someone like Stacy's bitter neighbor to draw it out for them.

A call came in through the car's system, redirected from Michowsky's phone, and he picked it up immediately.

"Go for Michowsky, Fradella, and Winnett," he said.

"Yeah, it's Detective Greene from Broward County. Just finished talking to Lisa Trask's manager and some of her colleagues. No one knew anything about an affair, or any romantic involvement with a coworker. She was the quiet type, nose to the grindstone, albeit a little sad."

"Okay, thanks," Michowsky replied, sounding just as disappointed as they all probably felt.

"One more thing, that's probably irrelevant. She worked as a key account manager at the bank branch. Her biggest client was University of Miami Hospital; it outsourced with the bank all its receivables processing, the checks from patients, through a service called, 'lockbox.' Lisa Trask managed the hospital receivables. I don't think it's that—"

"Greene, I could hug you right now," Tess replied, then ended the call. "I'll be damned," she muttered.

"Share," Fradella said. "What are you thinking?"

"It's this damn hospital. It ties in somehow. Two of the victims have it in common."

"And two don't," Michowsky said. "This is thinner than air; you're reaching."

"I know it's thin, but there's something in my gut that won't let go. The hospital ties in somehow."

Her phone chimed and she recognized Donovan's caller ID. She took the call on speaker. "Go ahead, make us happy."

"Now the Operational Technology Division won't talk to me either, just so you know. I have a list of almost 150 high-pedestrian traffic areas, from hotel lounges, to airports, downtown shopping, hospital lobbies, piers, and boardwalks. We need to narrow it down before I pull in the cell histories to cross-reference, or we'll be doing this all month," Donovan said.

"Did you just say hospitals?" she blurted out impatiently.

"This is how you piss me off, Winnett. If you know something, why waste my time?" he sounded angry.

"I don't, D, honestly. Which hospitals are showing up on the list?"

"Baptist, Mount Sinai, Holy Cross, Cleveland Clinic, University—"

"University of Miami?" she interrupted, although she already knew the answer.

"None other," Donovan grumbled. "Next time, just ask me to verify a theory. I can work as an adult, you know. I *can* be trusted."

"Come on, Donovan, it was just a hunch, and an implausible one at that. Were Sarah Thomas and Stacy Rodriguez at that hospital in the past few months?"

She heard the clacking of a rapidly typed-on keyboard, and Donovan mumbling something indecipherable. She held her breath, waiting for his findings.

"Yes, and yes, although I can't tell if they spent any amount of time there; I have no data for that. They could have been just passing by, nothing more."

"I'll take what you can give. Now we need to figure out why these women were at the hospital. Were they really at that hospital, or just passing by the street? Look at everything, family members who might be sick, relatives who work there. Ask around. Nothing came up during the background check we did the first time, so we'll have to dig even deeper."

"Already on it," Donovan replied morosely, then promptly cut the call.

They rode in silence for a while, then Michowsky tapped her on the shoulder.

"You know, that gut of yours, Winnett? It's scary."

A Name

51

When Tess, Fradella, and Michowsky arrived back at Palm Beach County Sheriff's Office, they found Doc Rizza buried in data. Squinting in front of the wall-mounted screen, he scrolled through endless lines in a report showing names, addresses, and drug regimens.

"What are you up to?" Tess asked.

"The rapist unsub has a genetic mutation, autosomal dominant polycystic kidney disease. Typically, once the disease has been diagnosed, the patient receives a prescription for tolvaptan, which slows the progression of cyst development. I've asked for a report on all tolvaptan prescriptions in southern Florida, male patients only, and this is it. More than six thousand names."

Fradella whistled and scratched his head, while Tess approached the screen with a deep frown marking her forehead.

"I thought this was a genetic mutation, Doc. It's supposed to be rare, right?"

"Polycystic kidney disease is a mutation, but more than half a million people suffer from it in the United States. To make things worse, tolvaptan is prescribed for a number of other ailments, such as congestive heart failure, hyponatremia—"

"All right, I get it. Doc, can you please send the list to Donovan, and ask him to cross-reference it against all hospital personnel? Maybe it's time to finally get lucky."

"The hospital, again?" Doc Rizza asked, raising his eyebrow.

"Long story, but I believe we're on to something."

Michowsky stepped out of the room to take a call, but then immediately returned and put the phone on speaker. "Go ahead, Mr. Thomas," he said.

"I received your message, saying to call you about Sarah."

"Yes… We need to know if Sarah ever visited anyone, or spent any time at the University of Miami Hospital."

Silence took over the open line.

"Mr. Thomas?" Michowsky said.

"She was doing that again, huh?" Matthew Thomas replied, the sadness in his voice clear, tangible.

"Doing what, sir?"

The man hesitated before speaking, and this time Michowsky gave him the time. When he eventually spoke, he sounded overwhelmed.

"Sarah's mother died four years ago in a car crash; a drunk driver in a pickup truck T-boned her Honda only a mile away from home. She was pronounced brain dead, but she was an organ donor. A nurse who worked in that hospital was next in line to get a heart." His voice was choked and faint. "Sometimes, Sarah went over there to see the nurse. She never talked to her, and, from what I know, that nurse didn't know who Sarah was. But Sarah, when she missed her mother, went over there and hung around in the cafeteria, waiting for that nurse to come downstairs for lunch. I asked her not to do that anymore; it wasn't healthy for her. She'd promised…"

His voice broke, and all they could hear for a few seconds were raspy, forced breaths of air, the kind people take when trying to control their emotions.

"Thank you, Mr. Thomas, we appreciate your help. Once again, we're very sorry for your loss."

As soon as Michowsky ended the call, Fradella jumped to his feet. "Sarah was a stalker?" he asked. "Got to admit I didn't see that coming."

Tess shook her head, while a cryptic smile bloomed on her lips. "Don't care a single bit, because now we're three out of four. We're on to something here, guys. Let's talk to Renata again, see if—"

The conference line cut her off, but she didn't mind.

"Donovan, I was just thinking of you," she said cheerfully. "What do you have?"

"A couple of things. Stacy Rodriguez worked for a software development company called Something Software."

"Yeah, yeah, we know that," Tess interjected impatiently. "What about it?"

"Well, that company won a bid to build the hospital's new EMR system. For all nonmedical personnel, that's short for an electronic medical records system."

Tess felt a wave of excitement bubble in her chest. "Yes!"

"Stacy attended project meetings and conducted user-acceptance testing with hospital personnel, at least two or three times per month. You nailed it."

"Awesome," she said, feeling the tension and the urgency to act on the information she'd just received.

"Next, I've cross-referenced the list of patients who take this, um, tolvaptan, against any payables and tax records the hospital has issued in the past year. The only match so far, because the thing is still grinding, is a new employee by the name of Michael Walden. He's an imaging technician who works on the main floor, in Diagnostic Imaging. He's been there only a few weeks. Before that, he was at Mercy."

"Great work, D, thanks!" She sprung to her feet and beckoned Fradella to grab his stuff. "It makes sense. The man who spiked my IV was very comfortable trolling that hospital; he knew where the cameras were, he knew how to disappear, and what clothes to wear to not draw any attention."

"Whoa, don't you rush arresting people, Winnett. The search is still running; it only went through the paystubs for now, because that's a single database, easy to search. Forms 1099 and vendor employees are a different ballgame, not to mention all long-term, patient family members who spend time in that hospital. This man has no criminal record whatsoever."

She felt a wave of frustration course through her brain, when she remembered the composite sketch drawn based on DNA markers. "D, can you push me his photo?"

Within a second, the photo of a man popped up on the wall-mounted screen. She took out her smartphone and pushed the composite to the same screen, positioning them side by side.

"It could work," she muttered, "it could be him. Keep in mind only a few of the facial features in the drawing are DNA-based. Hair type and color, eye color, skin color, the balding tendencies, the nose."

"He looks different, this Michael Walden. He looks... harmless," Michowsky said.

"To you, maybe. But there's something... haunting in his eyes," Tess replied. "Something too intense to be any good. Let's not waste any more time and bring him in. Donovan, you're my hero," she added, and, just before hanging up, she heard her analyst groan.

"Then why didn't Katherine Nelson recognize him? We've profiled this unsub as the kidnapper, right?" Michowsky asked.

"That hospital is huge," Tess replied. "Katherine worked in Pediatrics, and this guy is in Imaging, downstairs. I think it still holds."

Michowsky made a quick call to dispatch, requesting backup, then they all headed for the elevator. Tess pulled out her phone and dialed the hospital main number, then put the phone to her ear. She didn't want that particular call handled on speaker, thinking about her own privacy.

"What are you doing?" Fradella asked. "We shouldn't announce ourselves, you know that."

"You're forgetting I know people there. That tends to happen when you live somewhere for a week." As soon as the switchboard took the call, she requested, "Nurses' station on third floor, please."

A quick couple of rings, and then someone picked up. "Nurses' station," a man's voice said.

"Melissa Henderson, please."

There was a brief hesitation, then the man asked, "Who's calling?"

"It's Tess Winnett, her former patient," she said, feeling the bite of worry in her gut.

"Ah, Agent Winnett," the man said, sounding almost relieved. "It's Elliott Giraldo, Melissa's supervisor. She... didn't show up for her shift today. Didn't call, didn't leave a note or send an email. She's not picking up her phone, and we were just wondering what to do, considering Dr. Nelson's—"

"Got it, Elliott. We're on it; I'll be in touch." She hung up, then stared blankly ahead, while pallor took over her face and the chill of fear traveled through her veins. She didn't even register the speed at which Fradella drove the car, or the squealing tires as he took the on-ramp on the way to the hospital.

"They took Melissa, my nurse. The bastards have Melissa, and now they're going to kill Stacy."

Not a Fit

52

"We really have to move on this," Tess said. She felt the tension build in her neck, and blood rush to her head. "Gary, have one of the backup units pick up Michael Walden and put him in an interview room at county. Todd, take the next exit. Let's go to Melissa's home, see what we can find."

She entered the address Donovan had already sent into the car's GPS system, and for a few seconds, let her mind absorb the new facts. How did Melissa Henderson fit in all this? Quick and easy answer, she didn't. Not by a long shot.

As if reading her mind, Fradella turned to face her for a split second, then asked, "Was she cheating?"

"No," she replied quickly. "No, she wasn't. She doesn't fit the victim profile. I can't figure out why they took her."

"She has dark hair, but short," Michowsky said, "and she's about the right age, and pretty. Has a son, Charlie, age six," he continued, reading from the data Donovan had sent to their phones. "But how can you be sure she wasn't cheating? Was she depressed?"

"She was struggling with something," Tess admitted reluctantly, thinking of Melissa's red, swollen eyes, and the black circles that surrounded them. "I asked, and she said it was family problems. I read between the lines and assumed husband problems." She dialed Donovan as she was talking, and he picked up right away.

"Ask," he said simply.

"The background check you did for Melissa Henderson's husband, how deep did you go?"

"I did a good, thorough job, if that's your real question," he replied, sounding almost offended. "He came back squeaky clean, spotless."

"Family history? Work?"

"I looked at the whole thing, and nothing popped up. Whatever this is, I don't think Derek Henderson is a part of it."

"Okay. Send me the name and address for his place of employment. We'll pay him a visit anyway."

"You got it," he replied and hung up.

"What are you thinking?" Michowsky asked. "That gut of yours still talking to you?"

"All the time, Gary," she chuckled bitterly, "the damn thing won't shut up. Too bad I can't make much sense out of what it's telling me." She stopped talking for a little while, thinking through the information again. "This doesn't make sense, any sense whatsoever. Melissa doesn't fit the profile, and that means either something changed dramatically in the killing team dynamics, making them shift from their target victimology and signature, or something else happened, and Melissa's disappearance is not related to our case. We have to consider that, you know."

"Do you think it's possible she just left the guy?" Michowsky asked. "Maybe they argued and it got ugly. It's known to happen."

"Nah... I don't think so. She seems so responsible. She wouldn't just walk out on her job, on everyone. She'd send a note, a text, something."

Fradella came to a screeching stop in front of the Henderson residence, followed closely by two marked cars. Tess stepped out of the car, and beckoned the uniformed officers.

"Ask around, knock on doors, figure out the last time anyone saw her. Go!" She watched them walk away, and ignored their grumbling about chain of command and her authority over them.

Todd rang the bell, then pounded on the door. "This is the police, open up!"

His call remained unanswered, and, after looking in Tess's direction for approval, he kicked the door open. A minute later, the three of them reconvened in the living room.

"No one's here. No signs of struggle, nothing seems wrong," Michowsky said.

"Where's her kid? Do we need to put out an amber alert?" Tess asked, then immediately texted Donovan. Within a minute, he texted back, "Kid in PHX w Grandma, was on open ticket flight on 2/18. All good."

Tess swallowed a sigh of relief mixed with frustration, and, while thinking about the next steps, stared at the walls. Neatly framed photographs of the Henderson family hung in various spots on the cream-colored walls. The two Hendersons getting married; Melissa was beautiful, stunning in her wedding dress, and her husband was handsome too, looking proud. The two of them with their newborn child, smiling widely. The three of them on a camping trip, when the little boy was about four years old. That was the latest photo, although there was plenty room left on the wall to hang more recent snapshots of their life together. She turned to leave, and in passing, gave the wedding picture another look. They were beautiful people, the two of them, and Derek Henderson looked somewhat familiar, although she was sure they'd never met. An indistinct thought gnawed at the edges of her mind, but she shrugged it off and left the house, heading for the car.

"Time to have a conversation with Mr. Henderson," she said, and a frown slowly furrowed her brow. Nothing made sense; the entire case had been a senseless, agonizing mess.

Twelve minutes later, they waited for Derek Henderson to be called downstairs, to the reception lobby at the accounting firm he worked for. The lobby was neatly decorated and lush, a statement that the company, although midsized, was doing quite well financially. Tess studied the awards for professional excellence lined up on a side display, checking the time every minute and trying to refrain from stomping her foot.

"Yes, I'm Derek Henderson," a man said, approaching them with a spring in his step. "How can I help you?"

"Mr. Henderson," Tess said, then flashed her badge. "Special Agent Winnett, FBI; Detectives Michowsky and Fradella, Palm Beach County Sheriff's Office."

He turned pale. "What is this about?"

"It's about your wife. She hasn't shown up for work this morning, and she's not at home. Due to a series of circumstances, the hospital has contacted us and requested we look into her absence."

"What circumstances?" he asked, frowning. He had thick eyebrows, and the frown ruffled them, making them look thicker.

"Let's focus on your wife," Tess replied coldly. "When's the last time you saw her?"

He swallowed hard, and almost covered his mouth with his hand. There was panic in his eyes, and a thousand questions.

"This morning," he replied, stammering a little. "She was running a little late for work, but otherwise, everything seemed normal," he added, then gasped. "Oh, my God... Do you think they took her? Those people they were talking about on TV?"

"We don't know that yet, Mr. Henderson, and we can't assume. We'll be in touch," Tess added, and turned to leave.

"What can I do? You have to let me help," the man pleaded. "Just tell me what to do."

She stopped and gave Derek Henderson another scrutinizing look. He seemed genuinely worried, and acted normally, given the situation. No one would have stayed calm in his place; people tend to freak out when their families are threatened, and need something to do, to regain some illusion of control over their existence.

"Just go home, Mr. Henderson, and wait by the phone, in case there's a ransom call," she said. "We'll be in touch," she repeated, then walked out of the building, followed by Michowsky and Fradella.

"You're both awfully quiet," she said, "you didn't say a word in there. What's on your mind?"

Michowsky and Fradella exchanged a quick glance, and Tess could sense the frustration brewing in both of them. Countless hours, day after day, and they had very little to show for it. Another victim, snatched from right under their noses, and that only meant Stacy's hours were numbered.

"It just doesn't tie up right," Michowsky eventually said. "You know, when we're close to solving a case, the pieces of the puzzle fall where they belong, and you have the big picture? This time, it just isn't that way, and that means we're not getting any closer."

"Yeah, exactly what I'm thinking," Fradella added. "This guy, he doesn't know anything, and his wife, your nurse, doesn't belong on the victimology matrix. I was thinking we should have asked him if she was depressed, or if she'd seen the glimpse of death. I only thought of it now. But I don't think the same unsubs took her."

"Yeah, you're right about that, Todd," she admitted. "Melissa doesn't really fit. But I can't help thinking there's a connection, maybe because of the hospital. That place somehow ties in to all this."

"And he seems familiar somehow," Fradella added. "I keep racking my brain and can't figure out where I've seen him before. He's some hotshot forensic accounting investigator; maybe he was on TV."

"Yeah… maybe," Tess replied, frowning. The same thought bothered her. She tried to remember whether Melissa had his picture somewhere, in her room at the hospital, or maybe on her phone. Maybe he'd come to visit her while she was there… yeah, that must have been it. That's how Fradella remembered him too.

"Maybe he dropped by the hospital to see her while you guys were there?" she asked.

"I bet that's it," Michowsky replied. "I've definitely seen him before."

"Uh-huh," Fradella added.

The moment Fradella started the car, a call came through, from an unknown number.

"Yeah, this is Officer Naylor, down at the Henderson residence," the caller said.

"Yeah, what's up?" Fradella asked.

"The neighbor across the street saw Melissa Henderson climb into the next-door neighbor's car last night, at about seven o'clock, and they left together. She's one of those curious old ladies; she said the house stayed dark the entire evening, and she doesn't think anyone came home after Melissa left with the neighbor."

"How about the neighbor? Did he come back?"

"She doesn't know. I tracked down the guy. His name is Ryan Stafford. He's thirty-seven, and he runs an art gallery downtown, Stafford Art World. Want the address?"

"You need to ask?" she quipped, then disconnected the call.

She stayed silent, sunk in thought. How did the neighbor play in? She looked him up on the Internet and found a photo. He was also a bit intense, but not in a bad way. Darker hair, but still closer to blond, not brown. He was a little too old for the DNA profiles, but she was willing to assume there was a higher margin of error than they'd built into the physical profile. She stared at the photo for a while longer, then bit her lip angrily. There was no way she could be sure, one way or another. Maybe those DNA physical profiles were worthless after all.

They found Ryan Stafford behind his desk at the gallery, and he greeted them with a pleasant smile that died on his lips the second he heard what the visit was about.

"Oh, no," he whispered. "We had coffee together last night."

"Where did you two go?" Tess asked.

"I took her to the Bayside Café, at Biscayne and Port, by the water. She deserved a little break."

"What time was that?" Michowsky asked.

"We left the house about seven, and we were there until closing time, which is 8:30PM."

"Then where did you two go?"

Tess watched Ryan closely, noticing the signs of distress on his face. The pallor that painted a grayish hue on his skin. The hunched shoulders and the lowered head. The dilated pupils, overtaking the deep hazel of his irises, the small, beaded teardrops accumulating at the corners of his eyes. The slight tremble in his chin.

"You're in love with her, aren't you, Mr. Stafford?" she asked, not waiting for him to answer Michowsky's question.

He smiled awkwardly, staring at the floor. "Yes, that's me, the idiot who fell in love with the married woman next door."

"Where did you go, after the café closed?" Tess repeated the earlier question, but in a kinder tone of voice.

"I dropped her off at the hospital, at the main entrance. She said she had something to do at the lab, and she didn't want me to wait. She said she'd take a cab home. I would have waited, you know," he said, averting his eyes and clasping his hands together, anguished.

"Are you involved with her, Mr. Stafford?" Fradella asked.

"No… she doesn't know how I feel. I've been… I didn't want to tell her; I'm not a homewrecker. She might have noticed something, but no, we're not involved. I was just trying to be there for her. She's having a rough time lately."

"With what?" Tess asked.

"They argue sometimes, and I can hear them. I didn't tell her that, so she wouldn't feel embarrassed. One night, a few days ago, I heard her sobbing in the shower, and I think I heard her scream too, before that, but it was muffled, and I couldn't be sure. It could've been the TV; I could be wrong. I... didn't know what to do, so I didn't say anything, but now I sleep with the side window open and the AC cranked up, so in case she screams again, I'll hear her. If that man lays a hand—"

"So, these were more than the typical marriage disputes, you'd say?" Tess probed.

"Way more. Last night she was telling me about a former patient of hers, a fed, whom she thought about calling and asking for advice."

"So, you talked about her marriage problems yesterday?"

"She brought it up. I'd never... But she was visibly struggling lately, and I wanted her to know I was there for her, no matter what. If she felt threatened, or scared, all she had to do was knock on my door and I'd do anything for her. She said she thought her husband was cheating on her, but was terrified of asking him."

"I wish she'd have called me, Mr. Stafford, I really do."

"*You're* that fed?"

Tess nodded a couple of times, then touched his arm. "I like her too, you know. She's one hell of a gal. If you can think of anything else, give me a call." She extended her hand and Ryan Stafford shook it. "We'll find her, Mr. Stafford, I promise."

Back at the car, Fradella gave her a long look.

"What the hell was that all about?"

"What?" she asked, genuinely surprised.

"You were almost mushy in there, with that guy. That wasn't the Tess Winnett I know."

"Ah, Todd, it's a bit personal, but here goes. I don't know how Derek Henderson really fits in all this nightmare, but after we close this case, I need to have a sit-down with him. I'll give him a talk he'll remember so well, he won't even be able to raise his voice ever again. Not even to cheer for his favorite NFL team anymore, you hear me?" She grumbled a few well-chosen cusswords under her breath, and Fradella knew better than to ask more questions.

"Tess, Todd, we have a problem," Michowsky intervened, after checking a text message. "Michael Walden didn't show up for work today."

Through the Looking Glass 53

Melissa sat on the floor, in the farthest corner away from that horrible, dark window, and brought her knees up, hugging them, tightly interlacing her frozen fingers. She leaned her face against the cold wall and closed her eyes, finding little solace in her own internal abyss, where her unspeakable fears took more dimensions than she'd ever thought possible.

It felt like one of those nightmares that never ends, despite waking up screaming in the dead of the night. As soon as sleep returns, so does the nightmare. She couldn't believe how fast her life had been uprooted, and the only thing she was grateful for was that Charlie was safe with her mother. At least he wasn't home, wondering why his mom didn't come home last night.

Thinking of Charlie choked her. She wiped a tear from her eye but kept her eyes stubbornly closed. She couldn't stand to look at Stacy anymore. She felt she was about to scream at her and scratch her eyes out. After all, she was the woman her husband preferred to chase, instead of coming home to his family. She was to blame for all this...

She shook her head quickly, pushing away the irrational thoughts that troubled her mind. How could it be this young woman's fault, any of it, even Melissa's wandering spouse? Stacy was nothing more than a victim, one who was about to die.

Curled up in the armchair, the woman hadn't moved in what seemed like hours, other than to shudder or tremble every now and then, as if touched by a wintry gust. Earlier, Melissa had tried to lift her spirits, but she wasn't responding; she pulled away from her and even rejected the blanket Melissa had quietly offered. The unspoken word in that dreadful room was death, waiting for Stacy beyond the dark, deeply tinted window.

Melissa felt her gut twist in a knot, fearing the moment Stacy would die, fearing her turn would come to endure the torture, with no hope left. Earlier, with a trembling hand, she'd scribbled her name on the wall behind the bedpost, and tried to say her goodbyes to the world. Restless, she blamed herself for not opening up to Tess Winnett, who might have prevented this nightmare. What a ridiculous way to express loyalty to Derek, the man who'd been ignoring her for so long while chasing other women, the man who'd abused her son. She'd been so stupid...

Still, she didn't know if Derek was the strangler beyond that dark window. Stacy couldn't describe him; she'd only seen his hands holding that bloodied rope while he strangled Katherine. Melissa's worst fears haunted her, filling her blood with searing ice crystals that burned her mind and raced her heart. Anguish clenched with hope and denial in her weary mind, fighting to the death.

When did she take the leap from suspecting her husband of cheating, to assuming he was a cold-blooded serial killer? In which contorted reality was that making any sense? Just because the woman he showed interest in happened to be kidnapped? Many men lose their way and wander; some only once, then regret it forever, while others habitually turn matrimony into a farce and their extramarital affairs into a sport. And still, the vast majority of the philandering husbands of the world were just that: unfaithful. A far cry from serial killers.

Which one was Derek? Maybe it was her twisted imagination that spawned monsters, fueled by the hurt she'd felt watching Derek transformed by Stacy's presence. Maybe he'd just lost passion for her, the practical, chronically over-worked wife, and soon enough, some other woman filled the void in his heart, while the rest was a coincidence. It just so happened that her husband coveted the woman who was later kidnapped and held hostage by a serial killing duo. Derek might have been a cheater, but Melissa couldn't conceive the reality in which he was a killer; she could only fear it.

The door opened and she startled, pulling farther away into her corner. A man she didn't recognize came in and, within two steps, stopped next to the armchair where Stacy whimpered.

"No… no…" Stacy pleaded.

Paralyzed, Melissa looked at the man, wondering where she'd seen him before. He looked familiar, but also wasn't.

The man grabbed a handful of Stacy's hair, pulling her away. She fought to free herself, kicked and screamed and pleaded, but the man laughed in a raspy voice and slapped her across the face, hard. Stacy fell inert, and he just dragged her out of there, slamming the door behind him and closing the latch.

His laughter resonated in Melissa's mind, his voice sounding eerily familiar. Yet she'd never met someone so awful, or she would have remembered it. Obsessed that Derek could be the strangler in that terrifying duo, she racked her brain trying to remember the faces of his friends, colleagues, and old buddies from college. She came up empty.

The light turned on in the adjacent room, drawing a yellowish trapeze of light on the cement floor, and Melissa whimpered, knowing what was to come. Soon, Stacy's cries of pain would resonate through the tinted glass, while she could do nothing more than watch and listen, unable to help Stacy, unable to help herself.

Would they kill Stacy now? Was that it for her? Or would they just have their way with her again, and bring her back, bloody and broken, yet alive?

Melissa couldn't bear the thought, couldn't bear to be a part of something so horrifying, without being able to do anything about it. She didn't want to hear or see any of what was to come, and she wanted to cover her ears and squeeze her eyes shut until it was over. Yet she was drawn to that window, a helpless moth to the light, needing to see and hear what she didn't want, needing to be there for Stacy, even if just locking her eyes with Stacy's in her dire moments. She wanted to see if the man holding the rope was her husband, Derek. Not knowing was the worst.

The man who took Stacy threw her over the bench and tied her hands in front of her, then moved behind her and spread her legs with his knee. Then he crouched down and tied each of her ankles, forcing them apart with black zip ties secured against the bench legs. Stacy started to regain consciousness and opened her eyes, looking at Melissa for help.

Melissa pounded on the window with both her fists, shouting, screaming. "No, you bastard, leave her the fuck alone! No!"

The man finished tying Stacy's ankles and rose, taking position behind her. Then he grabbed a fistful of Stacy's hair and pulled abruptly, forcing her head up. She screamed, a blood-curdling scream ended in an open-mouthed sob.

That's when the man grinned widely and turned to look Melissa in the eye. His fierce eyes drilled into hers and his crooked grin widened, filled with contempt. She gasped as she thought she recognized a technician from the hospital, someone she'd run into casually, in the cafeteria and the hallways. But Mike, the young man she remembered from the hospital was a nice, seemingly gentle person; it couldn't be the monster she watched with eyes opened wide in horror, as he made Stacy scream over and over again, not taking his maniacal eyes from Melissa, as in a promise of vengeance and pain.

Then Melissa froze, and even Stacy's screams seemed to fade away in the distance. There was a second man in the room. He was shrouded in darkness, and, from where she stood, she couldn't see much of him. The side of his right arm. Coiled rope, held tightly with white-knuckled fists. A shoulder that seemed familiar, although it could have been anyone's. She couldn't bear to look anymore.

Oh, God… please, no.

Courage

54

Tess watched the officers break down Michael Walden's apartment door, barely hiding her frustration. It was an end-of-the-hallway, ground-floor apartment in a huge building; hardly the place he could hold women captive, rape and kill them, then haul their bodies unseen, unheard. A waste of time, another dead end.

She dialed Donovan as she entered the small apartment, barely registering any details. A typical bachelor apartment, relatively clean and organized. She didn't know what she was hoping to find, but nothing really stood out. No restricted drugs in the medicine cabinet. No rope in the tool closet. No blood-stained clothing in the laundry hamper. Nevertheless, she slid a glove on her hand and fished a few hair fibers from the bathroom counter, then sealed them in a Ziploc bag. Per Doc Rizza's instructions, she made sure at least some of the hairs had root follicles still attached, for DNA comparison. Then she pressed the green button on her phone and connected the call.

"I was just about to buzz you," Donovan said, in lieu of a greeting. "Michael Walden just got promoted from person of maximum interest to confirmed suspect. His grandmother, although ninety-one years old at the time and living in a retirement home, bought and registered a black Crown Vic, almost two years ago. Online auction; everything was done remotely."

"He's not here, D. Is his phone on?"

"That's a negative, and his car is too old to have GPS onboard. Even if it does, it was installed aftermarket, and I can't trace it."

"How about Melissa's phone? Is that pinging anywhere?"

"Nope. Last place it registered was the tower near the hospital, last night. Nothing since; I would've told you."

"Give me something, Donovan, don't leave me hanging. We're running out of time. Stacy and Melissa—"

"Yeah, I know," he interrupted. "Listen, I have an idea, but it might be a wild goose chase. Walden's phone history shows a weird behavior; it's like he goes to a particular place a lot, but whenever he's there, he switches his phone off, and the device doesn't ping for a few hours. Then, when he turns it back on, it pings the same tower. That's where it pinged last time it was on, and that was a few hours ago."

"Meaning?" Tess asked, frowning impatiently. Sometimes Donovan could pour endless amounts of nerd speak into her ear, managing to make very little sense while at it.

"Meaning he probably spends a lot of time there, and while he's there, the phone's always off."

"What's *there*? What are you talking about?"

"An abandoned warehouse, in the middle of nowhere, off Reagan Turnpike, near the Everglades. That place was part of a large building supply plant that was shut down a few years back. The only structures still standing are two warehouses and a loading ramp. It's the only thing that fits, within range of that cell tower."

"Send me the—"

"It's sent," Donovan replied. "Good luck, Winnett, go get them."

She ended the call and rushed to the car, briefing Fradella and Michowsky on the way. She looked at their faces and saw the same determination and urgency she felt; it was one of those moments where it actually felt like they were making progress, finally getting somewhere after endless days of stumbling and feeling their way in the dark.

The convoy of vehicles took almost twenty minutes to cross the city, despite the blaring sirens. Tess could barely contain her anxiety, worried they'd be too late. She didn't say a word the whole time, and neither did the detectives. Fradella's hands gripped the wheel tightly, while his eyes were focused on the road and on the many maneuvers he was making through the dense traffic. As for Michowsky, he pressed his lips together every now and then, but didn't say a word. Soon enough they'd know.

On the final stretch of the road they silenced the sirens, unwilling to give the perpetrators a warning and time to disappear. As soon as they entered the old factory yard, she noticed the black Crown Vic parked outside one of the warehouses, but Fradella was already headed there. He brought the SUV to an abrupt stop in front of the entrance, shooting loose gravel against the undercarriage, then rushed inside, gun drawn, followed closely by Michowsky. Tess unholstered her weapon and removed the safety, then entered the structure right behind them.

The warehouse was vast and almost completely dark. The only light came from the door they'd left open behind them, and from several small, dirty windows in the high ceiling. They turned on their flashlights and proceeded cautiously, checking behind each steel shelf or pile of cardboard debris.

Then Tess heard a scream, and felt the hair on the back of her neck stand on end. It was muffled, distant, and was coming from inside the warehouse. She signaled Fradella and he nodded, then they rushed ahead, following the direction the scream had come from.

They'd almost reached the far end of the warehouse, when they heard another scream, this one longer, ending in a heartbreaking sob. Tess squinted and projected the flashlight beam in all directions, seeking the source of the sound. The beam landed on a door to what seemed to be an enclosure of sorts, probably an office space built against the back wall of the warehouse.

They took positions left and right of that door, then Fradella kicked it wide open.

Tess froze for a split second, taking the disheartening image in. Stacy, barely conscious, was bound to a high bench, just as Doc Rizza had described based on the autopsy results. Michael Walden stood behind her, holding a handful of her hair twisted around his fingers and a long knife in his other hand. He had an expression of pure shock in his eyes, but that didn't dilute the viciousness of his lewd gaze.

"Step away from her," Tess commanded, approaching Walden. "Don't even breathe. I'm itching to put you out of your misery. You make me sick."

Walden dropped the knife and the clink of it hitting the floor resonated and echoed against the warehouse's metallic structure. Fradella grabbed him and handcuffed him quickly, then pushed him toward one of the uniformed officers.

"Keep him handy," Fradella said. "He'll need to answer some questions."

Tess rushed to Stacy and felt for her pulse. It was weak and fast, thready, but she was still alive.

"Get medical in here, now," she shouted, and someone confirmed they were already on their way. Two EMTs rushed inside with their emergency bags and huddled around Stacy. Tess stepped back to give them room to work.

That's when she noticed the window into the other room, and the arm-chair farther toward the back wall. She took a few steps closer and saw Melissa's tear-streaked face, as she was shouting something inaudible from behind the tinted, soundproof glass. She looked around, searching for an entrance to that room, and didn't see it at first. Almost at the back end of the warehouse there was another door, and Tess unlatched it and pushed it open.

Melissa rushed out and landed in Tess's arms, mumbling something unin-telligible, as she buried her face in Tess's shoulder and wept.

"It's all right," Tess said, "you're all right. We got you."

"Come with me," Melissa whispered and tugged at Tess's hand.

Tess turned and looked for Michowsky. "Don't let the bastard get away, Gary. He's got to be here, somewhere." Then she followed Melissa back into the room that had been a prison and watched her lead the way to the far wall, next to the bedpost. Without a word, Melissa pointed at the names scratched on the wall there, behind the bed.

Tess crouched and squinted, trying to read the scratched lettering in the fluorescent light. She turned on her flashlight and read the seventeen names, one by one, feeling her blood turn to ice. Many names were familiar; she'd seen them before, on the missing persons open-cases report. A few weren't familiar though, leaving unanswered questions for what would probably amount to months of additional investigations to come. The last name on the list was Stacy's, but for her, it wasn't too late. She didn't belong there, on that wall.

She stood and turned to leave, but Melissa grabbed her hand again.

"There's more," she whispered, then pointed at the dresser. She pulled open the center top drawer, and revealed a locked display of diamond rings. Each of them had its own red velvet box, showcased as if in a high-end store, and arranged neatly in a transparent case. A few empty boxes were lined up with their lids open, awaiting their bounty.

She recognized a few of the rings, based on the descriptions and photos she'd seen in case files. Sarah's yin-yang design with two stones was there, and so was Katherine's three-stone mounted in gold that had drawn her drug dealer's attention.

She counted the rings and then counted them again; there were twenty-three. Why so many? Maybe some of the first women didn't write their names on that wall. She looked at Melissa with an unspoken question in her eyes, but Melissa didn't have an answer; just a rebel tear hanging from her long eyelashes. Tess grabbed her arm and led her out of there. She noticed Melissa shivered and whimpered quietly when they re-entered the adjacent room, where Michael Walden was being searched and handcuffed.

"It's all right," Tess whispered, and hugged her gently. "He's finished. It's over."

Melissa lifted her head and looked around the room, then pushed herself away from Tess. She watched the uniformed officer haul Walden out of there, and shuddered.

"There's another one," she whispered. "A strangler, just like you said. You have to find him."

There was an undertone of urgency and fear in her voice, and Tess resonated with that. "We'll find him, don't worry. I bet by now Walden's singing like the proverbial birdie. Rapists are nothing but cowards. Let's get you some help."

She walked Melissa outside the warehouse, holding on to her arm, supporting each other. The adrenaline that had fueled Tess for so many days was starting to vanish, now that Stacy and Melissa were safe, and she felt light-headed and faint. The pain in her back had returned with a vengeance, making her feel like she'd been stabbed all over again. But there wasn't time to lick her wounds just yet. The strangler was still out there somewhere, and the manhunt wasn't over. She still had work to do.

When they exited the warehouse, the sun was almost setting, and Tess squinted a bit under its sharp rays. Melissa whimpered, smiling among fresh tears, and squeezed her arm. "I never thought I'd see the sun again," she said. "Thank you."

They were almost at the ambulance when Tess heard a man call Melissa's name. Then she saw Derek rush and lift her in his arms.

"Mel, thank God, you're okay," he said, then put her down and wrapped his arms around her. "I was so worried. Are you… did they hurt you?"

"N–no," she stammered, and wrapped her arms around her husband.

Tess watched the reunion with mixed feelings. It made her happy to see families reunited; it gave her work purpose and meaning. But she had a question she couldn't delay asking, and a gnawing uneasiness in her gut she couldn't put her finger on.

"Mr. Henderson, how did you know where we were?"

He kissed his wife's hair once more, then looked Tess in the eye, seemingly embarrassed. "I followed you from a distance the entire time," he replied. "When you left my office, I was right behind you. I forwarded our home line to my cell, to pick up any ransom calls, just like you said. But I would've gone crazy alone in that house, waiting for a sign from you. I hope you'll find it in your heart to forgive me." He buried his face in his wife's hair, rocking her gently back and forth, and whispered, "Oh, God, my darling, I love you so much."

Reluctantly, Tess turned and walked away, slowly, as if something wouldn't let her leave. It wasn't rational; after being held captive by the strangler, Melissa would have recognized him, no doubt, especially considering the layout of the crime scene. The room where the women were held captive had a window into what Tess could only call the torture room, so Melissa must have seen every gory detail, including the face of the strangler. So why was it that her gut felt so unsettled?

Tess shuddered, imagining how the women must have felt, seeing other victims raped and killed before their eyes, and knowing this was going to be their future. She let out a frustrated breath of air, thinking how the profile had failed to identify the sadistic streak in the strangler. Just because he wasn't a sexual sadist, that didn't mean he wasn't sadistic, skilled in the hellish art of physiological torture. That's why the victims overlapped, to allow the cruel son of a bitch time to break their spirits before ravaging their bodies.

She stopped and turned around to take another look at Melissa and her husband. He was facing away from Tess, and Melissa still kept her arms around his back, her face cuddled in his shoulder. But as she turned, Tess saw Melissa open her eyes wide and search hers in an unspoken cry for help. Tess approached them slowly, unsure what Melissa wanted to say. As if reading her uncertainty, Melissa extended her arm toward Tess in a pleading gesture.

Tess felt a chill and a tingling down her spine. She stopped a few yards away from them and pulled out her weapon. "Freeze," she shouted. "Step away from her with your hands up."

Her imperative got Fradella and Michowsky's attention, and they approached quickly with their guns drawn, taking positions around the couple.

Henderson pivoted half a circle to face Tess, and grabbed Melissa by the neck with one hand, while with the other he shoved a gun in her side.

"Don't be an idiot, Henderson. The moment you pull that trigger, you're history. Look around you."

Several other officers had their guns drawn and trained on him. His panic-filled eyes searched desperately for a way out. "No way," he shouted. "I've got the hostage, I make the rules, you hear me?"

"All right," Tess replied calmly. "Tell me what you want."

Tess looked at Melissa and repositioned her gun in her hand, as if to aim better, but in fact she was asking her a question. Melissa nodded once, almost imperceptibly, then closed her eyes and turned her face away, as much as her husband's grip allowed.

Then Tess fired her weapon, and Derek Henderson dropped to the ground, with a bullet hole in the center of his forehead. Melissa shrieked, then crouched to the ground sobbing, hugging herself. Tess rushed toward the fallen body and kicked Henderson's gun away, then kneeled with difficulty and slid on a glove to search him for other weapons. In Henderson's right jacket pocket, she found a neatly coiled piece of jute rope, with traces of blood on it. She let it drop in an evidence bag held by one of the officers, then took Melissa away from there, shielding her from viewing the corpse. Her frail body trembled hard, in shock.

"How did you know?" she asked Melissa.

"I felt the gun on his belt and…" she hesitated, then looked at Tess with pleading eyes, "I had suspicions. I'm so sorry I didn't tell you before. I couldn't believe he…"

"It's all right," Tess said. "What you did right there took a truckload of courage, Mel. Know that."

Tess handed her over to the EMTs, then walked toward the car where the handcuffed Michael Walden was already spilling his guts to Michowsky.

"You know that deal we just offered?" Michowsky was asking, while pointing at Henderson's body. "It's off the table."

"What? You can't do that," he argued. "I already told you—"

"You should've gotten it in writing, you moron," Michowsky said. "Feel free to shut up and be misunderstood. We're not curious about what a lecherous piece of scum like you really thinks."

"Argh…" Walden grunted. "You act so full of yourselves, but these women, they ain't no saints. Derek's right. They're whores, cheaters, even his own wife. They'd date anyone, except me. All of them refused me… I was a fucking virgin when I finished college! But no, Derek got them all; they'd line up for him, while with me, they were polite and making up excuses. How's that right?"

"I don't know, buddy, why don't you tell me? You and Derek were in college together?" Fradella asked. Tess glanced quickly in Fradella's direction, and he nodded. "You're an accountant, that's your background?"

"Me?" he replied, seemingly amused. "No, I did health sciences, but Derek and I took a few courses together in junior year. He had an edge, something I wanted to have, the way he looked at those bitches. I saw it in his eyes, and we talked some back then, but I guess he wasn't ready. I wanted him to take me there, to show me how it's done."

"Show you how what's done?" Fradella asked.

"Pfft…" Walden reacted, visibly disgusted. "You're not paying attention. I was itching to get even, to teach those sluts a lesson, but he still thought he could be normal, have a family like everyone else. He went his separate way. Such an idiot… wasted so much time," he spat the words like they burned his lips.

"Then what changed?"

"About two years ago, his dad had died a horrible death because of his whore of a mother. He buried him, then he looked me up the same day, mad as hell, livid. I'd be mad too, in his shoes."

"How did his father die?" Fradella asked.

"Cirrhosis. The loser drank himself dead after the slut left him."

"That must have been the trigger event," Tess said in a low voice.

"Uh-huh," Michowsky replied, just as quietly.

"So you were just the gofer for Derek," Tess said, looking Walden in the eye, and struggling to contain her disgust. "He'd snap his fingers and you'd just rush to do his bidding? Is that it?

Walden threw his legs out of the car, intending to get out. He was visibly agitated, frustrated, bursting with the urge to set the record straight, just where they wanted him to be to keep on talking.

Fradella placed his hand firmly on his shoulder. "Stay where you are," he said.

Walden put his legs back inside the car and cussed quietly. He didn't seem willing to say anything else, although he pressed his lips together tightly, as if to keep the bursting flood of words sealed inside his mouth.

Tess smirked at him, then said, turning casually toward Fradella. "Yep, just what I thought; gofer. Nothing more. Derek was the mastermind, not this putz."

"No!" Walden shouted. "You don't know shit! We were partners, Derek and I. He wanted them to look a certain way, that's true, but *I* got to choose. Then I'd tell him who, and he'd go pay them a visit or two, see if he liked them. Then I'd pick them up, and have fun with them for a while."

"You'd get to choose?" Tess asked again, although she already knew the answer, not only from Walden's statement, but also from the behavioral profile. "You? How come?"

Walden licked his lips and gave her a look that sent shivers of revulsion down her spine. His nostrils flared, as if he inhaled her scent, and just watching him made her sick.

"I had to like them," Walden said, "Derek only wanted to see the bitches whoring and hear them screaming, that's what got him off. And they'd all be whoring with me this time, not like in college. Not anymore," Walden added, then laughed, with a raspy, loaded voice. "Oh, man, were they whoring with me, and then some." His sickening laughter resounded strangely in the almost empty parking lot, getting a few other officers to turn and look.

"Keep talking," Tess said, crinkling her nose. "You're going down for murder, multiple counts. Probably you're going to hang for it. Can't wait."

"No, no, no," he shouted, "you can't do that! I never killed anyone, I swear! And you have to understand, it was their fault. They didn't even look at me; it was like I wasn't even a human being. They thought they were too damn good for me, but I showed them."

Fradella rolled his eyes, hearing his rant. "Did you read him his rights?" he asked Michowsky.

"Twice," Michowsky replied humorously.

"But I got them all in the end, didn't I?" Walden continued. "All of them!"

"You know what would make my day, Walden?" Tess asked, while a hint of a smile appeared on her tired face.

Walden stopped talking and looked at her with fear-dilated pupils and a gaped mouth.

"If you made a run for it right now," she said, "while I haven't yet put the safety back on my weapon." She chuckled, feeling a wave of relaxation ease the tension in her muscles. The case was finally closed. She could breathe. "Wanna go for it, huh? What do you say?"

"Uh-uh," Walden replied, then pulled away from them, sliding farther on the rear seat of the police car.

They laughed, as Walden remembered he had the right to remain silent.

"Don't worry, Mike," Tess added, "where you're going you'll get plenty of action, if you know what I mean. You won't be complaining of abstinence ever again."

An Invitation

55

Tess watched the marked car holding Walden in the back seat as it pulled away, then she noticed Melissa was still sitting on the bumper of the ambulance, shivering under a blanket. She headed toward her with a frown. Doc Rizza and AJ were about to load Derek Henderson's body onto the stretcher and she didn't want Melissa to see all that. The zipper closing on a black body bag was a sound she'd never forget.

"Why are you still here?" she asked an EMT, completely ignoring Melissa.

"She refuses to climb onto the stretcher," the young EMT replied. "She won't even let me start an IV. She might go into shock."

"I don't need an IV," Melissa replied, still shuddering at times under the warm sun and the thick blanket.

Tess crouched with some difficulty in front of her, keen on making eye contact at the same level with her.

"Woman, don't be an idiot. This EMT here's just trying to make a living, and you're giving him crap."

Melissa chuckled sadly.

"Remember what you told me about those know-it-all assholes who make a health professional's life hell?" Tess asked.

"Pricks," Melissa said.

"Huh?"

"I said pricks, not assholes."

"Same kind of schmuck altogether, Mel. Don't be one of them, all right?"

Melissa sighed and stood, then gave Tess a hand and helped her up. If the EMT had known to ask, Tess would've probably accepted a place on the second stretcher inside that bus. She felt bone-tired, but it was a good feeling.

"Your mom's on her way," she said, and squeezed Melissa's hand. "She's bringing Charlie. As soon as they land, someone will pick them up and bring them to you."

"Thank you," Melissa whispered, while fresh tears pooled in her eyes.

Tess hesitated for a second, unwilling to meddle in other people's business, but then, watching her climb quietly on the stretcher, thought she'd ask anyway. "Hey, listen. If you'd allow me, I could call your neighbor, Ryan Stafford, to be there when you wake up. Would you like that?"

She averted her eyes for a little while, then looked at her and whispered, "Yes, I'd love that."

"All right," Tess replied quietly, then continued a little louder and in a business-like tone of voice. "Are you back on duty tomorrow? I'm due to have my stitches removed, and no way in hell am I letting anyone else touch me."

She smiled between tears, but before she could answer, the EMT slammed the doors shut. "We need to roll, ma'am."

She tapped on the ambulance door twice, then walked away toward Fradella's vehicle.

"Winnett," she heard Pearson's voice call. He'd just pulled in, raising a cloud of dust and gravel around his car. She rolled her eyes but walked briskly toward him.

"Yes, sir," she acknowledged him with a timid smile.

"How did the DNA composites work for you? Anything you'd like to share?"

"Ugh," she blurted, but then swallowed her frustration and continued, in a more professional tone. "They worked really well as an elimination tool. We ruled out suspects faster. But that guy," she pointed toward Henderson's body, "all we could think of was he looked familiar and tried to place him, when the sketch was right in front of us the whole time. It pisses me off, sir, because it was right there, all of it. The dimple in his chin, the eyes, the hair, and we just—"

"I heard you managed to let a perp live," he cut her off, giving the crowded crime scene a thorough look. He wasn't smiling, but he wasn't frowning either. "You could've let both bastards live, you know. It would've helped your case with the committee."

She frowned, drawn back to the stark realities of her job. "I couldn't; I had to—"

"Crime Scene Unit will take over here, Winnett. You're dismissed."

"Sir?"

"Take some goddamned time off, for Chrissake."

She grinned. "Is that an order?"

He didn't reply; he climbed back into his black SUV and started the engine. Before pulling out of the lot, she thought she saw a hint of a smile tugging at his lips.

Fradella's phone chimed, and he approached quickly after reading the message.

"Donovan confirmed it was Derek Henderson who disposed of the bodies. He used a… three-dimensional analysis of the video surveillance imagery to ascertain the suspect's height, and it matches Henderson. Walden is too short."

"Was that you, speaking like that?" Tess asked, almost laughing. "All those big words?"

"It's all Donovan with the mouthfuls," he replied. "All I did was read the message. Hey, have you been cleared to eat like normal people do? Or are you still doing that green hospital Jell-O?"

"I don't think she knows what color hospital Jell-O is, Todd," Michowsky commented.

She laughed. "Nah… I haven't done hospital Jell-O in a few days," she added, and winked.

"How about some burgers at that fierce friend of yours, and some adult beverages?" Michowsky asked. "I can still smell those burgers he brought you. It was the first time in my life I thought about stealing food from a bedridden person."

"Whoa," Fradella reacted. "Are you about to confess a crime?"

She looked at Fradella, then at Michowsky, and her smile widened. It felt good to end a day like that, with friends, but she wasn't used to it, and her first thought was to refuse. She frowned a little, considering the invitation.

"You know, guys, what we have here, this interagency cooperation, this, um, partnership of ours is starting to feel a lot like friendship, and I don't know how to handle it," she admitted, then watched them fidget uneasily, waiting for her to continue. "But I'm a quick study. Let's grab that burger… I'm starving."

"Cool," Fradella said, then slapped his hands together, rubbing them in anticipation.

"Todd's buying," Michowsky said. "He lost the bet. Would twenty cover us for three burgers and some beers?"

"I'm sure we can work things out," Tess replied, then took Fradella's arm while walking to the car. "The bartender is a good friend of mine; he might run us a tab."

"Wait a minute," Fradella reacted, "what bet?"

~~ The End ~~

Read on for an excerpt from

Taker of Lives

An FBI Agent who doesn't know how to quit.
A serial killer who leaves no trace.
Who's watching you sleep tonight?

Thank You!

A big, heartfelt thank you for choosing to read my book. If you enjoyed it, please take a moment to leave me a four- or five-star review; I would be very grateful. It doesn't need to be more than a couple of words, and it makes a huge difference.

Join my mailing list for latest news, sale events, and new releases. Log on to www.WolfeNovels.com to sign up or email me at LW@WolfeNovels.com.

Did you enjoy Tess Winnett and her team? Would you like to see her return in another story? Your thoughts and feedback are very valuable to me. Please contact me directly through one of the channels listed below. Email works best: LW@WolfeNovels.com.

If you haven't already, check out *Dawn Girl,* a gripping, heart stopping crime thriller. If you enjoyed *Criminal Minds*, you'll enjoy *Dawn Girl*. Or, if you're in a mood for something lighter, try **Las Vegas Girl**; you'll love it!

Connect with Me

Email: LW@WolfeNovels.com
Facebook: https://www.facebook.com/wolfenovels
Follow Leslie on Amazon: http://bit.ly/WolfeAuthor
Follow Leslie on BookBub: http://bit.ly/wolfebb
Website: www.WolfeNovels.com
Visit Leslie's Amazon store: http://bit.ly/WolfeAll

Books by Leslie Wolfe

BAXTER & HOLT SERIES

Las Vegas Girl
Casino Girl
Las Vegas Crime

TESS WINNETT SERIES

Dawn Girl
The Watson Girl
Glimpse of Death
Taker of Lives
Not Really Dead
Girl With A Rose
Mile High Death

STANDALONE TITLES

Stories Untold
Love, Lies and Murder

ALEX HOFFMANN SERIES

Executive
Devil's Move
The Backup Asset
The Ghost Pattern
Operation Sunset

For the complete list of Leslie Wolfe's novels, visit: Wolfenovels.com/order

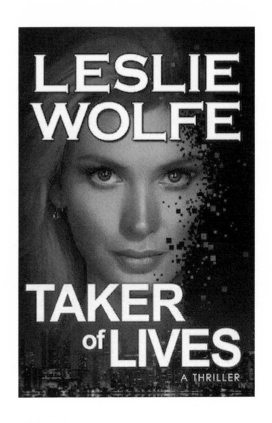

1

NIGHTMARE

She woke with a start, her heart instantly racing when the raw memory of strange, gloved hands on her body invaded her consciousness. She could still feel the cold latex on her skin, touching her, stripping her naked, manipulating her limbs, sending shivers of fear and aversion through her veins. She remembered feeling paralyzed, wanting to scream but staring powerlessly at the face of a monster hiding behind a mask, laughing in quiet, raspy gurgles that only she could hear, glaring at her with merciless, hateful eyes.

She rubbed her forehead with frozen, trembling fingers and forced herself to breathe, gasping in deep, long breaths of air to wash away the memory of the troublesome nightmare. Must've been a nightmare… she was in her own bed, wearing her favorite silk jammies, and she could hear her mother's rushed footfalls as she was getting ready for work. Nothing was out of place.

Just a night terror, that's all it was. The worst she could remember, a vivid one she won't be forgetting any time soon, still, just a nightmare. Her eyes fell on Pat's photo, framed on her night table, and she focused on his loving smile for a moment, imagining his strong arms wrapped around her body, making her feel safe again.

Better.

She stood, feeling a little weak at the knees, but pushed herself to walk out of the bedroom, heading toward the kitchen. Her throat was parched dry, as if she hadn't had a drink of water in ages. She filled a glass at the sink and gulped it down avidly, then breathed again.

"Good morning, sweetie," her mother greeted her, then grazed her cheek with a warm hand. "Feeling better?"

She frowned, a bit confused. What was her mother talking about?

Her mother stopped her morning get-ready rush and gave her a head-to-toe scrutiny, then a tiny smile stretched her lips.

"You were a little dizzy last night, and your blood pressure was lower than what I like to see."

"Ah," she reacted, still frowning, realizing she didn't remember much of the night before.

"Christina, we discussed this," her mother said in her clinical voice, the tone she reserved for her most disobedient patients. "You don't eat much, these photo shoots are a resource drain, so you *have* to pace yourself. You'll burn out. *Vogue* won't go bankrupt if you take a day off every once in a while."

It was the eternal conflict between the two of them. Her mother meant well but failed to realize a model's career span only lasted a few short years, and she couldn't afford to waste a single day. She was twenty-four years old, already on her way to becoming old news. Soon, the agencies would start sending her templated emails, saying stuff like, "After careful consideration, yadda, yadda, we have decided to proceed with a different candidate who suits our needs better at this time." Free translation? "You're too old for this game, sorry. We've got someone younger; find something else to do with yourself."

But that day hadn't arrived yet; she was still one of the most sought-after models in the industry, and her photo shoots took her around the globe, adorning her in designer clothing that she got to keep after showing on coveted catwalks under the incessant flicker of thousands of flashlights. Dizzy or not, she had a schedule, and she intended to keep it. Her pickup limo was due at nine, and she wasn't going to be ready in time.

She toughed it out and pushed her mother's concerns aside with a beaming smile and a hand gesture.

"I'll be fine, Mom, don't worry. I'll even do some blood tests if you'd like, but not today. Any coffee left for me?"

Her mother gestured toward the Keurig machine. "Got you some vanilla pods, the ones you like."

"Hazelnut too?"

"Hazelnut too, sweetie," she smiled, then placed a smooch on her cheek and rushed out of the house, jingling the car keys in her hand. "Have a safe flight! And get some rest."

"I will," Christina replied to the empty house, suddenly as cold and quiet and scary as her nightmare had been.

Still shivering, she threw the coffee maker a regretful glance as soon as she realized it was a quarter to nine. Not nearly enough time to put on makeup and get dressed. She forced herself to move quickly, although it felt like she moved in slow motion, the air thick as if it were water, opposing too much resistance for her weakened body to overcome.

She entered the bathroom and turned on the vanity lights, then gave her face a critical overview. Dark circles under her eyes that would require concealer, a pallor that asked for more blush than usual and maybe a darker foundation tone. Hollow, haunted eyes that needed a touch of eyeshadow to bring their faded color forward.

She turned on the shower and began undoing her buttons, still examining her face, but her fingers hesitated; she looked in the mirror and her breath caught. Her pajama top was buttoned wrong, the lowest button fastened through the second lowest buttonhole. Trivial.

Then why did she feel her blood turn to ice when she looked at the uneven hems?

She felt a new wave of dizziness wash over her and took a step back. A strangled whimper came out of her mouth as faint memories invaded her mind.

Cold, latex-gloved hands touching her, stripping her naked, manipulating her body. A piercing, evil stare from behind a mask, and a raspy, terrifying laugh, a stranger's snicker, yet eerily familiar. The sound of a camera shutter, over and over, in a familiar rhythm of rapid bursts. Her own skin, turning to goose bumps when those strange hands invaded her. The same hands dressing her, putting on her pajama top, grazing against her breasts while doing the buttons.

She wrapped her arms around her body and took faltering steps back until she ran into the wall, her eyes riveted on the mirror, on the image of her unevenly done buttons.

"Oh, God, please…" she whimpered, as tears rolled down her pale cheeks. "Please don't let it be true."

The nightmare was real.

~~~End Preview~~~

Like *Taker of Lives*?

Buy it now!

About the Author

Leslie Wolfe is a bestselling author who has been writing all her life, although it took until 2011 for her to publish her first book, *Executive*.

Since then, she has written many more, continuing to break down barriers of traditional thrillers. Her style of fast-paced suspense, backed up by extensive background research in technology and psychology, has made Leslie one of the most read authors in the genre, and she has created an array of unforgettable, brilliant, and strong women heroes along the way.

Reminiscent of the television drama *Criminal Minds*, her series of books featuring the fierce and relentless FBI Agent **Tess Winnett** would be of great interest to readers of James Patterson, Melinda Leigh, and David Baldacci crime thrillers. Fans of Kendra Elliot and Robert Dugoni suspenseful mysteries would love the **Las Vegas Crime** series, featuring the awkward relationship between Baxter and Holt. Finally, her **Alex Hoffmann** series of political and espionage action adventure will enthrall readers of Tom Clancy, Brad Thor, and Lee Child.

Leslie has received much acclaim for her work, including inquiries from Hollywood, and her books offer something that is different and tangible, with readers becoming invested in not only the main characters and plot but also with the ruthless minds of the killers she creates.

A complete list of Leslie's titles is available at https://wolfenovels.com/order.

Leslie enjoys engaging with readers every day and would love to hear from you. Become an insider: gain early access to previews of Leslie's new novels.

- Email: LW@WolfeNovels.com
- Facebook: https://www.facebook.com/wolfenovels
- Follow Leslie on Amazon: http://bit.ly/WolfeAuthor
- Follow Leslie on BookBub: http://bit.ly/wolfebb
- Website: www.WolfeNovels.com
- Visit Leslie's Amazon store: http://bit.ly/WolfeAll

Contents